John Timbs

Things Not Generally Known

John Timbs

Things Not Generally Known

ISBN/EAN: 9783742817655

Manufactured in Europe, USA, Canada, Australia, Japa

Cover: Foto ©Andreas Hilbeck / pixelio.de

Manufactured and distributed by brebook publishing software
(www.brebook.com)

John Timbs

Things Not Generally Known

Second Series.

THINGS

NOT GENERALLY KNOWN,

Familiarly Explained.

A BOOK FOR OLD AND YOUNG.

By JOHN TIMBS, F.S.A.,

AUTHOR OF "WALKS AND TALKS ABOUT LONDON;" "CURIOSITIES OF
SCIENCE;" ETC.

THRIFT OR CHRISTMAS BOX
From the Roach Smith Collection of London Antiquities in the British Museum.

Fourth Edition: Tenth Thousand.

LONDON:

LOCKWOOD AND CO., STATIONERS' HALL COURT.

MDCCCLXVI.

GENTLE READER,

Encouraged by the sale of Twenty-three Thousand copies of *Things not generally Known, familiarly Explained*, I have devised for its successor the volume which I now submit to your kind consideration as a "SECOND SERIES" of that Work. The success of the first volume has tempted several imitations: the title has been extensively applied to contents pretty "generally known," and the design has been parodied in various shapes; yet, despite this furtive ingenuity, the demand for the original has increased rather than diminished.

The interest of the present volume or series is especially of a *Domestic* character. By shaking off the dust of antiquities, it seeks to adapt their interest to the family fireside, and also to bring some of the truths of history from ponderous folios to the illustration of subjects of every-day occurrence and the usages of every hour. How much entertaining knowledge has been of late gained by archæological inquiry! And how often do these pursuits, while they realise the poet's beautiful line,—

　　　"'Tis distance lends enchantment to the view,"—

at the same time lead to researches which are rewarded with profit as well as pleasure!

In the sections on Domestic lore will be found many interesting glimpses of the Manners, Customs, and Ceremonies of our ancestors, and their modes of living,—how they were amused, and how their recreation was regulated. To these sections succeed notices of Laws,* Privileges, and Dignities, which will be useful in correcting erroneous notions of the Past, and showing us the better practice of the Present.

Under Phenomena of Life are given several subjects of a psychological character, treated in a popular manner, that is to say, without venturing too far into the doctrine of man's spiritual nature. The impressive interest of such inquiries need not here be insisted on: they relate to every stage of

---

* In this Section the Author has been greatly aided by Stephen's *Commentaries*, 4 vols. 8vo, of which a new edition has recently appeared.

man's life, offering phenomena in the prattle of childhood, the ardour of youth and adolescence, the graver inquiry of manhood, and the meditation of old age, with its cheerful contemplation of "rest unto the soul." In this section, the thoughts of the physician, the moralist, the speculative philosopher, and the poet, have been alike laid under contribution. *

To these are added sections on some salient points of the Philosophy and Science of our own time, as exemplified in the Economic Arts.

Throughout the work I have sought to epitomise, and aimed at that condensation which is "the result of time, and experience which rejects what is no longer essential." In these days of rapid book-multiplication, old Fuller's saying is as much to the purpose as when he wrote, "it is a vanity to persuade the world one hath much learning by getting a great library."

June 1859.   I. T.

* The Author desires here to acknowledge that he has received much assistance in this chapter from the experience of several Correspondents of *Notes and Queries.*

.*. The whole design, of which the present Volume may be considered a portion, now consists of

It is proposed to complete the Work (D.V.) by the publication of a second Volume of *Curiosities of Science* at no very distant period. Meanwhile it should be explained that each of the above volumes is complete in itself.

The Frontispiece.

PUPPET-SHOW: PUNCH AND JUDY.

At pp. 52-57 will be found an attempt to trace the history of this renowned street-play, which is

> . . by authority allowed
> To please the giddy gaping crowd,

as it did some two centuries since, in our metropolis. Since the above was penned, the writer's attention has been drawn* to what appears to be evidence of the existence, upwards of four centuries since, of the representation of a puppet-show identical with our modern Punch and Judy. This occurs in the manuscript of the French romance of *Alexander*, in the Bodleian Library at Oxford, which was written and illuminated in the fourteenth century. It is drawn with great distinctness, the figures bearing a strong resemblance to the modern portraits of Punch and Judy; the drapery of the lower portion of the puppet-show is richly coloured, and the figures of the children are drawn with much spirit. Strutt has copied several illustrations of his work on *British Sports and Pastimes* from the above manuscript; yet he has strangely overlooked this specimen, although he describes the modern Punch and Judy. Another illumination of a puppet-show occurs a few folios onward, but differs in the puppets.

THE CHILD'S WINDMILL

is engraved beneath the puppet-show. This toy is of great antiquity: it consists of two short sticks, with pieces of paper at the extremities attached crosswise to a longer stick; the cross is made to turn freely, and is caused to whirl round by running with it extended against the wind. It occurs as an illustration of childhood in a block-print of the "Seven Ages of Man," engraved about the middle of the fifteenth century, and now in the British Museum. Strutt states, the paper windmill has been seen in a painting nearly five hundred years old, with this difference only, that the sails are square. Fosbroke thought that he had seen it upon some classical marbles. It is now occasionally seen for sale in our streets; but we remember a time when its appearance was much more frequent.

The Vignette.

THRIFT OR CHRISTMAS BOX.

This specimen has been engraved from Mr. Roach Smith's Collection, now in the British Museum. It will be found described at page 31. The original is probably an apprentice's earthen Christmas-box, which closely resembles the Roman *Paganalia*, for the reception of contributions at rural festivals; from which custom, with certain changes, is said to have been derived Christmas-boxes. Those described in the Second Series of *Pompeiana* are earthen boxes, into which money was slipped through a hole. Aubrey found one filled with Roman denarii.

* As one of the illustrations, by F. W. Fairholt, F.S.A., of a series of able papers on the Domestic Manners of the English during the Middle Ages, by Thomas Wright, F.S.A., &c.,—in the *Art-Journal*.

CONTENTS.

* *Note to " The Spindle and Distaff,"* pp. 1-6.—A short time since, there died at
Reay, in Scotland, Margaret Sutherland, relict of the late Mr. Hugh Farquhar,
or Mackay, aged 100. She is stated to have excelled in using the distaff and
spindle, which she continued to use almost to her end, being the last in Caithness
who employed those ancient instruments.

Special acknowledgment is due to the Secretary of the Society of Antiquaries
for his admirable paper on the Distaff and the Spindle, which has furnished the
staple of the first article in the present volume.

THINGS

NOT GENERALLY KNOWN.

(SECOND SERIES.)

Old English Manners, Ceremonies, and Customs.

THE DISTAFF AND THE SPINDLE.

THESE implements appear to have been anciently the type and symbol and the insignia of the softer sex in nearly every age and country.

They are not unfrequently mentioned by the oldest authorities. Homer speaks of golden spindles as fitting presents for ladies of the highest rank; and Herodotus tells us that Euelthon's last and most significant gift to Pheretime was a golden spindle and a distaff with wool.

A very early allusion to spinning with the distaff and spindle occurs in Proverbs, the allusion being derived by Solomon from a still older authority: "She layeth her hands to the spindle, and her hands hold the distaff" (*Prov.* xxxi. 19). It shows, also, that the distaff was used by the Jewish women; although, from the representations on the tombs of Benihassen, the Egyptians appear to have spun their thread without it. One group of women spinners represents them as using a spindle in each hand, a proficiency which does not appear to have been ever attained by the moderns (*Rosellini*). A male spinner, in the same moment, uses both hands to the spindle. These representations show also that the Egyptians affixed the *vorticellum*, or whirl, to the upper part of the spindle, contrary to the practice of other nations. Nevertheless, in the picture of Leda on the walls of Pompeii, represented in the *Museo Borbonico*, we find two spindles and a *calathus*, but no distaff; moreover, the whirls of the spindle are affixed to the upper part, in the Egyptian manner; a very remarkable peculiarity, well deserving the attention of the archæologist.

B

Minerva, as the instructress of man in all the useful arts, is fabled as the author of the distaff and spindle ; hence, as Apollodorus informs us, the Palladium held in its right hand a spear, and a distaff and spindle in the left. Tertullian, however, says that the ancients ascribed the invention of spinning to Mercury. These traditions may perhaps be reconciled by the fact, that the spinning of wool, although as old as the days of Homer, was a later invention than that of flax, since the fibre of the latter would the more readily suggest its application.

Pliny, on the authority of an eye-witness, reports that the distaff and spindle of Tanaquil, or Cuia, the wife of Tarquinius Priscus, was long preserved in the Temple of Sangus, whilst the royal robe she had made for Servius Tullius was preserved in the Temple of Fortune. Hence, he continues, it was the custom to carry before the Roman bride a distaff charged with flax, and a spindle likewise furnished.

Plutarch says that the name Thalassius, chaunted at the nuptials of the ancient Greeks, had reference to the word for spinning ; and that when the bride was introduced to her new home, she brought with her a distaff and spindle, and hung her husband's door with woollen yarn.

From Pliny we learn that a rural law in Italy forbade the women to use their distaffs abroad, or even to carry them openly ; it being considered a bad omen to meet them thus employed. A similar superstition once obtained in France, and may have been derived from the Roman conquerors.

Many passages from the ancient poets might be cited in which the mode of spinning is described. It may suffice to name Catullus, who describes the Parcæ spinning the web of destiny ; and Martial styles the Fates "*lanificæ sorores.*"

Among the many beautiful coins of Tarentum in Calabria, are several representing the mythic hero Taras holding a spindle with the yarn wound upon it, which may allude to the manufacture of flax, wool, and especially the purple cloth for which the Tarentines were so famous. Strabo especially mentions the glossy wool of Tarentum.

Descending to later times, we find the distaff and the spindle still more conspicuous as the distinguishing badge of the female sex. Among our Saxon ancestors, the "spear half" and the "spindle half" expressed the male and the female line ; and the spear and the spindle are to this day found in their graves. It was the same with the Thuringians ; and among the Franks, the choice of a sword or a distaff decided the fate of a free woman who had attached herself to a slave.[*]

[*] Kersey, in his *Dictionarium*, 2d edit. 1715, has : " Distaff. an instrument used in spinning. The crown of France never falls to the distaff, i.e. is never inherited by women."

The science of the moderns has, however, banished (from this country, at least) even the spinning-*wheel*,—an improvement on the simpler process of the distaff and the spindle. The spinning-wheel is stated in the *Dictionnaire des Origines* to have been invented by a citizen of Brunswick in 1530, in which year also was printed the Dictionary of Palsgrave, wherein we find the phrase " I spyune upon a rock" rendered " je fille au rouet."

We have good evidence that a wheel was actually used in spinning at a much earlier date than the sixteenth century. A manuscript in the British Museum, written early in the fourteenth century, contains several representations of a woman spinning with a wheel; but she *stands* at her work, and the wheel is moved with her right hand, while with her left she twirls the spindle.* The spinning-wheel said to have been invented in 1530 was doubtless that to which *women sat*, and which was worked with the feet.†

In France and Italy were formerly current sayings referring to a personage identical with the *Frau Berchta* of German superstition. She is still said to live in the imaginations of the upper German races,—in Austria, Bavaria, Suabia, Alsace, Switzerland, and some districts of Thuringia and Franconia. "She appears in the Twelve Nights as a woman with shaggy hair to inspect the spinners, when fish and porridge are to be eaten in honour of her, and all the distaffs must be spun off."‡

This superstition was clearly once common in England. Herrick has in his *Hesperides* these lines on " Saint Distaff's Day, or the morrow after Twelfth Day :"

> Partly work and partly play,
> You must on Saint Distaff's Day :
> From the plough soon free your team ;
> Then come home and fother them.
> If the maides a spinning goe,
> Burn the flaxe and fire the tow ;
> Scorch their plackets, but beware
> That ye singe no maiden haire,
> Bring in pailes of water then,
> Let the maides bewash the men.
> Give Saint Distaff all the right,
> Then give Christmas sport good-night ;
> And next morning every one
> To his own vocation.

* This is, in fact, the wheel called "a torn," the term for a spinning-wheel still used in some districts of England.

† In Stow's *Chronicle*, edit. 1631, we find : "About the 20th year of Henry VIIth, Antony Bonvise, an Italian, came into this land, and taught English people to spin with a distaff, at which time began the making of Devonshire kersies and cotall clothes." Aubrey, in his *Natural History of Wiltshire*, says : " The art of spinning is so much improved within these last fourty years, that one pound of wool makes twice as much cloath (as to extent) as it did before the civill warres." Both these notices evidently allude to mechanical improvements.

‡ Thorpe's Northern Mythology, vol. I. 1851.

It is easy to perceive in these lines an allusion to some heathen divinity whose worship was peculiar to women, although the honours were affected to be rendered to a saint; and this can be no other than Frau Berchta.

In the Northern mythology, the three stars in the belt of Orion are called Frigga Rock, or Frigga's Distaff. This, in the days of Christianity, was changed to Maria Rock. Superstitious regarding spinning still survive among all the Northern nations. There is a Swedish tradition that there must be no spinning on Thursday evening, nor in Passion Week, or there will be spinning in the night. Among the Danes, nothing that runs round must be set in motion from Christmas Day till New-year's Day; there must consequently be neither spinning nor winding. Nor should there be any spinning on Saturday evening.

The well-known couplet, said to have been the rallying cry on the occasions of popular risings in England,—

> When Adam delve, and Eve span,
> Who was then the gentleman !—

well expresses the notion which our forefathers entertained of human industry in primitive times. Some such homely distich was probably in the mind of him who sculptured the curious font in East Meon Church, Hants, where one of the groups represents our first parents sent forth to labour after their expulsion from Paradise; Adam receiving a spade from the angel with a submissive and even abased air, while our common mother stalks away with head erect, plying her spindle and distaff.

In former times the distaff, or rock, was a formidable weapon in the hands of the gentler sex. In the *Winter's Tale*, Hermione exclaims:

> We'll thwack him hence with distaffs.

And Chaucer, describing the hue and cry after the fox, says:

> Ran Colle our dogge, and Talbot and Garland,
> And Malkyn with a distaf in hir hand.

The use of the distaff and spindle was not, however, confined to the humbler classes, but they were used by women of rank and condition, even down to a comparatively recent period. Lenoir found in the royal tombs in the Abbey of St. Denis, in 1793, in the coffin of Jeanne de Bourgogne, the first wife of Philip de Valois, her distaff and spindle; and in the tomb of Jeanne de Bourbon, wife of Charles V., among other relics, a spindle or distaff of gilt wood. Grose mentions the tomb of Alice, prioress of the nunnery of Emanuel or Manuel, in Stirlingshire, on which was sculptured a distaff. And in Germany the spindle was suspended over the tombs of women of high rank, as the helm and the sword were displayed above those of the knight and the noble. Ditmar tells us that a silver spindle was suspended above the tomb of the wife of Conrad duke of Franconia, and daughter of the Emperor Otho, in the church of St. Alban the Martyr at Mayénce.

And Sir Lewis Pollard, the judge, who died in 1540, was represented on his monument with eleven sons, each girt with the sword, and the like number of *daughters with their spindles;* thus proving them to have been the badge of the sex in the first half of the sixteenth century. Gwillim, in his *Display of Heraldry,* gives the coat of the family of Trefusis — Argent, a chevron between three wharrow spindles sable; adding, " This spindle differeth much from those preceding in respect of the crook above, and of the wharrow imposed under the lower part thereof. · This sort of spindle women do use most commonly to spin withall, not at the torn, as the former, but at a distaff put under their girdle, so as they oftentimes spin therewith going. The round ball at the lower end serveth to the fast twisting of the thread, and is called a whwrrow; and therefore this is called a wharrow spindle, where the others are called slippers, that pass through the yarn as this doth." A friend informed the writer, that on one occasion he saw in the Highlands of Scotland a small potatoe serving the office of a wharrow or spindle-whirl.

The use of the distaff in England by the recluses is shown by Aubrey, who tells us that Wiltshire was full of religious houses, and that old Jacques "could see from his house the nuns of Saint Mary's (juxta Kington) come forth into the Nymph Hay with their rocks and wheels to spin, and with their sewing work." And in his Ms. *History of Wilts,* Aubrey says : " In the old time they used to spin with rocks; in Staffordshire, &c. they use them still."

In the *Boke of Husbandry,* said to have been written by Antony Fitzherbert, a judge of the Common Pleas, temp. Henry VIII., the writer urges attention to the growth and preparation of flax, which, he observes, should be among the cares of the good housewife. " Thereof," he says, "maie they make shetes, bordclothes, towells, sherts, smockes, and such other necessaries; and therefore let thy distaffe be alwaye redye for a pastyme, that thou be not ydle. And undoubted a woman can not gette her lyvinge honestly with spynnynge on the dystaffe, but it stoppeth a gap, and must nedes be had."

This is, perhaps, one of the most significant notices to be found in our literature of the use of the distaff and spindle. ·It shows that spinning, although a needful art, was the occupation of female leisure, the employment of the rich and the poor in the intervals of more important business, and in the long nights of winter. Hence Chaucer sarcastically makes it one of the three resources of women at all times:

> Deceapt, wepynge, spynnynge, God hath give
> To wymmen kyndely, whil thay may live.
> *Prologue to the Wyf of Bathes Tale.*

The distaff was, in fact, like the fancy-work and crochet of our day, a remedy against idleness; and was rarely abandoned, except when other duties demanded attention and forbade its use. This is plainly shown in the life of Saint Bertha, who, though engaged in the important office of founding a religious house, carried her distaff with her, using it in the manner of a plough to trace a channel from the well which she had purchased, to the monastery, the water filling the trench and flowing after her as she desired!

The distaff and spindle afforded light and not irksome employment even to the invalid and the blind. Nothing, perhaps, shows more clearly their constant and inveterate use than the vulgar superstition recorded in the *Evangiles des Quenouilles*, where the thread spun by a woman in childbed is directed to be tied around warts in order to charm them away.

We have already seen that the distaff was a weapon of defence: when pointed with iron, it could even be rendered a stiletto. That it was stuck in the girdle, we find from mediæval representations. In the Loutrell Psalter, the good wife comes out to feed the hen and her chicks from a platter, her distaff in her girdle; and in the very beautiful Ms. of Valerius Maximus in the British Museum, Sardanapalus is depicted spinning among a company of women, whose distaffs are secured in the same way.

The art of spinning, in one of its simplest and most primitive forms, is yet pursued in Italy, where the countrywomen of Caia still twirl the spindle, unrestrained by that ancient rural law which forbade its use without doors. The distaff has outlived the consular fasces, and survived the conquests of the Goth and the Hun. But rustic hands alone now sway the sceptre of Tanaquil, and all but the peasant disdain a practice which once beguiled the leisure of high-born dames.

We have selected and abridged these illustrations from an able paper by Mr. John Yonge Akerman, F.S.A. and Secretary to the society, in *Archæologia*, vol. xxxvii. pp. 83-101.

The finding of some spindle-pins in Sunbia, in 1846; and a notice of the art, as preserved in the term *spinster*, or single woman, in law,—will be found in *Things not generally Known*, First Series, p. 117.

SHOES.

Shining Shoes were at one time ridiculed as part of the precise dress of a citizen. Kitely says, as a citizen,

Mock me all over,
From my flat cap unto my shining shoes.
Ben Jonson's *Every Man in his Humour*, act ii. sc. 1.

The ornamental shoe-tie, like other gay fashions, came to us from France. Ben Jonson, describing a mere Englishman, who affected to be French, asks,

Would you believe
That so much scarf of France, of hat, and feather,
And shoe, and tye, and garter, should come hither!

Plain strings were first used, and soon after the great roses
which figure so much in portraits.

The shoeing-horn is mentioned by Shakspeare in *Troilus
and Cressida*, as in a chain, hanging at the leg. The shoeing-
horn is frequently used metaphorically as a convenient incite-
ment to liquor, something to *draw on* another glass or pot:
as, "a gamond of bacon well dressed is a good shoeing-horn
to pull down a cup of wine" (Dr. Cogan's *Haven of Health*). In
the old play of *Gammer Gurton* we find, "a shoeing-horn to
draw on two pots of ale." And in *Pierce Pennilesse:* "When
you have done, to have some shoeing-horns to pull on your
wine, as a rasher of the coles, or a red-herring." This frequent
use of the shoeing-horn as a metaphor implies its general
service.

Slippers were originally made *rights and lefts*, which might
not have been suspected but for the following passage:

Standing on slippers, which his nimble haste
Had falsely thrust upon contrary feet.
                              Shakspeare's *King John*, act iv. sc. 2.

These were shaped to each foot, so that they could not be con-
veniently interchanged; but this exactness had once been so
long disused as to puzzle Dr. Johnson. Other commentators
have abundantly illustrated the fact; and now shoes are almost
invariably so made.—Nares's *Glossary*, new edit. 1858, abridged.

SHOE-BLACKS.

A century since, London had its "gentlemen trading in
black-ball," as Chesterfield and Walpole designated the street
shoe-blacks, in *The World*, No. 57, wherein they look up with
envy to the occupation of shoe-cleaning, and lament the severity of their fortune in being sentenced to the drudgery of a
less respectable employment—authorship. Gay makes "the
black youth," his mythological descent from the goddess of
mud, and his importance in a muddy city, the subject of an
episode in his *Trivia*. The blacking was carried in a pipkin;
an old wig was invariably used to wipe off the dirt or dust
from the shoes, which were cleaned on the feet, and so dexter-
ously, as not to soil the fine white cotton stocking (once the
extreme of fashion), or to smear the bright buckles.

Dr. Johnson speaks of the shoe-black at the entry of his
court (Bolt-court, Fleet-street); several shoe-blacks might be
seen on the steps of St. Andrew's Church, Holborn; and on
the site of Finsbury-square, when it was a field. On the gene-

ral manufacture of blacking, shoe-blacks rapidly disappeared; but we remember a shoe-black at the entrance to Johnson's-court, Fleet-street, in 1824.

In 1851 the trade was revived by the Ragged-School Union employing wholly destitute boys as shoe-blacks in the streets, each wearing a red jacket and a numbered badge. Their receipts in the second year were 1500*l.*, a portion being placed to the boys' credit in the savings-bank; and some lads yearly emigrate to the colonies, paying out of their earnings a portion of their own outfit. Little was it expected a century since, that the pence earned by cleaning shoes in the streets would ever become the means of enabling shoe-blacks of London to emigrate to its antipodes!

Chamberlayne, in his *Present State of Great Britain*, 1726, sarcastically says: "There is in England plenty of excellent leather for all sorts of uses: insomuch that the poorest people in England wear good shoes of leather; whereas in our neighbouring countries the poor generally wear either shoes of wood, or none at all."

SILK STOCKINGS FIRST WORN IN ENGLAND.

Silk Stockings were very rare long after they had been first seen in England. Sir Thomas Gresham had sent to him the memorable "payre of long Spauish silke stockings" which he presented to Edward VI., and which Stow has commemorated in his *Chronicle* as "a great present." The gift derived its value from the rarity of the object; "for you shall understand that King Henry VIII. did weare onely cloath hose, or hose cut out of ell-broade taffaty; or that by great chance there came a paire of Spaniah silke stockings from Spaine." So that, although silk stockings had been brought into England a few years prior to the reign of Edward VI., Gresham's gift constitutes the earliest distinct mention of the introduction of that article of dress into this country.

Sir Thomas Gresham, writing to Sir William Cecil in 1560, says: "I have written into Spayne for silk hose both for you and my lady your wife;" those for Cecil were black. Silk stockings were still of great rarity and value, as appears from an anecdote related of Queen Elizabeth by Stow. "In 1560," he says, "her silk-woman, Mistress Mountague, presented her Maiestie with a payre of blacke kuit silke stockings, for a new-year's gift; the which, after a few dayes wearing, pleased her Highnesse so well, that she sent for Mistris Mountague, and asked her where she had them, and if she could help her to any more: who answered, saying, 'I have made them very carefully, of purpose only for your Majesty; and seeing these please you so well, I will presently set more in hand.' 'Do so,' quoth the Queen ; ' for indeede I like silke stockings so well, because they are pleasant, fine, and delicate, that henceforth I will wear no more cloth stockings.' "

WEARING KNIVES.

The Knife was often used for a sword or dagger ; but in Shakspeare's time it meant rather the latter :

That my keen knife see not the wound it makes.
Macbeth, act i. sc. 5.

Here, however, they are expressly distinguished :

I wear no knife to murder sleeping men ;
But here's a revengeful sword.   *2 Henry VI.* act iii. sc. 2.

Spenser, who purposely employed a phraseology more anti-quated than his own, often used knife for a sword :

And after all his war to rest his wearie knife.
Faerie Queene, iii. iv. 24.

Knives and daggers were part of the customary accoutrements of brides ; they were, however, commonly worn by ladies, and the wedding-knives were only more highly ornamented than the others. Shakspeare, in the old quarto, 1597, makes Juliet wear a knife at the friar's cell, and when she is about to take the potion. Steevens thus illustrates the wearing of wedding-daggers :

See at my girdle hang my weidling-knives.
Dekker's Match me in London, 1631.

Here by my side do hang my wedding-knives.
King Edward III. 1599.

WORSTED AND BLANKETS.

Worsted is named from its having been originally manufac-tured in the reign of Henry II. at Worsted, in Norfolk, by the Flemings who fled from the persecutions under the Duke of Alva. *Blankets* are so called from their having been first made, in 1340, by one Thomas Blanket, of Bristol.

WEARING THE BAND.

The Band, as an article of ornament for the neck, was for-merly the common wear of gentlemen ; the clergy, and lawyers, who now exclusively retain them, formerly wore ruffs. The assumption of the band was doubtless originally a piece of coxcombry, as was the wearing of large wigs ; though both are now thought to be connected with professional dignity. It is rather remarkable that what, from the old usage, was within these forty years called a band at the universities, is now called a *pair of bands*, probably from a supposed resemblance to a pair of breeches.—Nares's *Glossary*.

WEARING POWDER.

Powder for the hair was introduced into England early in the seventeenth century, and became immediately ridiculed by the dramatists, and severely censured by the Puritans. In a play printed in 1618, the wearers are alluded to as "curled millers' heads;" and Ford, in *Love's Sacrifice*, 1633, talks of a lady powdering her hair. About 1654, Howell refers to our modern gallants as "all mad, or subject to be mad, because they ashe and powder their pericraniums all the year long."

The fashion again became ridiculed in 1705, when the duty of one guinea per annum was levied upon every person who wore hair-*powder;* and John Britton and E. W. Brayley wrote and printed a ballad entitled *The Guinea-Pig*, of which many thousands were sold at one penny each. The hair-powder duty in the first year was estimated at 200,000*l.*

KENDAL-GREEN, LINCOLN-GREEN,

was a sort of foresters' green cloth, for the manufacture of which Kendal, in Westmoreland, was famous. Shakspeare, in 1 *Henry IV.* act ii. sc. 4, has

> Three misbegotten knaves in Kendal-green.

It was the uniform of Robin Hood's followers :

> All the woods
> Are full of outlaws, that in Kendal-green
> Follow'd the outlaw'd Earl of Huntingdon.
> *Robert Earl of Huntingdon,* 1601.

Fuller, in his *Worthies*, being a Cambridge man, out of sympathy wishes well to the clothiers of Kendal, "as the first founders of Kendal-green."

Lincoln was also celebrated for the manufacture of green cloth and stuffs, or rather for the green dye employed upon them. Spenser has :

> All in a woodman's jacket he was clad
> Of Lincoln-green, belayed with silver-lace.   *Faerie Queene.*
> Whose swains in shepherds' gray, and girls in Lincoln-green.
> Drayton's *Polyolbion.*

Robin Hood's men were clad in Lincoln-green :

> An hundred valiant men had this brave Robin Hood,
> Still ready at his call, that bow-men were right good,
> All clad in Lincoln-green, with caps of red and blue.—*Drayton.*

Robin Hood himself wore a mantle of Lincoln-green ; but when he went to court,

> He clothed his men in Lincoln-green,
> And himself in scarlet-red.   *Robin Hood's Garland.*

SERVANTS' BADGES.

In the time of Shakspeare all the servants of the nobility wore silver badges on their liveries, on which the arms of their masters were engraved. The colour of the coat was universally blue. It was also called a cognizance.

According to Spenser, the livery which a serving-man wears is so called, as it is delivered and taken from him at pleasure.

USE OF STARCH.

In the reign of Elizabeth was introduced the fashion of using Starch of different colours, to tinge the linen. In 1561, a Dutch woman undertook to teach the art of starching for four or five pounds, with 20s. additional for showing " how to seethe the starch." In a masque by Middleton and Rowley, five differently coloured starches are personified, and introduced as contending for superiority in monstrous and starched ruffs, —all which were abused by Stubbs, who enumerates " white, redde, blewe, and purple" starch, but strangely omits yellow, which, in popularity, surpassed all the rest.

Yellow starch dates from 1616 ; for in the *Owle's Almanacke*, 1618, it is said : " since yellow bandes and saffroned chaperoones came up, is not above two yeares past ; but since citizens' wives fitted their husbands with yellow hoze is not within the memory of man." Mrs. Turner, who was executed for the murder of Sir Thomas Overbury, is said to have invented yellow starch : she was hanged at Tyburn in a yellow ruff, which threw the colour into temporary disgrace ; but the belles soon forgot this, and yellow starch afterwards became more fashionable than ever.

INDIAN MUSLIN.

The excellence of this fabric may be thus explained. The native cotton of India has a far shorter fibre than that of North America : little care is bestowed on its cultivation and collection, and little care is taken to protect it from injury after it is collected. That the fibre is good and fit for manufacturing purposes is evident ; for the muslins woven in the looms of India have long shown how the labour and ingenuity of the natives could with this cotton, even in spite of careless cultivation and imperfect methods, more than match European skill, though aided with all the appliances of modern science and mechanical invention.—*E. Solly, F.R.S.*

WEARING THE WATCH.

The Wearing of a Watch was, till late times, considered in some degree as a mark and proof of gentility ; though the invention may be traced back to the 14th century. Watches were even worn ostentatiously hung round the neck to a chain; which fashion has been revived in female dress.

A watch makes part of the supposed grandeur of Malvolio in his anticipated view of his great fortune :

> I frown the while, and perchance wind up my watch, or play with some rich jewel.—Shakspeare's *Twelfth Night.*

Even a repeater is introduced by Ben Jonson :

> It strikes one, two,
> Three, fc r, five, six. Enough, enough, dear watch.
> *Staple of News.*

In the *Alchemist*, a watch is lent to wear in dress :

> And I had lent my watch last night to one
> That dines to-day at the sheriff's.

In 1638, watches had become so common, that

> Every puny clerk can carry
> The time of day in his pocket.
> *Antipodes, a Comedy.*

But if the following story be true, which Aubrey tells of one Mr. Allen, a reputed sorcerer, who died, aged 96, in 1630, watches must have been in his day very uncommon :

> One time, being at Home Lacy, in Herefordshire, Allen happened to leave his watch in the chamber-window (watches were then rarities) [we may add, perhaps, particularly in Herefordshire]. The maydes came in to make the bed; and hearing a thing in a case crying *tick, tick, tick*, presently concluded that was his devil [or familiar], and took it by the string with the tongues (tongs) and threw it out of the window into the mote, to drowne the devil. It so happened that the string hung on the sprig of a elder that grew out of the mote, and this confirmed them that 'twas the devil. So the good old gentleman gote his watch again.—*Letter in the Bodleian Library.*

GENTLEMEN OF THE BEDCHAMBER.

Chamberlayne tells us that the Gentlemen of the Privy Chamber, first established by King Henry VII., as a particular mark of royal favour and trust, are empowered to execute the king's verbal commands, without producing any written order, their persons and character being sufficient authority. For example, in King Henry the Eighth's time, Cardinal Wolsey was arrested for high treason by a gentleman of the privy chamber, without any written order ; the cardinal obeyed, saying his person was a sufficient warrant, after the said cardinal had refused to submit to the arrest by a great lord and an order in writing. The date of Chamberlayne's work is 1726 (temp. George I.). He continues : The first of the eleven gentlemen of the bedchamber is the groom of the stole, that is, groom or servant of the long robe or vestment ; he having the office

and honour to present and put on his majesty's first garment
or shirt every morning, and to order the things of the bed-
chamber. Of the gentlemen, each in his turn waits one week
in the king's bedchamber, there to lie by the king on a pallet-
bed all night, and in the absence of the groom of the stole to
supply his place.

THE ROYAL HARBINGER.

The Harbinger, or Forerunner, is an officer in the royal
household, whose duty it was in ancient times to allot and
mark the lodgings of all the king's attendants in a progress;
and the term is derived from the word *harborough* or *harbergh*,
a lodging. This custom was in force in Charles the Second's
reign, when, on the removal of the Court to pass the summer at
Winchester, Bishop Ken's house, which he held in the right
of his prebend, was marked by the harbinger for the use of Mrs.
Eleanor Gwynn; but Ken refused to grant her admittance, and
she was forced to seek for lodgings in another place.

HENCHMAN

was the old name for a page or attendant; or *haunchman*,
from following the haunch of his master: it was also applied
to boy, as *hench-boy* or *haunch-boy*. Shakspeare speaks of the
haunch of winter as the latter end of it. Here etymologies
seem obvious enough: but Dr. Johnson derives the word from
hync, Saxon for servant, and man (*Skinner*); and from *hen-
gest*, a horse (*Spelman*). Still, it was most commonly used for
foot-attendant, or page. But Chaucer has mounted *henshmen*.
Still, this only affects the etymology, for they became pages afterwards. Minshew says expressly that "it is used for a man who
goes on foot attending upon a man of honour or great worship."

> I do but beg a little changling boy,
> To be my henchman.
> > Shakspeare's *Midsummer-Night's Dream*, act ii. so. 2.
>
> Three henchmen were to every knight assign'd,
> All in rich livery clad, and of a kind.   *Dryden.*

Henchmen were excepted from the operation of the statute
4 Edward IV. cap. 5, concerning excess of apparel.

Hench-boy was not uncommon: in the old play of *Wits:*

> Sir, I will match my lord mayor's horse, make jockeys of his hench-
> boys, and run 'em through Cheapside:

showing that to set hench-boys on horseback was to change the
nature of their service.

THE BOARD OF GREEN CLOTH.

This is the name of the office of the Lord Steward of her

Majesty's household in St. James's Palace, and is derived from
the table at which the Lord Steward and his officers usually sit.
Chamberlayne describes it (and Dr. Johnson follows him) as

A Court of Justice continually sitting in the King's House. To this
court is committed the charge and oversight of the King's Court-Royal
for matters of justice and government, with authority for maintaining
the peace within the verge wheresoever the court shall reside, and the
power of correcting all the servants therein that shall in any way offend.

It is called the *Green Cloth*, of a green cloth, where they sit ; over
whom are the arms of the Compting-house, bearing *vert*, a key, *or*, and
a staff *argent saultier*, signifying their power to reward and correct.

The jurisdiction of the board extended over "the verge of
the court," or twelve miles round the residence of the Sovereign,
and was extended to "progresses," though not to "huntings."
The limit was first defined by 13 Richard II. stat. 1. cap. 3.
All offences were tried within "the Sessions of Verges," and all
committals were made to the Marshalsea, of which "the Court
of Verges" was a branch. To the Board belonged the sole right
of arresting within the limits and jurisdiction of the palace.
The warrant-book, in the Lord Steward's office, contains several
entries of committals to the Marshalsea of persons for such
offences as serving a subpœna in the king's house, for serving
the Lord Chief-Justice's warrant in St. James's Park, and for
striking in the king's court. The punishment was forfeiture of
the right hand, and forfeiture of lands and goods. William Earl
of Devonshire (the patriot earl, and afterwards the first duke)
was fined by the Board 30,000l. for caning Colonel Colepepper
and pulling his nose in the Vane Chamber at Whitehall.

"It is to be noted," says Sir John Bramston, "that this Colepepper
had struck the Earl some months since in the same or in the next room,
and was tried for it at the verge, and was sentenced to lose his hand,
and was at the great instance of the Earl pardoned."—*Autobiography
of Sir John Bramston*, p. 275.

Mr. Cunningham (*Handbook of London*), to show the nature
of the duties of the Lord Steward, quotes the following order
from the warrant-book:

Board of Green Cloth, 12 *June* 1631.

Orders were this day given that the Maids of Honour should have
sherry tarts instead of gooseberry tarts, it being observed that cherrys
are at threepence per pound.

The Poets Laureate used to receive their annual tierce of
canary from this office : Cibber is stated to be the last who took
the tierce, and since his time there has been paid to the Poets
Laureate an annual allowance of 27l. in lieu of wine.

The practice of this notorious "Palace Court" was extended
to the holding plea of all personal actions arising within twelve
miles of the palace : the Court existed as an oppressive tribunal
until 1849, when it was abolished.

OFFENCES IN THE ROYAL PARKS.

The Park, as well as the Palace, formerly not only sheltered persons from arrest, but to draw a sword in the Park was also a very serious offence. Congreve, in his *Old Bachelor*, makes Bluffe say, " My blood rises at that fellow. I can't stay where he is; and *I must not draw in the Park*." Traitorous expressions, when uttered in St. James's Park, were punished more severely. Francis Heat was whipped, in 1717, from Charing Cross to the upper end of the Haymarket, fined ten groats, and ordered a month's imprisonment, for saying aloud in St. James's Park, " God save King James III., and send him a long and prosperous reign !" and, in 1718, a soldier was whipped in the Park for drinking a health to the Duke of Ormond and Dr. Sacheverel, and for saying he hoped soon to wear his right master's cloth." The Duke of Wharton, too, was seized by the guard in St. James's Park for singing the Jacobite air, " The king shall have his own again." In the letter-book of the Lord Steward's office are two letters, dated 1677, sent with two lunatics to Bethlehem : Deborah Lyddal, for offering to throw a stone at the queen; and Richard Harris, for throwing an orange at the king; in St. James's Park.—*Curiosities of London.*

COCK-CROW.

Mr. T. Forster, the meteorologist, observes, that during the still dark weather which usually happens about the Brumal Solstice, cocks often crow all day and all night : hence the belief that they crow all night on the vigil of the Nativity.

There is this remarkable circumstance about the crowing of cocks : they seem to keep night-watches, or to have general crowing matches at certain periods, as—soon after twelve, at two, and again at daybreak. These are the Alectrophones mentioned by St. John. To us these cock-crowings do not appear quite so regular in their times of occurrence, though they observe certain periods, when not interrupted by changes of the weather, which generally produce a great deal of crowing ; indeed, the song of all birds is much influenced by the state of the air.

It seems that *crepusculum*, or twilight, is the sort of light during which cocks crow most. This has been observed during the darkness of eclipses of the sun, as in that of September 4th, 1820.

It was long ago believed among the common people that at the time of cock-crowing the midnight spirits forsook these lower regions, and went to their proper places. This notion is very ancient; for Prudentius, the Christian poet of the fourth century, has a hymn, the opening of which is thus translated :

> They say the wandering powers that love
> The silent darkness of the night,
> At cock-crowing give o'er to rove,
> And all in fear do take their flight.

This idea is illustrated by Shakspeare in *Hamlet*, where the ghost was "about to speak, when the cock crew;" and "faded at the crowing of the cock." By a passage in *Macbeth*, "we were carousing till the second cock," it appears there were two separate times of cock-crowing; and in *King Lear* we have, "he begins at curfew, and walks till the first cock." And in *Romeo and Juliet*,

> The second cock has crow'd,
> The curfew bell has toll'd ; 'tis three o'clock.

Chaucer, in his *Assemblie of Foules*, has,

> The cocke, that horologe is of Thropes lite ;

i. e. the clock of the villages.

The disappearance of spirits at cock-crow is a frequent fancy of the poets. Herrick, in his *Hesperides*, "The old Wive's Prayer," has,

> Drive all hurtful fiends us fro'
> By the time the cocks first crow.

Spenser says of one of his spirits :

> The morning cock crew loud ;
> And at the sound it shrunk in haste away,
> And vanished from our sight.

In two lines ascribed to Drayton :

> And now the cocke, the morning's trumpeter,
> Play'd Hunts up for the Day-Star to appear.

Butler, in *Hudibras*, part iii. canto 1, has :

> The cock crows, and the morn draws on,
> When 'tis decreed I must begone.

And in Blair's *Grave*, the apparition evanishes at the crowing of the cock.

Tusser gives the order of crowing, in his *Five Hundred Pointes of Good Husbandrie*, as follows :

> Cocke croweth at midnight, times few above six,
> With pause to his neighbour to answer betwix :
> At three aclocke thicker, and then, as ye knowe,
> Like all into mattens neere day they doo crowe :
> At midnight, at three, and an hour yer day,
> They utter their language as well as they may.

Or, who can forget the allusion in Milton's *Comus*, where the two brothers, beulghted in the forest, implore that they may but hear the village cock

> Count the night-watches to his feathery dames ?

Bourne thus illustrates the sacredness and solemnity of the periods of crowing :

It was about the time of Cock-crowing when our Saviour was born. The Angels sung the first Christmas Carol to the poor shepherds in the fields of Bethlehem. Now it may be presumed, as the Saviour of the world was then born, and the heavenly Host had then descended to proclaim the news, that the Angels of Darkness would be terrified and confounded, and immediately fly away; and perhaps this consideration has partly been the foundation of this opinion. It was, too, about this time when our Saviour rose from the dead. A third reason is, the passage in the Book of Genesis, where Jacob wrestled with the Angel for a blessing; where the Angel says unto him, 'Let me go, for the day breaketh.'"

Bourne likewise attaches much importance to

the circumstances of the time of Cock-crowing, being so natural a figure and representation of the Morning of the Resurrection; the Night as shadowing out the Night of the grave; the third watch being, as some suppose, the time our Saviour will come to Judgment at; the noise of the Cock awakening sleepy man, and telling him, as it were, the Night is far spent, and the Day is at hand, representing so naturally the voice of the Archangel awakening the dead, and calling up the righteous to everlasting Day: so naturally does the time of Cock-crowing shadow out these things, that probably some good, well-meaning men might have been brought to believe that the very Devils themselves, when the Cock crew and reminded them of them, did fear and tremble, and shun the Light.

In the Great or Passion Week, as kept in the fourth century, the fast of Good Friday was prolonged, by all who were able to bear it, over the succeeding Saturday, while Christ continued in the tomb, till Cock-crow on the Easter morning.

During Lent, so late as the reign of George I., an officer of the Court, denominated "the King's Cock-crower," *crowed the hour* every night within the precincts of the palace, instead of calling it in the ordinary manner. In Debrett's *Imperial Calendar* for the year 1822, in the list of persons holding appointments in the Lord Steward's department of the royal household, occurs the "Cock and Cryer at Scotland-yard."

SEDAN-CHAIRS

are named from Sedan, on the Meuse, in France, where they were seen by Sir Sanders Duncombe, who subsequently introduced them for public hire. They were, however, first used in England by the Duke of Buckingham, in 1623, when Prince Charles, returning from Spain, brought with him three curiously-wrought sedans, two of which he gave to the Duke, who, first using one in the streets of London, was accused of "degrading Englishmen into slaves and beasts of burden." Massinger, in his *Bondman*, produced a few weeks after, refers to ladies

For their pomp and ease being borne
In triumph on men's *shoulders;*

doubtless in allusion to Buckingham's sedan, which was borne like a palanquin. But the popular clamour was ineffectual; and in 1634, Duncombe, now a pensioner, obtained a patent from the king "for carrying people up and down in close chairs," and had "forty or fifty making ready for use." The coachmen and chairmen soon quarrelled; and in 1636 appeared a tract entitled *Coach and Sedan pleasantly disputing for Place and Precedence.* The chairmen, however, no longer bore the sedan on their shoulders, but suspended by straps, as in our time; and the form of the chair was also changed.

Among the Exchequer papers has been found a bill for a sedan-chair made for Nell Gwyn, 34*l.* 11*s.*, the several items being charged separately; besides a bill for chair-hire, 1*l.* 11*s.* 6*d.* (See Cunningham's *Nell Gwyn*, p. 142.)

Defoe, writing in 1702, says: "We are carried to these places (the coffee-houses of Pall-mall and St. James's-street) in chairs (or sedans), which are here very cheap—a guinea a week, or a shilling per hour; and your chairmen serve you for porters, to run on errands, as your gondoliers do at Venice." Dryden has, "close mew'd in their sedans;" and Gay,

At White's the harnessed chairman idly stands.   *Trivia.*

"Two pages and a chair" are the outfit of Pope's Belinda (*Rape of the Lock*). Swift thus describes a fop in a sedan during a "City Shower:"

> Box'd in a chair, the beau impatient sits,
> While spouts run clattering o'er the roof by fits;
> While ever and anon, with frightful din,
> The leather sounds;—he trembles from within!

In St. James's Palace is the "Chair Court;" Hogarth's picture of "The Rake arrested by Bailiffs" shows us the arrival of chairs at the Palace-gate; and in Hogarth's "Beer-street" we have a pair of chairmen calling for a foaming mug. The chairmen of the aristocracy wore embroidered liveries, cocked-hats, and feathers; and the chair had its crimson-velvet cushions and damask curtains, such as Jonathan Wild recovered for the Duchess of Marlborough, when two of his rogues, in the disguise of chairmen, carried away her chair from Lincoln's Inn Chapel, while "the true men were drinking." There exists a curious print of Leicester-square in the reign of George II., showing the Prince of Wales borne in his sedan towards St. James's, attended by halberdiers and his suite.

Hannah More, during the Westminster election, in 1784, was carried in a chair from Henrietta-street through Covent Garden, when a great crowd followed her, crying out, "It is Mrs. Fox: none but Mr. Fox's wife would dare to come into Covent Garden in a chair. She is going to canvass in the dark!" "Though not a little frightened," says Hannah, "I laughed heartily at this; but shall stir out no more in a chair for some time."

Sedans are now very rare: the Duchesses of Gloucester, Hamilton, and Dowager Northumberland, and the Marchioness of Salisbury, are stated to have been the last persons who retained this antiquated mode of conveyance. In entrance-halls is occasionally kept the old disused family sedan, emblazoned with arms. A few link-extinguishers are to be seen in the iron-work facing old mansions; the sign of "the Two Chairmen," exists in Warwick-street, Cockspur-street; and on Hay-hill; and in Charles-street, Berkeley-square, is the old sign of "the Running Footman."

The Dowager Marchioness of Salisbury, who was buried at Hatfield in 1835, always went to court in a sedan-chair; and at night her carriage was known by the flambeaux of the footmen. We remember also to have seen the Dowager Duchess of Northumberland and Madame Catalani in their sedans.

Perhaps the longest journey ever performed in a sedan was the Princess Amelia being carried by eight chairmen from St. James's to Bath, between April 13 and April 19, 1728. The chairmen were relieved in their turns, a coach and six horses attending to carry the men when not on service.

EARLY COURT-BARBERS.

Glorieux comme un barbier is a French saying, which Duchat imputes to the very near contact of barbers with the faces of kings and great men. It appears from Rymer that the king's palace, in the time of Henry VI., was surrounded with little shops, which were to be entirely under the direction and control of the king's barber, together with the clerk of the ewry. As there were then no carriages, and the streets were very dirty, it is not improbable that those who went to court were shaved, as likewise dressed, in these stalls or shops before they appeared in the royal presence.

A considerable fee was also given to this barber for shaving every Knight of the Bath on his creation, as well as 40s. from every baron, 100s. from every earl, and 10l. from every duke, on the like occasion.

THE BARBER'S CHAIR.

The Chair in a Barber's Shop was long proverbial, from its capaciousness, for accommodating all occupants; whence arose the phrase *as common as a barber's chair.**

Plutarch remarks that barbers are naturally a loquacious race; and gives an anecdote of King Archelaus, who stipulated with his barber to shave him in silence. Not so, however, have thought most of barbers' customers: the cithern, or lute, was hung up in the shop, to be played for their diversion; and snapping his shears or fingers was a barber's qualification. Of his art, as practised of old, Lyly gives a curious sample in these phrases of "the elegant occupation:"

Now, sir, will you be trimmed? will you have your beard like a

* The Barber's Chair has lasted to our time as the oracle of news; and Douglas Jerrold used wittily to note the topics of the day under the head of the Barber's Chair, in *Lloyd's Weekly News.*

spade or a bodkin ! a penthouse on your upper lip, or an ally on your
chin ! a low curle on your head like a bull, or. dangling locks like a
spaniell ! your moustachios sharpe at the ends, like shomakers' aules,
or hanging down to your mouth, like goates' flakes ! your love-locks
wreathed with a silken twist, or shaggie to fill on your shoulders !

*

FORFEITS IN A BARBER'S SHOP.

Formerly Forfeits were enforced for certain breaches of conduct in a Barber's Shop : as,

For handling the razors,
For talking of *cutting throats*,
For calling *hair-powder flour*,
For meddling with any thing on the shopboard.

The custom is thus alluded to by Shakspeare :

The strong statutes
Stand, like the *forfeits* in a *barber's shop*,
As much in mock as mark.

Measure for Measure, act v. sc. i.

In 1856, there was hanging in a barber's shop at Stratford-
upon-Avon a set of rules, which the possessor mounted when
he was an apprentice, some fifty years previously; and his em-
ployer, who was in business as a barber at Stratford at the time
of Garrick's Jubilee (1769), frequently alluded to this list of
forfeits as being generally acknowledged by all the fraternity to
have been in use for centuries. The old man well remembered
large wooden bowls for lathering; which bowls were placed
under the chin, a convenient niche having been cut in the side
in which the chin dropped and kept the bowl suspended during
the lathering operation. He used to relate that some of the
customers paid by the quarter: for these an especial bowl was
set apart, and used only at the time when their shaving-money
was due; and inside this particular bowl, inscribed in perfectly
unmistakable characters, were the words, " Sir, your quarter's
up !" The following are the

Rules for seemly Behaviour.

First come, first served—then come not late;
And when arrived keep your state :
For he who from these rules should swerve,
Must pay the forfeits—so observe.

1.

Who enters here with boots and spurs,
Must keep his nook ; for if he stirs,
And gives with armed heel a kick,
A pint he pays for every prick.

2

Who rudely takes another's turn,
A forfeit mug may manners learn.

3.

Who reverentless shall swear or curse,
Must lug seven farthings from his purse.

4.

Who checks the barber in his tale,
Must pay for each a pot of ale.

5.

Who will or cannot miss his hat
While trimming, pays a pint for that.

6.

And he who can or will not pay,
Shall hence be sent half trimm'd away;
For will he, nill he, if in fault,
He forfeit must in meal or malt,
But mark, who is already in drink,
The cannikin must never clink.

This table of forfeits was published by Dr. Kenrick, in his review of Dr. Johnson's edition of Shakspeare, 1765; and was quoted by him from recollection of a list he had read many years before, at Malton, or Thirsk, Yorkshire.

Nares thinks these lines wear some appearance of fabrication; particularly in the mention of *seven farthings*, evidently put as equivalent to a pint of ale, but in reality the price of a pint of porter in London when Dr. Kenrick produced the above lines, and not at all likely to have been the price of a pint of ale many years previously.

UNLUCKY HAIR.

A Correspondent of *Notes and Queries*, No. 20, N.S. writes: "Among our peasantry, it is considered very unlucky to leave lying about, or to throw away, any, even the smallest scrap of human hair." They therefore pick it up, sweep up the place where hair has been cut, and scrupulously burn the sweeping in the fire, saying, that if left about, the birds would build their nests with the hair, a fatal thing for him or *her* from whose head it had fallen: they say, if a *pyet* (Anglicè magpie) got hold of it for any such purpose,—by no means an unlikely circumstance, considering the thievish propensities of the bird, —the person's death "within year and day" was sure.

LONG HAIR AND THE BEARD.

In 1102, at a council held in London by Archbishop Anselm, it was enacted that those who had Long Hair should be cropped, so as to show part of the ear and the eyes. Odericus Vitalis tells us how Bishop Serlo, preaching before Henry I. and his court, inveighed so successfully against the iniquity of long locks, that his audience saw the folly of their ways; and the prelate, seizing the favourable moment, produced a pair of scissors from his sleeve, and cropped the king and many of his courtiers with his own hand.

From Wace and the Bayeux tapestry we find that the Beard was not worn by the Normans at the time of the Conquest, though in fashion among the Anglo-Saxons. And the Normans continued their custom till the second half of the twelfth century. The monumental effigy of Henry II. at Fontevraud represents him without either beard or moustache. "The beard," says Stothard, "is painted and pencilled like a miniature, to represent its being close shaven." Among the English, however, the beard was often retained, and became a sort of protest against the new dynasty. In 1196, William Longbeard—"le dernier des Saxons," as he is named by M. Thierry—became conspicuous from his opposition to the Norman rule, the inveteracy of which was manifested to the world by the excessive length of his beard. At this time, however, a beard and moustache of moderate dimensions were in vogue among both races. The effigy of Richard II. at Fontevraud, and that of King John at Worcester, offer good examples of this change of fashion.— *Hewitt on Ancient Armour.*

THE FRANKLIN

of old was a freeholder or yeoman; a man above a vassal or villein, but not a gentleman. Still, the usage varied, as follows:

Not swear it, now I am a gentleman? let boors and *franklins* say it, I'll swear 't.— *Winter's Tale,* act v. sc. 2.

There is a franklin in the wilds of Kent hath brought three hundred marks with him in gold.—1 *Henry IV.* ii. 1.

Provide me presently
A riding suit, no costlier than would fit
A franklin's housewife.   *Cymbeline,* iii. 2.

In the following a franklin seems to mean a kind of waiting gentleman, or groom of the chambers:

But entered in a spacious court, they see,
* * * *
Where them does meet a franklin fair and free,
And entertaines with comely courteous glee.
              Spenser's Faerie Queene.

Thus low was the estimation of a franklin in the reign of Elizabeth. In earlier times he was a personage of much more dignity, and seems to have been distinguished from a common freeholder by the greatness of his possessions. Chaucer's *frankelein* is evidently a very rich and luxurious gentleman: he was the chief man at the sessions, and had been sheriff, and frequently knight of the shire.—Nares's *Glossary,* new edit. 1858.

THE HAYWARD

was the old name for the keeper of the cattle or common herd of a parish or village,—from *hay*, a hedge, and *ward;* because a chief part of his business was to see that the beasts did not break down or browse the hedges. Puttenham, in his *Art of English Poetry*, speaks of "the shepheards and haywards assemblies and meetings when they kept their cattel and heards." Like other disused words, it still remains in use as a surname. We have *Hayward's Heath*, on the London and Brighton Railway.

FOSTER, OR FORSTER.

This is a contraction of Forrester, in which form it still exists as a proper name. It is several times used by Spenser:

So where a griesly foster forth did rush.   *Faerie Queene.*

The word is also found in Chaucer, and the romance of Bevis of Hampton.

THE YEOMANRY OF ENGLAND.

Mr. Buckle, in his admirable *History of Civilization in England*, vol. i., gives the following account of this "once important class:"

Our municipal privileges, the rights of our yeomanry, and the security of our copyholders, were, from the fourteenth to the seventeenth conturies, the three most important gaurantees for the liberties of England. In France, such guarantees were impossible. The real division being between those who were noble and those who were not noble, no room was left for the establishment of intervening classes; but all were compelled to fall into one of these two great ranks. The French have never had any thing answering to our yeomanry; nor were copyholders recognised by their laws.

The history of the decay of that once most important class, the English yeomanry, is an interesting subject. Its decline was first distinctly perceptible in the latter half of the seventeenth century, and was consummated by the rapidly increasing power of the commercial and manufacturing classes, early in the eighteenth century. After losing their influence, their numbers naturally diminished, and they made way for other bodies of men, whose habits of mind were less prejudiced, and therefore better suited to that new state which society assumed in the last age. Some writers regret the almost total destruction of the yeoman freeholders; overlooking the fact, that they are disappearing, not in consequence of any violent revolution or stretch of arbitrary power, but simply by the general march of affairs; society doing away with what it no longer requires.

A Yeoman, in legal definition, is he that hath free land or forty shillings by the year; who was anciently thereby qualified to serve on juries, vote for knights of the shire, and do any other act where the law requires one that is *probus et legalis homo.*

MARRIAGE CELEBRATIONS.

When a man and his wife have been married in Germany fifty years, there is a sort of second marriage celebrated with the greatest festivity. And in Holland, after a man and his wife have been married twenty-five years, there is a solemnity which is called a *Silver Marriage;* after fifty, it is dignified with the name of a *Golden Marriage.*

A RACE FOR A MARRIAGE.

There is a custom in this barbarous country (Derbyshire), says Burton, in his *Admirable Curiosities,* 10th edit., 1737, that it is death to marry a maid without her friends' consent; so that if any man have affection for a maid, a day is appointed for both their friends to meet, and see the young couple run a race. The maid hath the advantage of starting, and the third part of the race, so that it is impossible, except she be willing, ever to be overtaken: if the maid outrun him, he must never make any further motion to her, under a penalty; but if she have any affection for him, though she at first run hard to try his love, yet she proceeds to stumble and halt, so that he may overtake her.

"THE SCRATCH-CRADLE."

The Cratch is a manger, particularly that in which our Saviour was laid; and the word is still used in Roman Catholic countries in that particular sense:

> The sun reduced the solemnised day
> On which, a King laid in a cratch to find,
> Three kings did come conducted from the east.
>   Fanshaw's *Lusiad.*
> There in a cratch a jewell was brought forth,
> More than ten thousand thousand worlds in worth.
>   Taylor's *Workes,* 1630.

This opens to us the meaning of the childish game corruptly called *Scratch-cradle,* which consists in winding pack-thread double round the hands into a rude representation of a manger, which is taken off by the other player on his hands so as to assume a new form, and thus alternately for several times, always changing the appearance. The art consists in making the right changes. But it clearly meant, originally, the cratch-cradle,—the manger that held the Holy Infant as a .radle.—Nares's *Glossary.*

WEDDING CUSTOMS.

The principal customs observed at Weddings, in the seven

teenth century, are curiously collected in the following passage from Beaumont and Fletcher's *Scornful Lady*:

> Bollove mo, if my wodding smock were on,
> Wore tho glovos bought and giv'n, tho liconso coms,
> Wore tho rosomary branches dipp'd, and all
> The hippocras and cakes eat and drunk off,
> Woro these two arms incompass'd with the hands
> Of bachelors, to lead me to the church,
> Wore my feet at the door—wore "I John" said,[*]
> If John should boast a favour done by me,
> I would not wed that year.

APOSTLE AND OTHER SPOONS.

Spoons of silver, sometimes gilt, the handle of each terminating in the figure of an apostle, were named Apostle Spoons—a set being *twelve*. They were the usual present of sponsors at christenings; and are still to be seen in the shops of our silversmiths, and in the cabinets of the curious. It is in allusion to the above custom, that, when Cranmer professes to be unworthy of being sponsor to the young princess, the king replies, "Come, come, my lord, you'd spare your spoons" (*Henry VIII.* act v. sc. 2). Ben Jonson, in his *Bartholomew Fair*, has, "And all this for the hope of two apostle spoons."

HEDGEHOG SUPERSTITIONS.

One cause of the superstitions attached to the Hedgehog is the peculiar noise it makes, which is alluded to by Shakspeare in *Macbeth*, where the witches round the caldron say:

> Twice the brindled cat hath mew'd,
> Twice and once the *hedge-pig whin'd*, &c.

The sound of its voice is that of a person snoring, or breathing very hard; and, as heard in the silence of the night, might be mistaken by the fearful and superstitious for the moaning of a disturbed spirit.—*Notes and Queries*, 2d S., No. 103.

THE HARE.—ITS MELANCHOLY AND OMENS.

A Hare was formerly esteemed a melancholy animal, probably from her solitary sitting in her form; and thence, in the fanciful physics of the time, its flesh was supposed to engender melancholy. It was not eaten by the Britons, in Cæsar's time. It was not only in England that the hare had this character; La Fontaine calls it "le mélancolique animal."

Prince Henry tells Falstaff that he is melancholy as a hare (1 *Henry IV.* i. 2). In the old play of the *White Devil* occurs

[*] Namely, "I John take thee Mary," in the marriage-service.

> Like your poor melancholy hare,
> Feed after midnight.

Drayton sings:

> The melancholy hare is formed in brakes and briers.

An old medical writer says: "hare fleshe engeudreth melancholy bloudds," and "more melancholy than any other, as Galen sayth." This was not quite forgotten in Swift's time: in his *Polite Conversation*, Lady Answerall, being asked to eat hare, replies: "No, madam; they say, 'tis melancholy meat."

But the strangest opinion about hares was that they annually changed their sex, which was countenanced by respectable ancient authorities, and not denied by Sir Thomas Browne with so much decision as might be expected. Fletcher, in his *Gentle Shepherd*, alludes to

> Hares that yearly sexes change.

We are not surprised to find that a hare crossing a person's way was supposed to disorder his senses; the ground of which conceit, Sir Thomas Browne says, "was no greater than this, that a fearful animal passing by us portended unto us something to be feared;" but Wren illustrates it more practically: "when a hare crosseth us, wee thinke itt ill lucke shee should soe neerly escape us, and we had not a dog as neere to catch her."

The hare was vulgarly supposed to be so fearful, that it never closed its eyes, even in sleep. Chapman has drawn from this notion a fine epithet in his Epicedium on the death of Prince Henry:

> Relentless Rigor, and Confusion faint,
> Frantic Distemper, and hare-eyed Unrest.

Thomson has this line upon hare-hunting:

> Poor is the triumph o'er the timid hare.

The bone of a hare's foot was considered to be a remedy against the cramp:

> The bone of a haires foote closed in a ring,
> Will drive away the cramp whenas it doth wing.
>
> Withal's *Dictionarie*, 1608.

To hare was also the same as to hurry, to harass, or scare. Thus, in Ben Jonson's *Tale of a Tub:*

> Hare the poor fellow out of his five wits
> And seven senses.

JEW'S EYE.

The extortions to which Jews in England were subject before and after the thirteenth century exposed them to cruel mutilations, as drawing their teeth if they refused to pay the sums demanded of them. The threat of losing an eye would have a still more powerful effect: hence the high value of a Jew's Eye. The allusion was familiar in the time of Shakspeare:

> There will come a Christian by
> Will be worth a Jewess' eye.
> *Merchant of Venice*, act II. sc. 5.

JEWS' BREAD.

In the *Plantarium* of Cowley we find it noted that "in old time the seed of the white poppy, parched, was served up as a dessert." By this we are reminded that white-poppy seeds are eaten to this day, upon bread made exclusively for Jews. The "twist" bread is generally so prepared, by brushing over the outside upper crust with egg, and sprinkling upon it the seeds.

JEWISH MARRIAGES.

The night before the celebration of the marriage is called the "watch night," and is kept as such by the family of the bride and the maidens who attend her on the occasion. If the bridegroom's residence be at a distance from that of the bride, he usually arrives some time in the course of this night, or very early in the morning. The bridemaids watch anxiously for his arrival; and, as soon as they are apprised of his approach by the joyful shout set up by some of the members of the family who have been on the look-out to catch the first glimpse of him, "The bridegroom cometh!" they go forth to meet him. The precision with which this answers to the parable in the 25th chapter of Matthew's gospel scarcely requires pointing out: "While the bridegroom tarried, they all slumbered and slept. And at midnight there was a great cry made, Behold the bridegroom cometh: go ye out to meet him" (*Matt.* xxv. 5, 6).—*R. H. Herschell.*

THE TWELFTH-NIGHT BEAN.

The old method of choosing King and Queen on Twelfth Night was borrowed from the French, who had their *roi de la fève* on the same occasion. A bean and pea were mixed up in the composition of the cake; they who found these in their portions of the cake were constituted king and queen for the evening:

> Now, now the mirth comes,
> With the cake full of plums,
> Where beans 's the king of the sport here;
> Besides, we must know,
> The pea also
> Must revell as queene in the court here.
> *Herrick's Hesperides.*

This chance of king and queen led to the Twelfth-Night characters, of which there were so many that each of the party might draw one. John Britton claims to have introduced these characters, in 1799, when they "led the way to a custom which annually led to an extensive trade" (*Autobiography*, p. 129). These were letter-press characters; next year they were accompanied by prints of the personages, by Cruikshank (father of the inimitable George), all comic.

ST. AGNES' EVE.

To fast on the eve of the festival of St. Agnes, Jan. 21, using certain ceremonies, was esteemed a certain way for maids to dream of their future husbands:

> As on sweet St. Agnes' night,
> Please you with the promised sight,
> Some of husbands, some of lovers,
> Which an empty dream discovers.　　　BEN JONSON.

Aubrey has this account of the ceremony: "Upon St. Agnes' night you take a row of pins, and pull out every one, one after another, saying a Paternoster, sticking a pin in your sleeve; and you will dream of him or her you shall marry."

One of Keats's most graceful and picturesque poems is the "Eve of St. Agnes."

FIG SUNDAY.

On Palm Sunday, or the Sunday before Easter, it is customary in certain parts of England, with rich and poor, to eat figs, whence the day is termed Fig Sunday. The observance appears to be local. Miss Baker, in her *Northamptonshire Glossary*, 1854, states, that on the Saturday preceding the above day "the market at Northampton is abundantly supplied with figs, and there are more purchased at this time than throughout the rest of the year; even the charity-children in some places are regaled with them." Hone, in his *Year-book*, states that it has long been the custom for the inhabitants to eat figs on this day at Kempton in Hertfordshire, where they also keep wassail, and make merry. We remember the observance as common in our school-days, at Hemel Hempstead, in Hertfordshire. It is thought to have originated in our Saviour's desire to eat the fruit of the fig-tree, on his way from Bethany, after his triumphant entrance into Jerusalem, on the Monday following.

GOOD FRIDAY—CRAMP RINGS.

Hospinian tells us that the kings of England had a custom of *hallowing rings* with much ceremony on Good Friday, supposed to have taken its rise from a ring preserved in Westminster Abbey, believed to have great efficacy against the cramp and falling sickness when touched by those who were afflicted with either of these disorders. This ring is reported to have been brought to King Edward (probably the Confessor) by some persons coming from Jerusalem. Lord Berners, when ambassador to Charles V., writing to Cardinal Wolsey from Saragoça, June 21, 1518, says: " If your grace remember me with some *Crampe Rings*, ye shall do a thing much looked for; and I trust to bestow them well with God's grace," &c. (*Harleian Ms.*) We have known rings made of jet sold as remedies for cramp.

THE PASCHAL LIGHT.

This was an enormously thick wax-candle, which was lighted on the morning of Easter Day; the wax itself being curiously adorned with grains of incense, and inscribed with the epact, dominical letter, &c.; also the names of the reigning pope, king, and bishop of the diocese, and the date of the consecration of the church.—Hart's *Ecclesiastical Records, &c.*

EGGS AT EASTER.

Pasch Eggs, that is, Easter Eggs, from *Pascha*, the Passover, have been given in many countries as a sacred observance of the Romish Church, and prevailed among our ancestors before the Reformation. The egg was doubtless considered as an emblem of the Resurrection. It was usually coloured for the purpose, yellow, red, or blue. These eggs were blessed by the priests in this form: " Bless, O Lord, we beseech thee, this thy creature of eggs; that it may become a wholesome sustenance to thy faithful servants, eating it in thankfulness to thee on account of the Resurrection of our Lord," &c. Thus Egg Saturday concluded the eating of eggs before the fasting of Lent; and Easter Day began it again. There is extant a curious book of emblems (1672), adorned with one hundred beautiful engravings of eggs, with devices within them.

SAINT BARNABAS' DAY.

Saint Barnabas, after a life spent in preaching the Gospel, suffered many torments, and was starved to death. His remains were found near the city of Salamis, with a copy of the Gospel of St. Matthew in Hebrew laid on them.

Saint Barnabas Day (June 11) was anciently a great feast among the English people. The almost nightless day of the solstitial season, already begun, was sung in the old popular distich :

> Barnaby bright, Barnaby bright,
> The longest day and the shortest night.

This was literally the longest day according to the old style
a century and more ago; and now there is very little difference
in its length, being so near the summer solstice. This day is
Solstitialis in the Ephemeris of Nature. Great bonfires used to
be lighted this evening, as well as on the eve of St. John the
Baptist. Garlands of roses, of lavender, of rosemary, and of
woodroof, were also worn and used to decorate the churches on
St. Barnabas' Day, as we find by many old entries and church-
books; and they were often paid for by the parish.

This Saint's Day is annually observed at the College of St.
Barnabas, Pimlico; when the school-children are feasted, and
the schools are profusely decorated with flowers. The church,
with its painted windows, decorated oak roof, rood, corona,
&c., is also richly dight with flowers and evergreens in honour
of the patron saint.

One of the favourite flowers on this festival was woodroof;
and we find entries of money paid for it on St. Barnabas' Day
as early as the reign of Edward IV. Gerard has the following:

Woodroofe *Asperula* hath many and square stalkes full of joynts,
and at every knot or joynt seven or eight long narrow leaves, set round
about like a star or the rowell of a spurre. The flowers grow at the
top of the stems, of a white colour and a very sweet smell, as is the rest
of the herbe; which being made up into garlands on bundles, and hanging up in houses in the heat of summer, doth very well attemper the
aire, coole and make fresh the place, to the delight and comfort of such
as are therein. . . . Woodrooffe is reported to be put into wine to make
a man merry, and to be good for the heart and liver.—*Herball*, p. 1124.

MARTLEMAS

is a corruption of Martin-mass, that is, the feast of St. Martin,
which falls on the 11th of November. Falstaff is jocularly called
Martlemas, being in the decline of life, as the year is at this
season. This was the customary time for hanging up provisions to dry which had been salted for winter; as our ancestors
lived chiefly upon salted meat in the spring, the winter-fed
cattle not being fit for use. So Tusser:

For Easter, at Martlemas hang up a beefe:
With that and the like, yer (ere) grass beefe come in,
Thy folke shall look cheerely when others look thin.

November.

At this feast it was common to sell rings of copper-gilt,
which were given as fairings, or love-tokens.

THE BELLMAN'S VERSES.

Part of the office of this guardian of the night was to bless
the sleepers whose door he passed, which was often done in
verse. Hence these lines of Herrick:

The Bellman.

From noise of scarafires rest ye free,
From murders *benedicite.*
From all mischances, that may fright
Your pleasing slumbers in the night,
Mercie secure ye all, and keep
The goblin from ye while ye sleep.
Past one o'clock, and almost two,
My masters all, good-day to you.

Thus Milton:

The belman's drowsy charm,
To bless the doors from nightly harme.—*Penseroso.*

Hence the printed sheet of Bellman's Verses at Christmas.

CHRISTMAS-BOXES.

In the very interesting collection of London Antiquities formed by Mr. Charles Roach Smith, and now in the British Museum, are specimens of "Thrift-boxes; small and wide bottles with imitation stoppers, from three to four inches in height, of thin clay, the upper part covered with a green glaze. On the side is a slit for the introduction of money, of which they were intended as the depositories;" and as the small presents were collected at Christmas in these money-pots, they were called "Christmas-boxes," and thus gave name to the present itself. These pots were doubtless of early origin; for we find analogous objects of the Roman period. (See *Caylus, Recueil d'Antiquités.*)

In the *English Usurer*, 1634, the author, speaking of the usurer and swine, says:

Both with the Christmas-boxe may well comply;
It nothing yields till broke.

Humphrey Browne, in his *Map of the Microcosme*, 1642, says: "A covetous wretch, he doth exceed in receiving, but is very deficient in giving; like the *Christmas earthen boxes* of the apprentices, apt to take in money, but he restores none till he be broken, like a potter's vessell, into many shares." And in Mason's *Handful of Essaies*, 1621, we find: "Like a swine, never good till his death; as *an apprentice's box of earth*, apt he is to take all, but to restore none till hee be broken."—*Halliwell's edit.* vol. i.; quoted in Mr. Roach Smith's catalogue.

A gilt Nutmeg was formerly a common gift at Christmas, or festive times. Mars gives Hector "a gilt nutmeg" in *Love's Labour 's lost.*

(For other Anniversary Customs and Observances, see "The Calendar," in *Things not generally Known*, First Series, pp. 148-160.)

Olden Meals and Housewifery.

THE DINNER-HOUR.

The proper Hour for Dinner is laid down by Thomas Cogan, a physician, in a book entitled the *Haven of Health*, printed in 1584, as follows:

When foure houres bee past after breakfast, a man may safely take his dinner; and the most convenient time for dinner is about *eleven* of the clocke before noone. The usuall time for dinner in the universities is at *eleven*, or elsewhere about noon.

Grace at meat was often said in metre in the time of Shakspeare. In the play of *Timon of Athens* there is an instance of a metrical grace said by Apemantus, act i. sc. 2. Dr. Johnson says that metrical graces are to be found in the Primers; but Archdeacon Nares could not meet with them.

TOOTH-PICKS.

The employment of Tooth-picks is very ancient. In the 12th volume of Mr. Grote's able *History of Greece*, p. 608, we find that Agathocles, "among the worst of Greeks," was poisoned by means of a medicated quill, handed to him for cleaning his teeth after dinner. Mr. Grote's authority is Diodorus, xxi. Fragm. 12, pp. 276-278.

Tooth-picks were in common use in the time of the Cæsars. Martial tells us those made of a chip of mastic wood (*lentiscus*) are the best; but that if you run short of such timber, a quill will serve your purpose; and he ridicules an old fop, who was in the habit of digging away at his gums with his polished *lentiscus*, though he had not a tooth left in his head.

Tooth-picks occur early of silver; but pieces of wood, or of feathers with a red end (as quills in our day), were most usual. The tooth-pick is the Anglo-Saxon *toth-gare.*

The old name was *Pick-tooth:* it was imported by travellers from Italy and France, and the using of it was long deemed an affected mark of gentility. It was worn as a trophy in the hat; and Sir Thomas Overbury describes a courtier, the pink of fashion, "with a pick-tooth in his hat." Bishop Earle says of an idle gallant, "his pick-tooth bears a great part in his discourse." Magnetic tooth-picks were made at the end of the seventeenth century.

A tooth-drawer of old was frequently called *Kind-heart:* it seems that he wore a particular costume in the reign of Elizabeth, when he is described as wearing his hat buttoned up on one side, and a feather therein.

This *old Remedy for Toothache* will be found in the *Pathway to Health:* Take vinegar and mustard, powder of pepper, pellitory of Spain, and the curnell of a nut-gall, and boil them all together, and put it into the hollow tooth.

THE BANQUET, OR DESSERT.

The Banquet of old was not, as now, a dinner, but the Dessert, and was usually placed in a separate room, to which the guests removed when they had dined. Massinger has:

> We'll dine in the great room, but let the musick
> And banquet be prepared here.

"The common place of banqueting, or eating the dessert," Gifford says, "was the garden-house, or arbour, with which almost every dwelling was furnished." To this Shallow alludes thus:

> Now you shall see mine orchard, where in an arbour we will eat a last year's pippin of mine own grafting.—2 *Hen. IV.*

Evelyn used the word in this sense so late as in 1685:

> The banquet (dessert) was twelve vast chargers piled up so high that those who sat one against another could hardly see each other.— *Memoirs,* vol. ii.

The banqueting-house built for Queen Anne, a short distance north of Kensington Palace, in 1705, is a still later instance. This was occasionally fitted up for *fêtes à la Watteau;* but when the court quitted Kensington, Queen Anne's building was converted into an orangery and greenhouse.

ABOVE OR BELOW THE SALT.

At the tables of our ancestors a large salt-cellar was usually set at about the middle of a long table; the places above which were assigned to guests of more distinction; those below to dependents, inferiors, and poor relations. Hence it is the characteristic of an insolent coxcomb, that "his fashion is not to take knowledge of him that is beneath him in clothes. He never drinks below the salt" (Ben Jonson's *Cynthia's Revels,* act ii. sc. 2): that is to say, not to any one who sits below it. Hence also it is the characteristic of a servile chaplain,

> that he do, on no default,
> Ever presume to sit above the salt.—*Hall's Satires.*

This phrase probably applied only when the company sat on both sides of a long table, the salt marking the dais of the board.

"It argues little for the delicacy of our ancestors," says Mr. Gifford, "that they should have admitted of such distinctions at their board ; but, in truth, they seem to have placed their guests *below the salt* for no better purpose than that of mortifying them."

But what can be said for the early law of Canute, by which a person sitting out of his proper place was to be pelted from it by bones, at the will of the company, without the privilege of taking offence ?

THE SEWER.

This was the officer who set and removed the dishes at a feast ; probably from *écuyer*. The word is used by Milton and Dryden. The inferior servants carried the dishes; the sewer placed them on the table, and took them off. It was the business of the sewer also to bring water for the hands of the guests : hence he bore a towel as the mark of his office.

RUSHES STREWED IN ROOMS.

Before the luxury of carpets was introduced into England, it was common to strew green rushes on the floors, or in the way where processions were to pass. Even in the palaces of royalty, the floors were generally strewed with rushes and straw, sometimes mixed with sweet herbs. In the Household Roll of Edward II. is an entry of money paid for sending from York to Newcastle, to procure straw for the king's chamber.

At the coronation of Henry V., when the procession is coming, the grooms cry, "More rushes, more rushes!"—*2 Henry IV.* act v. sc. 5. Thus also at a wedding :

> Full many maids, clad in their best array,
> In honour of the bride, come with their baskets
> Fill'd full with flowers ; others in wicker baskets
> Bring from the marsh rushes to o'erspread
> The ground whereon to church the lovers tread.
> Browne's *Brit. Pastorals.*

TURKEY CARPETS.

An illustration of the early traffic of the Gresham family with the Levant is supplied by the will of Lady Gresham (Sir John's sister-in-law), where particular mention is made of her "Turkey carpets ;" a great luxury for a private individual in an age when rushes formed part of the furniture of the court. The cost of these carpets must have been great ; for in 1602, a Turkey carpet sixteen feet long cost 27*l.*, equivalent to nearly 200*l.* at the present day.

THE ORDINARY.

A public dinner, where each person pays his share, is not unknown in these days; but was formerly the resort of a much higher class. Thus, in the reign of James I. ordinaries were the lounging-places of the men of the town, and the fantastic gallants who herded together. Ordinaries were the exchange for news, the echoing-places for all sorts of town-talk: there they might hear of the last new play and poem, and the last fresh widow sighing for some knight to make her a lady. These resorts were attended also to save the charges of housekeeping.

But a more striking feature in these ordinaries showed itself as soon as the voyder had cleared the table. Then began the shuffling and cutting on one side, and the bones rattling on the other. The ordinary, in fact, was a gambling-house.—D'Israeli's *Curiosities of Literature*, vol. iii.

Ordinaries are mentioned by Shakspeare and his contemporary dramatists. It was part of fashionable education for gallants to eat their way at an ordinary. In 1608, a common price for a genteel ordinary was 2s.; some ordinaries were 1s. 6d., others dearer, as "the ten-crown ordinary." And in Clitus's *Whims* we read: "The ordinarie is his (the gamester's) oratorie, where he preyes upon the countrey gull to feede himselfe."

Keepers of ordinary-tables were subject to the same laws as other victuallers; and in 1620 they had to enter into bonds and sureties that they would not "dress any flesh in their houses in the Lent-time for any respect, nor suffer it to be eat there."

Locket's (on the site of Drummond's banking-house at Charing Cross) was a famous ordinary, which survived the reign of Queen Anne; for Lord Foppington, in Vanbrugh's *Relapse*, 1708, tells us that at Locket's they "shall compose you a dish no bigger than a saucer shall come to fifty shillings." Mrs. Centlivre, in one of her prologues, says:

> At Locket's, Brown's, and at Pontack's inquire
> What modish kickshaws the wise beaux desire,
> What fam'd ragouts, what now-invented salad,
> Has best pretensious to regale the palate.

ALE AND ITS ASSOCIATIONS.

Ale being the olden drink of England, much of it was consumed at its rural festivals, to which it in part gave name. Thus there were bride-ales, church-ales, clerk-ales, give-ales, lamb-ales, leet-ales, Midsummer-ales, Scot-ales, Whitsun-ales, and several more. Nares emphatically says, "Other etymologies have been attempted, but this is the most natural and most probable."

Ale is read in the old dramatists for *alehouse*: thus, in *Thomas Lord Cromwell*: "Oh, Tom, that we were now at Putney, at the ale there."

Aleberry consisted of ale boiled with spice and sugar and sops of bread. *Alecie* signified being drunk with ale; a word coined in imitation of *lunacy*, which is being under lunar influence.

Ale-conner was an ale-taster, an officer appointed in every court-leet, to look to the assize and goodness of bread, ale, and beer. Thus, in an account of the progresses of Queen Elizabeth, we read of Captain Cox, who was of such credit and trust that he had been chosen ale-conner many a year when his betters had stood by; " and ever quitted himself with such estimation, as yet, to taste of a cup of nippitate, his judgment will be taken above the best in the parish, be his noze near so read."

Ale-cost was the herb *balsamita vulgaris*, which was frequently put into ale as an aromatic bitter; " as also into the barrels and stands, amongst those herbes wherewith they do make sage-ale."—*Gerard.*

Ale-draper was a humorous term for the keeper of an ale-house.

Ale-knight was a haunter of alehouses—a tippler :

> Come, all you brave wights
> That are dubb'd ale-knights,
>   Now set out your sleves in fight ;
> And let them that crack
> In the praises of sack
> Know malt is of mickle might.
> > *Wits' Recreations*, 1564.

Ale-stake was a stake set up for a sign at the door of an ale-house.

Ale-stanbearer is described in *Nomenclator*, 1585, as a porter that carries burdens (as a barrel) with slings, " as we see brewers doe, when they laye beere into the seller;" which describes the mode now in use as it was three centuries since.

Single Ale, Single Drink, or Single Beer, were all terms for Small Beer ; as Double Beer for Strong. Single Broth is another old name for Small Beer. A cup of Six was a cup of beer sold at Six Shillings the barrel, the price of Small Beer.

THE SCOTCH WHIGS AND SMALL BEER.

The nickname of Whig, as applied to a party, has been derived from Whig, a thin liquor made from whey ;—from *hwæg*, whey (Saxon), which was drunk by the poorer classes in Scotland as small beer. Bishop Burnet, however, derives the name from *Whiggamoor*, a cattle-driver in the south-west of Scotland, by contraction *whigg*. His opinion as a Scotchman (says Nares) must have more weight, because the name had been applied to the Scotch fanatics, before it was taken up as a term of ridicule against the country party in England, which was about 1680.

Nor does there appear much propriety in applying the name of a liquor not much in use to a party, which the Scotch Whigs were of themselves, and at one time a formidable one. Woodrow, the Scottish historian, inclines to the "small-beer" derivation; but Nares favours Burnet's opinion. (See "Whig and Tory," in *Things not generally Known*, First Series, p. 157.)

OLDEN CIDER-MAKING.

In 1657, Dr. John Beale, a Fellow of the Royal Society, wrote a curious account of making Cider in those days in Herefordshire. He says:

"Crabs and wild pears, such as grow in the wildest and barren cliffs and on hills, make the richest, strongest, the most pleasant, and lasting wines that England yet yields, or is ever likely to yield. I have so well proved it already by so many hundred experiments in Herefordshire, that wise men tell me that these parts of England are some hundred thousand pounds sterling the better for the knowledge of it. . . . . . The Bromsbury crab and the Barland pear, and the soft crab and white or red horse pear, excel them and all others known or spoken of in other counties." Of the red-horse pear of Felton or Longland he says, "that it has pleasant masculine rigour." Of the quality of the fruit he observes: "Such is the effect which the austerity has on the mouth on tasting the liquor, that the rustics declare it as if the roof of the mouth were filed away; and that neither man nor beast care to touch one of these pears, though ever so ripe." Of the pear called rinny winter pear, which grows about Ross, in Herefordshire, he observes that "it is of no use but for cider; and if a thief steal it, he would incur a speedy vengeance, it being a furious purger; but being joined with well-chosen crabs, and reserved to a due maturity, becomes richer than good French wine; but if drunk before the time, it stupefies the roof of the mouth, assaults the brain, and purges more violently than a Galenist."

Of the quality of the liquor he says: "According as it is managed, it proves strong Rhenish, Barrack, yea, pleasant Canary, sugared of itself, or as rough as the fiercest Greek wine, opening or binding, holding one, two, three, or more years, so that no mortal can say yet at what age it is past the best. This we can say, that we have kept it until it burn as quickly as sack, draws the flame like naphtha, and fires the stomach like *aqua vitæ.*"

THE POSSET

was a drink composed of hot milk, curdled by some strong infusion, which was much in favour with our ancestors, both as luxury and medicine. All the guards that attended the king in *Macbeth* seem to have had their possets; for Macbeth says, "I have drugged their possets." In Fletcher's *Scornful Lady*, two of the characters take a posset on the stage before they retire to rest. The Sack Posset was a treat usually prepared for a bridegroom:

> In came the bridemaids with the posset,
> The bridegroom eat in spight.—*Suckling.*

Dryden mentions a "pepper posset;" Dr. Sir John Floyer, a posset in which *althea* (marshmallow) roots are boiled; and Dr. Arbuthnot orders gruels and posset drinks to increase the milk.

Our nearest approach to the old posset is whey, or milk curdled with wine or acid; and treacle-posset.

SOPS IN WINE.

This was a fanciful name for the flowers now called pinks, considered as the second species of gillofers. At weddings, cakes, wafers, and the like were blessed and put into the sweet wine which was presented to the bride; and probably these flowers were thought to resemble them. It has, however, been inferred that such pinks were often put into the wine to give it a flavour; for we read in Blount's *Tenures* of "a sextary of July-flower wine."

The custom of taking the more substantial sops in wine at weddings is alluded to in Shakspeare's *Taming of the Shrew*, where, at his own wedding, Petruchio is said to have

> Quaff'd off the muscadel, and throw the sops
> All in the sexton's face.

AQUA VITÆ

was formerly in use as a general term for ardent spirits. In Beaumont and Fletcher's *Beggar's Bush* it is evidently used for brandy, or, as it is here termed, 'brand-wine;' for the cry of the aqua-vitæ man is, "Buy any brand-wine!" In the following passage it may be supposed to mean usquebaugh, or perhaps whisky: "I will rather trust a Fleming with my butter, Parson Hugh the Welshman with my cheese, an Irishman with my aqua-vitæ bottle," &c. (*Merry Wives of Windsor*, act ii. sc. 2.)

JUNIPER.

It was formerly supposed that the wood of Juniper, when once lighted, would remain on fire a whole year if covered with its own ashes. Hence Ben Jonson, in the *Alchemist*, talks of the "coal of juniper," which the tobacconist kept for his customers to light their pipes from.—Nares's *Glossary*.

FERINTOSH WHISKY.

The word Ferintosh signifies Thanes' Land, it having been part of the thanedom of Cawdor (Macbeth's), or Calder. The barony of Ferintosh belonged to the Forbeses of Culloden, and contained about 1800 arable acres. All barley produced on this estate was privileged to be converted into whisky duty free; the natural consequence of which was, that more whisky was distilled in Ferintosh than in all the rest of Scotland. In 1784, government made a sort of compulsory purchase of this privilege from the Culloden family, after they had enjoyed it a complete century. The sum paid was 21,500*l.*

COFFEE.

Coffee has three ingredients, very similar to those contained in tea. These are, a volatile oil produced during the roasting; a variety of tannic acid, which is also altered during the roasting; and the substance called theine, or caffeine, which is common to both tea and coffee. On the different properties of the volatile oil which coffees contain depend in great measure the aroma and consequent value of the several varieties of coffee. A higher aroma would make the inferior Ceylon, Jamaica, and East-Indian coffee nearly equal to the value of the finest Mocha; and Payen, the chemist, says, if the oil could be bought for the purpose of imparting this flavour, it would be worth in the market as much as 100*l.* sterling an ounce!

The great use of coffee in France is supposed to have abated the prevalence of gravel. In the French colonies, where coffee is more used than in the English, as well as in Turkey, where it is the principal beverage, not only the gravel, but the gout, is scarcely known. Among others, a case is mentioned in the *Pharmaceutical Journal* of a gentleman who was attacked with gout at twenty-seven years of age, and had it severely till he was upwards of fifty, with chalk-stones in the joints of his hands and feet; but the use of coffee, then recommended to him, completely removed the complaint.

In Burton's *Anatomy of Melancholy* we find this early notice of coffee:

The Turkes have a drink called *coffa* (for they use no wine), so named of a berry as black as soot, and as bitter (like that black drink which was in use among the Lacedæmonians, and perhaps the same); which they sip still of, and sup as warm as they can suffer. They spend much time in those coffee-houses, which are somewhat like our ale-houses or taverns; and there they sit chatting and drinking to drive away the time, and to be merry together: because they finde by experience that kinde of drink so used helpeth digestion and promoteth alacrity (vol. ii. part ii. sect. 5).

Coffee-grounds, as well as tea-grounds, once played a part in divinations. Thus a cast of the cup was regarded as a picture of all one's life to come; and in No. 56 of the *Connoisseur*, a girl, divining to find out what rank her husband shall be, sees him "several times in coffee-grounds with a sword by his side; and he was once at the bottom of a tea-cup in a coach-and-six with two footmen behind it."

WHAT WAS HIPPOCRAS?

A medicated drink, composed usually of red wine, but sometimes white, with the addition of sugar and spices.* As the apothecaries call it *vinum Hippocraticum*, Menage was convinced it is derived from Hippocrates, as being originally compounded by medical skill. Theobald observes, in a note on the *Scornful Lady*, that it was called *Hippocras* from its being strained through the woollen bag called by the apothecaries *Hippocrates's Sleeve*. It was a very favourite beverage, and usually given at weddings. In old books are many recipes for the composition of Hippocras. Here is one :

To make *Hyppocras* the best way.—Take 5 ounces of aqua vitæ, 2 ounces of pepper, and 2 of ginger, of cloves, and grains of paradise each 2 ounces, ambergrease 3 grains, and musk 2 grains; infuse them 24 hours in a glass bottle on pretty warm embers : and when your occasion requires to use it, put a pound of sugar into a quart of wine (claret or white wine) or cider ; dissolve it well, and then drop 3 or 4 drops of the infusion into it, and they will make it taste richly.—Lupton's *Thousand Notable Things*.

In *Poor Robin's Almanack*, 1696, for winter we have :

Sack, hippocras now, and burnt brandy,
Are drinks as warm and good as can be.

LAMBS'-WOOL.

This was a favourite liquor among the common people, and was composed of ale and roasted apples ; the pulp of the roasted apple being worked up with the ale till the mixture formed a smooth beverage. Herrick sings :

Now crown the bowls
With gentle lambs-wooll ;
Add sugar, and nutmegs, and ginger.

HONEY, MEAD, AND WAX, IN OLDEN TIMES.

The privilege insisted upon in the Great-Forest Charter of every man being entitled to the Honey which he finds on his own ground, denotes its great value in our early rural economy. Before the plantation of sugar in the West Indies, honey must necessarily have been in great request, and borne a high price. The Wax likewise must have been of considerable value ; and a statute of Henry VI., with regard to wax-chandlers, in the preamble sets forth that wax was used in great quantities, not only for making candles, but likewise images of saints. It was also much used for effigies in funerals, and figures employed by pretended witches.

* This resembles the contents of the loving-cups, which are passed round at the Lord Mayor's banquets, and at feasts in the City halls, to this day.

Mead was now the liquor of luxury, and continued in great request throughout Wales to a late date. Thus Drayton, in his *Polyolbion*, speaking of the Principality, says:

Fill me a bowl of meath, my working spirit to raise.

And in 1647, the gentry of Monmouthshire and Radnorshire gave a magnificent entertainment to the then Prince of Wales at Raglan and Radnor castles; at the latter feast metheglin was handed round in large goblets to the courtiers who attended the prince in his progress. And mead was made in many rural districts to our own time.

Honey and wax are frequently mentioned in the laws of Howel Dha, where the perquisite of the king's great chamberlain to as much as he can bite off the end of a candle is particularly recognised. And to this day there is at Conway, in Carnarvonshire, an annual "honey fair."

BLACK-JACKS.

These were olden pitchers made of leather, and in some cases lined with metal, for holding beer; they are thought to have been named from the *Jack*, a horseman's defensive upper-garment, quilted and covered with strong leather. The term *jack* was also used for a coat-of-mail; and our Guards to this day wear "*jack-boots*." Leathern jacks are used at Christ's Hospital for bringing in the beer, whence it is poured into wooden piggins. Black-jacks are of smaller size. The Rev. W. Brooke Kempson, of Stoke-Lacy, Herefordshire, possesses a fine set of four black-jacks, which has been in his family two centuries. They are a quart, pint, and two half-pints; they are of strong black leather, lined with pewter, and have deep silver rims, and silver shields bearing the family crest. "The Black-Jack" was occasionally a tavern sign; the Black-Jack in Portsmouth-street, Clare-market, was the haunt of Joe Miller the comedian, and here he uttered and collected his time-honoured jests.

HOOPED DRINKING-MUGS.

Hoop was the old name for a quart-pot, such pots being anciently made with staves bound together with hoops, as barrels are. Nash, in his *Pierce Penniless*, says: "I believe hoops in quart-pots were invented that every man should take his hoop, and no more." There were usually three in number to such a pot; hence one of Jack Cade's promised reforms was, "the three-hooped pot shall have ten hoops; and I will make it felony to drink small beer" (2 *Hen. VI.* act iv. sc. 2). Nares asks: "Will not this explain *cock-a-hoop* better than the other derivations?" A person is cock-a-hoop, or in high spirits, who has been keeping up the hoop, or pot, at his head.

Pewter pots are made with hoops to this day; but formerly, the hoop outside seems to have served the same purpose as the pegs inside in the older Peg-Tankards.

THE MANCHET.—MANCIPLE.

This is a fine white roll, named, according to Skinner, from *michette*, French; or from *main*, because small enough to be held in the hand (*Minshew*).

> No manchet can so well the courtly palate please
> As that made of the meal fetch'd from my fortil loam.
> Drayton's *Polyolbion.*

Here are two olden recipes for manchets : [*]

Lady of Arundel's Manchet.—Take a bushel of fine wheat-flower, 20 eggs, three pound of fresh butter ; then take as much salt and barm as to the ordinary manchet ; temper it together with new milk pretty hot, then let it lie the space of half an hour to rise, so you may work it up into bread, and bake it : let not your oven be too hot. — *True Gentlewoman's Delight*, 1676.

Take a quart of cream, put thereto a pound of beef-suet minced small, put it into cream, and season it with nutmeg, cinnamon, and rose-water ; put to it eight eggs and but four whites, and two grated manchets ;. mingle them well together, and put them in a buttered dish ; bake it, and being baked, scrape on sugar, and serve it. — *The Queen's Royal Cookery*, 1713.

Manchets (fine white rolls) are used in the colleges of Oxford and Cambridge to this day. The manchets and cheese, and fine ale, of Magdalen College are well known.

The Manciple, a purveyor of victuals, a clerk of the kitchen, or caterer, still subsists in the universities, where the name is therefore preserved ; but Archdeacon Nares believed nowhere else. One of Chaucer's pilgrims is a manciple of the Temple, of whom he gives a good character for his skill in purveying.

ANTIQUITY OF CHEESE.

Cheese and curdling of milk are mentioned in the book of Job. David was sent by his father Jesse to carry ten cheeses to the camp, and to look how his brother fared. "Cheese of kine" formed part of the supplies of David's army at Maha-naim during the rebellion of Absalom. As David, when too young to carry arms, was able to run to the camp with ten cheeses, ten loaves, and an ephah of parched corn, the cheeses must have been very small. Homer makes cheese form part of the ample stores found by Ulysses in the cave of the Cyclop Polyphemus. Euripides, Theocritus, and other early poets,

---

[*] Quoted in the Additions to the new edition of Nares's *Glossary*, by James O. Halliwell, Esq., F.R.S., &c., and Thomas Wright, Esq., M.A., F.S.A., 2 vols. 1858 ; a work abounding in learning and curious lore.

mention cheese. Ludolphus says that excellent cheese and butter were made by the ancient Ethiopians; and Strabo states that some of the ancient Britons were so ignorant that, though they had abundance of milk, they did not understand the art of making cheese. There is no evidence that any of these ancient nations had discovered the use of rennet in making cheese; they appear to have merely allowed the milk to sour, and subsequently to have formed the cheese from the caseous part of the milk, after expelling the serum or whey.

The county of Chester has been for ages famous for the excellence of its cheese. It is stated that the Countess Constance of Chester (reign of Henry II., 1100), though the wife of Hugh Lupus, the king's first cousin, kept a herd of kine, *and made good cheeses*, three of which she presented to the Archbishop of Canterbury. Giraldus Cambrensis, in the twelfth century, bears honourable testimony to the excellence of the Cheshire cheese of his day. Cheshire retains its celebrity for cheese-making: the pride of its people in the superiority of its cheese may be gathered from a provincial song, published with the music about 1746, during the Spanish war, in the reign of George II.

Next to Cheshire rank Gloucestershire, Wiltshire, and Somerset, for their cheese. In the latter county they have the proverb:

> If you wid have a good cheese, and hav 'n old,
> You must turn 'n seven times before ho is old.

To curdle the milk in cheese-making was formerly used the *Galium verum* of botanists, a wild flower with square stems, shining whorled leaves, and loose panicles of small yellow flowers, popularly known as *Cheese Rennet*.

AMBERGREASE.

This substance, *Ambergris*, literally gray amber, from its colour and perfume, has been long known, and was formerly much used in wines, sauces, and perfumes. It is found floating on the sea in warm climates, and is now generally agreed by chemists to be produced in the stomach of the *Physeter macrocephalus*, or spermaceti whale. There is no doubt that it is an animal secretion. Various other conjectures of its origin were formerly suggested.

Beaumont and Fletcher thus refer to its use in wine:

> 'Tis well, be sure
> The wines be lusty, high, and full of spirit,
> And amber'd all.

And, in an old play, for furnishing the banquet:

> I had clean forgot, we must have ambergrise,
> The grayest can be found.

Milton has inverted the word, in the banquet produced by
the devil to tempt our Saviour :

> Meats of noblest sort.
>
> *   *   *   *   *   *   *
>
> Gris-amber steam'd.   *Paradise Regained.*

Drayton, in *Moon-calf,* has

> . . . . capons with their fat bellies
> Stuff'd with ambergrise.

ADULTERATION OF FOOD.

In the Ms. regulations of the household of Henry VIII. are
the following punishments for the adulteration of food :

His Highness's baker shall not put alums in the bread, or mix rye,
oaten, or bean floor with the same ; and if detected, he shall be put in
the stocks. His Highness's attendants are not to steal any lock or keys,
tables, forms, cupboards, or other furniture, out of noblemen's or gentlemen's houses, where they go to visit. Master cooks shall not employ
such scullions as go about naked, or lie all night on the ground before the
kitchen fire. No dogs to be kept in the Court, but only a few spaniels
for the ladies. Dinners to be at ten, suppers at four. The officers of
his privy chamber shall be loving together, no grudging nor grumbling,
nor talking of the king's pastime. There shall be no romping with the
maids on the staircase, by which dishes and other things are often
broken. Care shall be taken of the pewter spoons, and that the wooden
ones used in the kitchen be not broken or stolen. The pages shall not
interrupt the kitchen-maids. Coal to be only allowed to the king's,
queen's, and Lady Mary's chambers. The brewers are not to put any
brimstone in the ale.

A LEASH OF GAME.

The word Leash, from *lesse,* French, signifies a string or
thong by which a dog is led along. Skinner says that a *leash,*
in the sense of three together, is derived from the same, it
being unusual to unite more than three dogs to lead together ;
and Nares presumes it usual to unite that number. From the
dogs it was easily transferred to the game caught by them, and
thence into general use. It was also used for the string by
which a hawk was held.

THAMES SHAD AND SALMON.

These fish are no longer taken in the neighbourhood of London. Shad Thames, a narrow street, running along the water-
side from Pickle-Herring Wharf to Dockhead, is in all probability named from the quantities of shad-fish formerly caught
in the river at this spot. Mr. Corner, F.S.A. (in the *Surrey
Archæological Society's Collections*), states that his friend Mr.
W. W. Landell informed him that his mother recollected in her
youth the shad-fish, caught in great numbers in the Thames off

Horselydown, being cried about the streets, as herrings, mackerel, and sprats now are.

In the *Gentleman's Magazine* for June 1749 is this record: "Wednesday, 7.—Two of the greatest draughts of salmon were caught in the Thames, below Richmond, that have been known some years; one net having thirty-five large salmon in it, and another twenty-one, which lowered the price of fresh salmon at Billingsgate from '1s. to 6d. per lb.'" Two salmon were taken in the Thames, at Brentford, about thirty-six years since.

BOILING LOBSTERS.

We may thus explain the change of colour in the lobster on being boiled, a transformation which served the witty author of *Hudibras* as a simile :

> Now, like a lobster boiled, the morn
> From black to red began to turn.

The shell of the lobster is imbued with a black or bluish-black pigment, secreted by the true skin, which also gives out the calcareous matter after each moult, so that lime and pigment are blended together. This pigment becomes red (pale or intense) in water at the temperature of 212 deg. Fahr.; and the same effect is produced by the action of alcohol, ether, and various acids.

THE EGG,

as a whole, is richer in fat than beef. It is equalled in this respect, among common kinds of food, only by pork and by eels. The white of the egg is, however, entirely free from fat ; and it is a very constipating variety of animal food, so that it requires much fat to be eaten along with it when consumed in any quantity, in order that this quality may be counteracted. It is, no doubt, because experience has long ago proved this in the stomachs of the people, that "eggs and bacon" have been a popular dish among Gentile nations from time immemorial.— *J. F. W. Johnston.*

TEWKESBURY MUSTARD.

The ancient town of Tewkesbury, in Gloucestershire, was famous very early for its mustard. Shakespeare speaks only of its thickness, but others have celebrated its pungency :

His wit is as thick as Tewkesbury mustard.—2 *Hen. IV.* ii. 4.

If he be of the right stamp, and a true Tewkesbury man, he is a choleric gentleman, and will bear no coals.—See "Durham Mustard," in *Things not generally Known*, First Series, p. 142.

MARCH-PANE.

This, one of the glories of olden confectionery, is a sweet

biscuit, composed of sugar and almonds, like those now called Macaroons. It is also called *massepain* in some old books. The word March-pane exists, with little variation, in almost all the European languages; yet the derivation of it is uncertain. In the Latin of the Middle Ages, March-panes were called *Martii panes;* which gave occasion to Hermolaus Barbarus to inquire into their origin, in a letter to Cardinal Piccolomini, who had some sent to him as a present. Balthazar Bonifacius says they were named from Marcus Apicius, the famous epicure. Minshew, following Hermolaus, will have them originally sacred to Mars, and stamped with a castle.

Whatever was the origin of their name, the English recipe-books show that they were composed of almonds and sugar, pounded and baked together. Here is a recipe :

To make a March-pane. —Take two pounds of almonds, being blanched and dryed in a sieve over the fire, beate them in a stone mortar, and when they bee small, mixe them with two pounds of sugar beeing finely beaten, adding two or three spoonefuls of rose-water, and that will keep your almonds from oiling : when your paste is beaten fine, drive it thin with a rowling pin, and so lay it on a bottom of wafers ; then raise up a little edge on the side, and so bake it ; then yce it with rose-water and sugar, then put it into the oven againe, and when you see your yce is risen up and drie, then take it out of the oven and garnish it with pretie conceipts, as birdes and beasts being cast out of standing-moldes. Sticke long comfits upright into it, cast biskst and carrowaies in it, and so serve it : you may also print of this march-pane paste in your moldes for banqueting dishes. And of this paste our comfit-makers at this day make their letters, knots, armes, escutcheons, beasts, birds, and other fancies.—*Delightes for Ladies*, 1608.

March-pane was a constant article in the desserts of our ancestors, and appeared sometimes on more solemn occasions. When Elizabeth visited Cambridge, the University presented their chancellor, Sir William Cecil, with two pairs of gloves, a march-pane, and two sugar-loaves. In the old play of *Wits,* we find a reference to

> . . . dull country madams, that spend
> Their time in studying receipts to make
> March-pane and preserve plumbs.

Castles and other figures were often made of march-pane for splendid desserts, and were demolished by shooting or throwing sugar-plums at them.

OLDEN CONFECTIONERY.

The following notes are curious :

Almonds are an olden delicacy of our table, and have for ages been very extensively used in a variety of preparations. Almond-milk, composed of almonds ground and mixed with milk or other liquid, was a favourite beverage, as was also almond-butter and almond-custard. The antiquity of the practice of serving almonds and raisins together at dessert seems to be shown from the name Almonds-and-raisins being given as that of an old English game in *Useful Transactions in Philosophy*, 1700. Almond-cakes were perhaps what we now call macaroons.

Biscuits (originally Biskets) of various kinds were in use in the sixteenth and seventeenth centuries; among which that most in repute was called Naples Biscuit, from the place where it was first made: it occurs in the Carpenters' Company's books in 1644.

Candied Angelica and Elecampane.—These two articles of confectionery originated in medicinal plants. The virtues of Angelica are thus described by Gerard:

The rootes of garden Angelica is a singular remedie against poison, and against the plague, and all infections taken by evill and corrupt aire; if you do but take a peece of the roote, and hold it in your mouth, or chew the same betweeen your teeth, it doth most certainly drive away the pestilentiall aire.

Angelica, which, eaten every meale,
Is found to be the plague's best medicine.

The New Metamorphosis, Ms. temp. Jac. I.
—Note to the new edition of Nares's *Glossary*.

Orange-Flower Water has been a favourite perfume in England since the reign of James I. It occurs in Copley's *Wits, Fits, and Fancies*, 1614; and in the *Accomplished Female Instructor*, 1719, is the following recipe: Take two pounds of orange flowers, as fresh as you can get them, infuse them in two quarts of white wine, and so distill them, and it will yield a curious perfuming spirit.—*Orange Butter* was made, according to the *Closet of Rarities*, 1706, by beating up new cream, and then adding orange-flower and red wine, to give it the colour and scent of an orange.

THE BAG PUDDING,

Or plum-pudding boiled in a long bag, seems to have been a favourite dish centuries since. Davies, in his *Scourge of Folly*, 1611, sings:

A big bag-pudding then I must command,
For he is full, and holds out to the end;
Seldom with men is found so good a friend.

True love is not like to a bag-pudding: a bag-pudding hath two ends, but true love hath never an end.—*Poor Robin*, 1709.

A Pudding Pie, a piece of meat baked in a dish of batter, is mentioned by Taylor, in 1630: how this dish came to be called "A Toad in a Hole," we are unable to divine.

HOW TO ROAST A POUND OF BUTTER.

We find this culinary folly of the last century in the third edition of *The Art of Cookery*, by a Lady, 1748. " Lay it (the butter) in salt and water two or three hours; then spit it, and rub it all over with crumbs of bread, with a little grated nutmeg; lay it to the fire, and as it roasts, baste it with the yolks of two eggs, and then with crumbs of bread, all the time it is roasting: but have ready a pint of oysters stewed in their own

liquor, and lay it in the dish under the butter; when the bread
has soaked up all the butter, brown the outside, and lay it on
your oysters. Your fire must be very slow."

SPITS, TURNSPITS, AND JACKS.

The Spit, as an implement for roasting meat, was formerly
often made of wood, with a projecting part, by means of which
it was turned by hand. Hence, in the old play of the *Four P's*,
we find mention of "turning the spit," which could not happen
in modern cookery:

> To so her ayt
> So byaely turnynge of the spyt ;
> For many a spyt here hath she turned,
> And many a good spyt hath she burned.

Lear speaks of "red burning spits, hissing." Iron spits, however, soon succeeded these clumsy instruments; but recourse
is still had to the wooden spit when ancient hospitality is imitated, in roasting animals whole.

Turnspits, *i. e.* poor boys, were hired to turn the spits; and
Aubrey tells us, "they licked the dripping-pan, and grew to
be huge, lusty knaves." Swift, in his *Miscellanies*, thus refers
to a royal turnspit:

> I give you joy of the report
> That he's to have a place at court ;
> Yes, and a place he will grow rich in,
> A turnspit in the royal kitchen.

To the turnspit succeeded dogs, thence called turnspit-dogs,
who turned the spit-wheel as the squirrel turns his wheel cage.
In the kitchen of the ancient castle of St. Briavel, on the edge
of the forest of Dean, may be seen this contrivance for the dog
to turn the spit. Who does not recollect Gay's charming fable
of " the Cook, the Turnspit, and the Ox" ?

> The dinner must be dish'd at one.
> Where's this vexatious turnspit gone ?
> Unless the skulking cur is caught,
> The sirloin's spoilt, and I'm in fault.

Then, the poor dog's lament of his lot :

> Was ever cur so cursed ? (he cried ;)
> What star did at my birth preside ?
> Am I for life by compact bound
> To tread the wheel's eternal round ?

At what date the spit was first turned by the smoke-jack it
is hard to trace; for this contrivance is ancient, there being a
smoke-jack represented in a painting at Nurnberg, which is
known to be older than 1350. By this apparatus, believed to
be of German origin, the rising current in a chimney, acting
upon the inclined vanes of a wheel fixed in the funnel, gives
motion by a train of wheels to any thing which is hung before
the fire to roast.

Beckmann calls the *Smoke-jack* a new invention of the 16th century ; but, in addition to the above earlier instance, it occurs in 1444. Evelyn mentions the smoke-jack which had been near a hundred years in his brother's kitchen ; adding : " I am told Mr. Smith of Mitcham's spits are turned by the water, which, indeed, runs through his house."

The smoke-jack is now almost superseded by jacks impelled by the descent of a weight, or the uncoiling of a spring. The hanging jack is old ; for we read of one two centuries since :

I met Spicer in Lincoln's Inn Court, buying of a hanging-jack, to roast birds upon.—Pepys's *Diary*, Feb. 4th, 1660.

In 1601, however, a jack-maker occurs as an exclusive trade. The jack was anciently ornamented with puppets, whence, perhaps, the name.

THE WARMING-PAN.

In the " Inventorye" of Goods of Will. More, Esquiere, of Loseley in Surrey, A.D. 1556, occurs "a warmynge," considered to be a warming-pan, and the earliest recorded notice of the article.—John Evans, F.S.A., *Archæologia*, vol. xxxvi. p. 289.

The old warming-pans were often engraved with armorial bearings, mottoes, and inscriptions.

In the *Welsh Levite tossed in a Blanket*, 1691, we read : " Our garters, bellows, and warming-pans wore godly mottoes, &c." We find a warming-pan engraved with the arms of the Commonwealth, and the motto : " ENGLANDS . STATS . ARMES." Another warming-pan has the royal arms, C. R., and " FEARE GOD HONNOR Yᵉ KING. 1662."

Some years ago, there was purchased at the village of Whatcote, in Warwickshire, a warming-pan engraved with a dragon, and the date 1601 ; probably brought from Compton Wynlatt, the ancient seat of the Earls (now Marquis) of Northampton ; the supporters of the Compton family being dragons.—*Notes and Queries*, No. 76.

TORTOISE-SHELL.

This beautiful material is procured from the marine tortoise called the Hawk's-bill turtle. The mottled plates are most prized in England ; but the Spanish ladies will give at least twice as much for a comb of uniform yellow colour as for a mottled one. Tortoise-shell is used for veneering ; and the Romans of the Augustan age had their couches and other articles of furniture veneered or inlaid with tortoise-shell.

THE TRENCHER

was a wooden platter long used instead of metal, china, or earthen plates. It was even considered a stride of luxury when trenchers were often changed in one meal. "And with an humble chaplain it was expressly stipulated," says Bishop Hall, " that he never change his trencher twice." The term " a good trencher-man" was then equivalent to a hearty feeder (Nares's *Glossary*). Maple-wood, being soft and white, was formerly in great request for trenchers.

The late Rev. Mr. Fosbroke remembered when no other but wooden dishes of this kind were used in farm-houses in Shropshire. The general form of the trencher was round; yet the *trencher-cap* of our Universities has a square top.

THE TRUE JAPAN WARE.

In lackering woodwork, or *japanning*, the Japanese excel the world. In this operation, they select the finest wood of fir or cedar, to be coated with varnish. They get the gum from which they obtain the varnish from the *Rhus vernix*, a tree abundant in Japan. On puncturing the bark, the gum oozes out of a light colour, and of the consistence of cream; but on exposure to the air, it grows thicker and blacker. It is so transparent, that when laid unmixed on wood, the grain and every mark of the wood can be seen through it. Sometimes they place beneath the varnish a dark ground, coloured partly by the dark sludge caught under a grindstone; they also use finely-powdered charcoal, and sometimes leaf-gold ground very fine. They then ornament the varnished surface with figures and flowers of gold and silver. They make and thus varnish screens, desks, caskets, cabinets, from whence we take our notions of Japanese ingenuity; but it is said that the best samples are never sent out of the country.—*American Expedition to Japan.*

TIND—TINDER.

The word Tind, though from the Saxon *tyndan*, and employed by Wickliff, Milton, and Dryden, is now little used. It signifies "to ignite either fire or candle; to light, to kindle;" as "tind up the candle:"

As one candle tindeth a thousand.—Sanderson's *Sermons*, 1689.

Miss Baker, in her *Northamptonshire Glossary*, says: "The form of this word is various: Skinner and Ray have, to *tine* or *tin* a candle. *Tine* is used in Somerset and Wilts; in Cheshire, *tin, tine, tend*, or *tind*; Devonshire, *teen:* all these are good old words. With us it is still current in the rural districts."

THE LINK.

That Links were early used is shown by reference in old writers to the strange mode of restoring the blackness of a rusty hat by smoking it with a link. Greene, quoted by Steevens, says: "This cozenage is used in selling old hats found upon dunghills, instead of newe, blackt over with the smoke of

an old link"—"fuliginous link," as Howel terms it. What a
help it must have been to a toper!

> Round as a globe, and liquor'd every chink,
> Goodly and great, he sails behind his link.   *Dryden.*

The linkmen of Gay's time were not, however, to be trusted:

> Though thou art tempted by the linkman's call,
> Yet trust him not along the lonely wall;
> In the midway he'll quench the flaming brand,
> And share the booty with the pilfering band.   *Trivia,* b. iii.

Here and there, in the old squares and streets of Western London, may be seen, attached to the iron railings, large extin-
guishers, formerly used by the linkmen for extinguishing their
links.

ANTIQUITY OF THE LATCH-KEY.

Among a variety of objects discovered at Salisbury, in excavations for sewerage, in 1853, the most remarkable are the
Latch-Keys, the age of which might be questioned if they were
not known to have been found with other keys at least as old
as the fifteenth century.—*J. Y. Akerman, F.S.A.; Archæologia,* vol. xxxvi. p. 72.

MECHANIC ARTS EARLY IN THE EIGHTEENTH CENTURY.

Chamberlayne, in his *Present State of Great Britain,* 1726,
says:

Here (in Great Britain) are the best clocks, watches, locks, barometers, thermometers, air-pumps, &c. in the world. The late Queen
Mary had a clock, made by Mr. Watson, late of Coventry, worth a thousand pounds, in which are all the motions of the celestial bodies. Locks
are here made of iron and brass, of fifty pounds a lock. Watches so
curious that one part of the movement of a repeating-watch comes to
ten pounds, which makes them ordinarily fifty or sixty pounds a watch;
and yet these prove profitable merchandise when we send them into
foreign countries, so valuable and so inestimable is the work. Curious
telescopes, microscopes, perspectives, mirrors, spheres, globes, charts,
maps, and all sorts of mathematical instruments, dials, balances, sea-
compasses, &c. The late improvement in making glass; of polishing
the insides of great iron guns; of weighing up ships that are sunk to
the bottom of the sea; in fishing, as they call it, for money lost it may
be 100 years ago, and many other noble inventions and improvements;
as, weaving silk stockings, mills of copper, gunpowder, polishing glass,
&c. Mortlake tapestry, earthenware of Fulham, speaking-trumpets,
making of lustring, engines for raising of glass, spinning of glass, cutting of tobacco, printing stuffs, linen, and paper; making damask
linen, watering silks; the way of separating gold from silver; boulting-
mills, lanterns of divers sorts, cane-chairs, making horn-ware, &c. All
these instances show how excellently the English nation is turned for
all manner of mechanical arts.

Punch and Judy,
Old Plays, Pageants, and Music.

PUNCH AND JUDY.

The origin of these puppets has been referred to "a corruption, both in word and deed, of *Pontius cum Judæis*, one of the old mysteries, the subject of which was, Pontius Pilate with the Jews; and particularly in reference to *Matt.* xxvii. 19." So states a Correspondent to *Notes and Queries*, No. 139.

Another Correspondent (No. 51, 2d Series) supports this origin from some mystery-play, by inferring Poncinello, the name of Punch in Italy, to be a very easy corruption of Pontiello, or Pontianello; and Judy to be from Giudei (the Jew), or Giuda (Judas). There were traditions of Pontius Pilate afloat in the middle ages, and they have very probably been embodied in a mystery-play. Theobald, in one of his notes to Shakspeare, says: "There was hardly an old play, till the period of the Reformation, which had not in it a devil and a droll character, who was to play upon and work the devil." Perhaps Judas was often introduced as a fit representative; and so in our street exhibitions we generally see both characters introduced (Judas corrupted into Judy), and Punch victorious over *both*.

Strutt, in his *Sports and Pastimes* ("Decline of Secular Plays"), regards Punchinello as supplying "the place of the Vice, or mirth-maker, a favourite character in the moralities. In modern days, this celebrated actor, who has something to say to the greater part of his auditory, is called plain Punch. In the moralities, the Devil usually carried away the Iniquity, or Evil, at the conclusion of the Drama; and, in compliance with the old custom, Punch, the genuine descendant of the Iniquity, is constantly taken from the stage by the Devil at the end of the puppet-show."

Galiani, in his Vocabulary of the Neapolitan Dialect, favours the secular origin, which he fixes on Puccio d'Aniello, at Acerra, near Naples, as the original Punch; and after whose death a Polecenella, or young Puccio, succeeded him.

Forsyth (*Italy*, vol. ii.) has the following interesting note:

Capponi and others consider Punch as a lineal representative of the Atelian farcers. They find a convincing resemblance between his mask and a little chicken-nosed figure in bronze which was discovered at Rome ; and from his nose they derive his name, "a pullicono pullicinella !"

Admitting this descent, we might push the origin of Punch back to very remote antiquity. Punch is a native of Atella, and therefore an Oscan. Now the Oscan farces were anterior to any stage. They intruded on the stage only in its barbarous state, and were dismissed on the first appearance of a regular drama. They then appeared as *Exodia* on trestles ; their mummers spoke broad Volscan ; whatever they spoke they grimaced, like Datus ; they retailed all the scandal that passed, as poor Malloula's wrongs ; their parts were frequently interwoven with other dramas ; and in all these respects the *Exodiarius* corresponds with the Punch of Naples.

Yet if we return from analogy to fact, we shall find that Master Punch is only a caricature of the Apulian peasant ; a character invented, as some suppose, by the Captain Mattamoros, improved by Cioccio the tailor, and performing the same part as the Fool or the Vice in our English plays and moralities.

* * * * *

What is a drama in Naples without Punch, or what is Punch out of Naples? Here, in his native tongue, and among his native countrymen, Punch is a person of real power ; he dresses up and retails all the drolleries of the day ; he is the channel, and sometimes the source, of the passing opinions ; he can inflict ridicule, he could gain a mob, or keep the whole kingdom in good-humour. Such was De Fiori, the Aristophanes of his nation, immortal in buffoonery.

The out-door Punch has, however, long been banished by kingly persecution from Naples ; he may probably fare better at the *Teatro di San Carlino,* the head-quarters of Pulcinella.

Mr. Macfarlane, nevertheless, has shown that Punch and the whole family of *barattini* (puppets) are the delight of many countries besides Italy. He is as popular in Egypt, Syria, and Turkey, as in London or Naples.* Under the name of Karaguse, or Black-Snout, he has amused and edified the grave bearded citizens of Cairo and Constantinople for many an age. Traces of him are found in Nubia, and far beyond the cataracts of the Nile ; and it is supposed types or symbols of him have been discovered among the hieroglyphics of the ancient Egyptians. The wandering Arabs cherish him. He is at home with the lively Persians, and beyond the Red Sea, and the Persian Gulf, and the Indian Ocean. Karaguse, or Black-Snout, is found slightly travestied in Hindostan, Siam, and Pegu, Ava and Cochin China, China Proper, and Japan. The Tartars behind the Great Wall of China are not unacquainted with him, nor are the Kamtchatkans ; and Herculaneum and Pompeii have given up Punch after being buried sixteen centuries.

But it is time to notice the arrival of Punch in England. Mr. Peter Cunningham has found in the overseers' books of St.

---

* The studious Bayle is stated to have repeatedly sallied from his retreat at the sound of Punch's cracked trumpet, announcing his arrival in Rotterdam.

Martin's-in-the-Fields four entries, in 1666 and 1667, of "Rec.
of Punchinello, y⁰ Italian popet player, for his booth at Charing-cross," the sums varying from 2l. 12s. 6d. to 1l. 2s. 6d.
Next are quoted some lines on why it was so long before the
statue of Charles the First was put up at Charing Cross, the
last line being,

Unless Punchinello is to be restored.

"These," says Mr. Cunningham, "are the earliest notices of
Punch in England" (*Handbook of London, voce* Charing-cross.)
Another early reference is that made by Granger, who,
speaking of one Philips, a noted merry-andrew in the reign of
James II., says, "this man was some time fiddler to a puppet-
show, in which capacity he held many a dialogue with *Punch*,
in much the same strain as he did afterwards with the mounte-
bank-doctor, his master, upon the stage."

Sir Richard Steele, in the *Tatler*, immortalises Powel, the
famous puppet-showman, who exhibited his wooden heroes
under the little piazza in Covent Garden, opposite St. Paul's
church, as we learn from the letter of the sexton in the *Spectator* (No. 14), attributed to Steele, who complains that the performances of Punch thinned the congregation in the church;
and that, as Powel exhibited during the time of prayer, the
tolling of the bell was taken by all who heard it for notice of
the commencement of the exhibition. The writer, in another
letter, decides that the puppet-show was much superior to the
opera of *Rinaldo and Armida* in the Haymarket: he adds, that
too much encouragement cannot be given to Mr. Powel, who
has so well disciplined his pig, that he and Punch dance a
minuet together.

In No. 44 of the *Tatler*, Isaac Bickerstaff, Esq. complains
that he has been abused by Punch in a prologue, supposed to
be spoken by him, but really delivered by his master, who stood
behind, "worked the wires," and by "a thread in one of Punch's
chops," gave to him the appearance of animation. No. 50 of
the same work contains a real or supposed letter from the showman himself, insisting on his right of control over his own puppets, and denying all knowledge of the "original of puppet-
shows, and the several changes and revolutions that have happened in them since Thespis." A subsequent No. (115) shows
that Punch was so attractive, particularly with the ladies, as to
cause the Opera and Nicolini to be deserted. Here also we learn
that then, as now, Punchinello had "a scolding wife;" and that
he was attended besides by a number of courtiers and nobles.

Punchinello was part of the Smithfield revels:

'Twas then, when August near was spent,
That Bat, the grilliado'd saint,

Had usher'd in his Smithfield revels,
Where Punchinelloes, popes, and devils
Are by authority allowed,
To please the giddy, gaping crowd.
Hudibras Redivivus, 1707.

Hence we collect that the popularity of Punch was completely established in 1711-12, and that he materially lessened the receipts at the Opera, if not at the regular national theatres. Still, no writer of the reign of Queen Anne speaks of him as a novelty, which may be established from poetry as well as prose. Gay, in his *Shepherd's Week* (Saturday), distinguishes between the tricks of "Jack-Pudding, in his parti-coloured jacket," and "Punch's feats;" and adds, that they were both known at rustic wakes and fairs. But the most remarkable account of Punch is given in No. 3 of the *Intelligencer*.

Nevertheless, the exact date of Punch's arrival in England is uncertain. Mr. Payne Collier concludes that he and King William came in together, and that the Revolution is to be looked upon as the era of the introduction of the family of Punch and of the glorious "House of Orange."

Mr. Collier humorously speculates on "the character of *Punch*," and attempts to prove it to be "a combination or concentration of two of the most prominent and original delineations on the stage"—King Richard III. and Falstaff: his costume closely resembles the Elizabethan peasecod-bellied doublets.

At various periods the adventures of Punch have been differently represented, and innovations have been introduced to suit the taste and to meet the events of the day. Thus, in Fielding's time, in consequence of the high popularity of *The Provoked Husband*, he complains (*Tom Jones*, book xii. chap. v.) that a puppet-show witnessed by his hero included "the fine and serious part" of the above comedy. Here is a later interpolation: after the battle of the Nile, Lord Nelson figured on one of the street stages, and held a dialogue with Punch, in which he endeavoured to persuade him, as a brave fellow, to go on board his ship, and assist in fighting the French: "Come, Punch, my boy," said the naval hero, "I'll make you a captain or a commodore, if you like it." "But I don't like it," replied the puppet-show hero; "I shall be drowned." "Never fear that," answered Nelson; "he that is born to be hanged, you know, is sure not to be drowned."

During one of the elections for Westminster, Sir Francis Burdett was represented kissing Judy and the child, and soliciting Mr. Punch for his vote.

Punch has amused ages. "We ourselves," says Mr. Collier, "saw the late Mr. Windham, then one of the secretaries of state, on his way from Downing-street to the House of Commons on a night of important debate, pause, like a truant boy, until the whole performance was concluded, to enjoy a hearty laugh at the whimsicalities of the motley hero." And in 1850 we frequently saw Punch exhibiting for the special amusement of an infant duke in Piccadilly.

"We are never ashamed of being caught gazing at Punch," says Albert Smith, in a piquant sketch in the *Mirror*, May 1st 1847; and this facete writer was one of the earliest contributors to *Punch, or the London Charivari*, established in 1841, which has ranked among its contributors Gilbert à Beckett, Douglas Jerrold, and W. M. Thackeray. Jerrold's "Mrs. Caudle's Curtain Lectures" introduced the work to the domestic circle, which it might not otherwise have reached. Previously Punch had, however, not been invariably a puppet; for we read of a farce named *Punch turned Schoolmaster*. In 1828, George Cruikshank published his grotesque etchings of Punch, in a volume of very agreeable histrionic matter by Mr. Payne Collier, F.S.A. Haydon painted, in 1829, his Hogarthian picture of Punch, which Wilkie esteemed very highly. And in 1840, Mr. Webster, R.A., painted, with equal success, Punch in the Country.

How to play Punch.—First, a few words as to the machinery or properties. The animating "thread in one of Punch's chops," mentioned in the *Tatler*, shows a method of performance not now followed. At present, the puppets are played only by putting the hands under the dress, and making the middle finger and thumb serve for the arms, while the fore finger works the head. The opening and shutting of the mouth is a refinement which does not seem to be practised in Italy. "How is Punch's unearthly voice produced?" asks Albert Smith. "Is it a natural sound, or the result of some peculiar instrument in the mouth? We were taught in infancy that two quadrangular pieces of tin, bound together by narrow tape, would produce the desired effect when placed between the lips. This is not the fact. A squeaking sound may be perpetrated through its use, but no articulation of words is practicable; and we opine that the noise is the result of much training, or natural conformation of the muscles of the organs of voice." A later authority, however, gives the secret:

Porsini and Pike were celebrated Punch exhibitors: the former is said to have frequently taken 10*l.* a day; but he died in St. Giles's workhouse. A set of Punch figures costs about 15*l.*, and the show about 3*l.* The speaking is done by a "call" made of two curved pieces of metal about the size of a knee-buckle, bound together with black thread, and between them is a thin metal plate. Porsini used a trumpet. The present artists maintain that "Punch is exempted from the Police Act." The most profitable performance is that in houses; and Punch's best season is in the spring, and at Christmas and Midsummer: the best "pitches" in London are in Leicester-square, Regent-street (corner of New Burlington-street), Oxford Market, and Belgrave-square. There are sixteen Punch-and-Judy frames in England, eight of which work in London. *Fantoccini* are puppets, which, with the frame, cost about 10*l.* *Chinese Shades* consist of a frame like Punch's, with a transparent curtain and movable figures; shown only at night, with much dialogue.— *Selected from a Letter by Henry Mayhew; Morning Chronicle,* May 16, 1850.

WHO WAS MOTHER BUNCH?

A celebrated ale-wife, apparently of the latter part of the sixteenth century, mentioned by Dekker in his *Satiromastix,* 1602; and in 1604 was published *Pasquil's Jests, mixed with Mother Bunch's Merriment.*

THE WHITSUN PLAYS AT CHESTER.

These Plays were acted, seven or eight on each day, during the Monday, Tuesday, and Wednesday of the Whitsuntide week, by the various crafts in the city, to each of whom a separate mystery was allotted. The drapers, for instance, exhibited the Fall of Lucifer; the water-carriers of the Dee reproduced the Deluge; the cooks had the Harrowing of Hell. The performers were carried from one station to another by means of a movable scaffold, a huge and ponderous machine, mounted on wheels, gaily decorated with flags, and divided into two compartments, the upper of which formed the stage, and the lower, defended from vulgar curiosity by coarse canvas draperies, answered the purposes of the green-room. The performers began at the abbey gates, where they were witnessed by the high dignitaries of the Church; they then proceeded to the High Cross, where the mayor and the civic magnates were assembled; and so on, through the city, until their motley history of God and His dealings with man had been played out.

The production of these pageants was costly: each Mystery has been set down at fifteen or twenty pounds, present money. The dresses were obtained from the churches, until, this practice being denounced as scandalous, the guilds had then to provide the costume and other properties. Our Lord was commonly represented wearing a gilt peruke, and a sheepskin coat, painted or illuminated. Lucifer appeared with the conventional horns, tail, cloven feet, and a red beard, illustrating, in the latter particular, the clumsy Pluto of the *Gerusalemme,* and, in the other, the grotesque conception of the *Renaissance.* The close connection between Judas Iscariot and the evil principle was typified by his *red hair,* against which colour, (latterly modified into the bewitching auburn of the Venetian artist,) the illiterate in these days entertained a curious antipathy. Besides the expenditure on dress, the players had to be remunerated; and among the entries we find: "Payd to the players for rehearsal—Imprimis, to God, iis. viiid.; itm. to Pilate his wife, iis.; itm. to the Devil and

Judas, is. vid." There is a charge for the cock that crew on Peter's denial,—"Payd to Fauston, for coc-croying, iiijd. ;" and to Fauston, for hanging Judas, vd." "The cross, with a rope to draw it up," and "two pair of gallows," are prominent items in the old accounts; but "hell-mouthe," and "setting the world of fyer," occur upon every page. "Hell-mouthe," as preserved in early engravings, represented the head of a devouring dragon, whose red eye-balls glared fiercely on the spectators, and whose open jaws disclosed a murky cavern, wherein were stationed "a great company of devils," and from which issued the despairing groans of the tormented.

The Mystery held possession of the English stage for nearly three hundred years; and the Whitsun Plays were last acted at Chester in 1577. But a Miracle-Play was preserved in England, though in a very different form, till the reign of Queen Anne, when we find at Bartholomew Fair a "Little Opera, called the Old Creation of the World," with the contemporary additions of Marlborough's victories, and the Humours of Sir John Spendall, and Punchinello!

The Moral Play, introduced in the reign of Henry VI., followed the Miracle-Play, which was modified into the Interlude, the favourite Court entertainment *temp.* Henry VII. and of his son, both of whom relished the drama; a taste which they transmitted to Elizabeth. Hence arose "the Players of Interludes," and the "Gentlemen of the Chapel;" and John Heywood, "Player of the Virginals to King Henry VIII.," is entitled to be considered the father of English comedy.—*Edinburgh Essays*, 1856, abridged.

ACTRESSES ON THE ENGLISH STAGE.

Women did not appear as actresses in the theatres of antiquity, as may be gathered from Cicero, Plato, and Horace; but Shakspeare, who, like his contemporaries, attributes to all times the customs of his own, certainly thought of nothing more in *Antony and Cleopatra*, act v. sc. 2.

It is, however, well known that there were no actresses in the English theatres till after the Restoration. Corynte, in his account of Venice, says:

Here I observed certaine things that I never saw before. For I saw women acts, a thing that I never saw before, though I have heard that it hath been *sometimes* used in London.—*Crudities*, vol. ii.

A prologue, spoken about June 1660, turns particularly upon this subject:

> I come unknown to any of the rest,
> To tell you news: I saw the lady drest;
> The woman players to-day, mistake me not,
> No man in gown, or page in petticoat;
> A woman to my knowledge, yet I can't,
> (If I should dye) make affidavit on 't.

Some French women, however, acted at the Black Friars in 1629, as we learn from Prynne's *Histriomastix*. James Duport, who translated the Psalms, &c., was much offended at the scandal of introducing actresses, and wrote some indignant Alcaics on the subject. Hart, Clun, and Burt played female parts when boys. Kynaston performed Juliet to Betterton's Romeo.

BANKS'S HORSE.

The story of this learned horse (whose name was Marocco), and who was more celebrated in his time than even the learned pig in ours, is thus briefly told in Nares's *Glossary*.

Banks's Horse has the honour to be mentioned by Sir Walter Raleigh, in his *History of the World:*

If Banks had lived in older times, he would have shamed all the inchanters in the world ; for whosoever was most famous among them, could never master or instruct any beast as he did his horse.

One of his qualifications was dancing; for which reason he is supposed to have been alluded to in *Love's Labour's lost*, act i. sc. 2, under the title of the Dancing Horse. One of his exploits is said to have been going up to the top of St. Paul's church. This feat is alluded to in some verses by Gayton, *from Bankes his horse to Rosinante:*

Let us compare our feats: thou top of bowlen
Of hills, hast oft been seen. I top of Paul's (*pron.* Powle's).
To Smithfield horses I stood there the wonder.

According to the *Owle's Almanack*, 1618, this happened in 1601 : "Since the dancing horse stood on the top of Powle's, whilst a number of asses stood braying below, 17 years."

The editors of the Glossary add : The first mention of Banks's Horse occurs about 1590. In 1595, a supposed dialogue between Banks and his horse appeared under the title of *Maroccus Extaticus*. The latter was exhibited not only in England but abroad, where it became suspected that the horse was a demon, and his exhibitor a sorcerer ; and it is said that eventually both were burnt at Rome by the Inquisition.

ANTIQUITY OF FIDDLERS.

The earliest use of Fiddler does not signify what we now understand by a player on the violin. Thus, in Fletcher's *Knight of the Burning Pestle:*

They say 'tis death for these fiddlers to tune their rebecks.

And in Shakspeare's *Taming of the Shrew:* "Call me a fiddler," which is applied to a lutanist.

The violin, according to Anthony Wood, seems not to have been known in England till the time of Charles I. It was bor-

rowed from the old Welsh instrument *cruth*, which was not,
however, tuned in the same manner as a violin ; and in Barrington's time there were not above two or three persons in
Wales who could play upon it.

The fiddler had, nevertheless, become common in Cromwell's
time; for, by an ordinance dated 1656, "any minstrel or fiddler
who shall be making musick in any inn or tavern, or shall
ask any one to hear his musick, is to be punished as a sturdy
beggar."

A fiddler was also called a Crowder, from *crowd*, a fiddle :
Sir Philip Sidney has, "*Chevy Chase* sung by a blind crowder."

THE HOBBY-HORSE.

This was the name for a small horse ; as well as a personage belonging to the ancient morris-dance, when complete,
and made, as Mr. Bayes's troops are on the stage, by the figure
of a horse fastened round the waist of a man, his own legs going through the body of the horse, and enabling him to walk,
but concealed by a long foot-cloth ;* while false legs appeared
where those of the man should be, at the sides of the horse.
(Such hobby-horses may be found in the property-rooms of more
than one of our London theatres at the present hour.)

The Hobby-Horse is represented in the plate subjoined to
1 Hen. IV. in Steevens's Shakspeare of 1778, and the subsequent
editions, and illustrated by Mr. Tollet's remarks. Latterly the
Hobby-Horse was frequently omitted, which led to a popular
ballad with this line or burden:

> For O, for O, the hobby-horse is forgot,

which is quoted in *Love's Labour's lost* and in *Hamlet*.

The Puritans, who were declared enemies of all sports and
games, were strongly inveterate against the hobby-horse.

Many tricks were expected of the dancer who acted the
hobby-horse, and some of a juggling nature, as pretending to
stick daggers in his nose (perhaps a false one), which is represented in the print from Mr. Tollet's painted window of the
Morris May Day ; whence the Hobby-Horse is presumed to be
the King of the May.

HOBBY,

• or Hoby, was the old name for a small horse, or a nag.   Hob-

---

* The mule was generally trained to wear the foot-cloth, as a spirited horse
would not be likely to bear such an incumbrance. Howel, in 1680, tells us that
the doctors of physic rode to visit their patients with their mules and foot-cloths,
when the fee was but two shillings. The judges also rode in similar state to
Westminster Hall, which practice ended with the death of Sir Robert Hyde,
lord chief justice. Lord Shaftesbury would have revived the custom, but several
of the judges, being old and ill horsemen, would not agree to it.

bies were strong and active. of rather a small size, and reported
to be originally natives of Ireland. It is pretended that they
were so much liked and used, that the word became a proverbial
expression for any thing of which people are extremely fond.

THE VIRGINAL.

This was an instrument of the spinnet kind; but made rect-
angular, like a small pianoforte. Archdeacon Nares remembered two in use, belonging to the master of the king's choris-
ters. Their name, he adds, was probably derived from their being
used by young girls. They had, like spinnets, only one wire to
each note. The spinnet, as many persons remember, was nearly
of a triangular shape, and had the wires carried over a bent
bridge, which modified their sounds; those of the virginal went
direct from their points of support to the screw-pegs, regularly
decreasing in length from the deepest bass to the highest treble.
Sometimes the instrument is called a pair of virginals, which is
as improper as a *pair of organs.*

LOSS OF THE TRUMPET.

This instrument seems to have been in what may be called
its civil uses superseded by the bell. In our early theatres the
Prologue was usually introduced by the sound of the trumpet.
The members of Queen's College, Oxford, are still summoned to
dinner by sound of the trumpet. Sheriffs retained till lately
their state trumpeters: and the Lord Mayor of London has
parted with this officer: nevertheless he proceeds to his inau-
guration banquet in Guildhall, on Nov. 9, by sound of trumpet,
and the toasts are introduced by the same; and we have seen the
Lord Mayor returning in full state from church on Sunday by
sound of trumpet.

To descend in our illustration, Punch's showman has lost
his trumpet; and instead of the coach-horn we have the rail-
way-whistle.

ORIGIN OF BLACKGUARD.

The origin of this term of reproach has been traced to the
office of the Board of Green Cloth. It was first applied to the
meanest drudges in royal residences, who carried coals (Gifford's
Ben Jonson). The term was afterwards extended to vicious,
idle, and masterless boys and rogues; and was so used, Mr.
Cunningham found, by the books in the Board of Green Cloth,
as early as 1683, if not before.

English Laws, Legal Customs, Privileges, and Dignities.

MAJORITY OF MONARCHS.

It is very extraordinary that in no country (where the government by an hereditary monarch prevails) it should have been settled, as a general regulation, at what age an infant king should be considered as a major. There is in the *Nouveau Traité de Diplomatique* an engraving of an ordinance of Charles V., which is entitled *Ordonnance de la Majorité de nos Rois à quatorze ans.* This ordinance relates, indeed, to the education of the royal children, but not to any declaration of the age at which they are to become majors.

Solomon is said to have been but nineteen when he made his famous decision between the two mothers. A Roman consul could not regularly be a candidate for the office till he was forty-three years of age. Minorities of kings are denounced by Isaiah, to complete the national calamities of the Jews: "And I will give children to be their princes, and babes shall rule over them; and the people shall be oppressed" (*Isaiah* v. 4, 5).—*Barrington on Ant. Stat.*, note.

Richard II. was but eleven years old when he became King of England; and it was not until the 25th year of Henry VIII. that it was enacted, a King of England was not to be a major till eighteen, whilst a queen became so at the age of sixteen.

LAWS OF RICHARD III.

The reign of Richard III. is a remarkable epoch in the legislative annals of this country; not only from the statutes being thenceforth in English, but likewise from their having been the first which were ever printed. We accordingly find in these laws exceptions in favour of scriveners (employed in copying books), alluminors (illuminators), printers, and readers of books.

The English of the statutes of Richard III. and Henry VII. is more pure than that of the reign of Henry VIII., which arises from the preambles of the latter being more figurative in expression.

Books, though printed, were now excessively dear; whence Daines Barrington conjectures the *readers* above mentioned were booksellers, who received money from an audience who were either incapable themselves of reading, or otherwise could not afford to purchase the books. Fitsherbert's *Abridgment* In the reign of Henry VIII. sold for 40s.; and the number of readers in the same reign was so small, that Grafton, in 1540, printed but 1500 copies of the Bible.

BOTH SIDES OF THE QUESTION.

Daines Barrington, in his work on the More Ancient Statutes, observes: " We shall find that some of the reigns of those kings who are so much celebrated for their victories, produced laws of infinite oppression." He then instances the statute of *quo warranto* of Edward I., extended to Ireland by Edward III.; and 2 Henry V. against heretics. To these is added the following emphatic denunciation from Hobbes's works :

The greatest sums that ever were levied (comparing the value of money with what it is now), were raised by King Edward III. and Henry V., kings of whom we glory now, and think their names an ornament to the English history.

Henry brought himself into great distress by carrying on his wars with greater expense than we have any account of in former reigns. His army was, in consequence, most miserably paid ; and the carrier of Henry's banner at the battle of Agincourt had to petition his successor for payment ; for though the banner-bearer had incurred great expenses in attending Henry to France, yet he had not received any reward or salary whatsoever ! Yet it was some glory to have borne unpaid the banner of Henry V. at Agincourt.—See *Rymer.*

RANSOMS.

By the statute Henry VI. c. 5, it was enacted that a third share of the booty should be allowed at the Exchequer to the late king's officers; one part was to be the ransom of the prisoners, and the remaining two-thirds were to be paid to the crown. The former distribution of the booty involved large sums. Thus Leland, in his *Itinerary,* gives two or three different accounts of great houses being built out of the price of a prisoner's ransom, particularly Sudely Castle, in Gloucestershire. Sir — Latimer, when impeached by parliament, 50 Edward III., alleged in his defence that he had never received above 10,000*l.,* and this chiefly from the ransom of prisoners at the battle of Orroye. Rymer shows that Henry IV. paid 10,000 marks to Owen Glendower for the ransom of Lord Grey of Ruthin, whose daughter Owen had married, having obliged the father to give his consent while he was his prisoner. St. Palaye gives an account of a French knight, Du Guesclin, when taken prisoner at the battle of Poictiers, who fixed his own ransom at a very high price. Upon the Prince of Wales expressing a doubt whether he would be able to raise such a sum, Du Guesclin replied, that he first depended upon the kings of France and Castile; and if they would not pay the ransom, he had at least one hundred friends who would sell their estates, and every woman in France would spin, for his deliverance: yet he is said to have been more than commonly deformed.

From the articles of war established by Henry V. for his first campaign in France, we learn that sometimes the king bought a prisoner from his captor, and sometimes sold one. There are instances of the king's forbidding the sale of prisoners for a certain time; but their right is acknowledged by the proclamation.

An old French chronicle, printed at Paris in 1508, speaks of the great pressing of the English to make King John of France their prisoner at the battle of Poictiers, he being considered as the 20,000*l.* prize in the lottery of war.

The ransom of a king was therefore the greatest sum of money of which the people could form an idea. Hence the ancient lines on Hinkston Hill, in Cornwall, supposed to be full of very valuable mines:

> Hinkston Hill, well wrought,
> Is worth a king's ransom dearly bought.

Hence also the more homely weather proverb: "A peck of March dust is worth a king's ransom."

Holinshed shows that in the reign of Richard II. a war with France was esteemed the only method by which an English gentleman could become rich. Drayton has, in his *Battle of Agincourt:*

> Some that themselves by ransoms would enrich,
> To make their prey of peasants did despise,
> Felt as they thought their bloody palms to itch
> To be in action for their wealthy prize.

And again:

> Except some few in some great captain's hands,
> Whose ransoms might his empty coffers fill.

We find, by the Rolls of Parliament, 8 Henry VI., that the ransom of the Lord Talbot, prisoner to the French, was unreasonable and importable.

THE FALCON A ROYAL BIRD.

From the provision made with regard to Falcons, &c. in the Great Forest Charter, it seems that the king claimed them, wherever found, as royal birds. Falconry and hunting were then the principal amusements of the great barons; consequently hawks were very valuable. Falconry was so expensive, and required so many attendants, that few could afford such an establishment; but they who did not themselves keep falcons, were frequently obliged, by the grants of their lands, to procure them annually for those under whom they held their estates; and sometimes a lease was granted on condition of furnishing every year a falcon.

Falcons are always represented on the hands of princes and their descendants. In the Bayeux tapestry, Harold sets out on the message of Edward the Confessor to William Duke of Normandy with a hawk on his wrist. When he is afterwards taken prisoner, the captor, Guy Count of Ponthieu, precedes him with a hawk on his hand; and Harold follows dejected, but still permitted to carry his falcon. Montfaucon represents the two sons of William the Conqueror with this bird on their hand, as also queens and princesses in the same attitude.

ROYAL FISH.

The Whale and Sturgeon, when either thrown ashore or caught near the coast, are the property of the sovereign, on account (as it is said in the law-books) of their superior excellence.* Indeed, our ancestors seem to have entertained a very high notion of the importance of this right, it being the prerogative of the kings of Denmark and the dukes of Normandy; and from one of them it was probably derived to our princes. It is expressly claimed and allowed in the statute *De Prærogativa Regis;* and the most ancient treatises of law now extant make mention of it.

Upon this Barrington notes: "I apprehend that the custom of sending a *present* (as it is styled) to the king of the Sturgeon taken in the Thames, arises from this ancient prerogative of the crown, as it is one of the royal fish. I find, however, by a case stated with regard to a right of fishery in the Thames, that the *taker* of the Sturgeon is entitled to a *mare*, though the fish belongs to the king, paying that satisfaction." —*Observations on the More Antient Statutes.*

STRIKING IN THE KING'S COURT.†

Contempts against the royal palaces have been always looked upon as high misprisions; and by the ancient law before the Conquest, fighting in the king's palace, or before the king's judges, was punished with death. By the statute of 33 Henry VIII. c. 12, malicious striking in the king's palace, wherein his royal person resides, whereby blood is drawn, was punishable by perpetual imprisonment and fine at the king's

* The Swan is also a royal fowl; and all Swans, the property whereof is not known, belong to the king by his prerogative.

† See also p. 14 ante.

pleasure, and also with the loss of the offender's right hand; the solemn execution of which sentence is prescribed in the statute at length; but by 9 Geo. IV. c. 31, this punishment is repealed. It appears, however, to be a contempt of the kind now in question to execute the ordinary process of the law, by arrest or otherwise, within the verge of a royal palace, or in the Tower, unless permission be first obtained from the proper authority.—Stephen's *Commentaries.*

Baker, in his *Chronicle*, thus minutely describes the execution of the above barbarous sentence:

On the 10th of June 1541, Sir Edmund Knevet of Norfolk, Knight, was arraigned before the officers of the Green Cloth for striking one Master Cleer of Norfolk, within the Tennis Court of the King's House. Being found guilty, he had judgment to lose his right hand, and to forfeit all his lands and goods; whereupon there was called to do execution, first, the Sergeant Surgeon, with his instruments pertaining to his office; then the Sergeant of the Wood-yard, with a mallet and block to lay the hand upon; then the king's Master Cook, with a knife to cut off the hand; then the Sergeant of the Larder, to set the knife right on the joint; then the Sergeant Ferrier, with searing-irons to sear the veins; then the Sergeant of the Poultry, with a cock, which cock should have his head smitten off upon the block, and with the same knife; then the Yeoman of Chandry, with sear-cloths; then the Yeoman of the Scullery, with a pan of fire to heat the irons, a chafer of water to cool the ends of the irons, and two forms for all officers to set their stuff on; then the Sergeant of the Cellar, with wine, ale, and beer; then the Sergeant of the Ewry, with bason, ewre, and towels. All things being thus prepared, Sir William Pickering, Knight-Marshal, was commanded to bring in his prisoner, Sir Edmund Knevet, to whom the Chief-Justice declared his offence, which the said Knevet confessed, and humbly submitted himself to the king's mercy; only he desired that the king would spare his right hand and take his left: "Because," said he, "if my right hand be spared, I may live to do the king good service:" of whose submission and reason of his suit, when the king was informed, he granted him to lose neither of his hands, and pardoned him also of his lands and goods.—Baker's *Chronicle*, ed. 1674.

Chamberlayne describes the ceremony as follows:

The Sergeant of the king's Wood-yard brings to the place of execution a square block, a beetle, and a staple and cords to fasten the hands thereto. The Yeoman of the Scullery provides a great fire of coals by the block, where the searing-irons, brought by the chief Farrier, are to be ready for the chief Surgeon to use. Vinegar and cold water are to be brought by the Groom of the Saucery; and the chief officers of the Cellar and Pantry are to be ready, one with a cup of red wine, and the other with a manchet, to offer the criminal. The Sergeant of the Ewry is to bring the linen to wind about and wrap the arm; the Yeoman of the Poultry, a cock to lay to it; the Yeoman of the Chandlary, seared cloths; and the Master Cook a sharp dresser-knife, which at the place of execution is to be held upright by the Sergeant of the Larder, till execution be performed by an officer appointed thereunto. After all, the criminal shall be imprisoned during life, and fined and ransomed at the king's will.

STRIKING IN A CHURCHYARD.

The 6 Edward VI. c. 4, punishes *Striking in a Churchyard* with the loss of ears; which statute, at the time it was enacted, was intended to prevent dangerous riots between the Papists and Protestants upon the first establishment of the Reformation. Daines Barrington, writing in 1775, notes that not many years previously there was an indictment under this Act at the quarter sessions in Somersetshire.

"MOST CATHOLIC."

Prescott gives in a note (*Hist. Ferd. and Isab.* ii. 378) this explanation of the epithet *Most Catholic.* The title, as applied to Ferdinand and Isabella, was given to them by the Pope, who, desirous of offering them a compliment upon their conquest of Granada, addressed them as the *Most Christian;* which, however, being a title hitherto only applied to the sovereigns of France, was objected to by the Cardinals, and the epithet of "Most Catholic" substituted for it. The term Catholic had been before applied to the Asturian prince Alphonso, and also to Pedro II.; so that it was not new either to the house of Castille or Arragon; and the phrase *Los Reyes Catolicos* is applicable either to a female or male, agreeably to the Spanish idiom, though sounding singularly incorrect to an English ear. The Spanish language requires that when a word having reference both to a masculine and feminine noun is employed, it should be expressed in the former gender.—*Archæologia*, vol. xxxvii. p. 61.

THE SCOTTISH NATIONAL MOTTO.

On a coin presented to the Kelso Museum, dated 1695, the National Motto is "Nemo me impune lacesset." The 'i,' therefore, though introduced into the motto on the Great Seal of that year, does not appear to have superseded the 'e' entirely till a somewhat later period. That "lacesset" is the original reading, there would seem no doubt. *Pinkerton* (vol. ii. published 1808, at p. 127) says: "In the time of James VI., 1571, the merk and half-merk, Scottish, were struck—the former being then worth about twenty-two pence, and the latter eleven pence, English. Upon these pieces the motto ' Nemo me impune lædet' was ordered, but does not appear. In 1578 the famous ' Nemo me impune lacesset' occurs first upon the coin; the same in sense with the other, but of a better sound. Its invention is ascribed to Buchanan."

PEERS' AUDIENCE OF THE SOVEREIGN BY RIGHT.

It is usually looked upon to be the right of each particular peer of the realm to demand an audience of the sovereign, and to lay before him, with decency and respect, such matters as he shall judge of importance to the public weal. And therefore, in the reign of Edward II., it was made an article of impeachment in parliament against the two Hugh Spencers, father and son, for which they were banished the kingdom, "that they by their evil covin would not suffer the great men of the realm, the king's good counsellors, to speak with the king, or to come near him," but only in their presence and hearing.

It may be useful to mention, that no *sealed* letter can be presented to the sovereign by the lord chamberlain; all such communications must be open and without seal.

GRANT OF ARMS.

According to the rule of the Heralds' College, the use of Arms for any length of time whatsoever will not make them legal. To legally bear them, according to the College, the party must either derive such Arms by descent from one whom the College acknowledges as entitled to bear them, or he must obtain a grant of arms to himself from the College. The grant of arms costs about 70*l.* or 80*l.*, and the application for it must be made to the Heralds' College. The grant to the head of a family must include him and his heirs; but his brothers, or collateral relations, will have to be specially mentioned. In Ireland and Scotland, we believe, the rule against length of user does not prevail; and a period of prescription is there allowed.

To obtain a *Grant of Arms*, the applicant may employ any member he pleases of the Heralds' Office, and through him present a memorial to the Earl Marshal, setting forth that he, the memorialist, is not entitled to arms, or cannot prove his right to such; and praying that his Grace will issue his warrant to the Kings of Arms authorising them to grant and confirm to him due and proper armorial ensigns, to be borne according to the laws of heraldry by him and his descendants. This memorial is presented; and a warrant is issued by the Earl Marshal, under which a patent is made out, exhibiting in the corner a painting of the armorial ensigns granted, and describing in official terms the proceedings that have taken place, and the correct blazon of the arms. This patent is registered in the books of the Heralds' College, and receives the signatures of the Garter and one of the Provincial Kings of Arms. Thus an "Armiger" is made. The fees on a Grant of Arms amount to seventy-five guineas; an ordinary search of the records is five shillings; a general search one guinea. Arms that are not held under a Grant must descend to the bearer from an ancestor recorded in the Herald's visitations. No prescription, however long, will confer a right to a coat-armour.

THE TABARD.

This is a coat or vest, without sleeves, close before and behind, and open at the sides, formerly worn by nobles over their arms to distinguish them in the field, but now only by heralds in royal processions, &c. Stow speaks of the tabard as worn only by heralds in his day, but having been " a stately garment of old time." In Queen's College, Oxford, eight of the scholars, whose original dress was a tabard, are still called *Tabarders.* [*]

In this College the following old customs are still preserved : On New-Year's day the bursar presents to each member a needle and thread, a rebus on the founder's name, *Aiguille et fil,* adding the wholesome moral, " Take this, and be thrifty." Also on Christmas-day, a boar's head, decked with rosemary, is carried in procession into the hall, ushered in by the well-known carol, " Apri caput defero." And in the buttery is a curious drinking-horn, richly ornamented with silver gilt, and said to have been given by Queen Philippa (consort of Edward III.), after whom the College is named.

PRESSING MINSTRELS, ETC.

Among many instances of the power of impressing in the early ages occurs, in Rymer, an order of Henry VI. to authorise certain persons to press *Minstrels in solatium regis.* It would seem also that, so late as the reign of Edward VI., whenever a boy had a promising voice, he was forcibly taken from his parents, to be educated as a scholar for the king's chapel, as may be inferred from these lines by Tusser, printed in 1577 :

> Then for my voyce, I must (no choyce)
> Away of force, like posting horse,
> For sundry men had placards then,
> Such childe to take.

Probably the last exercise of a prerogative of this class was in the reign of William III. The patentee of Drury Lane Theatre having a dispute with Dogget the actor, about articles, procured a message from the Lord Chamberlain's office to fetch Dogget up from Norwich. On being brought up by *habeas corpus,* he was released by Lord-Chief Justice Holt, who much censured the proceeding.

In the *Liber Niger Domus Regni* (*temp.* Edward IV.) is an ordinance naming " Children of the Chapelle vilj, founden by the King's privie coffers for all that longeth to their apperelle by the hands and over-syghts of the deane, or by the master of song assigned to teache them ;"

---

[*] The *Tabard* Inn, Southwark, celebrated as Chaucer's Pilgrims' Inn, has become corrupted to the *Talbot.* Although one of the most ancient inns in the kingdom, the present buildings are not earlier than the reign of Charles II. The original inn was destroyed by fire in the seventeenth century. There was formerly an inn with the sign of the Tabard in Gracechurch-street ; and there now is in Tothill Street, Westminster, the *Cock and Tabard* sign.

such being the origin of the present musical establishment of the Chapel-Royal. Ordinances were also issued for the *impressment of boys* for the royal choirs. In 1550, the master of the King's Chapel had license "to take up from time to time children to serve the King's Chapel." Tusser, the "Husbandrie" poet, was, when a boy, in Elizabeth's reign, thus impressed for the Queen's Chapel. The Gentlemen and Children of the Chapel-Royal were the principal performers in the religious dramas or *Mysteries;* and a "master of the children," and "singing children," occur in the chapel establishment of Cardinal Wolsey. In 1583, the Children of the Chapel-Royal afterwards called the Children of the Revels, were formed into a company of players, and thus were among the earliest performers of the regular drama. In 1731, they performed Handel's *Esther,* the first oratorio heard in England; and they continued to assist at oratorios in Lent, so long as those performances maintained their ecclesiastical character entire.—*Curiosities of London,* p. 166.

Masons, bricklayers, and other workmen, were also pressed for the king's works (*temp.* Richard III.) within the Tower of London and Palace of Westminster; and Windsor Castle was in part so built. The old law maxim was, "The king is entitled to every man's service;" and we even find goldsmiths pressed for the personal adornment of Edward IV.

A FALSE PEDIGREE.

Rushworth records, in his own quaint manner, the following curious proceedings in the Earl Marshal's Court, in the reign of Charles II.:

About this time, West, Lord Delaware, commenced a suit in the Court of Honour, or Lord Marshal's Court, against one who went by that name. The case was, a person of a far different name by birth, but an ostler, having, by his skill in wrestling in Lincoln's-inn-fields, got the name of *Jack of the West,* coming afterwards to be an innkeeper, and getting a good estate, assumes the name of West, and the arms of the family of the Lord Delaware, and gets from the heralds his pedigree, drawn through three or four generations, from the fourth son of one of the Lords Delaware; and his son, whom he bred at the inns of Court, presuming upon his pedigree to take the place of some gentlemen, his neighbours, in Hampshire, they procured him to be cited by the Lord Delaware in this court, where, at the hearing, he produced his patent from the heralds. But so it fell out, that an ancient gentleman, of the name of West, and family of Delaware, and named in the pedigree, who had been long beyond sea and conceived to be dead, and now newly returned, whose son, as it seems, this young spark would have had his father to have been, appeared in court at the hearing, which dashed the whole business; and the pretended West, the defendant, was fined 500*l.,* ordered to be degraded, and never more to write himself gentleman.

THE ENGLISH AND FRENCH GENTLEMAN.

M. Alexis de Tocqueville, in his *France before the Revolution of* 1789, has this interesting passage:

For several centuries the word *gentleman* has altogether changed its meaning in England, and the word *roturier* has ceased to exist. It would have been impossible to translate literally into English the well-known line from the *Tartuffe*, even when Molière wrote it in 1664 :

Et tel qu'on le voit, il est bon gentilhomme.

If we make a further application of the science of languages to history, and pursue the fate of the word *gentleman* through time and through space, the offspring of the French *gentilhomme*, we shall find its application extending in England in the same proportion in which classes draw near one another and amalgamate. In each succeeding century it is applied to persons placed somewhat lower in the social scale. At length it travelled with the English to America, where it is used to designate every citizen indiscriminately. Its history is that of democracy itself. In France the word *gentilhomme* has always been strictly limited to its original meaning. Since the Revolution it has been almost disused, but its application has never changed. The word which was used to designate the members of the caste was kept intact, because the caste itself was maintained as separate from all the rest as it had ever been. This caste had become far more exclusive than it was when the word was first invented, and in France a change had taken place in the opposite direction of that which had occurred in England.

EXCESS IN DRESS AND DIET.

Under the head of public economy (says Blackstone) may properly be ranked all sumptuary laws against luxury and extravagant expenses in Dress, Diet, and the like. Concerning excess in apparel, there were formerly a multitude of penal laws existing, chiefly made in the reigns of Edward III., Edward IV., and Henry VIII., against piked shoes, short doublets, and long coats; all which were repealed by statute 1 Jac. I. c. 25. But as to excess in diet, Blackstone goes on to remark, there still remained one ancient statute unrepealed (10 Edw. I. st. 3), which ordains that no man shall be served at dinner or supper with more than two courses; except upon some great holidays there specified, in which he may be served with three. This statute was also at length expressly repealed by 19 and 20 Vict. c. 64.

SIMONY.

Simony means the corrupt presentation of any one to an ecclesiastical benefice for money, gift, or reward. It is so called from its resemblance to the sin of Simon Magus, the magician, who is mentioned in the Acts of the Apostles (viii. 18-24) as having offered money to Peter and John, in order that he might obtain from them apostolical powers. Peter vehemently rebuked him, and he showed some appearance of penitence ; but he afterwards became one of the chief opponents of Christianity; and coming to Rome, it is pretended that he worked miracles, which gained him many followers, and obtained for him the favour of Nero. At last, it is said, as he was exhibiting in tho emperor's presence the feat of flying through the air in a fiery chariot, which he was enabled to perform by the aid of demons, the united prayers of Peter and Paul, who were present on the occasion, prevailed against him, and the demons threw him to the ground. There are other marvellous stories of his life and doctrine.

MERCHANTS' RELIGIOUS OBSERVANCES.

It is worthy of remark, that a pious spirit is more conspicuous in the domestic observances and habits of our ancestors than in our own. A Scripture posy was the common ornament of a chamber; it was found on a ring, or occurred as the heading of a letter. To speak of commercial matters,—there are many little religious formulæ now fallen into disuse which once prevailed universally, and show that a more religious feeling animated our ancestors than is now fashionable with their descendants. "*Laus Deo*" (Praise be to God) was once the usual heading of every page of a merchant's journal. When goods were sent to some foreign port, the bill of lading, as it is technically termed, invariably stated that they had been "shipped *by the grace of God* in and upon the good ship" called by such a name. A policy of insurance against sea-risks still begins with these words: "*In the name of God, Amen;*" and, up to a late date, all commercial appointments were made "God willing." — Burgon's *Life and Times of Sir Thomas Gresham*, 1839.

COMPULSORY PRACTICE OF ARCHERY ON SUNDAYS.

In the reign of Richard II. (1388), a law, which seems to have been more of a political than of a religious character, prescribes to servants of husbandry and artificers *the use of bows and arrows on Sundays and holidays,* enjoining such to "leave playing at tennis, or foot-ball, cartes, dice, casting of the stone, and other importune games;" and an act of Henry IV. enforced the observance of this law under the penalty of six days' imprisonment; while the execution of the law is sought to be secured by the imposition of a fine of 10s. on the superior, and 1s. 4d. on the inferior officers, if guilty of neglect in executing it. The object of this law was to enforce the practice of archery, so as to be available in time of war.

PARLIAMENT SITTING ON SUNDAYS.

For reasons of imperative necessity, the observance of holidays, however sacred, must give way to the preservation of the public peace against violent outbreaks; for an evil might

happen in the night which it would be too late to prevent in
the morning. The same principle extends to the meeting of
the Privy Council, and its offshoot the Cabinet Council, at the
present time; which, when the public welfare appears to demand it, meets on the Sunday or any other holiday without
scruple.

In like manner, parliament occasionally assembles on a
Sunday, as on the death of George II., when both Houses met
on that day, October 26, 1760, to take the oaths.* Our earlier
history will furnish us with similar instances. Thus, in the
reign of Edward III., parliaments met on a Sunday in the
17th and 43d years; and in the 16th of Charles I., in a case of
great necessity,† the Long Parliament, after hearing a sermon,
commenced business at nine in the morning of that day, and
sat all day; passing, however, a resolution "to enter upon no
matter which did not concern the interests of religion and the
welfare of the kingdom, and that it be not drawn into a precedent by any inferior court or private person for neglecting
the due observance of the Lord's day."

BAKING ON SUNDAYS.

The statute of Charles II. against labour on Sunday contains an exemption in favour of cooks' shops, which has been extended to the baking of meat, puddings, and pies on a Sunday;
it being held, on the general exception contained in the Act
in favour of works of piety and necessity, that the act of the
baker did not fall within the statute; Mr. Justice Wilmot observing, that it was "as reasonable that the baker should bake
for the poor, as that the cook should roast or broil for them"
(the magistrates). A conviction under the statute against a
baker for baking meat and pastry for his customers, for pay,
was quashed upon similar reasoning; Lord Kenyon maintain
ing that the laborious part of the community were entitled to
indulgence, many of them not having the means of dressing
their dinners at home. These cases led to the passing of statutes (first in 1794) for the regulation of baking and the sale
of bread on a Sunday; when a piece of hair-splitting was use-
lessly raised, as to whether the permission for the sale of bread
would include also the sale of rolls!

ORIGIN OF THE COURTS OF COMMON LAW AND EQUITY.

The policy of our ancient* constitution, as regulated and
established by the great Alfred, was to bring justice home to

* See Swann *v.* Broome, 1 Bl. 499, where Lord Mansfield says: "I myself
have sat in parliament on a Sunday."
† Viz. the resolution of the King to set out for Scotland on the Monday,
communicated to them on the Saturday (Rush. iv. 361).

every man's door, by constituting as many courts of judicature
as there are manors in the kingdom; wherein injuries were re-
dressed, in an easy and expeditious manner, by the suffrage of
neighbours and friends.   These little courts, however, communicated with others of a larger jurisdiction, and those with
others of a still greater power; ascending gradually from the
lowest to the supreme courts, which were respectively constituted to correct the errors of the inferior ones, and to determine such cases as, by reason of their weight and difficulty,
demanded a more solemn discussion.

This institution seems highly agreeable to the dictates of
natural reason, as well as of more enlightened policy; being
equally similar to that which prevailed in Mexico and Peru before they were discovered by the Spaniards, and to that which
was established in the Jewish republic by Moses; of whom we
read, that, finding the sole administration of justice too heavy
for him, he "chose able men out of all Israel, such as feared
God, men of truth, hating covetousness, and made them heads
over the people, rulers of thousands, rulers of hundreds, rulers
of fifties, and rulers of tens; and they judged the people at all
seasons; the hard cases they brought unto Moses, but every
small matter they judged themselves." — Stephen's *Commentaries.*

The names of our courts of judicature are singularly direct.
Thus the highest court in England at Common Law is named
the *King's Bench,* because anciently the sovereign sometimes
sat there in person, on a high bench, and his judges on a lower
bench at his feet.

The *High Court of Chancery,* from *Curia Cancellaria,* is named,
as some think, because the judge of this court sat anciently
intra cancellos, or *lattices;* the east end of our churches, being
separated *per cancellos* from the body of the church, as peculiarly belonging to the priest, were thence called Chancels.

The *Court of Common Pleas* is so called because here are debated the usual *pleas* between subject and subject.

Selden observes, that the *Barons of the Exchequer* were so
called because they were anciently made from such as were
barons of the kingdom or parliamentary barons.   The same
reason is given for the appellation of barons of the Cinque
Ports, now extinct.

Much of the old machinery of the Exchequer Court lasted
till our time.   Dugdale, in his *Origines Juridicales* thus explains the name of the court:

The Exchequer is a four-cornered board, about ten foot long and
five foot broad, fitted in manner of a table for men to sit about; on
every side whereof is a standing ledge, or border, four fingers broad.
Upon this board is laid a cloth bought in Easter Term, which is of black

colour, rowed with strokes distant about a foot or a span. . . . . That this court, then, had its name from the board whereon they sate, there is no doubt to be made ; considering that the cloth which covered it was thus party-coloured, which the French call *Chequy.*

Chamberlayne says : " The Exchequer is so called, as some think, from a chequer-wrought table in that court (as the Court of Green Cloth in the King's House is so called from the green carpet) ; or else from the French word *Eschiquier,* a chess-board, because the accomptants in that office were wont to use such board in their calculation."

The Chancellor is one of the judges of the court ; and in ancient times he sat as such, together with the Lord Treasurer and the Barons. His duties are now entirely ministerial. The Lord High Treasurer was also one of the judges ; and in the office of the Comptroller-General of the Exchequer in Whitehall Yard, is to this day preserved the ancient chair, covered with needlework, on which the Lord High Treasurer of England used to sit.

Certain officers of this court are the Clerk and Comptroller *of the Pipe,* from the documents passing *through a pipe.* Thus the office of the four Tellers of the court (says Chamberlayne) is to receive all moneys due to the king, and thereupon to throw down a bill, *through a pipe,* into the Tally Court, where it is received by the Auditor's clerk, who there attends to write the words of the said bill upon a tally, and then delivers the same to be entered by the Clerk of the Pells, or his under-clerk, who there attends to enter it in his book ; then the tally is cloven by the two Deputy Chamberlains, who have their seals ; and while the Senior Deputy reads one part, the Junior examines the other part with the other two clerks.

The *Clerk of the Pells* was named from his office being to enter the Teller's bill on a parchment-skin, in Latin *pellis.*

In the Tally Court (says Chamberlayne) sit the Deputies of the two Chamberlains, who cleave the tallies, and examine each piece apart ; also the Tally-cutter attends there.

A Tally in the Exchequer, from the French word *tailler,* and the Italian *tagliare,* to cut, is a very ancient and most certain way of avoiding all cosenage in the king's revenue, there is the like nowhere else in Christendom ; and is after this manner :

(Part of an Exchequer Tally, date 1816.)

He that pays or lends the king any moneys, receives for his acquittance or acknowledgment a Tally, which is a stick with words written on it on both sides concerning the acquittance proper to express what the moneys received is for : which being cloven asunder by the Deputy-Chamberlain, one part thereof, called the stock, is delivered to the party that pays the money ; and the other part, called counter-stock, or counter-foil, remains with them, who afterwards deliver it over to the other Deputies, to be kept till it be called for, and joined with the stock ; after which they send it, by an officer of their own, to the Pipe, to be applied to the discharge of the Accomptant.

This most ancient way of striking of tallies hath been found by long experience to be absolutely the best way that ever was invented ; for it is morally impossible so to falsify or counterfeit a Tally, but upon rejoining it with the counter-foil it will be obvious to every eye, either in the notches, or in the cleaving, in the length, or in the breadth, in the natural growth, or in the shape of the counter-foil.

It was the burning of heaps of these wooden records in the stoves of the House of Lords that caused the conflagration by which the old Houses of Parliament were destroyed, in 1834; in which year this old mode of reckoning was abolished.

OPEN COURT: ADMISSION-FEES.

In the statute 13 Edw. I. cc. 42-44, we find reference to fees claimed by certain officers; seeming to denote that the courts of law were not then *open courts*, in the sense that they are now understood to be so. An open court is at present generally so crowded by idle spectators as to inconvenience all who have real business. The above statute directs that the plaintiff or defendant should pay nothing; but by implication seems to allow that the idle part of the audience should pay one penny each for admittance, or nearly equal to one shilling at present: "so that," says Barrington, "if the spirit of the law was attended to, it would in a great measure prevent what is now so sensibly felt as an inconvenience."

ORIGIN OF "TERMS."

These forensic seasons are supposed by Selden to have been instituted by William the Conqueror; but Sir H. Spelman has proved that they were gradually formed from the canonical constitutions of the Church; being, indeed, no other than those leisure seasons of the year which were not occupied by the great festivals or fasts, or which were not liable to the general avocations of rural business. Throughout all Christendom, in very early times, the whole year was one continual Term for hearing and deciding causes; for the Christian magistrates, to distinguish themselves from the heathens, who were extremely superstitious in the observation of their *dies fasti et nefasti*, went into a contrary extreme, and administered justice upon all days alike: till at length the Church interposed, and exempted certain holy seasons from being profaned by the tumult of forensic litigations; and particularly the time of Advent and Christmas, which gave rise to the winter vacation; the time of Lent and Easter, which created that in the spring; the time of Pentecost, which produced the third; and the long vacation between Midsummer and Michaelmas, which was allowed for the hay-time and harvest. All Sundays also, and some particular festivals, as the days of Purification, Ascension, and some others, were included in the prohibition, which was established by a canon of the Church, A.D. 517, and was fortified by an imperial constitution of the younger Theodosius, comprised in the Theodosian code. Afterwards, when our own legal constitution came to be settled, the commencement and duration of

our Law Terms were appointed with an eye to the above canonical prohibitions.—Stephen's *Commentaries.*

WORDINESS OF LEGAL DOCUMENTS.

The true objection to modern statutes (says Barrington),
is rather their prolixity than their want of perspicuity; which
redundancy hath in a great measure arisen from the use of
printing. When manuscript copies are to be dispersed, the
trouble of writing an unnecessary word is considered; but a
page or two additional in print neither adds much to trouble
or expense.

From the reign of Robert I. words began to be multiplied; before
the reign of James III. the evil had increased; it is now familiar. How
the chimes are rung in our enlightened age upon any horse, mule, ass,
cattle, coach, berlin, landau, chariot chaise, calash, wagon, wain, cart,
or other carriage whatsoever! as if every quadruped and carriage would
not comprehend all particulars.—*Hist. Memorials*, by Sir David Dal-
rymple, Edinburgh, 1796.

The oldest conveyance we have any account of, viz. that of
the cave of Machpelah from the sons of Heth to Abraham,
hath some unnecessary and redundant words: "And the field
of Ephron, which was in Machpelah, which was before Mamre,
the field and the cave which was therein, and all the trees that
were in the field, that were in all the borders round about,
were made sure unto Abraham," &c. (*Genesis* xxiii.) The
parcels in a modern conveyance of 1859 cannot be well more
minutely particularised.

OYEZ! OYEZ!

Blackstone takes occasion, in reference to these words, to
remark upon the corruption which has taken place, and is still
observable, in the law French; viz. that in the prologue to all
our public proclamations, *oyes!* or *hear ye!* is generally pronounced most unmeaningly, *oh yes!*

EARLY SINECURES.

The statute 1 Hen. IV. c. 13, enacts that the comptrollers
and searchers of the Customs shall be resident in person at the
port, without making any deputy to execute their office. The
abuse of turning the Custom-house offices into sinecures had
begun to prevail in the reign of Edward III.; for by the grant
of the comptrollership of the port of London to Chaucer (and
no one hath so good a claim to a place of ease as a poet), there
is an express condition that he shall not only reside, but make
all the entries with his own hand. "I believe," says Barrington, "it will not be easy to find such a condition in a modern

patent; as Treasuries either know nothing of this law, or otherwise choose to be ignorant of it."

COUNSELS' FEES.

The ancient Roman orators practised *gratis*, for honour merely, or at most for the sake of gaining influence; and so likewise it is established with us that a counsel can maintain no action for his fees, which are given, not as *locatio vel conductio*, but as *quiddam honorarium;* not as a salary or hire, but as a mere gratuity, which a counsellor cannot demand without doing wrong to his reputation: as is also laid down with regard to advocates in the civil law, whose *honorarium* was directed, by a decree of the senate, not to exceed in any case ten thousand *sesterces*, or about 80*l.* of English money.— Stephen's *Commentaries.*

THE ALIAS.

In the statute 5 Hen. IV. c. 6, Barrington notes "that an accused person is styled John Salage, *otherwise Savage;* which is the first precedent that I find of the *alias* being used; and it is very remarkable that the Statute of Additious* passed the following year.

" A YEAR AND A DAY."

The addition of the day in this term seems to have been made with an intention of preventing all disputes about inclusive and exclusive. The term of a year and a day is likewise used in the Danish law; and it is the precise time during which the feudary is to apply to the lord for investiture.

ORIGIN OF " CULPRIT."

The ceremonies formerly observed on a criminal trial involve the true etymology of the word "culprit." When the prisoner pleaded not guilty, *non culpabilis*, or *nient culpable*, it was abbreviated on the minutes of the court thus, "*non* (or *nient*) *cul.*," and the joining of issue thereon by the prosecutor was expressed by the abbreviation "*prit;*" the precise origin of which latter expression is somewhat doubtful. In course of time it became the practice for the officer of the court to read aloud these words, without regard to their real meaning (which was beginning to be forgotten, owing to the disuse of law

---

* Shakspeare uses the word *addition* in its legal sense in

Where great *addition* swells, and virtue none,
It is a bloated honour.   *All's well that ends well.*

French), and to apply them as an appellation of the prisoner himself; for when a prisoner pleaded not guilty, the officer used to say, "*Culprit,* how wilt thou be tried?" to which the latter usually replied, "By God and the country;" meaning by a jury.

NORFOLK LAWYERS.

Norfolk has the old reputation of having been always a litigious county; insomuch that the number of attorneys allowed to practise in it was reduced, by a statute of Henry VI., to eight; and the county paid an annual composition at the Exchequer that they might be fairly dealt with. Hence the proverbial line of

Norfolk full of wyles;

and in the old play of the *City Match:*

Long more earnestly for the term than Norfolk lawyers.

THE OFFICE OF CORONER.

This officer is, in the Scotch law, termed the *crowner,* "in the manner that the common people now pronounce the word." Lord Coke derives the name "*a corond,* because he is an officer of the crown, and hath conusance of some pleas which are called *placita coronæ.*" Lord Bacon derives it *a corond populis;* which Barrington disputes, "the crowd attending in a circle being by no means peculiar to this particular magistrate." The name has also been referred to *corphonner,* or view of the corpse. By the statute 3 Edw. I. c. 10, coroners are required to be knights; and by the 28 Edw. III., they must be of the most meet and lawful men in the county.

OATHS : SWEARING WITH THE GLOVE ON.

There is (it has been well observed) perhaps no single ceremony connected with the administration of civil or criminal justice to which so much and so deserved importance is attached as the taking of an oath, especially in a court of justice. It is indispensable to the due course of judicial procedure that this should be the case; and seeing that statements made upon oath have daily the effect of disposing of the property, characters, liberties, and even of the lives of persons in every grade of society, we cannot wonder that from the very earliest period of our constitutional history the taking of an oath was, for its greater solemnity, accompanied by various ceremonies, which, though individually perhaps of no great moment, add, when taken collectively, very materially to the dignity of the proceeding.

Prior to the Reformation, indeed, oaths could only be taken before the sovereign himself, the bishops and other dignitaries of the church, and persons specially licensed by them; and during the ceremony the hand was laid upon the Gospels, the missal, relics of saints and martyrs, or matters of like reverence; while the person swearing invoked "God and the holy angels," "God and the holy evangelists," &c.

Fynes Morryson informs us (in his *Precepts to Travellers*), that the custom of *holding up the hand* is always observed in France when a witness is sworn. They have either borrowed this from us, or we from them, though we differ in the use of it. The ceremony of the prisoner's holding up his hand after being arraigned seems to have been introduced to distinguish him from the crowd which stands around him. Lord Bacon, in his *Apophthegms*, mentions a Welshman's having supposed the judge to be a fortune-teller, from the ceremony of the criminal's holding his hand up at the bar.

In our own time, as is well known, the ceremony of "swearing" a witness in a court of justice is simple enough. In ordinary cases, a copy of the New Testament is held in the hand, the person is adjured to speak "the truth, the whole truth, and nothing but the truth; so help you God;" and he kisses the sacred volume. The person has the head uncovered; he holds the book in his right hand, and *the glove of that hand is to be off* at the time of making the oath.

The latter observance was, however, dispensed with by Baron Bramwell, at the Liverpool assizes, in December 1858, when a witness coming before him, and finding some difficulty in removing the glove, was allowed to be sworn "holding the sacred volume in a gloved hand;" the learned judge remarking that "he knew no reason why a witness should be required to remove his glove when taking an oath." Now though there may be no legal reason why the hand should in such case be bare, it is well known that the gloved hand is esteemed very differently from the ungloved hand. Thus it is not permitted to enter the presence of the sovereign with a glove on, it being considered disrespectful to do so. On the entrance of the queen, or of a judge of assize, into Oxford or Cambridge, gloves are always presented to them by the vice-chancellor, to intimate that their exalted rank renders them worthy of covering their hands, although in the presence of the highest functionaries of the University.

If a somewhat rigid etiquette has caused so much importance to be attached to the glove in these matters, it seems not unreasonable that the removal of the glove upon receiving the Holy Gospels, prior to the invocation of the name of the Almighty, should be insisted upon; and the judge's remark on the above occasion must be regarded by right-minded persons as neither calculated to increase the respect for the solemnity of the judgment-seat, nor the dignity of his own high office.

In Scotland, the oath to witnesses is administered with a grand solemnity. The judge rises from his seat, and raising his right hand, requires the witness to do the same; and then, their han ds remaining elevated, the witness repeats after the judge the following words: "I swear by Almighty God, and as I shall answer to God at the great Day of Judgment, that I will tell the truth, the whole truth, and nothing but the truth." What could be more calculated to solemnise the mind, to search and quicken the conscience, than such an oath so administered? It might be as well, perhaps, if such were to be the practice in our own courts.—*S. Warren, Q.C.*

The earliest notice of the oath is, probably, that in *Genesis* xxiv. 2, 3: "And Abraham said unto his oldest servant of his house, that ruled over all that he had, Put, I pray thee, *thy hand under my thigh;* and I will make thee swear," &c.

The kiss in the oath opens the way to evasion and perjury in the unconscientious; and our judges and magistrates can testify to the number of persons who constantly shuffle out of the stringency of an oath by the device of kissing the thumb, or the cuff of the coat, in place of the book itself.

SWEARING UPON THE SWORD.

The singular mixture of religious and military fanaticism which brought about the Crusades, gave rise to the extraordinary custom of taking a solemn oath upon a sword. In a plain, unenriched sword, the separation between the blade and the hilt was usually a straight transverse bar, which, suggesting the idea of a cross, added to the devotion which every true knight felt for his favourite weapon, evidently led to this practice. The sword or the blade were often mentioned in the ceremony, without reference to the cross; yet the cross of the sword is also mentioned frequently enough to illustrate the true bearing of the oath.—Nares's *Glossary.*

That, at an earlier period than the above, the soldier swore by his sword, is shown by the following passage in the Anglo-Norman poem on the conquest of Ireland by Henry II., published by Thomas Wright, M.A. :

> Morice par sa espé ad juré,
> N'i ad vassal si osé.

SEALING AND SIGNING.

The use of Seals, as a mark of authenticity to letters and other instruments in writing, is extremely ancient. We read of it, among the Jews and the Persians, in the earliest and most sacred records of history. And in the book of Jeremiah there is a very remarkable instance, not only of an attestation by seal, but also of the other formalities usual on a Jewish purchase:

And I bought the field of Ilanameel, and weighed him the money, even seventeen shekels of silver. And I subscribed the evidence, and sealed it and took witnesses, and weighed him tho money in the balances. So I took the evidence of the purchase, both that which was sealed according to the law and custom, and that which was open. (*Jer.* xxxii.)

In the civil law also seals were the evidence of truth; and were required, on the part of the witnesses at least, at the attestation of every testament. But in the times of our Saxon ancestors they were not much in use in England. For though Sir Edward Coke relies on an instance of King Edwy's making use of a seal about a hundred years before the Conquest, yet it does not follow that this was the usage of the whole nation; and perhaps the charter he mentions may be of doubtful authority from the very circumstance of being sealed, since we are assured by all our ancient historians that sealing was not then in common use.

The method of the Saxons was for such as could write to subscribe their names; and whether they could write or not, to affix the sign of the cross; which custom many uneducated persons to this day keep up, by signing a cross for their mark when unable to write their names. For the same unsurmountable reason, the Normans, a brave but illiterate nation, at their first settlement in France, used the practice of sealing only, without writing their names; which custom continued when learning made its way among them, though the reason for doing it had ceased: and hence the charter of Edward the Confessor to Westminster Abbey, himself being brought up in Normandy, was witnessed only by his seal, and is generally thought to be the oldest sealed charter of any authenticity in England.

At the Conquest, the Norman lords brought over into this kingdom their own fashions; and introduced waxen seals only, instead of the English method of writing their names and signing with the sign of the cross. In the reign of Edward I., every freeman, and even such of the more substantial villeins as were fit to be put upon juries, had their distinct particular seals. The impressions of these seals were sometimes a knight on horseback, sometimes other devices; but coats of arms were not introduced into seals, nor, indeed, into any other use, till about the reign of Richard I., who brought them from the Crusade in the Holy Land, where they were first invented, and painted on the shields of the knights, to distinguish the variety of persons of every Christian nation who resorted thither, and who could not, when clad in complete steel, be otherwise known or ascertained.

This neglect of signing, and resting only on the authenticity of seals, remained very long among us; for it was held in all our books that sealing alone was sufficient to authenticate a deed; and so the common form of attesting deeds—" sealed and delivered"—continues to this day.* The Statute of Fraud, however (29 Car. II. c. 3), revives the Saxon custom, and expressly directs the signing in all grants of lands, and many other species of deeds ; in which, therefore, signing seems to be now as necessary as sealing, though it hath been sometimes held that one includes the other.—Stephen's *Commentaries*, vol. i.

Seals often furnish minute historical evidence. Thus Sir Thomas Gresham is traditionally said to have adopted for his crest a grasshopper, from that insect having saved his life when he was a poor famished boy, by attracting a person by its chirpings to the spot where he lay in a helpless condition. But this story is refuted by the fact of eleven of the letters of James Gresham, an ancestor of Sir Thomas, being sealed with a grasshopper, which was therefore the family crest of the Greshams.

CHARTERS SIGNED WITH THE CROSS.

The practice of affixing the sign of the cross proceeded from the inability of the signers to write : this is honestly avowed by Caedwalla, a Saxon king, at the end of one of his charters. A similar circumstance is related of the Emperor Justin in the East, and Theodoric king of the Goths in Italy. Procopius, in his *Historiæ Arcana*, says:"Justin,not being able to write his name, had a thin, smooth piece of board, through which were cut the four letters of his name, J. V. S. T., which, laid on the paper, served to direct the point of his pen, his hand being guided by another. Possibly this may likewise have given the hint to the first of our card-makers, who paint their cards in the same manner, by plates of pewter or copper, or only pasteboard, with slits in them in form of the figures that are to be painted on the cards."—*Philosophical Transactions*, vol. xl. p. 393.

Charlemagne used his monogram for his signature, for which Eginhard gives this as the reason : namely, that Charlemagne could not write ; and, having attempted in vain to learn in his grown age, he was reduced to the necessity of signing with his monogram.

The probable reason why the cross was always used in the middle ages in the testing of ecclesiastical charters was not only that it was a sacred symbol, but that Justinian had decreed it should have the strength of an oath.

* Merely placing the finger on a seal already made is equivalent to sealing (Shep. Touch. 57). And there is no necessity that the seal should be made either with wax or with a wafer, but only that some impressions should be made on the parchment or paper with the intent of sealing. (See the Queen v. Trustees of Covent Garden, 7 Q.B. 238 n.)

THE HANAPER AND PETTY-BAG OFFICE.

Consistently with the simplicity of ancient times, the writs under the Great Seal (relating to the business of the subject), and the returns to them, were originally kept in a hamper (*in hanaperio*); and the others (relating to matters wherein the crown was concerned) were preserved in a little sack or bag (*in parva baga*): thence has arisen the distinction of the Hanaper Office and Petty-Bag Office, which both belong to the common-law court in Chancery.

THE GREAT SEAL.

The custody of the Great Seal of the Sovereign is now intrusted to the Lord Chancellor, who was originally, in England, the king's chief secretary, to whom petitions were referred, patents and grants approved and completed, &c.: hence he was sometimes styled Referendarius, as in a charter of Ethelbert, A.D. 605; whereas the term Chancellor does not occur until about 920. When seals came into use, one of his duties was to affix the royal seal to documents; and as, in early times, he was usually an ecclesiastic, he became keeper of the king's conscience, examiner of his patents, the officer by whom prerogative writs were prepared, and *Keeper of the Great Seal.* The last Lord-Keeper was Lord Henley, in 1757.

The several Great Seals are interesting from their bearing portraits of the sovereigns; as in the seals of Offa and Ethelwulf, and that of Edgar with a bust in profile. After William I. all the kings are on one side on horseback, the face turned to the right, except that of Charles I., which is to the left. Edward IV. first carries the close crown. Edward the Confessor, Henry I. and II., are seated with the sword and dove. Henry VI. is the first king who has a close crown over his arms.

Wax was not uniformly used for seals: impressions occur in gold, silver, and lead; various other substances were used, but wax has been the most usual. The colours were white, yellow, red, green, mixed blue and yellow; but red appears to have been the most ancient. William I. generally sealed his grants with green, to signify the act continued for ever fresh and of force. William Rufus used red, and the Black Prince sealed with green; but the English kings generally preferred white down to Charles I.; though Beckmann considers it doubtful whether their seals were not originally yellow, and have been bleached by age. Sealing-wax, like that now used, was not known in Europe before the sixteenth century. The oldest authenticated seal of this kind is shining dark red wax, on a letter dated London, August 3, 1554. The oldest seal with red wafer is dated 1654.

The Great Seal made upon the accession of Queen Victoria

is a beautiful work of the late Benjamin Wyon, R.A., the chief engraver of her Majesty's Mint.

The details of the design are,—*Obverse:* An equestrian figure of the Queen, attended by a page; her Majesty wearing, over a habit, a flowing and sumptuous robe, and the collar of the Order of the Garter; in her right hand she bears the sceptre, and on her head is placed a regal tiara. The attendant page, with his bonnet in his hand, looks up to the queen, who is gracefully restraining the impatient charger, which is richly caparisoned with plumes and trappings. The legend, "Victoria Dei Gratiâ Britanniarum Regina, Fidei Defensor," is engraved in Gothic letters, the spaces between the words being filled with heraldic roses. *Reverse:* The Queen, royally robed and crowned, holding in her right hand the sceptre, and in her left the orb, is seated upon a throne, beneath a niched Gothic canopy; on either side is a figure of Justice and Religion; and in the exergue are the royal arms and crown: the whole encircled by a wreath or border of oak and roses.

The seal itself is a silver mould in two parts, technically called a pair of dies. When an impression is to be taken or cast, the parts are closed to receive the melted wax, which is poured through an opening at the top of the seal. As each impression is attached to a document by a ribbon, or slip of parchment, its ends are put into the seal before the wax is poured in; so that when the hard impression is taken from the dies, the ribbon or parchment is neatly affixed to it. The impression of the seal is six inches in diameter, and three-fourths of an inch in thickness. On every accession to the throne a new seal is struck, and the old one is cut into four pieces and deposited in the Tower of London: formerly the fragments were distributed among certain poor people of religious houses.

The keeping of the Great Seal is intrusted to the Lord Chancellor, who formerly wore it on his left side; now his lordship merely carries the bag in which the seal is deposited when he receives it from the sovereign, or when, upon his retirement from office, he delivers it into the royal hands. This bag is about twelve inches square, and of rich crimson silk-velvet,* superbly embroidered with the royal arms on both sides, fringed with gold bullion; and to the bag is attached a stout cord, by which it is carried as may be required. Thus it is borne before the sovereign upon high state occasions; and is always laid upon the table with the mace, before the Chancellor, in the House of Lords and in the Court of Chancery.

ORIGIN OF TRIAL BY JURY.

Blackstone considers this mode of trial as having been "universally established among all the northern nations, and so interwoven in their very constitution, that the earliest accounts of the one give us also some traces of the other" (*Commentaries*). He also says that it is mentioned in England as early as the laws of Ethelred; for which he cites Wilk. *Ll. Anglo-Sax.* 117

* This bag, or purse, was formerly renewed every year; and when Lord Hardwicke was Chancellor, Lady Hardwicke, notable for her parsimony, took care that the bag should not become the seal-bearer's perquisite; for she annually retained the purse herself, having previously ordered that the velvet of which it was made should be the length of the height of one of the state rooms at Wimpole, Lord Hardwicke's seat in Cambridgeshire. And so many of the old bags were thus saved, that the Chancellor's Lady had enough velvet to hang the state room throughout, and make curtains for the state bed.

(though the passage cited will be found to refer, not to trial by jury, but to an inquisition by twelve persons in the nature of a grand jury). He speaks, however, of the date of its first establishment among us as unknown ; and the same uncertainty is confessed in a much later work, where, though trial by jury is considered as having been in use among the Anglo-Saxons, it is observed that "no record marks the date of its commencement." (Turner's *Hist. Anglo-Sax.* vol. iii. p. 233, 6th edition.) We must add, that when the Anglo-Saxon memorials are carefully scrutinised, we find them to be such as even to justify a doubt whether Trial by Jury (in any sense corresponding to our use of that term) did actually exist among us at any time before the Norman Conquest. The most probable theory seems to be, that we owe the germ of this (as of so many other of our institutions) to the Normans. At the date of Bracton's work, in the time of Henry III., it had taken among us, in substance, the shape which it now wears; but its rudiments appear as early as the reign of Henry II. Indeed, the particular species of it called the *grand assize*, which was appropriate to the trial of the question of *mere right*, was established by a law of that monarch's reign.—Stephen's *Commentaries*, note.

WHY TWELVE JURYMEN ?

In the patriarchal and apostolical number of twelve, of which a jury in the superior courts always consists, "Lord Coke has discovered," says Blackstone, vol. iii. p. 366, "abundance of mystery" (See *Co. Litt.* 155). And he proceeds to remark, that Dr. Hickes, who attributes the introduction of this number to the Normans, tells us that among the inhabitants of Norway, from whom the Normans as well as the Danes were descended, a great veneration was paid to the number twelve. Mr. Hallam also (*Hist. Mid. Ages*, vol. ii. p. 401, 7th edit.) remarks upon the veneration with which this number was regarded in Scandinavia generally, and cites Spelman's *Glossary*, *voce* Jurata; Ducange, *voce* Nembda ; and the *Edinb. Review*, vol. xxxi. p. 115. He observes, that Spelman has produced several instances of the regard paid to twelve in the early German laws ; and there is distinct evidence that twelve jurors were in use among the Anglo-Saxons for an *inquisition*, though there seems no sufficient proof that it was used by them as the number for trial.—Stephen's *Commentaries*, note.

The persons exempted from serving on juries are : all peers, judges of the superior courts, clergymen, Roman Catholic priests, dissenting ministers, whose place of meeting is duly registered, and who follow no secular occupation but that of schoolmaster; serjeants, barristers, and advocates, actually practising ; attorneys, solicitors, and proctors, actually practising and taking out their certificates; officers of all courts of law or equity, or of ecclesiastical or admiralty jurisdiction, actually exercising their duties; coroners, gaolers, and keepers of houses of correction; physicians, surgeons, and apothecaries, duly practising; officers of the royal army or navy on full pay; licensed pilots, or masters of vessels in the buoy or light service, duly licensed; servants of the royal household, officers of customs and excise, sheriffs' officers, high-constables, and parish-clerks.

DISSENTIENT JURYMEN.

The Jury, having withdrawn from the court to consider their verdict, in order to avoid intemperance and causeless delay, are kept without meat, drink, fire, or candle, unless by permission of the judge, till they are all unanimously agreed; "a method of accelerating unanimity," says Blackstone, "not wholly unknown in other constitutions of Europe, and in matters of greater concern. For by the Golden Bull of the Empire, if, after the congress is opened, the electors delay the election of a King of the Romans for thirty days, they shall be *fed with bread and water* till the same is accomplished."

And, by the ancient rule (which, in strictness, seems to be still in force), if the jurors do not agree in their verdict before the judges are about to leave the town, though they are not to be threatened or imprisoned, the judges are not bound to wait for them, but may carry them round the circuit, from town to town, *in a cart.*

The jury being denied candles is referred to an ancient canon enjoining that they could not exercise an honest judgment during the night.

Sir Thomas Smith mentions that in his time (the Commonwealth) it was usual for the party who obtained the verdict to give the jury a dinner.

FORMER CORRUPTION OF LONDON JURIES.

It is remarkable, that partiality as well as perjury in jurors of the city of London is more particularly complained of than in other parts of England by the preamble of 2 Hen. VII., and other statutes. Stow informs us, that in 1468 many jurors of this city wore punished by having papers fixed on their heads, stating their offence of being tampered with by the parties to the suit. This offence continued in the reign of Elizabeth, and Stow knew one of these perverters of justice "who was carted and banished out of Billingsgate Ward." Fuller, in his *English Worthies,* mentions a proverbial saying, that *London Juries hang half and save half;* and Grafton records the opinion of the Bishop of London, that "London juries were so prejudiced, they would find Abel guilty of the murder of Cain." Ben Jonson, in his *Magnetick Lady,* has

And there's no London jury but are led
In evidence as far by a common fame
As they are by present deposition.

In the *Dance of Death*, written originally in French by Macclabree, and translated in the reign of Henry VII. with some additions to adapt it to English characters, a juryman is mentioned who had often been bribed to give a false verdict, which shows the offence to have been very common. The sheriff who returned the jury was greatly accessory to this crime, by summoning those who were most partial and prejudiced ; and Carew, in his account of Cornwall, informs us that it was common in an attorney's bill to charge *pro amicitia vicecomitis*, in other words, for the collusion of the sheriff.

HOW TO EXECUTE A WILL.

Lord St. Leonards, in his *Handy Book on Property Law,* somewhat reluctantly gives the following instructions for making your will without the assistance of a professional adviser. His lordship condemns the printed forms, which have misled many men. Such, however, as have resolved to *make their own will*, Lord St. Leonards advises thus :

Take care that, if written on several separate sheets of paper, they are all fastened together, and that the pages are numbered. Sign your name at the bottom of each sheet, and state at the end of your will of how many pages your will consists. If there are any erasures or interlineations, put your initials in the margin opposite to them, and notice them in the attestation. The attestation should be already written at the end of the will. . . . . The two persons intended to be the witnesses should be called in, and told that you desire them to witness your will ; and then you should sign your name in their presence, and desire them each to look at the signature. Your signature should follow your will, but should precede the signatures of the witnesses ; for if you were to sign after they had signed, your will would be void. When, therefore, you have signed, they should sign their names and residences at the foot of the attestation. You will observe, that according to the attestation, neither of the witnesses, although he has signed the attestation, should leave the room until the other witness has signed also. Remember that they must both sign in your presence ; and therefore you should not allow them to go into another room to sign, or even into any recess, or any other part of the room where it is possible that you may not be able to see them sign.

CUTTING OFF THE HEIR WITH A SHILLING.

The Civilians carried the doctrine of presumption so far as to hold every will void in which the heir was not noticed, on the presumption that his father must have forgotten him. From this, as Blackstone reasonably conjectures, has arisen that groundless vulgar error of the necessity of giving the heir a shilling, or some other nominal sum, to show that he was in the testator's remembrance. The practice is to be deprecated, as it wounds unnecessarily the feelings of a disinherited child. This, you may say, does not always happen. An assembled family, as the legacy to each was read aloud, sobbed, and wished that the father had lived to enjoy his own fortune. At last came the bequest to his heir—"I give my eldest son Tom a shilling, to buy him a rope to hang himself with." "God grant," says Tom, sobbing like the rest, "that my poor father had lived to enjoy it himself."—Lord St. Leonards' *Handy Book.*

WILLS AT DOCTORS' COMMONS.

To obtain perusal of a Will.—Apply at the Prerogative Will Office, at the first small box or recess, where a clerk, on receiving a shilling *stamp for search,* and the surname of the maker of the will required, directs the applicant to the *Indexes,* which are arranged chronologically and alphabetically on the left-hand side of the room. A search must then be made through these volumes for the entry of the will; which being found, a clerk at the further end of the room, on being furnished with the exact title and date of the will, ushers the inquirer into another apartment, lit by a skylight, and furnished with a table and benches. Here two clerks are seated; and the actual will being brought to the inquirer, he may inspect it at his leisure. He must not, however, copy any thing from it, or make even a pencil memorandum; and if he attempt to do so, he will be checked by the clerks.

To obtain the copy of a Will.—Apply to the clerks in the room, and they will state the expense per folio. The order for a copy must be left at the box at the entrance of the office, where the time will be named for the delivery of the copy, within a few days, on payment of the cost. To insure correctness, the copy is read out to the applicant in the office, and compared with the original will; and the copy is moreover duly attested by certain authorities of Doctors' Commons.

If the applicant merely desires to see the copy of a Will, the clerk in the outer room, on being shown the entry in the *Index,* will refer him by a written note to an attendant, who will at once bring the copy to him; the same rules against copying and making extracts prevail here.

The Prerogative Office is open (except on holidays) from October till March from 9 till 3, and the remaining six months till 4.

WIDOWS.

The Danish and Swedish laws speak of *annus luctûs* (year of grief) which is expected from the widow, during which she hath particular exemptions and privileges; and Tacitus observes, that amongst the ancient Germans it was esteemed *fœminis lugere honestum, viris meminisse.* The time for the widow's mourning has been circumscribed, not only by the ancient laws of Rome to ten months, but by the more modern ordinances of the *Code Frédérique* to six. By the ordinances of Canute, if the wife marries within the year, she forfeits her dower; and by the ancient laws of Spain, "if the wife, after the

death of her husband, marries again, she forfeits half her effects
to the children of the first marriage."—*Barrington.*

By ancient custom, in distributing intestates' effects in the
city of London and the province of York, if the deceased left
a widow and children, there were first deducted for the widow
her apparel and the furniture of her bed-chamber, in London
called *the widow's chamber.*

MARRIAGE-FINE.

In the custom-roll of Westhall Manor, in Norfolk, it is entered, that every tenant of that manor who marries out of the
fealty is obliged to pay the lord a bed, bolster, sheet, and pillow.
This was constantly observed, and there are several entries in
the roll of such payments. But in the time of Richard II.
the bed was omitted, by the lord's kindness; though the rest
were paid in Elizabeth's time, or a composition for them.

INNS OF THE OLDEN TIME.

Inns, being intended for the lodging and receipt of travellers,
may be indicted, suppressed, and the innkeepers fined, if they
refuse to entertain a traveller without a very sufficient cause;
for thus to frustrate the end of the institution is held to be
disorderly behaviour. The laws of Norway punish in the se-
verest degree such innkeepers as refuse to furnish accommoda-
tion at a just and reasonable price.

The innkeeper of former times seems to have been a person of less
humble station than now—he shared his calling with the monastery
and with the village pastor. Travellers had to choose (as they still
have in Roman-Catholic countries,) between the refectory of the monks,
the parsonage of the minister, and the tavern of mine host; payment
for the night's lodging, where he was in a condition to pay, being expected of him, in one shape or other, at all. The Keeper of the Tabard,
in the *Canterbury Tales,* appears to be upon a level with his guests both
in rank and information, and to play the part of one who felt that he
was receiving his equals, and no more, under his roof: yet his company
was not of the lowest; and in those times it seems to have been usual
for the landlord to preside at the common board, and act in every respect as the hospitable master of the house, save only in exacting the
shot; as, indeed, is the custom in many parts of Germany at the present
day. When the system of lay impropriations had begun to take effect,
it was by no means an uncommon thing for the minister himself to be
also a tavern-keeper; a circumstance, however, which, it must be confessed, may be thought to argue the extreme impoverishment of the
Church, which drove the clergy to such expedients for a living, rather
than the respectability of the calling to which they thus betook themselves.—*Quarterly Review,* 1832.

FIRE-TAX.

It is curious to find that a tax was once paid upon a fire in
England. Such was "the smoke farthings," levied by the clergy

upon every person who kept a fire. The "hearth money" was a similar tax, but was paid to the king : it was first levied in 1653, and its last collection was in 1690. Thus we see that by means of the Window-Tax, in addition to the above imposts, even the naturally free blessings of light and heat were not spared.

SHIPWRECK LAWS.

By the civil law, to destroy persons shipwrecked, or prevent their saving the ship, is capital. And to steal even a plank from a vessel in distress, or wrecked, makes the party liable to answer for the whole ship and cargo. The laws also of the Wisigoths, and the most early Neapolitan constitutions, punished with the utmost severity all those who neglected to assist any ship in distress, or plundered any goods cast on shore.—*Note to* Stephen's *Commentaries.*

The plundering of shipwrecked goods was likewise made capital by an ordinance of Sicily, in 1221 ; and Barrington says : " It is rather to our reproach that the same offence hath not been punished with death in England till the 26th year of the late king (Geo. II.)."

There is a remarkable exception to general humanity in the case of the Cypriots, who made a law that if any Jew should be thrown on their coasts, he should be immediately knocked on the head ; but this is said, by Dion Cassius, to have been caused by the Jews having been guilty of great cruelty to the inhabitants of Cyprus.

" JETSAM, FLOTSAM, AND LIGAN."

In order to constitute a legal wreck, the goods from the ship must come to hand. If they continue at sea, the law distinguishes them by the barbarous and uncouth appellations of *Jetsam, Flotsam, and Ligan.* Jetsam is where goods are cast into the sea, and there sink and remain under water ; Flotsam is where they continue swimming on the surface of the waves ; Ligan is where they are sunk in the sea, but tied to a cork or buoy, in order to be found again. These are the Crown's, if no other appears to claim them ; but if any owner appears, he is entitled to recover the possession. They are accounted so far distinct from a wreck, that by the royal grant to a man .of *wrecks,* things *jetsam, flotsam, and ligan* will not pass.

THE COVENTRY ACT.

By this Act, 22 and 23 Car. II. c. 1, specific provisions were made against the offence of maiming, cutting off, or disabling a limb or member.

This statute was occasioned by a barbarous assault on Sir John Coventry in the street. Sir John was on his way to his house in Suffolk-street, Haymarket, from the Cock tavern in Bow-street, where he had supped, when his nose was cut to the bone at the corner of the street, "for reflecting on the king." A motion had been made in the House of Commons to lay a tax on play-houses. This the Court opposed, when Coventry indulged in a licentious remark upon what another member had termed "the king's pleasure." For this Charles determined to *leave a mark* upon Sir John Coventry, and he was watched on his way home. "He stood up to the wall," says Burnet, "and snatched the flambeau out of the servant's hands; and with that in one hand, and his sword in the other, he defended himself so well, that he got more credit by it than by all the actions of his life. He wounded some of his assailants, but was soon disarmed; and then they *cut his nose to the bone*, to teach him to remember what respect he owed to the king." Burnet adds, that his nose was so well sewed up, that the scar was scarce to be discerned. The Act was then passed, to prevent the recurrence of such barbarity.

On this statute Mr. Coke, a lawyer in Suffolk, and one Woodburn, a labourer, were indicted in 1722; Coke for hiring and abetting Woodburn, and Woodburn for the actual fact of slitting the nose of Mr. Crispe, Coke's brother-in-law. The case was somewhat singular. The murder of Crispe was intended, and he was left for dead, being terribly hacked and disfigured with a hedge-bill; but he recovered. Now the bare attempt to murder was, at common law, no felony; but to disfigure with an intent to disfigure is made so by this statute, on which they were therefore indicted. And Coke, who was a disgrace to the profession of the law, had the effrontery to rest his defence upon this point, that the assault was not committed with an intent to disfigure, but to murder, and therefore was not within the statute. But the court held that, if a man attacks another to murder him with such an instrument as a hedge-bill, which cannot but endanger the disfiguring him, and in such an attack happens not to kill, but only to disfigure him, he may be indicted on this statute; and it may be left to the jury to determine whether it were not a design to murder by disfiguring, and consequently a malicious intent to disfigure as well as to murder. Accordingly the jury found them guilty; and they were both condemned and executed.—*Stephen*, note.

WHAT IS CHANCE-MEDLEY?

Blackstone defines Chance-medley to be such killing as happens in self-defence upon a sudden rencounter; which is called by Mr. Justice Foster "homicide *se defendendo* upon Chance-medley." Blackstone confines the term to a sudden affray; but it is equally applicable to manslaughter on a sudden quarrel. It is written both *Chance-medley* and *Chaud-medley;* the former signifying a casual affray, the latter an affray in the *heat* of blood or passion; both of them of pretty much the same import. But the former is, in common speech, too often erroneously applied to any matter of homicide by misadventure; whereas it appears by the statute 24 Hen. VIII. c. 5, and our ancient books, that it is properly applied to such killing as happens upon a sudden rencounter.

Chance-medley is also where one is doing a lawful act, and a person is thereby accidentally killed; for if the act be unlawful, it is felony. Thus, if a person, not intending harm, cast a stone, which happens to hit one, and he dies of the blow, or a schoolmaster in correcting his scholar, or an officer in whipping a criminal in a reasonable manner, happens to occasion his death, this is Chance-medley and misadventure. This is also applicable to death caused by the administration of poison by mistake for a certain medicine. Thus, in September 1855, at Liverpool, an inquest was held upon the body of an infant, who had died through a nurse giving the child oil-of-vitriol instead of castor-oil, which a little girl had been told to fetch from an adjoining room. The jury returned a verdict of "Chance-medley," which the coroner said was as near as possible to manslaughter, and had been passed as a mark of censure upon the nurse for not using more care on the occasion.

LYDFORD LAW.

The Law of Lydford (Devon) is a proverbial saying, expressive of too hasty judgment; as where the judge condemns first, and hears the cause afterwards. Ray gives the proverb thus:

> First hang and draw,
> Then hear the cause, by Lidford law.

A facetious ballad (*Harl. Ms.* 2307) begins thus:

> I oft have heard of Lydford law,
> How in the morn they hang and draw,
>   And sit in judgment after.
> At first I wonder'd at it much;
> But since I find the reason's such
>   As yet deserves no laughter.

It is then jocularly accounted for by the bad state of the castle, where imprisonment was worse than death. Here were probably held stannary courts, the proceedings of which were very summary.

THE LAW OF SELF-DEFENCE.

In the defence of one's self, or the mutual and reciprocal defence of such as stand in the relations of husband and wife, parent and child, master and servant,*—if the party himself, or any of his relations, be forcibly attacked in his person or property,—it is lawful for him to repel force by force; and the breach of the peace which happens is chargeable upon him only who began the affray.

Self-defence, therefore, as it is justly called the primary law of nature, so it is not, neither can it be, in fact, taken away by the law of society. In the English law particularly, it is held an excuse for breaches of the peace, nay, even for homicide itself; but care must be taken that the resistance does not exceed the bounds of mere defence and prevention, for then the defender would himself become an aggressor.—Stephen's *Commentaries*, 4th edit. 1858.†

THE LAW OF RECAPTION.

Recaption, or Reprisal, is another species of remedy by the mere act of the party injured. If he can so contrive it as to gain possession of his property again without force or terror, the law favours and will justify his proceeding. But as the public peace is a superior consideration to any one man's private property; and as, if individuals were once allowed to use private force as a remedy for private injuries, all social justice must cease, the strong would give law to the weak, and every man would revert to a state of nature,—for these reasons it is provided that this mutual right of recaption shall never be exerted where such exertions must occasion strife and bodily contention, or endanger the peace of society. If, for instance (says Stephen), my horse is taken away, and I find him in a common, a fair, or a public inn, I may lawfully seize him to my own use; but I cannot justify breaking open a private stable, or entering on the grounds of a third person, to take him, except he is feloniously stolen, but must have recourse to an action at law.

ANCIENT CONVEYANCING.

In the ninth and tenth centuries, the Franks, Goths, and Germans, on the transfer of land, gave with the *signum*, or mark cut on a piece of wood, a small knife for notching the mark, in the same manner as the inkstand and pen were lifted

---

* On the master's right to defend the servant, there has, however, been a difference of opinion.

† To this excellent work we are frequently indebted for citation in the present section.

up with the chart, as symbols of a transfer of land.   Amongst
the archives of Nôtre Dame, at Paris, is preserved a pointed
pocket-knife of the eleventh century, on the ivory handle of
which is engraved the record of a gift of land ; and a similar
knife is attached to a charter at Trinity College, Cambridge.
Madox records the grant and release of a church to the Abbot
of Thorney *per quandam virgam* (by a certain rod).

The surrender of copyholds by the rod or glove, and occasionally by a straw or rush (whence the word "stipulation," from
stipula, straw), is not rare in England ; and in the manor of
Paris Garden, Surrey, is preserved an ebony rod with a silver
head, on which are engraved the royal arms, with E. R. and a
crown, and an inscription, purporting that it is kept for the
surrender of copyholds of the manor (*Watkins on Copyholds,*
ii. 544, 506).   The inscribed sticks mentioned in *Ezekiel,* xxxvii.
16, appear to relate to this ancient mode of conveyancing.—
Mr. E. Williams, F.S.A.; Archæologia, vol. xxxvii. p. 390.

PANNAGE OF HOGS.

It appears, from a chapter of the Great Charter of Forests,
that Pasuage, or Pannage, was considered as being of great
profit to those who lived in the neighbourhood of a forest, for
the feeding of swine.   The people of this country in the winter chiefly subsisted on salt meat, even in the castles of the
great men and barons ; we therefore find in Domesday, that it
is generally stated for how many hogs the estate hath mast or
pasnage ; and the author of *Fleta* has a whole chapter *de cus-
todiâ porcorum.*   The care of hogs was anciently the occupation
of great men : in the time of Homer, Eumæus, one of the
most considerable persons in the isle of Ithaca, tended hogs.
In later ages, the famous Pope Sextus Quintus originally followed the same occupation.   The Saxon chronicle states, A.
1131, that there was then such a mortality among these animals, that they who kept 200 or 300 did not perhaps save one out
of the number ; and Ethelne, by his will, directs that 200 hogs
shall be fattened for his wife wherever she shall choose.   Camden notes, that in his time swineherds were not uncommon in
Bedfordshire, a county to this day famous for its breed of pigs.

HOW THE HABEAS CORPUS ACT WAS OBTAINED.

Bishop Burnet relates a circumstance respecting the Habeas Corpus Act which is more curious than creditable ; and
though we cannot be induced to suppose that this important
statute was obtained by a jest and a fraud, yet the story proves

that a very formidable opposition was made to it at the time. "It was carried" (says he) "by an odd artifice in the House of Lords. Lord Grey and Lord Norris were named to be the tellers; Lord Norris, being a man subject to vapours, was not at all times attentive to what he was doing, so, a very fat lord coming in, Lord Grey counted him for ten, as a jest at first, but seeing that Lord Norris had not observed it, he went on with his misreckoning of ten : so it was reported to the House, and declared, that they who were for the Bill were the majority, though it indeed went on the other side ; and by this means the Bill passed."—*Hist. Car. II.* 485 ; Christian's *Blackstone.*

LAW AGAINST GROWING TOBACCO.

It was in 1624 that James I. ordered by proclamation that thenceforth no tobacco should be grown in Great Britain, and that none should be imported other than was the produce of Virginia and Bermuda. This prohibition was not intended so much for the advantage of the colonists — although it really produced that effect—as it was to facilitate the collection of revenue upon the article, it being of course more easy to levy a duty at the Customs House upon importation than to collect a tax from every farmer in the country who might be disposed to cultivate tobacco. The same motive, undoubtedly, has induced the governments of several other European states to prohibit its culture. Tobacco, however, is extensively grown in Holland; in the states of the German Confederation; in Alsatia, in Hungary, the Ukraine, and Turkey in Europe. It thrives well as far as the 54th degree of latitude in Mecklenburg and Pomerania.

The law (says Barrington), which hath been perhaps most completely executed of any in the Statute-book, is the statute of Charles II. which directs the sheriff to root up all the tobacco growing in the country. Before this it was much planted in different parts of England, particularly in Gloucestershire. The Acts prohibiting its cultivation did not, however, apply until lately to Ireland.

An attempt was made, about the year 1837, to grow tobacco in Ireland. It proved very remunerative to the growers, but the authorities interfered to prevent its cultivation. The reasons assigned for prohibiting its home-growth were, that it would impoverish the soil, militate against West-India interests, and injure the revenue. This Irish tobacco was milder than the Virginian or Havannah, but ill-flavoured and wanting in aroma.

Aubrey, in his *Natural History of Wiltshire*, has some interesting notes on tobacco. "We have it" (he says) "in gardens for medicine; but in the neighbouring county of Gloucester it is a great commodity."

"Memorandum.—Tobacco was first brought out of the West Indies into England by Ralph Lane, in the eight-and-twentieth yeare of Queen Elizabeth's reigne" (Sir Richard Baker's *Chronicle*). Rider's *Almanack* (1682) says, "Since tobacco was first brought into England by Sir Walter Raleigh, 99 years. Mr. Michael Weekes, of the Custom-House, assures me that the custom of tobacco is the greatest of all others, and amounts now (1688) to 400,000 pounds per annum" (in 1857 it exceeded 5,000,000*l*.).

The best tobacco-pipes in England wore formerly made at Amesbury, of clay brought from Chiltern. Aubrey says, "made by —— Gauntlet, who markes the heele of them with a gauntlet, whence they are called gauntlet-pipes." (See also *Things not generally Known*, First Series, p. 100.)

MONASTERIES AND THE POOR-LAW.

The statute of Elizabeth for the maintenance of the poor is generally supposed to have been framed on the dissolution of the monasteries, whereas sixty years intervened; and if the poor were at any time distressed by there being no religious houses, it must have been immediately after the Reformation. Nor were the monasteries sufficiently numerous in England, or so equably dispersed, that in all parts of the country the poor could have subsisted by their charity.

Fynes Morryson, who wrote about this time, was not "moved with the vulgar opinion preferring old times to ours; because it is apparent that the cloysters of monkes (who spoiled all, that they might be beneficial to few) and gentlemen's houses (who nourished a rabble of servants), lying open to all idle people for meate and drinke, were cause of greater ill than good to the commonwealth."

VAGABONDS IN THE SIXTEENTH CENTURY.

In the reigns of Henry VIII. and Elizabeth nothing could exceed the severity of the law against vagabonds. The strolling beggar, if above the age of fourteen, was whipped, and burned through the ear with a hot iron the compass of an inch; and for the second offence he suffered death. As soon as they had been whipped, they received a sort of ticket, or permit, from the parish-officer, which if they could not produce, the punishment was again inflicted by every justice into whose hands they might fall.

James I. boasted to his Parliament of this clearance of the country. "Look," said the king, "to the houses of correction; remember that in the time of Chief-Justice Popham there was not a wandering beggar to be found in all Somersetshire, being his native county." This Popham is said to have been, in his younger days, "a knight of the road;" yet he prevented many notorious thieves and robbers from being pardoned by

James I. According to Anthony Wood, Popham "was well acquainted with their ways and courses in his younger days."
He was much dreaded by criminals, from the severity with which
he passed sentence. Dr. Donne, in a letter to Ben Jonson, says :

> With guilty conscience let me be worse stung
> Than with Popham's sentence thieves.

REMOVAL OF NUISANCES.

If a house or wall (says Stephen) is erected so near mine
that it stops my ancient lights, which is a private nuisance, I
may enter my neighbour's land, and peaceably pull it down ;
or, if the boughs of my neighbour's tree are allowed to grow so
as to overhang my land, which they had not been accustomed
to do, I may, on his refusal to remove such part of them as are
in that position, effect the removal myself. Or, if a new gate
be erected across the public highway, which is a common (or
public) nuisance, any of the king's subjects passing that way
may cut it down and destroy it. And the reason why the law
allows this private and summary mode of doing one's self justice is, because injuries of this kind, which obstruct or annoy
such things as are of daily convenience and use, require an immediate remedy, and cannot wait for the slow progress of the
ordinary forms of justice.

THE CITY GREEN-YARD.

The Green-yard was originally a portion of the garden of
the Nevilles in Leadenhall. In the new edition of Nares's *Glossary*, we find

> With that one of the officers went and took the fore-horse by the
> head, in order to drive the waggon to the Green-yard, which is a prison
> for all waggons, carts, and coaches, for all them that transgress against
> the city laws.—*Great Britain's Honycombe*, 1712, Ms.

The present City Green-yard is in Whitecross-street, Cripplegate, opposite the Debtors' Prison. Here, in the Green-yard
(the only *green* of which is its gate), are kept the Lord Mayor's
state-coach and horses. The coach, with its allegorical paintings,
is minutely described in *Curiosities of London*, pp. 688, 689.

OLD ABDUCTION LAW.

The old law of Abduction was so strict on the point of en-
ticement, that, if one's wife missed her way upon the road, it
was not lawful for another man to take her into his house, unless she was benighted, and in danger of being lost or drowned ;
but a stranger might carry her behind him to market, to a justice of the peace for a warrant against her husband, or to the
spiritual court to sue for a divorce.

PLAGUE LAW.

Very stringent enactments were introduced by 1 Jac. I. c. 31, a statute which made it a capital felony for any person having an infectious sore upon him uncured to go abroad and converse in company, after being commanded by the proper authority to keep his house. The necessity, however, of any regulations adapted to an actual prevalence of this disease among us has been long since at an end; no plague having, by the blessing of Providence, been known in this island for more than 170 years past; and the statute of James, after remaining for so long a period dormant, was at length, in the first year of the reign of her present Majesty, repealed.—*Stephen.*

How much more violent in London was the Last Great Plague, 1665-6, than the more recent visitation of the Cholera, will be seen by these tabular results:

Metropolis.	Years.	Duration.	Population.	Highest no. of deaths in one week.	Total deaths.
Plague	1665-6	13 months	000,000	7,165	68,500
Cholera ...	1832-3	17 months	1,682,641	445	6,729
"	1848-9	13 months	2,206,076	2,026	14,001
"	1853-4	17 months	2,372,728	2,050	10,026

W. D. Cooper, F.S.A. ; *Archæologia*, vol. xxxvii. p. 22.

SMALL-POX LAW.

It cannot be too generally made known, that to expose persons ill with small-pox, or having the virus of small-pox about their clothes or persons, in any "footpath, street, passage, road, lane, or way," so as to endanger others taking this disease, is an offence against the law, which may be punished with three months' imprisonment. To inoculate another with the small-pox is also held to be an indictable offence, for which six months' imprisonment may be awarded. — See The King *v.* Burnett, Maule and Selwyn's *Reports.*

ANCIENT AND MODERN LAW OF LUNACY.

In the case of persons of unsound mind, the civil law of Rome agrees with ours, in assigning them tutors to protect their persons, and curators to manage their estates. But in another instance, the Roman law goes much beyond the English; for, if a man by notorious prodigality was in danger of wasting his estate, he was looked upon as *non compos*, and committed to the care of curators or tutors by the prætor. And by the laws of Solon, such prodigals were branded with perpetual infamy. But with us, when a man on an inquest of idiotcy hath been returned an *unthrift*, and not an idiot, ne further proceedings have been had.—*Stephen.*

EARLY LAWS AGAINST THE ADULTERATION OF FOOD.

This low cheating was punished by our early laws. perhaps, with more stringency than by the enactments of the present day. Thus bakers, for offences relating to bread, had to stand in the pillory, by statute 51 Hen. III.; especially for breaking the assize of bread,—that is, violating the rules laid down for the regulation of its price. By the above act also knavish brewers had to stand in the tumbrel, or dung-cart; and we learn from Domesday Book, that brewers in the city of Chester were so punished as early as the reign of Edward the Confessor.

By the statute Frank-pledge, 18 Edward II., the butcher was to be set in the pillory if he sold measled pork a second time: for the fourth offence he was to leave the town or village in which the offence was committed; this being the only instance in our law of punishing by banishment from a particular place or district.

KENTISH ALE.

In the reign of Henry II., according to Giraldus Cambrensis, the Kentish Ale was reputed superior to that of any other county. Yet, by 33 Hen. VI., no person was allowed to make above 100 quarters of malt into beer or ale for his own use. This singular regulation Daines Barrington attributes to the great quantity of ale found in the cellars of the gentry of this county in Jack Cade's rebellion, which arose in Kent, and was much fomented and increased by the very free use which the rioters made of this animating liquor to an Englishman.

LAW OF THOROUGHFARES.

By the existing law of "Highways and Byways," viz. the 5th and 6th William IV. cap. 50, no thoroughfare can be lawfully stopped until a "nearer and more commodious way" is given in exchange, and any person is justified in removing obstructions so illegally raised; the police and magistrates will assist, if applied to: but few villagers are acquainted with this charter of their rights and liberties.

THE LAWS UPON DRUNKENNESS.

Our law looks upon Drunkenness as an aggravation of the offence, rather than as an excuse for any criminal misbehaviour. A drunkard, says Sir Edward Coke, who is *voluntarius dæmon*, hath no privilege thereby; but what hurt or ill soever he doth, his drunkenness doth aggravate it. It hath been observed, that the real use of strong liquors, and the abuse of them by drinkiug to excess, depend much upon the temperature of the climate in which we live. The same indulgence which may be necessary to make the blood move in Norway, would make an Italian mad. "A German, therefore," says the President Montesquieu, "drinks through custom, founded upon constitutional necessity; a Spaniard drinks through choice, or out of the mere wantonness of luxury; and drunkenness," he adds, "ought to be more severely punished, where it makes men mischievous and mad, as in Spain and Italy, than where it only renders them stupid and heavy, as in Germany and more northern countries." And accordingly, in the warm climate of Greece, a law of Pittacus enacted "that he who committed a crime when drunk, should receive a double punishment; one for the crime itself, and the other for the ebriety which prompted him to commit it." The Roman law, indeed, made great allowances for this vice: *per vinum delapsis capitalis pœna remittitur.* But the law of England, considering how easy it is to counterfeit this excuse, and how weak an excuse it is (though real), will not suffer any man thus to privilege one crime by another.—Stephen's *Commentaries.*

THE LAST WITCHES HANGED IN ENGLAND.

The destruction of the old notions respecting Witchcraft was effected, so far as the educated classes are concerned, between the Restoration and the Revolution: that is to say, in 1660, the majority of educated men still believed in witchcraft; while in 1688, the majority disbelieved it. In 1665, the old orthodox view was stated by Chief-Baron Hale, who, on a trial of two women for witchcraft, said to the jury: "That there are such creatures as witches, I make no doubt at all; for, first, the Scriptures have affirmed so much; secondly, the wisdom of all nations hath provided laws against such persons, which is an argument of confidence of such a crime." This reasoning was irresistible, and the witches were hung; but the change in public opinion began to affect even the judges, and after this melancholy exhibition of the Chief Baron's, such scenes became gradually rarer. Three persons were executed at Exeter for witchcraft in 1682, and Hutchinson says: "I suppose these are the three last that have been hanged in England." Dr. Parr, however, states that two witches were hung at Northampton in 1705; and that in 1712, five other witches suffered the same fate at the same place. (*Parr's Works,* vol. iv. p. 182.) This is the more shameful, because a disbelief in the existence of witches had become almost universal among educated men; though the old superstition was well defended on the judgment-seat and in the pulpit. However, all was in vain; every year

diminished the old belief; and in 1736 the laws against witchcraft were repealed, and another vestige of superstition effaced
from the English statute-book.—Note to Buckle's *History of
Civilization in England*, vol. i. p. 334.

All our executions for this dubious crime (says Stephen) are now
at an end; our legislature having at length followed the wise example of
Louis XIV. in France, who thought proper, by an edict, to restrain the
tribunals of justice from receiving information of witchcraft. And accordingly it is with us enacted, by statute 9 Geo. II. c. 5,* that no pro-
secution shall for the future be carried on against any person for witchcraft, sorcery, enchantment, or conjuration; or for charging another
with any such offence. But by the same statute persons pretending to
use witchcraft, tell fortunes, or discover stolen goods, by skill in any
occult or crafty science, are punishable by imprisonment; and by 5
Geo. IV. c. 83, persons using any subtle crafty means or device, by
palmistry or otherwise, to deceive his majesty's subjects, are to be
deemed rogues and vagabonds, and to be punished with imprisonment
and hard labour.

DARK-LANTERN: ROUND-HOUSE.

The vulgar error that it is not lawful to go about with a Dark-
Lantern, Barrington refers to the statute of the City of London,
13 Edw. I., which directs that, in consequence of continual
affrays in the streets, every person during the night should have
a light with him; in default of which, he should be sent to the
Tonel, or Round-house; the *tonel* having been an old butt or
hogshead, or something built in the shape of one. The name
of Round-house was long retained for this temporary gaol;
though sometimes the building was octagonal, or hexagonal, as
that at the end of the New Church in the Strand, and another
in the churchyard of Westminster Abbey, at the time Barrington wrote.

The Round-house (Watch-house) of St. Giles's was probably one of
the last that remained: it stood in an angle of Kendrick-yard, and its
back windows looked upon the burial-ground of St. Giles's Church; it
was built in a cylindrical form, like a modern Martello tower, though,
from bulging, it resembled an enormous cask set on its end: it was two
stories high, and had a flat roof, surmounted by a gilt vane in the shape
of a key. (See W. H. Ainsworth's *Jack Sheppard*.)—*Curiosities of London*, p. 329.

Elsewhere Barrington refers the above error to Guy Fawkes's
Dark-Lantern in the Gunpowder Plot.

EARLY SLAVE-TRADE IN ENGLAND.

It appears by Hakluyt, that in the year 1553, four-and-
twenty negroes were brought into England from the coast of

* This act is said to have been passed in consequence of an old woman being
drowned at Tring, in Hertfordshire, by her too credulous neighbours, who suspected her of witchcraft.—Christian's *Blackstone*.

Africa. These negroes must, therefore, have been sold in this country ; and if it had been contrary to law, they must have been set at liberty, or the point discussed, of which we do not find the least traces : such a question being also a liberal one, could not well have escaped the notice of Lord Bacon, who would undoubtedly have mentioned it in some of his treatises. —*Barrington.*

Giraldus Cambrensis writes, that so many villains were in his time exported to Ireland, that the slave-market there was quite glutted. Another author declares, that from the reign of King William to King John, there was scarcely a cottage in Scotland that did not possess an English slave.

Slaves were *sold* in England late in the last century; for, in the *Public Advertiser,* March 28, 1769, we find the following advertisement :

To be sold, a Black Girl, the property of J. B—, eleven years of age, who is extremely handy, works at her needle tolerably, and speaks French perfectly well; is of excellent temper, and willing disposition. Inquire of W. Owen, at the Angel Inn, behind St. Clement's Church in the Strand.

UNLAWFUL DETENTION OF CHATTELS.

This form of action was formerly subject (as were some other of our legal remedies) to the incident of *Wager of Law (vadatio legis)*, a proceeding which consisted in the defendant's discharging himself from the claim on his own oath, bringing with him at the same time into court eleven of his neighbours, to swear that they believed his denial to be true. This relic of a very ancient and general institution, which we find established not only among the Saxons and Normans, but amongst all the Northern nations that broke in upon the Roman Empire, continued to subsist among us even till the last reign, when it was at length abolished by 3 and 4 William IV. An instance of it occurred in the practice of our courts as lately as in 1824.

The origin of the above may be traced as far back as the Mosaical law: "If a man deliver unto his neighbour an ass, or an ox, or a sheep, or any beast, to keep ; and it die, or be hurt, or driven away, no man seeing it: then shall an oath of the Lord be between them both that he hath not put his hand unto his neighbour's goods : and the owner of it shall accept thereof, and he shall not make it good" (*Exod.* xxii. 10).

CRIMINAL LAWS IN THE EIGHTEENTH CENTURY.

"If bills introductory of new penal enactments were first referred to some of the learned judges before they were entertained in parliament, it is impossible," says Blackstone, vol. iv. p. 4, "that in the eighteenth century it would ever have been made a capital crime to break down, however maliciously, the mound of a fish-pond, whereby any fish should escape; or cut down a cherry-tree in an orchard,—as provided respectively by statute 9 Geo. I. c. 22, 21 Geo. II. c. 42. And were even a committee appointed but once in 100 years to revise the criminal law, it could not have continued to this hour a capital felony to be seen for one month in the company of persons who are called Ægyptians, as provided by 1 Philip and Mary, c. 4, and 5 Elizabeth, c. 20." It is scarcely necessary to remark, that all these sanguinary laws have been repealed.

CRIMINAL REVIVED.

If, upon the intended execution of the judgment to be hanged by the neck till he is dead, the criminal be not thoroughly killed, but revives, the sheriff must hang him again. For the former hanging was no execution of the sentence; and if a false tenderness were to be indulged in such cases, a multitude of collusions might ensue. Nay, even while abjurations were in force, such a criminal, so reviving, was not allowed to take sanctuary and abjure the realm; but his fleeing to sanctuary was held an escape, for which the officer was punishable.

PUNISHMENT IN ENGLAND: PRESSING TO DEATH— THE RACK.

The first of these terrible punishments, for "standing mute," first appears on the statute-books, 8 Henry IV., and was not abolished until by statute 12 Geo. III. c. 20.

Regularly, a prisoner is said to stand mute when, being arraigned for treason or felony, he either makes no answer at all, or answers foreign to the purpose, or with such matter as is not allowable, and will not answer otherwise. In such case, the rule of the ancient law was, that a jury was to be empannelled to inquire whether the prisoner stood obstinately mute, or was dumb *ex visitatione Dei.* If the latter appeared to be the case, the Judges were to proceed to the trial, and examine all points as if he had pleaded not guilty. But if found to be obstinately mute, then, in treason, it was held that standing mute was equivalent to conviction; and the law was the same as to all misdemeanours. But upon indictment for any other felony, the prisoner, after *trina admonitio,* and a respite of a few hours, was subject to the barbarous sentence of *peine forte et dure;* viz. to be remanded to prison and put into a low dark chamber, and there laid on his back on the bare floor naked, unless where decency forbade; that there should be placed on his body as great a weight of iron as he could bear, and more : that he should have no sustenance, save only ou the first day three morsels of the worst bread, and on the second three draughts of standing water that should be nearest to the prison-door ; and that, iu this situation, such should be alternately his daily diet *till he died*, or, as anciently the judgment ran, *till he answered.*—*Stephen.*

In the *Perfect Account of the Daily Intelligence*, April 16th, 1651, we find it recorded : " Mond. April 14th.—This Session, at the Old Bailey, were four men pressed to death that were all in one robbery, and, out of obstinacy and contempt of the court, stood mute and refused to plead."

It appears from the Sessions Papers that tying the thumbs together of criminals, in order to compel them to plead, was practised at the Old Bailey in the reign of Queen Anne. Among the cases cited by Daines Barrington is that of Mary Andrews, in 1721, who continued so obstinate that three whipcords were broken before she would plead. And in 1711, Nathaniel Haws had his thumbs squeezed, after which he continued seven minutes under the press with 250 lbs., and then submitted.

In the same chapter, Barrington notes that in the year 1659, Major Strangewayes was tried before Lord Chief-Justice Glyn for the murder of Mr. John Fussel ; and refusing to plead, was *pressed to death*. By the account of this execution, which is added to the printed trial, he died in about eight minutes, many people in the press-yard casting stones upon him to hasten his death. From the description of *the press*, it appears that it was brought nearly to a point where it touched his breast. It is stated likewise to have been usual to put a sharp piece of wood under the criminal, which might meet the upper part of the rack in the sufferer's body. Hollinshed states that the back of the criminal was placed upon a sharp stone. Other precedents mention the tying his arms and legs with cords, fastened at different parts of the prison, and extending the limbs as far as they could be stretched.*

The following extract from No. 674 of the *Universal Spectator* records two instances of *pressing* in the reign of George II. : " Sept. 5. 1741.—On Tuesday was sentenced to death at the Old Bailey, Henry Cook, the shoemaker, of Stratford, for robbing Mr. Zachary on the highway. On Cook's refusing to plead, there was a new press made, and fixed to the proper place in the Press-yard ; there having been no person pressed since the famous Spiggot the highwayman, which is about twenty years ago. Barnworth, *alias* Frasier, was pressed at Kingston in Surrey, about sixteen years ago."

These horrible details have often been discredited ; but records of pressing, so late as 1770, exist ; with the addition, however, that " the punishment was seldom inflicted, but some offenders have chose it *in order to preserve their estates for their children.* Those guilty of this crime are not now suffered to undergo such a length of torture, but have so great a weight placed on them that they soon expire."

---

* The Press-Yard, the scene of this torture, is between the Court-house and Newgate prison.

Afterwards, however, it was provided, by 12 Geo. III. c. 20, that standing mute in felonies should be equivalent to a conviction; and now, by 7 and 8 Geo. IV. c. 28, he shall, by the plea of not guilty, without any further form, be deemed to have put himself upon his country for trial; and the court shall order a jury for the trial of such persons accordingly.

Blackstone remarks upon this strange proceeding of *pressure*, that it is a practice of a different nature from the *rack*, or *question*, to extort a confession from criminals,—*this* having been only used to compel a man to put himself upon his trial, *that* being a species of trial itself. As to the rack, he says that "it is utterly unknown to the law of England; though once, when the Dukes of Exeter and Suffolk, and other ministers of Henry VI., had laid a design to introduce the civil law into this kingdom as the rule of government, for the beginning thereof they erected a rack for torture; which was called, in derision, the Duke of Exeter's daughter; and still remains in the Tower of London, where it was occasionally used as an engine of state, not of law, more than once in the reign of Queen Elizabeth. But when, upon the assassination of Villiers Duke of Buckingham, it was proposed, in the Privy Council, to put the assassin to the rack, in order to discover his accomplices, the judges (being consulted) declared unanimously, to their own honour and the honour of the English law, that no such proceeding was allowable by the laws of England."

Mr. Hallam observes, that though it be most certain that the English law never recognised the use of torture, yet there were many instances of its employment in the reigns of Elizabeth and James; and among others, in the case of the Gunpowder Plot. He says, indeed, that in the latter part of the reign of Elizabeth "the rack seldom stood idle in the Tower;" and cites Lingard for a specification of the different kinds of torture used (*Constit. Hist.* vols. i. and ii.).

We have much evidence of the use of the rack in England. Sir Walter Raleigh, at his trial, mentioned that Kentish was threatened with the rack, and that the keeper of this horrid instrument was sent for. Bishop Laud told Felton that if he would not confess, he must go to the rack. Campion, a Jesuit, was put to the rack in the reign of Elizabeth; and in Collier's *Ecclesiastical History* are mentioned other instances during the same reign. Bishop Burnet, likewise, in his *History of the Reformation*, states that Anne Askew was tortured in the Tower, in 1546; and that the Lord Chancellor, throwing off his gown, drew the rack so severely that he almost tore her body asunder. It appears from the Cecil papers that all the Duke of Norfolk's servants were tortured by order of Queen Elizabeth, who also threatened Hayward the historian with the rack.

Ben Jonson alludes to the rack being threatened in his time: "And like the German lord, when he went out of Newgate into the cart, took order to have his arms set up, &c. . . . . . . The judges entertained him most civilly, discoursed with him, offered him the courtesy of the rack; but he confessed," &c.

BREAD-AND-CHEESE ORDEAL.

The most easy method of a criminal proving his innocence, amongst all the extraordinary modes of trial which prevailed anciently, seems to have been what Muratori styles the *judicium panis et casei* (the judgment of bread-and-cheese). If, after the priest had blessed this food, the prisoner was able to swallow it, he was acquitted. Hence, perhaps, the expression, "*I wish it may choke me.*"—*Barrington.*

PUNISHMENT OF THEFT.

Theft, by the Jewish Law, was only punished with a pecuniary fine, and satisfaction to the party injured. And in the civil law, till some very late constitutions, we never find the punishment capital. The sanguinary laws of Draco, at Athens, punished theft with death; but Solon changed the penalty to a pecuniary mulct. And so the Attic laws in general continued, except that once, in a time of dearth, it was made capital to break into a garden and steal figs; but this law, and the informers against the offence, grew so odious, that from them all malicious informers were styled *sycophants,* a name which we have much perverted from its original meaning.

In this country, our ancient Saxon laws nominally punished theft with death, if above the value of twelve pence; but the criminal was permitted to redeem his life by a pecuniary ransom, as amongst their ancestors, by a stated number of cattle. But in the 9th year of Henry I. this power of redemption was taken away, and all persons guilty of larceny above the value of twelve pence were directed to be hung. So that stealing to above this value (which was called *grand* larceny), became a felony absolutely capital, and so continued to our own times: while *petit* larceny, that is, theft to inferior amount (although described as felony), was punished with imprisonment or whipping only. These denominations of grand and petit larceny are now at an end by 7 and 8 Geo. IV. c. 29, which gives to thefts to the amount of twelve pence or under the same effect as to thefts of greater amount.—*Stephen.*

The value of twelve pence was the standard in the time of Athelstan. Afterwards, in the reign of Henry I., one shilling was the stated value, at the Exchequer, of a pasture-fed ox; and if we suppose this shilling to mean that *solidus legalis* mentioned by Lyndewoode, or the seventy-second part of a pound of gold, it would be equal to 13s. 4d. of the present standard.—*Blackstone.*

The progressive reduction in the value of money, while death continued to be the sentence for theft to the same amount as before, justi-

Ged the complaint of Sir H. Spelman, that while every thing else living became dearer, the life of man had continually grown cheaper.

PUNISHMENT OF BRIBERY.

In England, this offence of taking bribes is punished in inferior officers with fine and imprisonment; and in those who offer a bribe, though not taken, by the same. But in judges, especially the superior ones, it has always been looked upon as particularly heinous; and there is a tradition, that in the reign of Edward III. a chief-justice (Thorpe) was hanged for this offence.* By the statute 11 Hen. IV., all judges and officers of the king convicted of bribery shall forfeit treble the bribe, be punished at the king's will, and be discharged from the king's service for ever.

THE PILLORY, TUMBREL, STOCKS, AND WHIPPING-POST.

These modes of the punishment of barbarous ages have almost disappeared from practice. The most ancient of them, *the Pillory*, existed in England before the Norman Conquest, and was in frequent use in our criminal law from that period until within the last forty years. In the laws of Canute it was called *healfonge*, or more properly *halsfang*, *i.e.* catchneck, a name derived, doubtless, from the form of the instrument used, and the mode in which the punishment was inflicted. Hence also the Latin name of the pillory, *collistrigium* (quasi collum stringens), is said to be taken. (Cowell's *Interpreter*.)

Barrington, however, maintains that *collistrigium* has been improperly translated Pillory; and, according to Sir Henry Spelman, pillory was formerly used to signify the offence, and not the mode of punishment. *Pilleurie* is frequently used in the old French chronicles in this sense; and, even by later writers, as Faviu, who, in his *Théâtre d'Honneur*, has, "Nos François libertins et désobéiss par leur désordre et *pilleurie*."

The form of the pillory, as used in England in the time of Henry VII., may be seen in a collection of prints published by the Society of Antiquaries. In modern times it was nothing more than a wooden frame, or screen, raised several feet from the ground, and behind which the culprit stood, supported upon a platform, his head and arms being thrust through holes in the screen, so as to be exposed in front of it; and in this position he remained for a definite time, usually assigned by

* Blackstone says Thorpe was actually hanged; but Lord Coke denies that Thorpe was hanged, or could be hanged, for this offence; and Lord Campbell, in his *Lives of the Chief-Justices*, considers the tradition that sentence of death was actually passed on him to be unfounded, and to have been invented by Oliver St. John in inveighing against the judges, who, in the reign of Charles I., decided in favour of the legality of ship-money.

the judge who passed the sentence.[*] The pillory was intended
" *magis ad ludibrium et infamiam quam ad pœnam*," i.e. more
for its exposure to mockery and infamy than corporeal punishment; upon which Barrington observes:

> It may therefore well deserve the consideration of a judge who in-
> flicts the punishment of the pillory, as it becomes at present (1769) the
> great occasion of mobs and riots, whether it can be reconciled to the
> original intention of the law in this mode of punishment; and parti-
> cularly if this riotous scene ends in the death of the criminal (as in the
> case of one Egan in 1756), whether the judge is not, in some measure,
> accessory both to the riot and the murder (*Obs. Ant. Stat.* pp. 48, 49).

The punishment being found inefficacious, and in other respects liable to many abuses, the pillory was generally abolished
by 56 Geo. III. c. 138, being retained only for the punishment of
perjury and subornation; and was altogether abolished in 1837,
by the statute 1 Vict. c. 23. The pillory of France, the *carcan*,
was discontinued upon the revision of the Code Pénal, in 1832.

The last person who stood in the pillory in London was
Peter James Bossy, who had been tried for perjury, and sentenced to transportation for seven years; previous to which he
was to be imprisoned for six months in Newgate, and to stand
in the pillory in the Old Bailey for one hour. The pillory part
of the sentence was executed June 22, 1830.

The *Tumbrel* (trebuchetum), an obscure punishment, which
is said to be the same as the *ducking* or *cucking stool*, and was
used for women, who were exempted, on account of their sex,
from the pillory, is often spoken of in the ancient English
laws in conjunction with the pillory. In early periods of English history, the right of having a pillory and tumbrel, and
sometimes also *furcæ*, or gallows, within their jurisdiction,
was claimed and insisted on as a beneficial franchise by lords
of leets, but subsequently became a burden to the public.

Stocks,—the wooden machine formerly much used for the
punishment of disorderly persons, by securing their legs, occurs as early as the Statute of Labourers, 25 Edw. III. A.D.
1350, where it is enacted that refractory artificers shall be put
in the stocks by the lords, afterwards bailiffs or constables, of
the towns where their offence has been committed, for three
days, or sent to the next gaol, there to justify themselves; and
that stocks be made in every town for such occasion between
that time and the feast of Pentecost. In 1376, the Commons
prayed the king for their establishment in every village. In

---

[*] " Defoe was carried from the pillory to Newgate, where he wrote his Hymn
to the Pillory, that

> Hieroglyphic state machine
> Contrived to punish Fancy in."
> Hepworth Dixon's *Memoir of John Howard.*

King Lear, Shakspeare has introduced the stocks upon the stage. Farmer, commenting upon the passage (see Malone's *Shakspeare*), says: "Formerly in great houses, as still in some colleges, there were movable stocks for the correction of the servants." The last pair of stocks seen in London was that for the parish of St. Clement Danes, which remained till 1827, in Portugal-street, Lincoln's-Inn-Fields. A Whipping-post usually adjoined the stocks. The whipping-post of the parish of St. Martin's-in-the-Fields is preserved to this day in a vault beneath the church; the upper portion of this post is ornamented with carving.

THE PARISH-TOP.

This was a large Top formerly provided in every village, to be whipped in frosty weather, that the peasants might be kept warm by exercise, and out of mischief, while they could not work. Shakspeare, in *Twelfth-Night*, has "his brains turn like a parish-top;"—Ben Jonson, in *New Inn*, he "spins like a parish-top;" and Beaumont and Fletcher, he "dances like a town-top, and reels, and hobbles." Evelyn, speaking of the uses of willow-wood, among other things made of it, mentions "great town-topps." And Sir W. Blackstone states that "to sleep like a town-top" was proverbial in his time.

WHO WAS JACK CADE?

Mr. M. A. Lower, F.S.A., in his very ingenious *Essays on English Surnames*, thus corrects an error, into which most of our historians have fallen, relative to the arch-traitor Jack Cade, *temp.* Hen. VI.:

They uniformly state that he was an *Irishman* by birth, but there is strong presumptive evidence that to Sussex belongs the unenviable claim of his nativity. Speed states that he had been servant to Sir Thomas Dagre. Now this Sir Thomas Dagre, or Dacre, was a Sussex knight of great eminence, who had seats at Hurstmonceaux and Heathfield, in this county. Cade has, for several centuries, been a common name about Mayfield and Heathfield, as is proved, as well by numerous entries in the parish registers, as by lands and localities designated from the family. After the defeat and dispersion of his rabble-rout of retainers, Cade is stated to have fled into the woods of Sussex, where, a price being set upon his head, he was slain by Sir Alexander Iden, sheriff of Kent. Nothing seems more probable than that he should have sought shelter from the vindictive fury of his enemies among the woods of his native county, with whose secret retreats he was, doubtless, well acquainted, and where he would have been likely to meet with friends. The daring recklessness of this villain's character is illustrated by the tradition of the district that he was engaged in the rustic game of bowls, in the garden of a little alehouse at Heathfield, when the well-aimed arrow of the Kentish sheriff inflicted the fatal wound.

Money, Weights, and Measures.

Dr. J. H. Gibbon, of the United-States Mint, in the third of his historical papers on "Weights in Modern Coinage," states: "The Avoirdupois ounce and pound were originally used in Babylon, a city of merchants; and were thence carried to Phœnicia and to Spain, whence they came to England and America. The Hebrew shekel was at least very nearly half an ounce avoirdupois, and it seems to be the oldest weight known in human history. According to tradition, it weighed 320 grains of barley. The purchase by Abraham of the cave of Machpelah is distinctly stated to be a cash transaction, to be settled by the payment of a certain weight of silver of a certain fineness 'current with the merchants.' The sum paid to Joseph's brethren by the Egyptians, in payment for the boy, was twenty pieces of silver; doubtless twenty avoirdupois pounds. Wherever the precious metals are mentioned by Hebrew writers, we are to understand the numbers as referring to avoirdupois weights. These weights came into use in England in the 14th century. A conventional avoirdupois ounce was adopted by the United States from Spain as the value of our moneyed unit. The word *dollar* and the word *coin* are both probably of Greek origin, *eidolon* and *eikon*, each signifying an image or idol, and the first coins having been stamped with the images of gods or kings. The 'images' which Rachel stole from her father, and hid in the camel's furniture, were probably coins,—not of Hebrew coinage, but of neighbouring *idol*atrous nations. The law requiring a hireling to be paid at sundown, and Jonah's paying his fare to Tarshish, indicate the use of small coins among the Hebrews. Our arbitrary unit does not agree exactly with any ancient or modern weight. The ancient Tyrian ounce contained 438 grains of very great fineness; while our modern dollar contains only 384 grains of inferior silver, as coined in halves. It was originally 416 grains. The half-shekel of the Hebrew was, therefore, worth 63 cents of our modern American money. A troy ounce is 480 grains, taking all the grains the same. The sterling—that is, Easterling—ounce was still different. Thus, all our modern weights and coinage are the remains and vestiges of ancient civilisations, now lost. In ancient times coinage was common in every colony and city.

The ancient laws of Deuteronomy are similar to those Newton sought to establish when Master of the English Mint, and declare emphatically that justness and accuracy in dealings are favourable to [or "have the promise of"] longevity."

THE STANDARD OF MEASURE.

At the Great Exhibition of 1851, Mr. Whitworth showed a machine which measured to the millionth part of an inch, and which enabled any one to calculate the expansion caused in a bar of iron a yard long, by touching it lightly for a moment with the finger tip. The same arrangement is now adopted by him for the production of standards of measure; the principle being, that the standard is obtained by measuring the distance between the perfectly flat ends of a solid bar having true surfaces on its sides and ends. His test is that of the touch; by it he can correct errors in dimensions up to the millionth of an inch; whereas the plan depending on the sight, aided by the microscope, can only correct errors to the 60,000th of an inch.

It affords a simple explanation of the relative merits of the two systems to state, that in line measurement the eye has only to pass over the distance actually measured; and when that is very small, the limited power of the sight, aided even by the microscope, in distinguishing difference, operates as a great check; whereas in the apparatus employed in end-measuring, the eye has to travel over a distance of about 40 inches to trace the variation of a thousandth of an inch.

By the application of this instrument, standard gauges for parts of machinery, which it is desirable to maintain uniform, are constructed; and so minute is its operation, that, as before stated, magnitudes can be estimated that do not exceed the one-millionth part of an inch.*

ORIGIN OF THE ELL AND YARD.

Most nations have regulated the standard of measures of length by comparison with parts of the human body; as the palm, the hand, the span, the foot, the cubit, the ell (*ulna*, or arm), the pace, and the fathom. But as these are of different dimensions in men of different proportions, in England a new standard of longitudinal measure was established by

---

* In 1758, the House of Commons issued a commission to adjust the standard of weight; and under the superintendence of officers of the Mint, and eminent scientific men, the standard was determined, and two troy pounds, of extreme accuracy, were produced. One of these pound-weights was deposited in the House of Commons, and was destroyed in the fire in 1834; and the other, until recently, has been in private hands. This duplicate of the original standard troy pound has been, since the destruction of its fellow, the weight always appealed to in any commission for the trial of weights. It was sold amongst other effects of the late S. Alchorne, Esq., formerly King's assay-master. The weight produced 17*l.*,

King Henry I., who commanded that the *ulna*, or ancient ell, which answers to the modern yard, should be made of the exact length of his own arm. King Richard I., in 1197, further ordained, that there should be only one weight and one measure throughout the kingdom; whence was derived the ancient officer of *the King's aulnager*, whose duty it was, for a certain fee, to measure all cloths made for sale, till the office was abolished by the statute 11 and 12 Will. III. c. 20.

THE MILE AND YARD IN VARIOUS COUNTRIES.

Scarcely any two countries have the same measures, though the same name is used to designate them in many countries. Take the Mile measure, for instance:

	Yards.		Yards.
England and the United		France	3,025
States	1,760	Scotch	1,984
Netherlands	1,093	Irish	2,038
Germany	10,120	Spanish	2,472
(or nearly 6 English miles.)		Swedish	11,700

These are computed in English yards; but the Yard itself, of three feet in length, represents divers distances in different places.

	Inches.		Inches.
The English yard is	36	The Spanish yard is	33·04
„ French „	39·13	„ Prussian „	36·57
„ Genoa „	57·60	„ Russian „	39·51
„ Austrian „	37·35		

ORIGIN OF COMMERCIAL TERMS AND USAGES.

The earliest money-dealers in England were the Jews. To them succeeded the Lombards, by which general appellation the early Italian merchants of Genoa, Lucca, Florence, and Venice, were designated. They obtained a footing in this country about the middle of the thirteenth century, and established themselves in Lombard-street, making it their business to remit money to and from their own country by bills of exchange.

Hence, as might be expected, a number of commercial terms have crept into our language of Italian derivation. Debtor and creditor, for instance; cash, from *cassa*, the case or chest where money was kept; usance, from *usanza*; bank and bankrupt, from *banco* and *banco rotto*; journal, from *giornale*; the abbre-

and was understood to have been purchased for the Government. The hydrostatic balance, used for the trial of the standard in 1758, with several boxes of extremely accurate weights, were withdrawn. The sale included many curious Mss. on Mint affairs. Amongst these was Crocker's Register Book of drawings for medals, certified under the hands of various officers of the Mint, and containing thirty autographs of Sir Isaac Newton, which sold for 40*l.*, and is now in the British Museum. A 5*l.*-piece of George III., dated 1820, and in very fine condition, sold for 8*l.*

viations £ *s. d.* for *liri, soldi,* and *denari;* and the often-recurring *ditto,* which should be spelt with an *e* instead of an *i.*

Macpherson gives instances of general letters of credit as early as the year 1200. Mention is made of *literæ cambitoriæ,* or negotiable bills of exchange, in an instrument bearing the date of 1364; and in 1400, bills were drawn in acts, and worded exactly as at present. In 1560, we find Gresham writing to Sir Thomas Parry, as to buying for the queen's majesty a great *iron chest* " with a littil key."

HANDSEL.

Anciently, among all the northern nations, shaking of hands was held necessary to bind the bargain; a custom which we still retain, says Blackstone, in many verbal contracts. A sale thus made was called *handsale;* till in process of time the same word was used to signify the instalment, or earnest which was given immediately after the shaking of hands, or instead thereof. Handsel is also now the first act of using any thing.

Handsel likewise denotes the first money received for the sale of goods, which is considered as fortunate or unfortunate to the seller, according to circumstances; whence the word is commonly used in a figurative sense.

PAWNBROKING IN ENGLAND.

Pawnbroking is said to have been established in England by Mich. de Northburg, Bishop of London, in the reign of Edward III.; and, according to Dugdale, and other authorities, if any sum so borrowed was not paid at the expiration of a year, the preacher at St. Paul's Cross was to announce that the pledge would be sold in fourteen days, unless previously redeemed. For the origin of the Pawnbroker's sign, Three Balls, see *Things not generally Known,* First Series, p. 128.

MONEY-LENDING IN THE OLDEN TIME: RATE OF INTEREST.

The practice of lending Money on Interest appears to be as old as the use of money itself. What was the rate of interest amongst the Jews does not appear very clearly from the Old Testament; but from a passage in Nehemiah (v. 11) it is conjectured by commentators that it was one per cent per lunar month; and as an additional month was intercalated every second or third year, this interest was equivalent to at least 13 per cent paid yearly. In Rome, according to Niebuhr, the rate was 8⅓ per cent for the old year of ten months, *i. e.* 10 per cent per annum; but though this restriction was in force at Rome, in the conquered provinces enormous interest was ex-

acted. After the expulsion of the Jews, the history of interest
in England is obscure till, in the third year of Henry VII.
(1488), a statute was passed forbidding interest to be taken;
and from a passage in the Act it would seem that 20 per cent
had been the usual rate charged. In the thirteenth year of
Elizabeth (1571), the Act of Edward VI. was repealed, and interest at the rate of 10 per cent legalised. This Act, which was
to continue in force for five years, was several times renewed,
and subsequently, in the thirty-ninth year of the same reign
(1597), made perpetual.—W. B. Hodge; *Proc. Institute of Ac-
tuaries.*

The rate of Interest has been gradually decreasing in this
country in proportion to the increase of specie, and has been
regulated by law, from time to time, as circumstances required
or allowed. The statute of 37 Henry VIII. c. 9, confined it
to *ten* per cent, as did also the 13 Eliz. c. 8. By 21 Jac. I.
c. 17, legal interest was reduced to *eight* per cent, which being
mentioned as quite recent in the *Staple of News*, marks the date
of that play; but in the *Magnetick Lady ten* per cent is spoken
of as the usual rate. The subsequent reductions of interest
were—to six per cent, 12 Car. II. c. 13; and to five, 12 Ann.
st. 2, c. 16.

ORIGIN OF THE FUNDS.

The term *Fund* applied originally to the taxes or funds set
apart as security for repayment of the principal sums advanced,
and the interest upon them; but when money was no longer
borrowed to be repaid at any given time, it began to mean the
principal sum itself. In the year 1751, Government began to
unite the various loans into one fund, called the Consolidated
Fund (which you must not confuse with that of the same name
into which part of the revenue is collected), and sums due in
this are now shortly termed Consols. These come under the
general denomination of Stocks.—*Albany Fonblanque's Handbook.*

A CUNNING FILE.

The first remarkable "clipper" of coin was an Alexander of
Byzantium, who was the chief officer of the public treasury, and
raised an immense and sudden fortune by clipping the money
in such a manner that the difference could only appear by the
weight. The Byzantines gave him the nickname of *the file,*
from his making such dextrous use of it; whence the term of
File became applied to various shades of cunning next door to
dishonesty.

SAVINGS-BANKS.

These valuable institutions originated with the Rev. Joseph

Smith, of Wendover, who, in 1799, proposed to his parishioners to receive Twopence and upwards every Sunday evening during the summer months; and to repay at Christmas the amount of the deposit, with the addition of one-third as a bounty. The next Savings-Bank was founded in 1804, at Tottenham, Middlesex, by Mrs. Priscilla Wakefield, the amiable writer of several books for young persons; this institution bore a nearer resemblance to the savings-bank of the present day than the Wendover one.

LAC—LAC OF RUPEES.

From *lakh*, the name of the Indian insect, is said to have been derived the well-known Indian word lac (*lakh*), meaning figuratively any very large amount, a figure suggested by the immense number composing each community of insects. For example, Lac signifies one hundred thousand, and a lac of rupees, 10,000*l*.

RENT IN VARIOUS COUNTRIES.

In England and Scotland, the rent paid by the cultivator for the use of the land is estimated in round numbers, taking one farm with another, at a fourth of the gross produce. In France the average proportion is about a third; while in the United States of North America, it is well known to be much less, and indeed, in some parts, to be merely nominal. But in India, the legal rent, that is, the lowest rate recognised by the law and usage of the country, is one half of the produce.

PURITY OF ANCIENT COINS.

Silver coins, after having been long in the earth, are often found covered with a salt of copper. This may be explained by supposing that the alloy of copper, at the surface of the coin, enters into combination with the carbonic acid of the soil, and being thus removed, its place is supplied by a diffusion from within; and in this way, it is not improbable that a considerable portion of the alloy may be exhausted in process of time, and the purity of the coin be considerably increased.—*Professor Henry*, U.S.

ORIGIN OF PIN-MONEY.

"There is," says Barrington, "a very ancient tax in France for providing the Queen with Pins; from whence the term of Pin-Money hath been, undoubtedly, applied by us to that provision for married women, with which the husband is not to interfere." Barrington gives this illustration of the use of the phrase: "Quand nous donnons argent à quelque chambrière, nous disons, *pour les épingles*."—*Bellon's Voyages*, 1533.

The Pin Manufacture is one of the most extraordinary branches of our national industry. By aid of improved machinery, more than three times the number of pins is made that could have been produced by the same number of workmen a few years since; yet the pins are sold at not more than twopence per pound over the cost of the metal of which they are formed. Upwards of 150 tons weight of copper and spelter are annually worked up into pins by one Birmingham house alone. Were the whole of this metal converted into ribbon pins, half an inch in length, it would produce 100,800,000,000, or about one hundred to each inhabitant of the globe. If placed in a straight line, these pins would be 787,500 miles in length, or sufficient to extend upwards of thirty times round the globe, or more than three times the distance of the moon from the earth. Hence we cannot be surprised at the unanswerable question,—"What becomes of all the pins?"

THE ANGEL—ANGEL-WATER.

The Angel was a gold coin worth about ten shillings, which, it appears from the following epigram, was a lawyer's fee:

Upon Anne's Marriage with a Lawyer.

Anne is an angel,—what if so she be!
What is an angel but a lawyer's fee?

Wits' Recreations.

Angel-gold was gold used for coining angels, and was of a finer kind than crown-gold.

Angel-Water was a very fashionable perfume in the seventeenth century. We find in the *Accomplished Female Instructor* the following recipe:

Angel-Water, an excellent perfume; also a curious wash to beautify the skin. Prepare a glaz'd earthen pot, and put into it 16 ounces of orange-flower water, a quarter of a pound of benjamine, two ounces of storax, half an ounce of cinnamon, and a quarter of an ounce of cloves grosly bruised, with three drams of calamus aromaticus; set them over hot embers or a gentle fire to simmer or bubble well up; when about a fifth part is consumed, add a bladder of musk, and a few minutes after take it off and let it cool, pour it off by inclination from the settlings, and put it into a thick glass bottle; and of the dross you may make perfumed cakes, or sweet bags, to lay among clothes.

GALLEY-HALFPENCE.

These were a coin of Genoa, brought in by the Galley-men, or men that came up in the galleys with wine and merchandise, and thence called *Galley-Halfpence*, broader than the English halfpenny, but not so thick; and probably base metal, because two years afterwards a statute (13 Henry IV. cap. 6) was made to confirm the former law, considering the great deceit as well of the said galley-halfpence as other foreign money.—*Martin Leake.*

The galleys unloaded at the east end of Lower Thames-street, thence called Galley Quay, where, in the seventeenth century, were struck tradesmen's tokens, therefore called "Galley-Quay Halfpence."

FIDDLERS' MONEY.

, "A fit of mirth for a groat," a frequent phrase in the seventeenth century, denotes that coin to have been the usual requital to the fiddlers or minstrels of that period, and hence led to the groat being called "fiddlers' money;" but after the Restoration, in 1660, it is noticed in various poetical productions and comedies that the sixpence had taken place of the groat ; and the phrase is still current : when several sixpences are given in change, the exclamation arises, " What a lot of fiddlers' money !"—J. H. Burn ; Introduction to *The Beaufoy Catalogue of London Tradesmen's Tokens.*

KIMMERIDGE COAL-MONEY.

Various theories have been brought forward by antiquarian writers to account for the frequent discovery of the so-called Kimmeridge Coal-Money on the coast of Dorsetshire. It is described by Hutchins, in his History of Dorset ; and in 1826, a treatise on the subject, by W. A. Miles, ascribed these remains to the Phœnicians, and indulged in some very fanciful speculations as to their use and origin. Mr. Sydenham, however, in 1844, explained to the Archæological Association, that this so-called "money" is the chuck or waste pieces of coal from the turning lathe. Several remains since discovered fully confirm these views: among them are cylindrical boxes and vases formed of separate annular portions, all turned on the lathe: and these discoveries show that an extensive manufacture of objects from Kimmeridge Coal had been in existence during the Roman occupation of Britain.—*Proc. Soc. Antiquaries,* 1858.

WHAT IS A PLUM OF MONEY ?

" In the cant of the City," says Dr. Johnson, " the sum of one hundred thousand pounds ;" and then illustrates its use by quotations from Addison, Prior, Arbuthnot, and Pope.

A Correspondent of *Notes and Queries,* Second Series, No. 79, considers the expression Spanish, and to have been borrowed by our London merchants from those of Spain.

Pluma, which in Spanish signifies *plumage,* bears also in that language the metaphorical and colloquial signification of *wealth.* The Spaniards, speaking of a man who has acquired riches, and of whom we should say that he had "feathered his nest," use the expression "*tiene pluma*" (he has got plumage). Hence our English expression, *he has got a plum.*

The same writer thinks the phrase may also have been taken from *plume*, which, in old English, stands for the prize of a struggle or contest, the emblem of success: thus Milton speaks of winning a *plume*.

Richardson, in his *Dictionary*, says that *Plum* is perhaps *plump*, or *plumper;* that *Plim* is a provincialism, to swell, to increase in bulk; and a *plum* may be a sum swelled or increased to 100,000*l.*,—a fortune considered, say at the beginning of the last century, a great success. Addison favours this origin when he says: "A man will swell into a plum."

But why should this be applied specifically to 100,000*l.* ? Another Correspondent of *Notes and Queries*, No. 83, replies, that a favourite expression amongst the merchants of the Continent in former days was "a ton of gold," which always meant 100,000 pieces of coin, *whatever their value.* Thus, in German currency, it was 100,000 rix-dollars; in English, 100,000*l.* sterling; in Dutch, 100,000 Dutch gilders, &c. (From Multzo's *Curieuses Muntz-Lexicon.*) Thus, foreign merchants having connected "a ton of gold" with the sum of 100,000*l.* sterling, may it explain why, in saying that a successful merchant was worth a plum, the particular amount was this "ton of gold," or 100,000*l.* ?

ALLOY: STERLING: STANDARD.

Neither gold nor silver is ever used in its pure state, either in coinage or manufacture. With gold a certain portion of silver or copper, or of both, is mixed; and with silver is mixed copper, or other baser metals.

Our forefathers, considering that silver in its finest degree would be too soft for use and service (for the finest silver is almost as soft as lead), did consult to reduce or harden the silver (by alloying it with baser metal) to such a degree, that it might be both serviceable in the works, and also in the wearing keep its native whiteness.—*Touchstone for Gold and Silver Wares,* 1607.

The proportions of the pure and baser metals are determined by law; and hence the added metal is called the "allay," or "alloy," from *à la loi*. Some think that alloy is derived from *allier*,—to mix, to combine,—and the French call the alloy *alliage*. Butler uses *allay:*

> For fools are stubborn in the way,
> As coins are hardened by th' allay.   *Hudibras.*

The whole is called standard, or *sterling*, from Easterlings, which the English denominated the Germans, from their living eastward; they were first called in by King John to reduce English silver to its due fineness, and such money is in ancient writings *Easterlings.—Camden.*

There are two standards for *gold* and two for *silver*: the standards for gold are twenty-two and eighteen carats of pure metal in every ounce, the ounce containing twenty-four carats; so that in each ounce there may be two or six carats, or one-twelfth, or one-fourth, of the weight of alloy. The coinage is of the higher standard, twenty-two carats, as are also usually wedding-rings. Other manufactures are of the lower standard.

The standards for silver are 11 oz. 10 dwt., and 11 oz. 2 dwt., of pure metal in every pound troy; or, in other words, 10 or 18 dwt. of alloy are permitted in every 12 ounces. The higher standard is never used. The silver coinage is of the lower standard,—*Ryland on the Assay, &c.* 1852.

THE GOLD AND SILVER COINAGE STANDARD.

The standard has frequently varied, but is now settled as follows: The pound troy of gold, consisting of 22 carats (or twenty-fourth parts) fine, and two of alloy, is divided into 46·725 sovereigns, or into 46*l.* 14*s.* 6*d.* And the pound troy of silver, consisting of 11 ounces and 2 pennyweights pure, and 18 pennyweights alloy, is divided into 66 shillings.

"JEWELLERS' GOLD."

Gold of the quality of 12 carats or less, if alloyed with zinc, instead of the proper quantity of silver, presents a colour very nearly equal to that of a metal at least 2½ or 3 carats higher, or of 8*s.* or 10*s.* an ounce more value. A large quantity of jewellery is made of gold alloyed in this manner, as gold chains, pencil-cases, thimbles, and lockets; and in addition to the above loss, a galvanic action is produced after a time upon gold so alloyed, by means of which the metal is split into separate pieces, and the article rendered useless.—*Watherston's Art of Assaying.*

TRONAGE AND TROY-WEIGHT.

Tronage, according to Ducange, is a right of toll for weighing goods, probably at a fair; *trona* signifying a pair of scales. Ducange likewise derives Troy-weight from *trona.* Upon this Barrington, in his *Observations on the More Ancient Statutes*, notes:

There is at Edinburgh a church which is called the Trone Church, and probably from the *trona*, or public scales, having hung opposite to it. There is likewise in the *Rolles Gascoynes*, published by Carte, a record, "De officio trongii, et pesagii lanarum," which agrees with Ducange's signification of the word. In the north of England, the stilyard, with which butcher's meat is weighed, is still called the *trones.*

HALL-MARKS ON PLATE.

All plate, and gold and silver wares, bear certain Hall-Marks, or assay-marks, generally five in number:

Characters of mark.	Signification.
1. The marker's initials	The maker.
2. One of the marks hereafter stated as standard-marks.....................	The quality of the standard.
3. The arms of the Company	The place of assay.
4. A letter, changed every year, and used throughout the year: the letter is appointed by each Company	The payment of duty.
5. The Sovereign's head.	

The standard-marks are:

A crown and figures 22	For gold of 22 carats.*
A crown and figures 18	For gold of 18 carats.
Lion's head ornsed, and Britannia (except at Birmingham and Sheffield, and there Britannia alone)	For silver of 11 oz. 10 dwt.
Lion passant	For silver of 11 oz. 2 dwt.

Arms of the Companies.

Leopard's head..........................	London.
Anchor	Birmingham.
A sword between three garbs	Chester.
A castle with three towers..............	Exeter.
Three castles...........................	Newcastle-upon-Tyne.
Crown..................................	Sheffield.
Cross and five lions	York.

The marks for gold of 22 carats, and for silver of 11 oz. 10 dwt., were, up to the year 1844, the same; and hence a great facility to fraud was afforded. An article of silver of the standard mentioned being duly assayed and marked, had only to be gilt, and who, but those more skilled than ordinary purchasers, could say it was not gold? This was changed by 7 and 8 Vict. c. 22, which required all wares of 22 carat gold to be marked by a "crown and the figures 22, instead of the mark of the lion passant."—*Ryland on the Assay, &c.* 1852.

HOW PLATE IS ASSAYED AND MARKED.

The silversmith, having mixed his metal, so as not to have more than 18 dwt. of alloy in every pound, and from it made the plate, stamps it with his initials; and then, before it is quite finished, lest the plate should be damaged in the process of scraping and marking it at the office, he sends it, with the amount of the duty and charges for marking, to the Assay Office, where a punch with his mark is entered. It is here ex-

* The Carat is an Abyssinian weight: it is divided into four parts, called grains, and these again into quarters; so that a carat-grain is equal to 2½ dwts.

amined by the wardens and assayers, to ascertain if it bears
the maker's registered mark; whether all the parts which
were intended to be affixed together are put together; whether they are sufficiently advanced in the work; and whether
there is any unnecessary solder. If they are not satisfied on
these points, the work is returned to the maker; if the wardens and assayer are satisfied, then a scraping is taken from it
and handed over to the assayer, who subjects it to analysis, to
ascertain the quality of the metal in reference to such of the
legal standards as the worker states it to be of. If it be found
deficient, then two other assays are made; if it be still deficient, the work is cut through, and the pieces are returned to
the owner. If any fraud be suspected by the introduction of
base metal which could not be discovered by assay, the wardens and assayer are authorised to cut the work through; and
if their suspicion prove well founded, it is forfeited to the
office; otherwise a compensation is made to the owner for the
destruction of his work. But if, as is generally the case, the
assayer finds the plate as good as, or better than the standard,
it is marked and returned to the owner, who finishes it ready
for sale.—*Ryland on the Assay, &c.* 1852.

The stocks were early used for punishment by the Goldsmiths' Company. Thus, in 1442, the wardens, accompanied
by the Prior of St. Bartholomew, went in search of an "un-
true worker," who stole away, "or else he had be set in the
stokkes." And in 1529-30, one John Caswell, for working silver
less pure than sterling, was first publicly set in the stocks, and
then sent by the warden to Newgate, where he died.

Counterfeiting the Hall-marks was made a capital offence
by 31 Geo. II. c. 32.

HOAR-STONES.

The frequent mention of Hoar-Stones in land-limits prior to
the Norman Conquest shows that our Saxon ancestors respected
these sepulchral monuments, and adopted them as land-marks;
and it favours the supposition that they found them already
desecrated and ruined on their arrival in this country. Near
Enstone, within the forest of Wychwood, is a Hoar-Stone, a
ruined cromlech, which gives name to two villages in the neighbourhood. The antiquary will require no proofs of its remote
age, of which the designation, Hoar-Stone, is the best voucher.
—J. Y. Akerman, F.S.A.; *Archæologia*, vol. xxxvii. p. 133.

TO MEASURE THE BREADTH OF AN OBJECT.

When the distance of the base is found, this operation is
most simple. Take the apparent angle formed by a pair of

compasses directed to the object, which lay down upon paper, and produce the sides till the base is reached, when the width will be that of the object upon the scale by which the distance has been found. Thus one position only is required.—*Mechanics' Magazine.*

WHAT IS TIME?

There is, perhaps, nothing of which the mind is less capable of forming a distinct idea than time, unconnected with the notions of sensible objects; yet, on account of this connection, every one thinks it a subject with which he is familiarly acquainted, until an explanation be required.

The query is,—Is absolute time any thing distinct from motion? But supposing the earth, planets, &c. had been without motion from the Creation, still would not the duration of this state of rest have been equal to the time which has elapsed since the Creation?

Every one has his own measure of time, in the quickness or slowness with which his ideas succeed each other; for time appears long to us when the ideas succeed each other rapidly in our minds, and *vice versâ.*

The only universal measure of time is the present instant; and yet some deny the existence of the present time, as being gone before we can note it. If there be no present, there cannot be any future time, and the past certainly has no existence. —*Notes to assist the Memory in various Sciences.*

GENERATIONS.

A generation is admitted to occupy, on an average, a space of thirty-three years.

Horace Walpole relates the following amusing instance of seeing six generations: " I was ten when I was presented to George I., two nights before he left England for the last time. This makes me appear very old to myself, and Methuselah to young persons, if I happen to mention it before them. If I see another reign, which is but too probable, what shall I seem then? I will tell you an odd circumstance. Nearly ten years ago, I had already seen six generations in one family, that of Waldegrave. I have often seen, and once been in a room with, Mrs. Godfrey, mistress of James II. It is true she doted. Then came her daughter, the old Lady Waldegrave; her son, the ambassador; his daughter, the Lady Harriot; her daughter, the present Lady Powis; and she has children who may be married in five or six years; and yet I shall not be very old if I see two generations more; but if I do, I shall be superannuated, for I think I talk already like an old nurse."

EXPECTATION OF LIFE.

For the sake of easy calculation, De Moivre assumed 86 as the boundary of human life; from which having deducted the person's age (if 30 or upwards), the half of the remainder is the average time that a man may expect to live. Thus:

	Years.
Boundary of human life	86
Suppose an individual's age to be	40
	$\frac{1}{2}$)46
Average Expectation of Life	23

The period of life at which man (under all circumstances) has the probability of the greatest number of years to come, is the age of 33.

If the probability that one man, A, shall live a year be $\frac{9}{10}$, and the probability of the life of another man, B, for one year be $\frac{9}{10}$, the probability that both shall live another year is as 100 to 48, viz. $\frac{9}{10} \times \frac{9}{10} = \frac{81}{100}$.

The probability of the death of A within the year being $\frac{1}{10}$, and of the death of B $\frac{1}{10}$, the probability that both shall die within the year is $\frac{1}{10} \times \frac{1}{10} = \frac{1}{100}$.

The probability that one of the events shall happen, and the other fail, is as the probability of the happening of the one multiplied by the probability of the failure of the other. So, in the above case, the probability that A shall live and B die is $\frac{9}{10} \times \frac{1}{10} = \frac{9}{100}$; and the probability that B shall live and A die is $\frac{9}{10} \times \frac{1}{10} = \frac{9}{100}$.—*Notes to assist the Memory in various Sciences.*

De Moivre's hypothesis has, however, now become obsolete, from the greater accuracy of mortality tables; and Mr. Charles Willich has established an easy rule for expressing the Expectation of Life for any age from 5 to 60. His formula stands thus: $s = \frac{2}{3}(80 - a)$; or, in plain words, the Expectation of Life is equal to two-thirds of the difference between the age of the party and 80. Thus, say a man is now 20 years old. Between that age and 80 there are 60 years. Two-thirds of 60 are 40; and this is the sum of his Expectation of Life. If a man be now 60, he will have an Expectation of nearly 14 years more. By the same rule, a child of 5 has a lien on life for 50 years. Every one can apply the rule to his own age. The results obtained by the new law correspond very closely with those from Dr. Farr's English Life Table, constructed with great care from an immense mass of returns.

CLIMACTERICS: THE GRAND CLIMACTERIC.

The term Climacteric is applied to certain years of a person's life, which are supposed to mark a certain degree in the scale of his existence; and also to a particular disease observed in persons advanced in life, wherein a general decay of the system takes place without any assignable cause being observed.

Among the superstitions of the Middle Ages, Climacterics, or Critical Periods of Life, were very strong; "and even down to rather recent times, the mystic numbers 7 and 9, so frequently occurring in the Bible, and the combination of these numbers, have had their influence with many persons" (*Notes and Queries*, 2d S., No. 86).

It was believed that the constitution of man changed every seven years : at seven years of age, a child had left infancy; at twice seven, or fourteen, he had attained puberty; at three times seven, or twenty-one, he had reached manhood, and so on. Combinations of the numbers 3, 7, and 9 were mostly employed; and $3 \times 7 = 21$, $7 \times 7 = 49$, $7 \times 9 = 63$, and $9 \times 9 = 81$, were important periods.

The Grand Climacteric was "the perilous or dangerous yeare of one's lyfe;" all the periods were to be feared, but the two Grand Climacterics, or most momentous, are fixed at 63 and 81 by Sir Thomas Browne.

According to some, the climacteric is every seventh year; but others allow only those years produced by 7 and the odd numbers 3, 5, 7, and 9 to be climacterical. These years, they say, bring with them some remarkable change with respect to health, life, or fortune. The Grand Climacteric is the 63d year; but some, making two, add to this the 81st. The other remarkable climacterics are the 7th, 21st, 35th, 49th,* and 56th (*Encyclopædia Britannica*, 4th edit. 1810).

WHAT IS THE NORMAL PERIOD OF A MAN'S LIFE ?

M. Flourens replies, One Hundred years; and on the following grounds. It is admitted that the length of each man's life is in exact proportion to the period it is growing. Now, as long as the bones are not united to their epiphyses, the animal grows ; as soon as the bones are united to their epiphyses, the animal ceases to grow. Now, in man, this union takes place at the age of twenty: consequently the natural duration of life is five times twenty years. Applied to domestic animals, M. Flourens' theory has, he tells us, been proved correct. "The union of the bones with the epiphyses," he says, "takes place in the camel at eight years of age, and he lives forty years; in the

* This year 40 has much less support from vital statistics than the age of 63, which Dr. Southwood Smith (*Phil. of Health*, I. 123) has shown from physiological views, and from Finlaison's tables, to be very susceptible of sickness; for taking a million of males, members of London benefit-societies, the proportion constantly sick

At 23 is 19,410		At 43 is 26,260
„ 28 „ 19,670		„ 48 „ 36,960
„ 33 „ 19,400		„ 53 „ 27,060
„ 38 „ 23,870		„ 63 „ 57,000
		And at 68 is 106,040

From this table it appears that there are not many more persons on the sick list at 53 than at 43 years of age; whilst at 63 the number is more than double. And at 48 the number of sick is more by one-third than at 53 years of age.—J. T. Buckton, *Notes and Queries*, 2d S., No. 69.

horse at five years, and he lives twenty-five years; in the ox at four years, and he lives from fifteen to twenty years; in the dog at two years, and he lives from ten to twelve years; and in the lion at four years, and he lives twenty." As a necessary consequence of the prolongation of life to which M. Flourens assures man he is entitled, he modifies very considerably his different ages. " I prolong the duration of infancy," he says, " up to ten years, because it is from nine to ten that the second dentition is terminated. I prolong adolescence up to twenty years, because it is at that age that the development of the bones ceases, and consequently the increase of the body in length. I prolong youth up to the age of forty, because it is only at that age that the increase of the body in bulk terminates. After forty the body does not grow, properly speaking; the augmentation of its volume, which then takes place, is not a veritable organic development, but a simple accumulation of fat. After the growth has terminated, man enters into the period of invigoration, that is—when all our parts become more complete and firmer, our functions more assured, and the whole organism more perfect. This period lasts to sixty-five or seventy years; and then begins old age, which lasts for thirty years."

To those who may be disposed to ask why it is that of men destined to live a hundred years so few do so, M. Flourens answers triumphantly, " With our manners, our passions, our torments, man does not die, he kills himself!" and he speaks at great length of Cornaro, of Leasius, and mentions Parr and others, to show that, by prudence, and, above all, *sobriety*, life can easily be extended to a century or more.

DURATION OF LIFE IN THE LEARNED PROFESSIONS.

Dr. Guy, in a paper read by him to the Statistical Society, has assembled from the most accredited records many interesting facts, from which it appears that physicians and surgeons live longer than clergymen, and that the latter live longer than lawyers. In his tables, Dr. Guy commences with those who have died after attaining the age of fifty-one; and of the persons of eminence in the three professions it is stated that the average age of clergymen is 69·48, of medical men 70·94, and of lawyers 68·50. This proportion, so far as can be ascertained from the present means of calculating, is also maintained at ages below fifty-one as well as above; and it shows a duration of life in favour of the three professions compared with the general mass of society. Dr. Guy has extended his investigations into the subject to the sixteenth, seventeenth, and eighteenth centuries; and though the latter are insufficient to establish positive conclusions, they indicate that the duration of life at those periods nearly corresponds with the present in length and in relative proportions, with the exception of lawyers, who seem to have been more shortlived in the eighteenth century, in the ratio of 1½ per cent.

MORTALITY AMONG SOLDIERS AND SAILORS.

In Britain, the number of deaths among the troops generally is 15 per 1000 per annum; while among officers and the civil population it is only 9 per 1000. In France, the mortality among troops is 18 per 1000; among civilians it is 10 per 1000. In the island of Barbadoes, the mortality among civilians is not more than 14 per 1000; while among European troops it is 58 per 1000. At the Cape of Good Hope and West Africa, the mortality among troops is 450 per 1000, or 45 per cent; in the navy at the same places, it is only 25 per 1000, or 2½ per cent. In general, the mortality among the sailors of the Navy is much less than among the troops.—*Keith Johnson.*

THE DAYS OF THE WEEK.

Ancient deeds are frequently dated the day of the week on which they were executed, *e. g. Die Jovis, Die Mercurii*, &c.; each day being dedicated to a heathen deity, as follows:

Dies Solis	Sunday.
Dies Lunæ	Monday.
Dies Martis	Tuesday.
Dies Mercurii	Wednesday.
Dies Jovis	Thursday.
Dies Veneris	Friday.
Dies Saturni	Saturday.

In some ancient deeds we find the equivalent terms *Dies Dominica* for Sunday, and *Dies Sabbati* for Saturday.

These Latin designations are also generally used in entries in the account-books of surgeons and apothecaries.

MARRIAGE: RESPONSIBLE AGES.

By the common law of England, all persons under the age of twenty-one are infants; twenty-one is the age of majority; and in the five following years of age, half of the marriages in England are now contracted. Males at fourteen, females at twelve, may consent to marry, but cannot legally marry until the age of twenty-one without the consent of their guardians. The English law regards fourteen as the age at which a person is competent to distinguish right and wrong; under seven children are irresponsible; between the ages of seven and fourteen, they are in some cases responsible.—*The Registrar-General.*

Olden Herbs and Fruit.

THE OLD HERB-GARDEN.

THE writer of a charming paper on "The Flower-Garden," in the *Quarterly Review*, No. 139, thus sketches the Herb-Garden of our ancestors, and adds a note suggesting its reproduction.

The olitory, or herb-garden, is a part of our horticulture now comparatively neglected; and yet once the culture and culling of simples was as much a part of female education as the preserving and tying down of "rasps and apricockes." There was not a Lady Bountiful in the kingdom but made her dill-tea and diet-drink from herbs of her own planting; and there is a neatness and prettiness about our thyme, and sage, and mint, and marjoram, that might yet, we think, transfer them from the patronage of the blue serge to that of the white-muslin apron. Lavender, and rosemary, and rue, the feathery fennel, and the bright-blue borage, are all pretty bushes in their way, and might have their due place assigned them by the hand of beauty and taste. A strip for a little herbary, halfway between the flower and vegetable garden, would form a very appropriate transition stratum, and might be the means, by being more under the eye of the mistress, of recovering to our soups and salads some of the comparatively neglected herbs of tarragon, and French sorrel, and purslane, and chervil, and dill, and clary, and others whose place is now nowhere to be found but in the pages of the old herbalists. This little plot should be laid out, of course, in a simple geometric pattern; and, having tried the experiment, we can boldly pronounce on its success. We recommend the idea to the consideration of our lady-gardeners.

Our plants used in the medicine of a still earlier period were certain herbs, of which many superstitious associations are recorded. The Druids were then the only physicians, and blended some knowledge of natural medicines with the general superstition by which they were characterised. Their famous Mistletoe, or *all-heal*, was considered as a certain cure in many diseases, an antidote to poison, and a sure remedy against infection. (A nostrum called *Heal-all* is compounded at this day.) Another plant, called Samoclus, or Marchwort, which grew chiefly in damp places, was believed to preserve the health of swine and oxen, when it had been bruised and put in their water-troughs. But it was required to be gathered fasting, and with the left hand, without looking back when it was being plucked. A kind of hedge-hyssop called Selago was esteemed to be a gene-

ral charm and preservation from sudden accidents and misfor-
tunes; and it was to be gathered with nearly the same ceremonies as the mistletoe. To these might be added Vervain,
the herb Britannica, which was either the great water-dock or
scurvy-grass, and several other plants; the virtues of which,
however, were greatly augmented by the rites in plucking them,
—superstitions not entirely out of use whilst the old herbals
were regarded as books of medicine.

ROUNCIVAL PEAS.

"Rouncival" was an old word for large and strong; derived
from the gigantic bones of the old heroes pretended to be shown
at Roncesvalles. Hence the word became a common epithet
for any thing large or strong, as Rouncival Peas, the large sort,
now called marrow-fats. Kersey, in his *Dictionary*, 1715, has:
"Rouncevals, a kind of large and sweet pease."

SKIRRET.

Skirret, Skerret, or Skirwort, is the Water-Parsnep, a root
formerly used in salads, and other dishes; and supposed to have
the same qualities which were attributed to potatoes, which,
Gerard says, were "by some called Skyrrits of Peru." Drayton
has

The skirret, which some say in sallads stirs the blood.   *Polyolbion.*

Evelyn describes the Skirret as eaten boiled, stewed, roasted
under the embers, baked in pies, whole, sliced, or in pulp, and
very acceptable to all palates. Skirret was served with melted
butter and sack, and its pulp was fried in fritters.

RIPENING SEEDS.

Cobbett and other writers on horticulture have ridiculed the
practice of gardeners carrying some seeds—melon, for instance
—in their pockets for a considerable time to improve them.
There may, however, be some truth in this notion; for it has
been suggested by an eminent botanist, that the seeds thus
carried probably became more fruitful after having been kept
some time, for the same reason that plants are more likely to
come to full flower after a lengthened season of rest.—*Proceedings of the British Association,* 1857.

THE SNAP-DRAGON.

The Snap-dragon is much cultivated in gardens for its
showy flowers, and is often found on old walls (especially in
the neighbourhood of London). Vogel observes, that the com-

mon people in many countries attribute some supernatural influence to this plant, believing it to have the power of destroying charms, and rendering maledictions of none effect.

FLEABANE.

Does any one remember a hardy herbaceous plant, of no mean beauty, once called *Chrysanthemum coccineum*, and afterwards *Pyrethrum carneum?*—a bright-green tufted thing, with rose-coloured flower-heads as large as a half-crown, and leaves not unlike camomile, for which reason it is called on the Continent *Camomille rouge.* This is one of certain plants which are reputed to *drive away fleas.* One of our common roadside plants is called Fleabane (*Inula pulicaria*), which, says Dodoens, an old Flemish herbalist, "laid, strowed, or burned in any place, driveth away all venomous beasts, and killeth knats and fleas." We are also assured by a certain Professor Cantraine that the common ox-eye daisy (*Chrysanthemum leucanthemum*), which whitens the meadows of slovenly farmers in early autumn, is used in Bosnia and Dalmatia as a specific against such unpleasant visitors. Professor Morren confirmed the fact of the ox-eye daisy being *pulicifugous, i. e.* repellent of fleas, by his own personal experience at Liège. But it seems that Caucasian, Persian, and Koordish fleas have a still worse enemy in the beautiful red pyrethrum, of the flower-heads of which is made the Persian flea-powder, which "not only causes the death of all sorts of disagreeable or injurious insects, but when distilled yields a spirit, of which a small quantity mixed with water may be used with the greatest success in the open air or in greenhouses against green-fly, house-flies, &c., without doing the least injury to plants." A powder of pyrethrum is very largely used as a Fleabane among the nations of Western Asia. It begins to flower in June, and lasts for more than a month. In dry weather the flower-heads are hand-plucked. They should be dried in the shade three or four days. Five-and-thirty tons of this flea-powder are manufactured annually for Russian use in Transcaucasia alone. More than twenty villages in the district of Alexandropol are occupied with the cultivation of the red camomile, whose powder will preserve them from fleas, will kill flies, gnats, &c. When winged creatures are to be dealt with, the powder is to be mixed with any substance which they like, such as sugar when house-flies are to be killed. Of this powder, it is believed, there is a specimen in the museum at Kew, sent to this country from Erzeroum by Mr. H. Calvert, with the following memorandum: "Piré-oti (which means Fleawort) is exported from Koordistan to various parts of Turkey for the destruction of fleas, which it certainly accomplishes most effectually. It suffices to strew some of the powder inside a bed or over a sofa or carpet, to kill or drive the intruders away. The English and French officers made an excellent use of this drug in the Turkish barracks."—Abridged from the *Gardeners' Chronicle.*

TO LAY IN LAVENDER.

The plant Lavender was formerly considered as an emblem of affection. Drayton, in one of his eclogues, sings :

> Some of such flow'rs as to his hand doth pass,
> Others such as a secret moaning bear ;
> He for his lass him lavender hath sent,
> Showing his love, and doth requital crave :
> Him rosemary his sweetheart, whose intent
> Is that he should her in remembrance have.

To *Lay in Lavender* was also a current phrase for to pawn ; because things pawned are carefully laid by, like clothes which, to keep them sweet, have lavender scattered among them. Ben Jonson, in *Every Man out of his Humour*, refers to a black satin suit, which, "for the more sweet'ning, now lies in lavender." Hence, in an old drama, translated by Cotgrave :

> A broker is a city pestilence ;
> A moth that eats up gowns, doublets, and hose.
> * * * * * * *
> And upon them
> Strews lavender so strongly, that the owners
> Dare never smell them after.

It is also a phrase generally for any thing nicely laid by for use : "He takes on against the pope without mercy, and has a jest still in lavender for Bellarmine" (Earle's *Microcosm*).

Sometimes it was used for laying by in any way, *even in prison.*

ASTROPHELL.

Astrophell, or Astrofel, was a bitter herb, probably what the old botanists called Star-wort. It occurs in Spenser ; a contemporary of whom, the celebrated Sir Philip Sidney, under the name of Astrophell, transforms a pair of lovers

> Into one flowre that is both red and blew :
> It first grows red, and then to blow doth fade,
> Like astrophel, which thereunto was made ;
> And in the midst thereof a star appeares,
> As fairly formed as any star in skyes.

THE BACHELOR'S BUTTON

is the flower of the Campion, or *lychnis sylvestris*, and was supposed by country-people formerly to have some magical effect upon the fortunes of lovers, who practised with them a sort of divination, to try whether they should marry their mis-

tresses or not. It seems to have grown into a phrase for being
unmarried—"to wear bachelors' buttons ;" and they are also
described as having sometimes been worn by the young women.

The form of the flower perpetuates a fashion of a long-
past age ; for Gerard tells us :

Now the similitude that these flurs have to the jagged cloth-buttons
antiently worn in this kingdom, gave occasion to our gentlewomen,
and other lovers of floures in these times, to call them bachelors' buttons.

ELECAMPANE.

Elecampane has been esteemed for ages in the domestic
herbal. The leaves are aromatic and bitter, but the root is
much more so. The former were used by the Romans as pot-
herbs; and appear to have been held in no mean repute in
after times, from the monkish line, "Elena campana reddit
præcordia sana." When preserved, it is still eaten as a cordial
by eastern nations; and the root is used in England to flavour
the confectionery in small sugar-cakes which bear its name.
It is tonic and stimulating.

SAFFRON AND SAGE.

These two plants, in their history and economy, present
some points of curious interest.

Saffron consists of the dried stigmas of the *Crocus sativus*,
a native of Asia Minor; and formerly so extensively cultivated
in Essex, as to give to one of its ancient towns, in the neighbourhood of which it was grown, the epithet of *Saffron* (*Walden*).
Hakluyt was told at Saffron Walden, that a pilgrim brought
from the Levant to England, in the reign of Edward III., the
first root of Saffron, which he had found means to conceal
in his staff, made hollow for that purpose : "and so," says Hakluyt, "he brought this root into this realm with venture of his
life ; for if he had been taken, by the law of the country from
whence it came, he had died for the fact."

The culture of Saffron at Saffron Walden has long been
abandoned : it must have been costly, for we find the Corporation of Saffron Walden paying five guineas for a pound of
Saffron, to present to Queen Elizabeth upon her visit to the
town. Nearly 40,000 flowers are required to yield one pound
of Saffron : the old statement that 203,920 flowers are requisite
is a gross exaggeration.

Saffron Hill, in the parish of St. Andrew's, Holborn, was
formerly a part of the gardens of Ely House, and derives its
name from the crops of Saffron which it once bore.

Beckmann has a curious chapter upon the ancient history

of Saffron, and its medicinal use among the Orientals: the Europeans, who adopted the pharmacy of the Greeks, sent to the Levant for Saffron until they learnt to rear it themselves; and in Hertodt's *Crocologia*, Jena, 1670, may be found the several uses of Saffron, even to the simplest form of preparing it. The ancients employed it strangely as a perfume, strewing their halls, theatres, and courts with it, and preparing with it scented salves.

The medicinal properties of Saffron are chiefly due to its volatile oil: the *Hay Saffron* is now only in demand, the *Cake Saffron* being an artificial compound of the florets of the saffron-flower, made up with gum, &c. and pressed into layers. Saffron formerly enjoyed high repute, both as a perfume, and as a nervine, stomachic, and narcotic drug. Its odour may affect some very susceptible individuals; and we have known saffron to be worn in silken bags to prevent infection. It is still a popular remedy for eruptive diseases, as measles,—a remnant of the old doctrine of colours; and to the same notion is to be referred the giving Saffron to canary-birds when moulting, a practice reprobated by Bechstein, who judiciously recommends iron to be put in the water at such times. On the Continent Saffron is used as a condiment for food; in England it is employed to colour cheese and confectionery, and as a dye.

The colour appears to have been forbidden at one time by law; for in 1446, a parliament, held at Trim, forbade the Irish to wear shirts stained with saffron, which they seem hitherto to have worn without any change till they dropped off their backs. Saffron was much used in the yellow starch so fashionable in England in the seventeenth century.

Saffron was used to colour the Warden-Pear Pies, mentioned by Shakspeare:

I must have saffron, to colour the warden-pies.

Henry says: "Saffron must be put into all Lent soups, sauces, and dishes: without Saffron we cannot have well-cooked *peas.*" In John Tradescant's catalogue of his garden at South Lambeth, we find "meadow saffrons from Constantinople."

Sage, Salvia (perhaps from *salvus,* healthy), is much used in cookery, and is supposed to assist the stomach in digesting fat and luscious foods. Sage-tea is also a stomachic and slight stimulant. The Chinese are said to prefer the infusion of Sage-leaves to that of their own tea; and the Dutch once carried on a profitable trade by carrying sage-leaves to China, and bringing back four times the weight of tea-leaves. Clary is a kind of Sage: it is used for making wine, which resembles Frontignac, and is remarkable for its narcotic qualities.

Sage has lost much of its medicinal reputation since the age when the school of Salernum thought so highly of it as to leave this dictum of old Saracenic pharmacy:

Cur moriatur homo cum Salvia crescit in horto?
(Why should man die when Sage flourishes in the garden?)

The practice of mixing Sage and other herbs, and the flowers or seeds of other plants, with cheese, was common among the Romans; and this led to the herbs, &c. being worked into heraldic devices in the middle ages. Charlemagne once ate cheese mixed with parsley-seeds at a bishop's palace, and liked it so much, that ever after he had two cases of such cheese sent yearly to Aix-la-Chapelle.

Our pastoral poet of the last century has noted this device:

Marbled with sage, the hardened cheese she press'd.　　*Gay.*

USES OF GINGER.

The medicinal properties of this very useful plant are much neglected. It is an aromatic stimulant of considerable power, and its action on the mucous membranes is great. When chewed, it relieves toothache, rheumatism of the jaw, and relaxed uvula. When received into the stomach, it promotes digestion in languid habits, and relieves flatulent colic. Gouty subjects are much benefited by Ginger, and it formed the basis of the once-celebrated Portland Powder. For such persons *preserved ginger,* taken at dessert, after a mixture of viands, is most beneficial; the finest being that in small, round, tender pieces, sent from the West Indies. Ginger-tea is an excellent stimulant for languid habits. Some headaches are relieved by applying to the forehead a poultice of scraped ginger and warm water. Ginger-beer often disagrees with persons owing to the sugar; for if made without it, it agrees with such persons well. Ginger, it should be remembered, however, loses much of its efficacy with age, so that old pieces are worthless.

CHAMOMILE.

Chamomile-flowers, from cultivated plants, yield an excellent bitter and tonic agent. They should be infused with cold water, as heat dissipates their oil. When made tepid, the infusion may be given beneficially in dyspepsia, and at the commencement of influenza and hooping-cough. The infusion, either warm or cold, furnishes an excellent application to weak eyes, or after exposure to the wind in travelling, especially by railway: this, used early, will often ward off inflammation.

M. Ozanam has also lately discovered that Chamomile infusion will prevent suppuration when the local disease is not too far advanced, and will gradually stop it when it has existed for a long time.

FRUITS INTRODUCED INTO ENGLAND.

That sound antiquary, the late Mr. Hudson Turner, has left the following very interesting information in his *Manners and Household Expenses in England in the Thirteenth and Fifteenth Centuries, from Original Records.* The only fruits named in records of the thirteenth century are apples and pears. Three hundred of the latter were purchased at Canterbury, probably from the gardens of the monks. And it is believed that few other sorts were generally grown in England before the latter end of the fifteenth century; though Matthew Paris, describing the bad season of 1257, observes that "apples were scarce, and pears scarcer, while quinces, vegetables, cherries, plums, and all shell-fruits, were entirely destroyed." These shell-fruits were probably the common hazel-nut, walnuts, and perhaps chestnuts. In 1256, the sheriffs of London were ordered to buy two thousand chestnuts for the king's use. In the Wardrobe Book of the 14th of Edward the First, before quoted, we find the bill of Nicholas, the royal fruiterer, in which the only fruits mentioned are pears, apples, quinces, medlars, and nuts. The supply of these from Whitsuntide to November cost 21*l.* 14*s.* 1½*d.* This apparent scarcity of indigenous fruits naturally leads to the inquiry, What foreign kinds besides those included in the term spicery—such as almonds, dates, figs, and raisins—were imported into England in this and the following century? In the time of John and of Henry the Third, Rochelle was celebrated for its pears and conger-eels. The sheriffs of London purchased a hundred of the former for Henry in 1223. In the 18th of Edward the First, a large Spanish ship came to Portsmouth; out of the cargo of which the queen bought one frail of Seville figs, one frail of raisins or grapes, one bale of dates, and two hundred and thirty pomegranates, fifteen citrons, and seven *oranges.* The last item is important, as Le Grand d'Aussy could not trace the orange in France to an earlier date than 1333. Here we find it known in England in 1290; and it is probable that this was not its first appearance. Thus, it appears certain that Europe is indebted to the Arab conquerors of Spain for the introduction of the orange, and not to the Portuguese, who are said to have brought it from China. An English dessert in the thirteenth century must, it is clear, have been composed chiefly of dried and preserved fruits,—dates, figs, apples, pears, nuts, and the still common dish of almonds and raisins.

HISTORIC PLUMS.

The Plum-tree is a native of, or naturalised in, Britain, and has been frequently found in our hedges; but its original country is supposed to be Asia, and according to Pliny it was brought

from Syria into Greece, and thence into Italy. Among the 200
or 300 varieties, some few are of historic origin. Thus the blue
Perdrigon has been for a long time in our gardens: Hakluyt,
in 1582, says: "Of late time, the plum called the *Perdigevena*
was procured out of Italy, with two kinds more, by the Lord
Cromwell after his travel." The Violet is an old plum, and was
cultivated by John Tradescant, gardener to Charles I.   The
Greengage was sent from France by the Earl of Stair to the
second Duke of Rutland, by the name of Green Spanich.   The
name of Greengage is said to have originated from accident :
the Gage family, in the last century, procured from the monks
of the Chartreuse, at Paris, a collection of fruit-trees : when
they arrived in England, the ticket of the Reine Claude had
been rubbed off in the passage ; the gardener, being from this
circumstance ignorant of the name, called it, when it bore fruit,
Greengage. The Fotheringham plum was cultivated by Sir William Temple, at Sheen, near Richmond, before the year 1700,
whence it was called the Sheen plum. The red Magnum Bonum
and the Jaune Hâtive are as old as the time of John Tradescant.
The Wentworth plum is said to have been first planted in the
gardens of Thomas Wentworth, Earl of Strafford, at Twicken-
ham.

CHERRIES IN ENGLAND.

Cherries were first planted in Britain one hundred years
before Christ ; and afterwards brought from Flanders, and
planted in Kent with such success, that an orchard of thirty-
two acres produced, in the year 1540, one thousand pounds !
Sir Hugh Platt, in his *Garden of Eden*, relates an anecdote of a
cherry-tree at Beddington, in Surrey ; "a conceit of that delicate knight Sir Francis Carew, who, for the better accomplish-
ment of his royal entertainment of our late Queen Elizabeth of
happy memory at his house at Beddington, led her Majesty to
a *cherry-tree*, whose fruit he had of purpose kept back from
ripening at the least one month after all cherries had taken
their farewell of England. This secret he performed by so
raising a tent or cover of canvas over the whole tree, and
wetting the same now and then with a scoop or horn, as the
heat of the weather required ; and so, by withholding the sun-
beams from reflecting upon the berries, they grew both great
and were very long before they had gotten their perfect cherry-
colour : and when he was assured of her Majesty's coming, he
removed the tent, and a few sunny days brought them to their
full maturity." At that time, as appears from Aubrey, there
was a summer-house in the grounds, at the top of which was
painted the "Spanish Invasion."

Cherries were cried about the streets of London, and sold, tied upon sticks, as at the present day, two centuries and a half since:

> Cherry ripe, ripe, ripe, I cry,
> Full and fair ones; come and buy.   *Herrick.*

Peacham, author of the *Complete Gentleman*, published in the reign of James I., who was reduced to poverty in his old age, and chiefly subsisted by writing little penny books for children, says: "July I would have drawn in a jacket of light yellow, eating *cherries*, with his face and bosom sunburnt."

The famous cherry-orchard just mentioned was planted at Teynham, near Faversham; from which orchard much of Kent was afterwards supplied. "No English fruit is dearer than cherries at first, cheaper at last, pleasanter at all times; nor is it less wholesome than delicious. And it is much that, of so many feeding so freely on them, so few are found to surfeit."

According to Busino, Venetian ambassador in the reign of James I., it was a favourite amusement in the Kentish gardens to try who could eat most cherries. In this way, one young woman managed to eat 20lbs. of cherries, beating her opponent by 2¼lbs.: a severe illness was the result. Busino finds fault with the English cherries, which are, however, praised by Fynes Morison. Kent still maintains its superiority in the number and flavour of its cherries: the chief orchards are in the parishes on the borders of the Thames, the Darent, and the Medway; and delightful is the scene in early spring, when

> Sweet is the air with the budding haws; and the valley stretching
>   for miles below
> Is white with blooming cherry-trees, as if just covered with lightest
>   snow.

OLDEN APPLES.

The *Apple-John*, or *John-Apple*, Kersey tells us, is a good-flavoured apple, which will keep two years. It will, consequently, become very withered:

> I am withered like an old apple-john.
>   Shakspeare, 2 *Henry IV.* act iii. sc. 3.

This apple is well described by Phillips as

> John-apple, whose wither'd rind, entrench'd
> By many a furrow, aptly represents
> Decrepit age.   *Cider,* b. i.

The *Renate* apple is said to have been introduced in the reign of Henry VIII., by his fruiterer, Richard Harrys, who also planted, "by his great coste and rare industrie, the sweet cherry and the temperate pipyn." Drayton sings, in his *Poly-olbion:*

> The renat: which though first it from the pippin came,
> Growne through his pureness nice, assumes that curious name,
> Upon the pippin stock the pippin being set.

The *Russeting*, or *Russet*, is thus mentioned by Drayton :

> Nor pippin, which we hold of kernell fruits the king,—
> The apple-orendge ; then the savoury russeting.

This apple was named from the russet colour of the shepherds'
holiday clothes, a sort of dingy brown.

The *Pearmain* is likewise mentioned by Drayton as

> The Pearmaine, which to France long ere to us was knowne,
> Which careful fruit'rors now have denizend our owne.

Aubrey notes: "The chronicle tells us, that in the reign of
Henry VIII. pear-mains were so great a rarity, that a baskett-
full of them was a present to the great Cardinall Wolsey." In
the previous reign (Henry VII.), as we learn from a manuscript
roll of that king's expenses, apples were from 1s. to 2s. each.

An Apple has not only caused the fall of the goodliest man,
Adam, but the death of one of the oldest of men since born.
Poor Robin, in his Almanac, 1694, says: "Venus is in a trine
with Sol, therefore it will be very dangerous to eat roasted
apples; because old Thomas Parr, the Salopian wonder (who
lived till he was an hundred and two-and-fifty years old), eat a
roasted apple, and died presently after it."

WHEN WERE ORANGES FIRST BROUGHT INTO ENGLAND?

The introduction of Orange-trees has been assigned to about
the year 1595, by Gibson, in his additions to Camden's *Britannia*, who states, that the Orange-trees at Beddington in Surrey,
brought from Italy by Sir Francis Carew, were the first that ever
reached England; and that when he (Gibson) wrote, 1695, the
trees had been growing at Beddington for more than a hundred years. Gibson, however, received this information from
Aubrey, who began his collections for his *Natural History of
Surrey* twenty years earlier, so that the introduction of Orange-
trees has been referred to the year 1575; and though Sir Francis Carew was, at the time of his death in 1611, of the age of
eighty-one, there seems good reason to doubt whether some one
had not been beforehand with him in bringing the Orange-tree
into England. According to a family tradition, Carew raised
three trees from oranges given him by Sir Walter Raleigh, who
first imported them, and whose wife was niece to Sir Francis. No
part of this story is, however, entitled to credit; and Raleigh
can certainly have had nothing to do with the introduction of
Orange-trees, as is proved by a letter written when Raleigh was
only nine years old, stating that the writer, Sir William Cecil,
had already "an orrange-tree."

Oranges were, however, known in England many years before either of the preceding dates. They are mentioned in the Privy-Purse expenses of Elizabeth of York, under the year 1502; and in Henry the Eighth's Privy-Purse expenses, about the year 1530, there is frequent entry made of a reward being given to James Hobart (probably a gardener), "for bringing of *oranges*, dates, and other pleasurs to the king's grace."

A curious use appears to have been made of the Orange soon after its first introduction. Cavendish describes Cardinal Wolsey entering a crowded chamber, "holding in his hand a very fair Orange, whereof the meat or substance within was taken out, and filled up again with the part of a sponge, wherein was vinegar and other confections against the pestilent airs; the which he most commonly smelt unto, passing among the press, or else when he was pestered with many suitors."

In the celebrated portrait, by Sir Antonio More, of Sir Thomas Gresham, he holds in his left hand a small object resembling an orange, but which is called a *pomander*. This sometimes consisted of a dried Seville orange, stuffed with cloves and other spices; and being esteemed a fashionable preservative against infection, it is frequently represented in ancient portraits, either suspended to the girdle or held in the hand. In the eighteenth century, the signification of this object had become so far forgotten, that, instead of pomanders, *bona-fide* oranges were introduced into portraits; a practice which Goldsmith has so happily satirised in his *Vicar of Wakefield*, where seven of the Flamboroughs are drawn with seven oranges, &c. See Burgon's *Life and Times of Sir Thomas Gresham*.

A pomander was sometimes made of silver, and perforated with small holes to let out the scent. Among pieces of plate sold in 1546, we find "a pommander, weying 3 oz. and ½" (Cotes's *History of Reading*). This probably gave rise to a silver inkstand in the shape of an apple.

ILLUSTRIOUS SIMPLERS.[*]

The vegetable drug Mithridate long handed down the name of the king of Pontus, its discoverer; "better known," says Gerard, "by his soveraigne Mithridate, than by his sometime speaking two-and-twenty languages. . . . What should I say," continues the old herbalist, "of those royal personages, Juba, Attalus, Climenus, Achilles, Cyrus, Massynissa, Semyramis, Dioclesian,"—all skilled in "the excellent art of simpling!"

[*] Collectors of Simples, or physical herbs.

Phenomena of Life.

THE BEGINNING OF CREATION.

MATERIALISTS have long entertained the question, Did the first egg proceed from a bird, or the bird from the egg? But the hundred and ninety-nine theories on the sources of life and organisation, and on the origin of animals, whether by ancient or modern philosophers, are all fanciful, wild, and unphilosophical, having no ground to rest upon. Nothing is satisfactory until it is declared and believed that it has been the will of an Omnipotent Being to create,—to form the earth and to give life; and that it was He who appointed the changes to be wrought on the material, and gave the animating principle to produce organisation in correspondence with these changes.—*Sir Charles Bell on the Hand.*

MAN'S PROPER PLACE IN CREATION.

Professor Daubeny, in his eloquent address to the British Association in 1856, observed, with equal force and beauty:

When we reflect within what a narrow area our researches are necessarily circumscribed; when we perceive that we are bounded in space almost to the surface of the planet in which we reside, itself merely a speck in the universe, one of innumerable worlds invisible from the nearest of the fixed stars; when we recollect, too, that we are limited in point of time to a few short years of life and activity,—that our records of the past history of the globe and of its inhabitants are comprised within a minute portion of the latest of the many epochs which the world has gone through; and that, with regard to the future, the most durable monuments we can raise to hand down our names to posterity are liable at any time to be overthrown by an earthquake, and would be obliterated as if they had never been by any of those processes of metamorphic action which geology tells us form a part of the cycle of changes which the globe is destined to undergo,—the more lost in wonder we may be at the vast fecundity of nature, which within so narrow a sphere can crowd together phenomena so various and so imposing, the more sensible shall we become of the small proportion which our highest powers and their happiest results bear, not only to the cause of all causation, but even to other created beings, higher in the scale than ourselves, which we may conceive to exist.

SECRETION OF MILK.

M. Lamperrière has exhibited to the French Academy an instrument constructed by him of India-rubber,—an artificial mouth, as it may be called,—with a view to ascertain and determine the quantity of Milk-Secretion in the female breast. It is made to embrace the nipple closely, and is provided with an apparatus to rarefy or exhaust the air, so as to produce a vacuum. The conclusion at which the inventor arrives, after sixty-seven experiments, is, that the secretion in each breast every two hours is from one and a half to two ounces. He met with one instance in which the quantity amounted to nearly three pounds in twenty-four hours.

IMPORTANCE OF THE LIVER.

Were it possible to say that one organ of digestion was more important than another, where all are essential, that organ would be the Liver. It is the largest organ in the body; it is the common portal of admission for all the more compound articles of food in their conversion into blood; it is a main agent in producing that conversion. Its importance is best shown by the evils which attend its derangements. If it does not clear the blood sufficiently of bile, a man is bilious—which is synonymous with being moody, moped, and miserable. If it makes too much sugar, a dangerous complaint results. If it makes too much oil for the amount of exercise taken, a man becomes too fat. On the other hand, if it cannot make sugar and oil enough, the person becomes thinner and thinner, and we then seek to spare his enfeebled liver by giving him a liver oil ready made, and perhaps more of sugar than he was accustomed to take. This stimulates his liver to make a fresh start in the manufacture of sugar and oil, to such an extent, that not unfrequently the taking of one pound of cod-liver oil occasions an increase of weight of six or seven pounds. When the liver strikes work, as it often does in the inveterate gin-drinker, the blood on the one hand is starved, because the liver does not let in nor prepare the most nutritious portion of the food, and on the other hand is poisoned, because the liver does not let out the impurities which ought to be removed as bile. Hence the unfortunate sufferer from confirmed disease of the liver is both bile-poisoned and emaciated.—*Dr. Radclyffe Hall.*

HOW HARVEY DISCOVERED THE CIRCULATION OF THE BLOOD.

William Harvey, after studying at Cambridge, went to Padua, where the fame of Fabricius attracted medical students from all parts of Europe.

There, excited by the discovery of the valves of the veins, which his master had recently made, and reflecting on the direction of the valves.

which are at the extremes of the veins, into the heart, and at the exit of the arteries from it, he conceived the idea of making experiments in order to determine what is the course of the blood in its vessels. He found that when he tied up veins in various animals, they swelled below the ligature, or in the parts furthest from the heart ; while arteries, with a light ligature, swelled on the side next the heart. Combining these facts with the direction of the valves, he came to the conclusion that the blood is impelled by the left side of the heart in the arteries to the extremities, and thence returns by the veins into the right side of the heart. He showed, too, how this was confirmed by the phenomena of the pulse, and by the results of opening the vessels. He proved also that the circulation of the lungs is a continuation of the larger circulation ; and thus the whole doctrine of the double circulation was established.—Whewell's *History of Inductive Sciences*, vol. iii.

Harvey made his experiments in 1616 and 1618 ; and first announced his discovery to the College of Physicians in the former year. He was always supported by the Fellows of the Royal Society ; but his practice as a physician fell through his discovery, and the medical profession stigmatised him as a fool. Nevertheless he lived to see his own doctrine established.

INSENSIBILITY OF THE HEART.

Harvey relates : A noble youth of the family of Montgomery, from a fall, and consequent abscess on the side of the chest, had the interior marvellously exposed ; so that after his cure, on his return from his travels, the heart and lungs were visible, and could be handled ; which, when it was communicated to Charles I., he expressed a desire that Harvey should be permitted to see the youth, and examine his heart. "When," says Harvey, "I had paid my respects to this young nobleman, and conveyed to him the king's request, he made no concealment, but exposed the left side of his breast ; when I saw a cavity in which I could introduce my finger and thumb. Astonished with the novelty, again and again I explored the wound ; and, first marvelling at the extraordinary nature of the cure, I set about the examination of the heart. Taking it in one hand, and placing the finger of the other on the pulse of the wrist, I satisfied myself that it was indeed the heart which I grasped. I then brought him to the king, that he might behold and touch so extraordinary a thing ; and that he might perceive, as I did, that unless when we touched the outer skin, or when he saw our fingers in the cavity, this young nobleman knew not that we touched the heart."

Other observations confirm this great authority, and the heart is declared insensible. Not only, however, does every emotion of the mind affect the heart, but every change in the condition of the body ; motion during health, the influence of disease,—is attended with a response in the action of the heart.

THE HUMAN HEART.

That wonderful machine, the Heart, goes, night and day, for eighty years together, at the rate of 100,000 strokes for every twenty-four hours, having at every stroke a great resistance to overcome. Now each ventricle will contain at least one ounce of blood; the heart contracts 4000 times in an hour, from which it follows that there pass through the heart every hour 4000 ounces, or 350 pounds of blood. The whole mass of blood is said to be about twenty-five pounds; so that a quantity equal to the whole mass of blood passes through the heart fourteen times in one hour, which is about once in every four minutes.

PROPORTION IN THE BIRTHS OF THE SEXES.

It has always been suspected that, on an average, the male and female births are tolerably equal; but, until very recently, no one could tell whether or not they are precisely equal, or if unequal, on which there is an excess. Goodman, early in the seventeenth century, supposed that more females were born than males. Turgot rightly says, there are rather more men than women born; but the evidence is too incomplete to make this more than a lucky guess: and Herder, writing in 1785, takes for granted that the proportion was about equal.

Yet this is a question to which all the resources of physiologists, from Aristotle down to our own time, afford no means of reply. But at the present day we, by the employment of what now seems a very natural method, are possessed of a truth which the united abilities of a long series of eminent men have failed to discover. By the simple expedient of registering the number of births and their sexes; by extending this registration over several years, in different countries,—we have been able to eliminate all casual disturbances, and ascertain the existence of a law which, expressed in round numbers, is, that *for every twenty girls there are born twenty-one boys:* and we may confidently say, that although the operations of this law are of course liable to constant aberrations, the law itself is so powerful, that we know of no country in which, during a single year, the male births have not been greater than the female ones.—Buckle's *History of Civilisation in England,* vol. i.

CHANGES IN THE BODY DURING LIFE.

Is it not surprising, that an individual, who retains every peculiarity of body and of mind, whose features, whose gait and mode of action, whose voice, gestures, and complexion, we are ready to attest as the very proof of personality,—should, in the course 'of a few days, change every particle of his solid fabric; that he, whom we suppose we saw, is, so far as his body is concerned, a perfectly different person from him whom we now see? That the fluids may change, we are ready to allow; but that the solids should be thus ever shifting, seems at first improbable. And yet, if there be any thing truly established in physiology,—if there be truth in the science at all,—that fact is incontrovertible.

In these revolutions of the living animal substance, the material is alternately arranged, decomposed, and rearranged. The end of this is, that the machinery of the body is ever new, that it possesses a property within itself of mending that which is broken, of throwing off that which was useless, of building up that which was insecure and weak, of repelling disease, or of controlling it, and of substituting that which is healthful for that which is morbid.

This property of the living body to restore itself when deranged, or to heal itself when broken or torn, is an action which so frequently assumes the appearance of reason, as if it were adapting itself to the particular occasion, that Mr. John Hunter speaks of parts of the body as "conscious of their imperfection," and "acting from the stimulus of necessity;" thus giving the properties of mind to the body as the only explanation of phenomena so wonderful.—*Sir Charles Bell on the Hand.*

HEAT OF THE HUMAN BODY.

The temperature of the Human Body is always a fixed one; and if we place a thermometer upon the tongue, or under the arm, or in any other unexposed part of the body, we shall find that it stands at the point in the index of Fahrenheit's thermometer marked 98°. This heat the human body maintains equally at the poles and under the tropics. No external temperature alters it, and we have thus conclusive evidence that it is produced from within. The cause of this heat is the combustion of the carbon and hydrogen contained in the carbonaceous group of foods. Starch, sugar, and oil, are conveyed from the stomach into the blood; and whilst in the blood they are brought in contact with oxygen gas, which is taken in during respiration; and the consequence of this contact is the union of the carbon and hydrogen with the oxygen, the foundation of carbonic-acid gas and water, and the giving out of heat.

Man inspires annually about seven hundredweight of oxygen, and about one-fifth of this burns some constituent, and produces heat. The whole carbon in the blood would, then, be burned away in about three days unless new fuel were introduced as food. The amount of food necessarily depends upon the number of respirations, the rapidity of the pulsations, and the relative capacity of the lungs. Cold increases the number of respirations, and heat diminishes them; hence the voracity of residents in the Arctic regions.

INFLUENCE OF SUGGESTION ON MUSCULAR MOVEMENT, INDEPENDENTLY OF VOLITION.

Numerous phenomena perplex many who are convinced of their genuineness, but cannot see any mode of reconciling them with the known laws of nervous action. For example, the movements of the Divining Rod, and the vibration of bodies suspended from the finger, have been clearly proved to depend on the state of expectant attention on the part of the performer; his will being temporarily withdrawn from control over his muscles by the state of abstraction to which his mind is given up, and the anticipation of a given result being the stimulus which directly and involuntarily prompts the muscular movements that produce it.—*Dr. Carpenter.*

HOW DOES THE FUNCTION OF MEMORY TAKE PLACE?

Berzelius, in his treatise on Animal Chemistry, asks this striking question:

Those registers of objects and occurrences which are formed in the course of a man's life; those dark but still sufficiently distinct tablets, the results of recitals or of reading; those numberless words of many languages understood by the same individual; the systems of facts which belong to the entire circuit of many sciences, and are preserved in a single human brain always ready for use, prepared to exhibit themselves intuitively to the individual,—where do they all lie in this narrow space, in this convulsive mass? What part has the matter (the water, the albumen, and the cerebral fat) in that sublime activity, which nevertheless does not exist without it, and which through its least derangement is altered or entirely lost?

WHAT IS THE NERVOUS FLUID?

Professor Faraday replies: "Though I am not yet convinced by facts that the nervous fluid is only electricity, still I think that the agent in the nervous system may be an inorganic force; and if there be reason for supposing that magnetism is a higher relation of force than electricity, so it may well be imagined that the nervous power may be of a still more exalted character, and yet within the reach of experiment."

RAPIDITY OF THOUGHT, OR NERVOUS ACTION.

The method of transforming the valuation of time into space by the rapid revolution of a cylinder, proposed by Mr. Fizeau, has been applied to the measurement of the rapidity of nervous impulse. Such a cylinder rotating 1000 times a second, and divided into 360 degrees, may measure 1-360,000th part of a second ; or, rotating 1500 times a second, 1-540,000th part of a second; and even this may be subdivided by a microscope, so as to obtain the ten-millionth, or perhaps 100-millionth part of a second. By this extreme minuteness of subdivision of time, it is not difficult to measure even the rapidity of a nervous impulse. If an electric shock be given to the arm, it produces a sensation and a contraction of the muscles. Hence, by noting the interval of time between the shock and the contraction, the time occupied by the transmission of the sensation and the action of the brain, however quick, will be determined. By trying the experiment with different parts of the body, sensible differences have been observed, the shock applied to the thumb being one-thirtieth of a second behind that applied to the face ; and this difference pertains to the transmission, and not to the action, of the brain, and hence enables us to eliminate the latter in the experiments.

In this way, it has been found by M. Helmholtz, by whom these experiments have been made with the most care,—1. That sensations are transmitted to the brain with a rapidity of about 180 *feet per second*, or at one-fifth the rate of sound; and this is nearly the same in all individuals. 2. The brain requires *one-tenth of a second* to transmit its orders to the nerves which preside over voluntary motion ; but this amount varies much in different individuals, and in the same individual at different times, according to the disposition or the condition at the time, and is more regular the more sustained the attention. 3. The time required to transmit an order to the muscles by the motor nerves is nearly the same as that required by the nerves of sensation to pass a sensation ; moreover, it passes nearly one-hundredth of a second before the muscles are put in motion. 4. The whole operation requires one and a quarter to two-tenths of a second. Consequently, when we speak of an active, ardent mind, or of one that is slow, cold, or apathetic, it is not a mere figure of rhetoric.—M. Ule, *Revue Suisse.*

THE " MEDULLA OBLONGATA."

Dr. Herbert Mayo, in his *Truths contained in Popular Superstitions,* thus felicitously illustrates the poetic prevoyance of one of the greatest physiological discoveries of our time.

At a point situated between the organs of the understanding and those of the will,—that is to say, somewhere at the junction of the spinal marrow and the brain,—Magendie has ascertained that there is a small portion of nervous matter, pressure upon which causes immediately heavy sleep or stupor, while its destruction,—*for instance, the laceration of the little organ with the point of a needle,*—instantaneously and irrevocably extinguishes life. This precious link in our system is beneficently stowed away in the securest part of our frame, that is to say, within the head, upon the strong central bone of the base of the skull. The fancy of Shakspeare, in the happy figure which follows, seems to adumbrate Magendie's discovery of to-day in poetry written three hundred years ago :

> Within the hollow crown,
> That rounds the mortal temples of a king,
> Keeps death his court; and there the antic sits,
> Mocking his state, and grinning at his pomp :
> Allowing him a breath, a little hour,
> To monarchise, be feared, and kill with looks ;
> Infusing him with self and vain conceits,
> As if the flesh that walls about our life
> Were brass impregnable. Till, humoured thus,
> He comes at last, and with a little pin
> Bores through his castle-wall—and farewell, king.

PERSISTENCE OF IMPRESSIONS.

There is reason to believe that *no idea which ever existed in the mind can be lost.* It may seem to ourselves to be gone, since we have no power to recall it ; as is the case with the vast majority of our thoughts. But numerous facts show that it needs only some change in our physical or intellectual condition to restore the long-lost impression. A woman servant, for instance, twenty-four years old, who could neither read nor write, in the paroxysm of a fever commenced repeating, fluently and pompously, passages of Latin, Greek, and Hebrew ; and it afterwards appeared that in her early days a learned clergyman with whom she lived had been in the daily habit of walking through a passage in his house, that opened into the kitchen, and repeating aloud the very passages which the servant uttered in her fever.—*D. E. Hitchcock,* Boston, U.S.

PRE-EXISTENCE OF SOULS.

This ancient doctrine has been variously treated by many eminent writers.

That the Deity, at the beginning of the world (when we are taught that He "rested from all His works which He had made"), created the souls of all men,—which, however, are not united to the body till the individuals for which they are destined are born into the world,—was (to omit any reference to Plato and his followers) a very general belief among the Jewish Kabbalists, a common opinion in our Saviour's time, and holden and taught by many fathers of the Christian Church; as Justin

Martyr, Origen, and others. It was, however, opposed by Tertullian.

Mede, in chap. iii. of his *Mystery of Godliness*, combats the vulgar opinion of "a daily creation of souls" at the time the bodies are produced which they are to inform. He calls "the reasonable doctrine" of pre-existence "a key for some of the main mysteries of Providence, which no other can so hand-somely unlock." Sir Harry Vane is said by Burnet to have maintained this doctrine. Joseph Glanvil, Rector of Bath (the friend of Meric Casaubon and of Baxter, and a metaphysician of singular vigour and acuteness), published in 1662, but with-out his name, a treatise to prove the reasonableness of the doctrine.* It was afterwards republished, with annotations, by Dr. Henry More.

In 1762, the Rev. Capel Berrow published *A Pre-existent Lapse of Human Souls demonstrated;* and in the *European Magazine* for September 1801 is a letter from Bishop War-burton to the author, in which he says: "The idea of a pre-existence has been espoused by many learned and ingenious men in every age, as bidding fair to resolve many difficulties."

Southey, in his published Letters, says: "I have a strong and lively faith in a state of continued consciousness from this stage of existence, and that we shall *recover the consciousness of some lower stages through which we may previously have passed* seems to me not improbable." Again: "The system of *progressive existence* seems, of all others, the most benevolent; and all that we do understand is so wise and so good, and all we do, or do not, so perfectly and overwhelmingly wonderful, that the most benevolent system is the most probable." Traces of be-lief in this doctrine also occur in Wordsworth's "Ode on the Intimation of Immortality in Childhood."

An illustration of the belief has been quoted from Dr. Leyden's beautiful "Ode to Scottish Music:"

> Ah, sure, as Hindoo legends tell,
> When music's tones the bosom swell,
> The scenes of former life return,
> Ere, sunk beneath the morning-star,
> We left our parent climes afar,
> Immur'd in mortal forms to mourn.

And in a note to this passage it is stated that the Hindoos ascribe the effect which music sometimes produces on the mind to its recalling undefinable impressions of a former state of existence.

The notion enters more or less into the majority of Oriental

* Among the Baxter Mss. in the Red-cross-street Library, Cripplegate, is a long letter, full of curious learning, from Glanvil to Baxter, in defence of the doctrine of the soul's pre-existence.

creeds and philosophies, and found a believer in·Plato. Indeed,
that "all knowledge is recollection" is a doctrine Platonic,
and probably pre-Platonic into depths of ages unfathomable.
(Abridged from Four Communications to *Notes and Queries*, 2d
Series, No. 49.)

Another Correspondent of *Notes and Queries* asks, in explanation, whether it be not very possible that previously to
this life the human soul has passed through different phases of
existence, and that it is destined to pass through many more
before it arrives at its final rest.

As an historical illustration, he adds : " We are told that
Pythagoras recollected his former self in the respective persons
of a herald named Æthalides, Euphorbus the Trojan, Hermoti-
mus of Clazomenæ, and others ; and that he even pointed out
in the temple of Juno, at Argos, the shield he used when he
attacked Patroclus."

Another Correspondent, in·No. 52, notes, confirmatory of
this opinion, the feeling which many persons have at some
moment experienced, that what they were then seeing or hearing, apparently for the first time, has been seen or heard by
them before, though their reason assures them of the contrary.
We ourselves have frequently experienced this feeling, which
has ever impressed us with the *sameness* of human existence.

Sir E. Bulwer Lytton thus notices this day-dream :

How strange it is that at times a feeling comes over us, as we gaze
upon certain places, which associates the scene either with some dim-
remembered and dream-like images of the Past, or with a prophetic
and fearful omen of the Future ! . . . . Every one has known a similar
strange indistinct feeling at certain times and places, and with a similar
inability to trace the cause.—*Godolphin*, chap. xv.

Elsewhere the same writer describes this feeling of reminis-
cence as " that strange kind of inner and spiritual memory
which often recalls to us places and persons we have never
seen before, and which Platonists would resolve to be the un-
quenched and struggling consciousness of a former life."

Does not Milton, who had imbibed from his college-friend
Henry More an early bias to the study of Plato, hint at the
same opinion in these exquisite lines in *Comus ?*

> The soul grows clotted by contagion,
> Imbodies and imbrutes, till she quite lose
> *The divine property of her first being.*
> Such are those thick and gloomy shadows damp,
> Oft seen in charnel vaults and sepulchres,
> Lingering and sitting by a new-made grave,
> As loth to leave the body that it loved.

Lord Lindsay, in his *Letters*, gives this very interesting experience :

We saw the river Kadisha, like a silver thread, descending from

Lebanon. The whole scene bore that strange and shadowy resemblance to the wondrous landscape delineated in *Kubla Khan* that one so often feels in actual life, when the whole scene around you appears to be re-acting after a long interval ; your friend seated in the same juxtaposi-tion, the subjects of conversation the same, and shifting with the same "dream-like ease," that you remember at some remote and indefinite period of pre-existence ; you always know what will come next, and sit, spell-bound, as it were, in a sort of calm expectancy.

Dr. Wigan, in his able work, *The Duality of the Mind*, has well described this sensation, adding : "all seems to be *remembered*, and to be now attracting attention, for the second time ; never is it supposed to be the *third* time." After observing that the delusion occurs only when the mind has been exhausted by ex-citement, the persuasion of the scene being a repetition comes on when the attention has been *roused* by some accidental cir-cumstance,—Dr. Wigan gives the explanation as follows :

Only one brain has been used in the immediately preceding part of the scene ; the other brain has been asleep, or in an analogous state nearly approaching it. When the attention of both brains is roused to the topic, there is the same vague consciousness that the ideas have passed through the mind before, which takes place on re-perusing the page we had read while thinking on some other subject. The ideas *have* passed through the mind before ; and as there was not a sufficient con-sciousness to fix them in the mind without a renewal, we have no means of knowing the length of time that had elapsed between the *faint* im-pression received by the single brain, and the *distinct* impression by the double brain. It may seem to have been many years.

Dr. Wigan often discussed this matter with his friend Dr. Gooch, who took great interest in subjects occupying the de-batable region between physics and metaphysics ; but neither of the doctors could devise a satisfactory explanation of the above phenomenon.   Dr. Wigan's theory of duality of mind has been much controverted ; but we think there is some probability in the view by Mr. W. L. Nichols, in *Notes and Queries*, Second Series, No. 55, that the cause is "some incon-gruous action of the double structure of the brain, to which perfect unity of action belongs in a healthy state."

William Hone, the author of the *Every-day Book*, has left this remarkable evidence. He relates that, being called to a house in a certain street in a part of London quite new to him, he had noticed to himself, as he walked along, that he had never been there before.

"I was shown," he said, "into a room to wait. On looking round, to my astonishment, every thing appeared perfectly familiar to me : I seemed to *recognise* every object. I said to myself, 'What is this ? I was never here before, and yet I have seen all this : and if so, there is a very peculiar knot in the shutter.'"

He opened the shutter, and found the knot ! Now then, thought he, " Here is something I cannot explain on any principles ; there must be some power beyond matter." The thought never left him; and it happily led him to doubt the truth of the system of materialistic atheism which, for thirty years of his life, he had adopted. "The strong intimation which the incident seemed to convey to his mind of the independence of the soul of the body, gave rise to inquiries which terminated in his becoming a convert to the truth of the Christian religion."

Next to this escape from "the horror of great darkness," the most remarkable fact in this mysterious impression is Hone's proposal as a test to himself of the reality of the impression,—the finding of a certain knot in the wood of the window-shutter,—and that he actually did discover it.*

Sir Walter Scott, a man of sound mind, made the following entry in his diary, under the date February 17, 1828 :

> I cannot, I am sure, tell if it is worth marking down, that yesterday, at dinner-time, I was strongly haunted by what I would call the sense of pre-existence, in a confirmed idea that nothing which passed was said for the first time; that the same topics had been discussed, and the same persons had stated the same opinions on them. . . . . . The sensation was so strong as to resemble what is called a *mirage* in the desert, or a calenture on board of ship. . . . . . It was very distressing yesterday, and brought to my mind the fancies of Bishop Berkeley about an ideal world. There was a vile sense of want of reality in all I did and said.—Lockhart's *Life of Scott.*

Tennyson has the following impressive sonnet upon this strange subject :

> As when with downcast eyes we muse and brood,
> And ebb into a former life, or seem
> To lapse far back in a confused dream
> To states of mystical similitude;
> If one but speaks, or hems, or stirs his chair,
> Ever the wonder waxeth more and more,
> So that we say, All this hath been before,
> All this *hath* been, I know not when or where:
> So, friend, when first I looked upon your face,
> Our thoughts gave answer, each to each, so true,
> Opposèd mirrors, each reflecting each,—
> Although I knew not in what time or place,
> Methought I had often met with you,
> And each had lived in the other's mind and speech.

And he thus explains the mystery :

> Moreover something is, or seems,
> That touches me with mystic gleams,
> *Like glimpses of forgotten dreams—*

---

* We were well acquainted with Mr. Hone, and give implicit credence to the truth of his account of his conviction. He had hitherto been an almost unvarying sceptic: but, like many sceptics, he appears to have believed what most men doubt,—for he asserted that he had seen an apparition.

Of something felt, like something here ;
Of something done, I know not where ;
Such as no language may declare.

Considerable space has been devoted to this inquiry, from our conviction of its great interest and importance : the subject has haunted the author of the present volume from his earliest years of thought.

PHRENOLOGY DEMOLISHED.

When the late Mr. George Combe, the disciple of Gall and Spurzheim, first appeared as the expositor of their system of Phrenology, which pretends to furnish not only a sure index of mental character and endowment, but, theoretically and practically, a system of philosophy and an instrument of education, Sir William Hamilton proceeded to test the worth of the so-called science. He selected several leading physiological points, —such as the relative size and function of the cerebellum, the age at which the brain is fully developed, the presence and value of the frontal sinus,—and found, after a series of experiments, that the dictum of the phrenologist on each point was not only erroneous, but absolutely false. Sir William went through a laborious course of comparative anatomy, made numerous experiments on the living animal, and dissected with his own hand several hundred different brains ; while, in order to ascertain the truth with regard to the frontal sinus, he sawed open a series of skulls, of different nations, both sexes, and all ages. The practical result was, that the points in which Sir William Hamilton had convicted the phrenologists of fundamental error, being reproduced against them by others in this country and on the Continent, weakened the confidence of the public in their statements, and thus helped to arrest the progress of the system, with its spurious science, materialistic philosophy, and demoralising art.—Sir W. Hamilton ; *Transactions of the Royal Society of Edinburgh*, 1826.

DISTANCE AT WHICH BELLS MAY BE HEARD.

It happened once, on board a ship sailing along the coast of Brazil, 100 miles from land, that the persons walking on deck, when passing a particular spot, heard most distinctly the sound of Bells, varying as in human rejoicings. All on board listened, and were convinced. Some months afterwards, it was ascertained that at the time of observation the bells of St. Salvador, on the Brazilian coast, had been ringing on the occasion of a festival. The sound, therefore, favoured by a gentle wind, had travelled over 100 miles of smooth water ; and striking the wide-spread sail of a ship, rendered concave by a gentle

breeze, had been brought to a focus and rendered perceptible.
—*Dr. Arnott.*

SMELL OF NEW-MOWN HAY.

New Hay has a peculiar smell, which is not perceptible
while the grass is growing; because (says Sir E. J. Smith,
the eminent botanist) this smell proceeds from the whole herb-
age, and seems to escape from the orifices of its containing
cells only when the surrounding vessels, by growing less tur-
bid, withdraw their pressure from such orifices. When this
scent of new hay is concentrated, it becomes the flavour of
bitter almonds.

HOW A FRACTURED BONE IS REPAIRED.

This is effected by a beautiful process of splicing, during
which phosphates, first very soluble, then moderately so, then
slightly so, are finally succeeded by dense insoluble bone-earth,
filling up the breach till it becomes the strongest part of the
reunited bone. And as counterpart of this, we have the most
solid bone dissolving under the pressure of a throbbing (aneu-
rismal) blood-vessel, which, unless the bone gave way, would
first torture, and then kill the whole body. Particle by particle the petrified ivory is pressed, softened, melted, dissolved,
and washed away, by the same potent acid which hardened it
from a thin liquid into a compact solid.

WHY THE FINGERS ARE NOT OF EQUAL LENGTH.

A master, in illustration of this question, made his scholar
grasp a ball of ivory, to show him that the points of the fingers
are then equal; it would have been better (says Sir Charles
Bell) had he closed the fingers upon the palm, and then asked
whether or not they corresponded. This difference in the length
of the fingers serves a thousand ends, adapting the form of the
hand and fingers for different purposes,—as for holding a rod,
a switch, a sword, a hammer, a pen or pencil, engraving-tools,
&c.—in all which a secure hold and freedom of motion are admirably combined.

NAMES OF THE FIVE FINGERS.

Our ancestors had distinct names for each of the five fingers,—the thumb being generally called a finger in old works.
The reasons are thus quoted by Mr. Halliwell, in his *Dictionary
of Archaisms,* from an old Ms.: The first finger was called
toucher, because "therewith men touch, I wis;" the second finger *longman,* "for long it is;" the third finger was called *leche-*

man, because a leche or doctor tasted every thing by means of
it. Elsewhere (in Brand's *Popular Antiquities*, vol. i.) the latter name is referred to the pulsation in the third finger, which
was at one time supposed to communicate directly with the
heart. The other finger was, of course, called *little-man*, because it was the least of all. Some of these names are preserved
in a nursery rhyme commencing thus, the fingers being kept
in corresponding movements :

> Dance, thumbkin, dance;
> Dance, ye merry men, every one :
> Thumbkin he can dance alone,
> Thumbkin he can dance alone;

and so on for four more verses, taking each finger in succession, and naming them *foreman, longman, ringman*, and *little-
man*.

POWER OF THE THUMB.

Look at the bones of the paw of the adult Chimpanzee, and
the remarkable peculiarity that distinguishes it from the human
hand is the smallness of the thumb ; it extends no further than
to the root of the fingers. Now it is upon the length, strength,
free lateral motion, and perfect mobility of the thumb, that the
superiority of the human hand depends. The thumb is called
pollex, because of its strength ; and that strength being equal
to that of all the fingers, is necessary to the perfection of the
hand. Without the fleshy ball of the thumb, the power of the
fingers would avail nothing ; and accordingly, the large ball
formed by the muscles of the thumb is the distinguishing character of the human hand, and especially of an expert workman.

The loss of the thumb amounts almost to the loss of the hand; and
were it to happen in both hands, it would reduce a man to a miserable
dependence ; or, as Adonibezek said of the threescore and ten kings,
the thumbs of whose hands and whose feet he had cut off, "they gather
their meat under my table."

Johnson derives "Poltroon" from *pollice truncata*, the thumb cut
off; it being once a practice of cowards to cut off their thumbs, that
they might not be compelled to serve in war.

Albinus characterises the thumb as the lesser hand, the assistant of
the greater.

The "great toe" is more peculiarly characteristic of the genus *Homo*
than even its homotype, the thumb ; for the monkey has a kind of *pollex* on the hand, but no brute mammal presents that development of
the *pollex* (great toe), on which the erect posture and gait of man
mainly depend.—*Owen on Limbs*, p. 37. (Selected and abridged from
Sir *Charles Bell on the Hand.*)

INCREASE OF THE NAILS AND THE HAIR IN MAN.

The following details are recorded in the Journal of the Institute of France, No. 846 :

The *Growth of the Nails* is more rapid in children than in adults, and slowest in the aged. It goes on faster in summer than in winter; so that the same nail which is renewed in 132 days in winter, requires only 116 in summer. The increase of the nails of the right hand is more rapid than those of the left; moreover, it differs for the different fingers, and in order corresponds with the length of the finger; consequently it is fastest in the middle finger, nearly equal in the two on either side of this, slower in the little finger, and slowest in the thumb. The growth of all the nails on the left hand requires 82 days more than those of the right.

The *Growth of the Hair* is well known to be much accelerated by frequent cutting. It grows more rapidly in day than night, in hot seasons than cold; but it is difficult to determine the precise rates. The growth of the hair and nails, as well as the epidermis, pertains to the secretions, and not to the organic structure proper; for the quantity of each formed corresponds very nearly with that of the peripheric secretions, especially with transpiration, increasing in the summer, whilst, on the contrary, the growth and nutrition of the body are most rapid in winter; so that the weight of man, as observed by Sanctorius and others, is greatest in winter. The small growth of the hair during the night accords with the fact of the diminution of all the secretions.

ACTION OF SUGAR ON THE TEETH.

M. Larez, of France, has proved that Sugar, from either cane or beets, is injurious to healthy teeth, either by immediate contact with them, or by the gas developed, owing to its stoppage in the stomach. If a tooth is macerated in a saturated solution of sugar, it becomes gelatinous, and its enamel opaque, spongy, and easily broken. This modification is due, not to free acid, but to a tendency of sugar to combine with the calcareous basis of the teeth.

OVERWORKING THE EYES.

Mr. Dixon, surgeon to the Royal Ophthalmic Hospital, gives as his opinion that *weakness of sight*, as a general thing, is owing to over-use of the eyes, and not to any special employment of them, since every day's experience teaches us that the most trying work for the eyes may be followed, provided due moderation is observed.

Dr. Caplin, of Manchester, observes:

The question whether the eye, or any other of the organs of sense, is capable of improvement in proportion to its use, is a very serious one. A great deal of our conduct in daily life depends on the way we answer it to ourselves. It is probable that the "wearing out," contrasted in the popular saying with "rusting out," is often falsely attributed to the human body, and that perfectly healthy organs are made more efficient by use, provided that such use does not diminish the nutrition of the system; but at the same time local injury is certainly experienced in many parts of the body, especially the eye, by working too long hours. The explanation appears to be this, viz. that after the body has been long employed, sufficient vigour does not remain in each separate organ to enable it to do its duty ; it cannot be called healthy after the general strength is exhausted. Overworking the eyes means working the eyes in an unnatural condition.

In using artificial light, the light should be above the level of the face, so as to allow, as in nature, the brow, the lashes, and the iris, to shelter the pupil, and thereby the expansion of the optic nerve, from the direct rays. Neglect of this precaution is two-fold injurious ; first, the influx of such rays, long continued, tends to exhaust the normal sensibility of the retina; and secondly, by eclipsing the brilliancy of the rays reflected from the object, so that the light must be increased to a degree otherwise superfluous, dazzling, and pernicious.

WEARING SPECTACLES.

There is a common but erroneous notion, that when you have once taken to wear spectacles, you will not be able to dispense with them. A Correspondent of *Notes and Queries* relates that a lady, seventy-eight years of age, recovered her eyesight after a severe fit of illness, before which she had worn "glasses" for thirty years; and could then read without spectacles the smallest print, and thread the smallest needle.

Dr. Caplin observes : Full blue and green glasses, which are often worn by persons having weak eyes, are highly objectionable, being of definite colours, and exciting complementary colours. Neutral-tinted glasses being, as the name implies, of no definite hue, screen the eye from all colours alike, and produce an effect most grateful to irritable eyes.

COLOUR-BLINDNESS.

This term is applied to an inability to distinguish different colours. It includes all varieties and degrees of the affliction. In some cases there is total blindness to colour, the distinction of black and white alone being perceived. More frequently there is inability to discern a single colour, such as red ; or inability to distinguish between two colours, such as red and green. Dr. George Wilson, who has paid much attention to this subject, estimates, from his own inquiries, the percentage of colour-blind persons in the community as high as one in twenty, and strongly-marked cases about one in fifty. Amongst its results, the danger attending the present system of railway and marine coloured signals Dr. Wilson considers very great.

MOON-BLINDNESS.

Sir G. Robinson has related to the British Association several instances of his men, who had slept on deck exposed to the moonbeams, being so blind on landing that they had to be led by the hand. The sailors were also in the habit of waking up the soldiers who attempted to sleep on deck, and warning them that they would be blinded.

REMEDY FOR NEAR-SIGHTEDNESS.

Mr. J. Ball, of New York, has invented, for the cure of imperfect vision, an instrument consisting of a circular cup, attached to an India-rubber ball. The cup is placed over the central portion of the globe of the eye, the eyelids being closed, and the air of the ball is pressed out so as to form a vacuum; the ball is then allowed to expand, thus producing a strong compression on the globe, by which the capillary vessels are speedily filled with blood. The instrument operates precisely on the principle of the ordinary cupping-glass. It is well adapted to that condition of the eye—the great flatness of the globe—which is a frequent cause of imperfect vision, and to chronic weakness of the eye from deficient circulation.

HOW THE EYE JUDGES OF DISTANCES.

The most plausible hypothesis as to the determination of proximity or remoteness of objects from the eye is that suggested by Hermann Meyer, of Zurich, namely, that proximity of an object is determined by divergence of the two optic axes. The reflective stereoscope has demonstrated the correctness of M. Meyer's hypothesis. If, after having placed the two pictures in the stereoscope in such a manner that their centres correspond, and when, consequently, one single image in relief appears, the two designs be drawn simultaneously towards the eyes, the dimensions of the image in relief seem to grow greater. If, however, the two designs be simultaneously removed from the eyes, then the image in relief seems to grow smaller than before. Now it is obvious that the convergence of the two optic axes increases in proportion as the two screens are brought near to the eyes, and decreases in proportion as they are removed.—From the *Art Journal.*

AT WHAT SEASON MAN WEIGHS MOST.

Season has an influence on the weight of man. Thus Mr. Milner weighed the prisoners in Hull gaol for five years, and found that they regularly increased in weight from April to November, and decreased in weight from November to March. The diet was the same all the year round, as was also the temperature.

QUANTITY OF AIR BREATHED BY A MAN DURING THE DAY.

Dr. Edward Smith, in a communication to the Royal Society, from a series of 1200 personal observations, declares the following detailed and average quantities of Air breathed by him at various periods of the day, and under certain defined conditions, so as to permit an approximate estimate to be made of the quantities breathed by various classes of the community, and of the quantities of chemical elements required to combine with the oxygen.

Thus, an unoccupied gentleman probably spends nine hours in the lying posture, eleven in the sitting posture, one in walking at the rate of two miles per hour, and three hours in standing, or walking at the rate of one mile per hour. The quantity of air thus inspired by him daily may be estimated as follows:

9 hours in the lying posture	. . .	243,000 cubic inches.	
11	,,	sitting	,,	. . .	361,780	,,
1	,,	walking	,,	. . .	66,000	,,
3	,,	standing	,,	. . .	144,000	,,

giving a total of 804,780 cubic inches of air breathed daily. An ordinary tradesman may be estimated to pass eight hours and a half in the lying posture, six in the sitting posture, three in walking, and four in standing. He will then breathe a total daily quantity of 958,580 cubic inches. The hard-working labourer will probably breathe 1,368,390 cubic inches of air daily. The three classes thus differ greatly in the quantity of oxygen which they inspire, and therefore in the quantity of food required by them; and if each obtained a suitable quantity of material to unite with the oxygen, the labourer would still have greater wear of system than the unoccupied man.

INFLUENCE OF CLIMATE AND TEMPERATURE ON MAN.

The influence of Climate is most powerfully evinced in the mental and physical degradation produced by malaria on the inhabitants of the moor and marshy districts of tropical regions; but even in Europe its effect on the amount of mortality is much greater than is generally understood. Thus in the smiling plains of Southern Italy the rate of mortality is twice as great as in the cold region of Scandinavia; and this proportion appears to be held in all countries. Temperature alone has a great effect on the production of diseases. It is calculated from the returns of mortality, that a fall of the mean temperature of the air from 45° to 4° or 5° below zero destroys from 300 to 500 of the population of London.—*Keith Johnson*.

WHY DO MEN IN HOT CLIMATES EAT LESS THAN MEN IN COLD ONES ?

Because, when men live in a hot country, their animal heat is more easily kept up than when they live in a cold one; therefore they require a smaller amount of non-azotised food, the sole business of which is to maintain at a certain point the temperature of the body. In the same way, men in the hot country require a smaller amount of azotised food, because, on the whole, their bodily exertions are less frequent, and on that account the decay of their tissues is less rapid.

The evidence of a universal connection in the animal frame between exertion and decay is now almost complete. Carpenter, in his *Human Physiology,* says : " There is strong reason to believe the waste or decomposition of the muscular tissue to be in exact proportion to the degree in which it is exerted." This, perhaps, would be generally anticipated, even in the absence of direct proof; but what is more interesting is, that the same principle holds good of the nervous system. The human brain of an adult contains about one and a half per cent of phosphorus; and it has been ascertained that, after the mind has been much exercised, phosphates are excreted, and that, in the case of inflammation of the brain, their excretion (by the kidneys) is very considerable. The existence of phosphorus in the brain was first announced by Hensing, in 1779.

FATAL CLIMATE OF THE WEST COAST OF AFRICA.

Commander Lynch, U.S. Navy, in his account of his recent expedition to Western Africa, states :

There is but one Englishman known to have survived the climate of Sierra Leone for five years, at the end of which time the fever carried him off. About forty years since, the Portuguese colonised an island in the immediate vicinity of Guinea, sending thither 7000 souls. At this time, there is but a single individual living in whose veins the blood of any of those colonists is believed to course.

SUPERIOR SALUBRITY OF ENGLAND.

The Registrar-General says :

It is now well established by extensive observation, that England is the healthiest country in Europe. France stands next to England in salubrity. In the continental cities the annual rate of mortality is seldom less than 30 in 1000; and frequently as high as 40. In London the rate of mortality is only 25 in 1000. Statistical records prove that " the climate of England is eminently salubrious ;" and it has not yet been shown that the climate of any part of the Continent is more salubrious than this island,—crowned with hills of moderate elevation, sloping towards the east and the south ; bathed by the showers of the Atlantic ; drained naturally by rivers running short courses to the sea ; cultivated more extensively than other lands, and producing those unequalled breeds of sheep, cattle, and horses which flourish only in healthy places. The healthiest parts of England are not yet places of general resort ; but the annual mortality in the various districts comprising watering-places seldom exceeds 21 in 1000 of the population, and is probably lower in those regions of the district to which visitors resort. The lowest mortality at the English watering-places, as they are rather vaguely designated, occurs at Eastbourne—only 15 in 1000 ; Worthing, the Isle of Wight, Mutford (including Lowestoft), Barnstaple (Ilfracombe inclusive), and Anglesey, 17 in 1000 ; Hastings, Upton-on-Severn (including Malvern), and Aberystwith, 18 in 1000 ; the Isle of Thanet, Newton-

Abbot (including the east and south-east of Devon), 19 in 1000. After these, the rates of mortality rise gradually to 23 and 24, which numbers represent the somewhat less salubrious districts of Yarmouth and Bath. Clifton also stands as high as 23, but a part of Bristol is included. Tunbridge Wells stands at 20, Dover at 21, Cheltenham at 20, Warwick (Leamington) at 20, Derbyshire (Buxton, Matlock, &c.) at 20, Scarborough at 21, Harrogate at 20, Whitby at 21, Kendal at 20, and Bangor at 21.

IMPROVED HEALTH OF ENGLAND.

The effects of the means adopted for checking disease in England, France, and Germany, during the past century, are such, that while formerly 1 out of every 30 of the population died each year, now the average is 1 in 45, reducing by one-half the number of deaths in these countries. In the year 1700, 1 out of every 5 of the population died in England. In 1801, the proportion was 1 in 35; in 1811, 1 in 38; and in 1848, 1 in 45 : so that the chances of life have nearly doubled in England within 60 years.—*Keith Johnson.*

THE HEALTHIEST AND UNHEALTHIEST SPOTS IN ENGLAND.

From a paper by Dr. Greenhow, lecturer on public health at St. Thomas's Hospital, it appears that the highest death-rate in the kingdom exists in Liverpool ; the lowest in Glendale and Rothbury, in Northumberland, and Eastbourne in Sussex. "Liverpool is the unhealthiest town in England," says Dr. Greenhow. "Glendale is one of the healthiest rural districts. The annual average mortality of Liverpool, from all causes, is at the rate of thirty-six in the thousand ; the deaths in each thousand of the people of Glendale amount to only fifteen annually."

HOW THE BIOLOGIST INDUCES AND DETERMINES SLEEP.

It is well known that the expectation of sleep is one of the most powerful means of inducing it, especially when combined with the withdrawal of the mind from every thing else which could keep its attention awake. Now the mind of the biologised subject has been possessed with the conviction that sleep is about to supervene, and is closed to every source of distraction. The waking at a particular time may also be explained by the influence of expectation. These phenomena are essentially conformable to facts whose genuineness every physiologist and psychologist is ready to admit. It is not, however, in any large proportion of individuals that this state can be induced ; probably not more than one in twenty, or at most one in twelve.

There is one phenomenon of the biological state which has

been considered preëminently to indicate the power of the operator's will over his subject; namely, the induction of sleep, and its spontaneous determination at a given time, previously ordained, or by the sound of the operator's voice, and that only.

HOW TO AVOID SLEEPLESS NIGHTS.

Mr. A. J. Ellis has announced to the Scottish Curative Mesmeric Association, that persons wishing to avoid sleepless nights should lie with their heads to the north, and not on any account lie with their heads to the west.

Mr. Alfred Smee, F.R.S., the well-known surgeon, has found the application of cold produce refreshing sleep, when all other medicaments have failed and been inapplicable; and many a time he has assuaged a sufferer's pain by applying a little cold water to the top of the brain, and has thus obtained for him rest when every other means have failed.

Mr. Smee also observes: "We have some voluntary power of being able to get to sleep. We perhaps lower the action of the heart, and the temperature of the body, when sleep takes place, and do not again awake until some unusual impression excites the bio-dynamic circuit to action, or the excitability becomes so exalted as to allow weaker impressions to have the same effect."—*Elements of Electro-Biology,* p. 59.

DEGREES OF SLEEP AND SENSITIVENESS.

A friend of Sir David Brewster fixed his attention on a certain object, and by marking the time with a watch, recorded his sensations between the period of perfect wakefulness and profound sleep. Different parts of the body (says Sir David) fall asleep at different times; and it might perhaps be argued by analogy, that different parts of the brain fall asleep at different times. It is a fact equally well known, that different parts of the body get intoxicated sooner than others: first the eyes begin to glare, then the tongue to get flabby, then the muscles begin to give way in the arms, then in the limbs, and so on.

Experiments have also been made to ascertain the different sensitiveness of various parts of the human body by means of a pair of compasses. At a distance of only one-eighth of an inch between the legs of the compasses, the two points will be distinguished on some parts of the body; whilst on the back the effect will be that of only one point, unless the compasses are stretched several inches.

Sir William Hamilton, in his *Lectures on Metaphysics,* on the authority of Jemker, a celebrated physician and professor of Halle, relates the following of a postman, whose daily journey lay between Halle and a town some eight miles distant, a considerable part of which was unenclosed champaign meadow-land. In walking over this smooth surface, the postman was generally asleep: but at the termination of this

part of his road, there was a narrow foot-bridge over a stream ; and to
reach this bridge it was necessary to ascend some broken steps. Now
it was ascertained, as completely as any fact of the kind could be,
(1) that the postman was asleep in passing over this level course;
(2) that he held on his way in this state without deflection towards
the bridge; and (3) that just before arriving at the bridge, he awoke.
This case, besides showing that the mind must be active though the
body is asleep, shows also that certain bodily functions may be dormant while others are alert. The locomotive faculty was here in exercise while the senses were in slumber.

This suggests another example found in a story told by Erasmus in
one of his letters, concerning his learned friend Oporinus, the celebrated
professor and printer of Basle. Oporinus was on a journey with a bookseller, and on their road they had fallen in with a manuscript. Tired
with their day's travelling,—travelling was then almost exclusively performed on horseback,—they came at nightfall to their inn. They were,
however, curious to ascertain the contents of their manuscript; and
Oporinus undertook the task of reading it aloud. This he continued for
some time, when the bookseller found it necessary to put a question
concerning a word which he had not rightly understood. It was now
discovered that Oporinus was asleep; and being awakened by his companion, he found that he had no recollection of what for a considerable
time he had been reading. This is a case concurring with a thousand
others to prove: (1) that one bodily sense or function may be asleep
while another is awake; and (2) that the mind may be in a certain state
of activity during sleep, and no memory of that activity remain after
the sleep has ceased. The first is evident; for Oporinus, while reading,
must have had his eyes and the muscles of his tongue and faces awake,
though his ears and other senses were asleep. And the second is no
less so; for the act of reading supposed a very complex series of mental energies. Physiologists have observed, that our bodily senses and
powers do not fall asleep simultaneously, but in a certain succession.
We all know that the first symptom of slumber is the relaxation of the
eyelids ; whereas hearing continues alert for a season after the power
of vision has been dormant. In the case last alluded to, this order was,
however, violated; and the night was forcibly kept awake while the
hearing had lapsed into torpidity.

DEATH FROM WANT OF SLEEP.

The following terrible mode of punishment is peculiar to the
criminal code of China. In 1850, a Chinese merchant at Amoy,
convicted of the murder of his wife, was condemned to die by
the total deprivation of sleep. The condemned was placed in
prison, under the surveillance of three guardians, who relieved
each other every alternate hour, and who prevented the criminal from taking any sleep night or day. At the commencement
of the eighth day, his sufferings were so intense, that he begged
to be killed by strangulation ; and the terrible request was carried into execution.—*From a Communication to the Royal Asiatic
Society.*

CURE FOR STAMMERING.

Dr. Warren, of the United States, has devised an easy and effectual Cure for Stammering, which is known to be generally a mental, and not a physical, defect. The method is, simply, at every syllable pronounced to tap at the same time with the finger; by doing which the most inveterate stammerer will be surprised to find that he can pronounce quite fluently, and by long and constant practice he will pronounce perfectly well. This may be explained in two ways: either by a sympathetic consentaneous action of the nerves of voluntary motion in the finger and those of the tongue,—which is most probable, for we know that a stammerer, who cannot speak a sentence in the usual way, can articulate perfectly well when he introduces a rhythmical movement, and sings it; or it may be that the movement of the finger distracts the attention of the individual from his speech, and allows a free action of the nerves concerned in articulation.

"A CHILD WITH A GOLDEN TOOTH."

At the end of the sixteenth century, terrible excitement was caused by a report that a golden tooth had appeared in the jaw of a child born in Silesia. It became impossible to conceal it from the public; and the miracle was soon known all over Germany, where, being looked on as a mysterious omen, universal anxiety was felt as to what this new thing might mean. Its real import was first unfolded by Dr. Horst. In 1595, this eminent physician published the result of his researches, by which it appears that, at the birth of the child, the sun was in conjunction with Saturn, at the sign Aries. The event, therefore, though supernatural, was by no means alarming. The golden tooth was the precursor of a golden age, in which the emperor would drive the Turks from Christendom, and lay the foundation of an empire that would last for thousands of years. And this, says Horst, is clearly alluded to by Daniel, in his well-known second chapter, where the prophet speaks of a statue with a golden head.—Buckle's *History of Civilization in England*, vol. i.

LEACH, OR LEECH,

from *læc*, Saxon, was the old name for a physician or surgeon. Shakspeare has :

> Make war breed peace; make peace stint war; make each
> Prescribe to other as each other's leach.
> *Timon of Athens,* act v. sc. 6.

The word has been retained to our time in the veterinary art, as horse-leech, cow-leech, &c.

A DOMESTIC MEDICINE-CHEST.

Very many persons are not aware that they have in their house a medicine-chest, in the shape of a set of well-filled cruets. The *Salt*, for example, is a decided cathartic, in the dose of half an ounce or an ounce; it is also a vermifuge in large doses, and its power is great in preventing as well as killing worms. Many of our readers remember the popular remedy of " Brandy and Salt."

The *Vinegar*, again, is refrigerant and diaphoretic, and is moderately stimulant and astringent when applied externally. It formerly had great reputation in cases of poisoning by narcotics; but here it is of doubtful efficacy. It is certainly useful, however, when soda, potash, or ammonia, are taken in overdoses, as the acetic acid which it contains combines with and chemically neutralises them. Vinegar-and-water is restorative of overworked eyes.

The *Mustard* comes next. In our time, it has been the fashion to attribute every medicinal virtue to mustard-seeds. More lately, a mustard-emetic was extolled as infallible in cholera; to be superseded by salt-and-water. A mustard-poultice (two spoonfuls of bread-crumbs and one of mustard, mixed with vinegar and hot water) is no mean rival to a blister.

Olive-Oil is demulcent and laxative. It is a good antidote to acrid poisons, and seems to be obnoxious to worms. Lastly, my Lord Bacon is of opinion that rubbing the skin with oil is very conducive to longevity.

Nor is our cruet-frame deficient in stimulants. First is pepper, black or white; the latter stronger. When infused in water, it will cure a relaxed sore throat; and *piperin*, the alkaloid from pepper, has cured ague. The Dublin Pharmacopœia has an ointment of black-pepper, which has been recommended for ring-worm. Cayenne, the king of peppers, possesses similar virtues to the above, but in a very exalted degree: in stimulating ulcerated sore throat it is very efficacious as a gargle. Poultices of capsicum are used for the fevers of tropical climates; and in ophthalmia from relaxation, the diluted infusion of capsicum is a good remedy.

INFINITESIMAL DOSES IN HOMŒOPATHY.

Of the system of minute doses mostly adopted by Hahnemann's followers the following is an illustration:

A grain of medicine is dissolved in 99 grains of alcohol, or alcohol and water; then one drop of this solution (first dilution) is mixed with 99 drops more of alcohol; one drop of this further attenuation (second dilution) with 99 drops more of alcohol; and so on to the 10th, 20th, 30th, or 600th to 1000th dilution, as the case may be. The result of this extraordinary and inconceivable process of subdivision is stated by Dr. Simpson, in the form of a calculation, revised by competent mathematical authorities, from which the following are illustrations: At the 6th dilution, had the entire original grain been furnished with its proper amount of alcohol, that quantity would have amounted to 13,000,000 gallons; at the 12th dilution, to a sea six times the size of the Mediterranean; at the 15th, to 46,000 times the whole waters contained in all the oceans of the globe; at the 30th dilution (the ordinary one employed by Hahnemann), to a "quantity sufficient to make one hundred and forty billion spherical masses extending from limit to limit of Neptune's orbit, or a quantity equal to many hundred spheres, each with a radius extending from the earth to the nearest fixed star."

We quote the above from Dr. Gardner's able paper on Homœopathy, in the *Edinburgh Essays*, 1856. The writer remarks, with well-placed humour,—this strange doctrine "was only feebly expressed by Lord Jeffrey, when he said that an ounce of medicine, put into the Rhone at the upper end of the lake of Geneva, would physic all the Calvinists at the lower end."

ERYSIPELAS AND ST. ANTONY'S FIRE.

Erysipelas is also called St. Antony's Fire, as thus explained by a note to the Life of St. Antony, by Butler:

In 1089, a pestilential erysipelas distemper, called the Sacred Fire, swept off great numbers in most provinces of France. Public prayers and processions were ordered against the scourge. At length it pleased God to grant many miraculous cures of this dreadful distemper to those who implored His mercy through the intercession of St. Antony, especially before his relics. The church in which they were deposited was resorted to by great numbers of pilgrims, and his patronage was implored over the whole kingdom against this disease.

BENEFITS OF COLD BATHING: COLD-WATER CURE.

The Emperor Severus, who died in England A.D. 213, practised Cold Bathing for the gout; and Sir Henry Coningsby, who lived to the age of 88, imputed his long life to 40 years of cold bathing. John Locke recommends the washing of feet in cold water for the prevention of corns. Sir John Floyer, M.D., of Lichfield, who wrote an Essay on Cold Bathing in 1702, maintains that we may learn the benefits of cold immersion from the practice of the lower animals. Ælian states that wild-pigs, when convulsed by eating henbane, go into the water, and, by drinking it, recover; whence we may learn the use of cold baths in narcotic poisons and sleepy diseases. Our water-fowl commonly wash themselves in wet weather; and Celsus recommends the use of cold baths against rainy seasons, to cure the pain of the limbs and the dullness of the senses occasioned before rains. Canary birds are subject to convulsions, and are usually cured by immersing them in cold water. Sir John Floyer was informed by a lady, whose lapdog he had seen in convulsions, that it was cured of them by being thrown into a tub of water; and he adds: "By these two instances we may observe the usefulness of cold baths in convulsions."

Sir John further tells us, that in Staffordshire, at Willow-bridge, the people go into the water in their shirts; and when they come out, they dress themselves in their wet linen, which they wear all day, and much commend for closing the pores, and keeping themselves cool; and, adds Sir John, "that they do not commonly receive any injury, or catch any cold thereby, I am fully convinced, from the experiments I have seen made with it." Thus we had the Cold-Water Cure a century and a half ago. Half a century later, Horace Walpole, in a letter to Mr. Cole, dated June 5, 1775, says:

Dr. Heberden (as every physician, to make himself talked of, will set up some new hypothesis) pretends that a damp house, and even damp sheets, which have ever been reckoned fatal, are wholesome. At Malvern, they certainly put patients into sheets just dipped in the spring.

THE ORIENTAL BATH

This Bath is of great antiquity; for we read of its existence amongst the ancient Egyptians, Chaldeans, and Persians. The Greeks and Romans used it; by the latter it was introduced into Spain, and afterwards into France and the British islands.

The price of a bath in ancient Rome was about one-eighth of a penny of our money. There is no drug to be compared to it in a sanitary point of view, as a purifier of the system. Gout, rheumatism, and chronic and skin diseases, were not known among the Turks, who were seldom ill. The physicians believe that those effects were owing to the great attention which they bestowed upon the functions of the skin, which the most eminent physiologists now consider to be analogous to the functions of the lungs. Deformed people were also rarely to be met with amongst the Turks.—*Dr. Haughton.*

HUMMUMS,

Arabic for "sweating-baths," is thus noted in Herbert's *Travels*, 1638: "The Hummums, or sweating-places, are many, resplendent in the azure pargetting and tyling wherewith they are ceruleated."

They were introduced into England soon after this date,

and are mentioned not unfrequently by the writers of the seventeenth century.

"Hummums" (says Hatton, in his *New View of London*, 1708), "is a bagnio, or place for sweating, kept in Covent Garden, by one Mr. Small." The site is now occupied by an hotel, which bears the name of *Hummums*.

EFFECT OF TEA UPON NERVOUS PERSONS.

It used commonly to be thought that Tea had a prejudicial effect upon persons of weak nerves; but it now appears that it actually contributes to recruit the nerves. Persons who cannot consume a sufficient quantity of food to yield the carbon necessary for generating animal heat, have recourse to tea, and find it actually a nutritious article of diet; "and it is only," says Liebig, "by such means as this that it can act as a nutritious agent." But another theory has been advanced by Dr. Lyon Playfair. He says thein, the principle of tea, has a composition very similar to nervous matter, the loss of which attends every operation of the mind. Hence there is a necessity for a supply of that nervous matter to enable the mind to carry on its operations. A large supply of proteinaceous matter would be required to be supplied to form the nervous matter with proper constituents, if taken in by means of bread or meat. But thein at once becomes a constituent of nervous matter; and this accounts for the agreeable stimulus and permanent effect on the mind produced by the use of tea, particularly by studious persons, as well as those whose nervous systems are exhausted from various causes.*

VARIOUS SIZES OF THE HUMAN BRAIN.

Dr. S. G. Morton, of Philadelphia, from the measurement of 623 human crania, by means of leaden shot one-eighth of an inch in diameter, which give the absolute capacity of the cranium, or bulk of the brain, in cubic inches, has elicited these facts:

1. The Teutonic, or German race, embracing the Anglo-Saxons, Anglo-Americans, Anglo-Irish, &c., possess *the largest brain of any people.*

2. The ancient Peruvians and Australians have the smallest heads.

3. The barbarous tribes of America possess a much larger brain than the semi-civilised Peruvians or Mexicans.

4. The ancient Egyptians have the least-sized brain of any Caucasian nation, except the Hindoos.

* Dr. Smith has shown by experiment, that tea very largely increases the exhalation of carbonic acid from the lungs.

5. The Negro brain is nine cubic inches less than the Teutonic, and three cubic inches larger than the ancient Egyptian.

6. The largest brain in the series is that of a Dutch gentleman, and gives 114 cubic inches; the smallest head is an old Peruvian's, of fifty-eight inches: the difference between these two extremes is no less than fifty-six cubic inches.

7. The brain of the Australian and Hottentot falls far below the Negro, and measures precisely the same as the ancient Peruvian.

This extended series of measurements fully confirms Dr. Morton's previous statement, that the various artificial modes of *distorting the cranium* occasion no diminution of its internal capacity, and consequently do not affect the size of the brain.

RANGE OF THE HUMAN VOICE.

There are in the Human Voice about nine perfect tones, but 17,592,186,044,415 different sounds. Thus 14 direct muscles, alone or together, produce 16,383; 30 indirect muscles produce 173,741,823; and all in coöperation produce the above total, independently of different degrees of intensity.

ARE QUALITIES HEREDITARY?

This curious inquiry is thus replied to by Mr. Buckle:

We often hear of hereditary talents, hereditary vices, and hereditary virtues; but whoever will critically examine the evidence, will find that we have no proof of their existence. The way in which they are commonly proved is in the highest degree illogical; the usual course being for writers to collect instances of some mental peculiarity found in a parent and in his child, and then to infer that the peculiarity was bequeathed. By this mode of reasoning we might demonstrate any proposition; since in all large fields of inquiry there are a sufficient number of empirical coincidences to make a plausible case in favour of whatever a man chooses to advocate. But this is not the way in which truth is discovered; and we ought to inquire, not only how many instances there are of hereditary talents, &c., but how many instances there are of such qualities not being hereditary. Until something of this sort is attempted, we can know nothing about the matter inductively; while, until physiology and chemistry are much more advanced, we can know nothing about it deductively.

These considerations ought to prevent us from receiving statements (Taylor's *Medical Jurisprudence*, pp. 644, 678, and many other books), which positively affirm the existence of hereditary madness and hereditary suicide; and the same remark applies to hereditary disease (on which see some admirable observations in *Phillips on Scrofula*, pp. 101, 102), and with still greater force does it apply to hereditary vices and hereditary virtues, inasmuch as ethical phenomena have not been registered as carefully as physiological ones, and therefore our conclusions respecting them are even more precarious.—*History of Civilization in England*, vol. I.

SPECIAL PROVIDENCES IN NATURE.

Dr. E. Hitchcock, in his able work on *Religious Truth illustrated from Science*, adduces the following example, on a gigantic scale, indicative of special Providence for the wants of civilised life untold ages before man's existence. In those early times, vast forests, for instance, might have been seen growing along the shores of estuaries: and these, dying, were buried deep in the mud, there to accumulate thick beds of vegetable matter over large areas; and this, by a long series of ages, was at length converted into coal. This could be of no use whatever till man's existence; nor even then, till civilisation had taught him how to employ this substance for his comfort, and for a great variety of useful arts. And is this an accidental effect of nature's laws? Is it not rather a striking example of special protective Providence? What else but Divine power, intent upon a specific purpose, could have so directed the countless agencies employed through so many ages as to bring about such marvellous results?

Thus it is ascertained that, by the process of vegetable growth and decay in the hoary past, thick beds of coal have been accumulated in the rocks of the United States over an area of more than 200,000 square miles; and probably many more remain to be discovered. Yet, upon a moderate calculation, those already known contain more than 1100 cubic miles of coal, one mile of which, at the rate it is now used, would furnish the country with coal for a thousand years; so that a million of years will not exhaust this supply. What an incalculable increase of the use of steam, and a consequent increase of population and general prosperity, does such a treasure of fuel open before this country! If the numbers should become only as many to the square mile as in Great Britain, or 223, there is room enough on this side of the Rocky Mountains for 600,000,000, and including the western slope of these mountains, for 700,000,000; equal almost to the present population of the globe. And yet all that has been thus far seen in this country, and all that is in prospect, is only an accidental, or incidental, event in his theology who admits no special Providence in Nature. We are not (adds Dr. Hitchcock) of that number; for we believe that God, through vast cycles of duration, directed and controlled the agencies of nature, so as to bury in the bosom of this continent the means of future civilisation and prosperity.

HOW TALL WAS ADAM?

This question has been debated with much earnestness by

very learned men of different ages and countries, who, however they may have differed in their computation, agree in one respect, that the stature of our first father was prodigious.

Some of the mystical writers of the Talmud assert, that when Adam was first created, his head lay at one end of the world, while his toes touched the other end; but that his figure was much shortened after his transgression, at the prayer of the angels, who were afraid of such a giant. These Talmudists, however, left him the height of 900 cubits;[*] and others pretend that on being expelled from Paradise, he walked through the ocean, which he found every where fordable. Other Rabbins reject as fabulous the account of Adam's stature equalling the length of the world: they fix it at 1000 cubits at his creation, and say that God deprived him exactly of one hundred cubits when he had eaten the forbidden fruit. These notions prevailed among the Turks, Arabs, and many people who certainly could never have read the old Jewish writers, but who all agree in attributing to Adam a most superhuman size. The stature of Eve, his wife, was, of course, proportionate: in the neighbourhood of Mecca is shown a hill which served as Eve's pillow, and afar off, in the plain, the spot where her legs rested, the distance from one of her knees to the other being computed at two musket-shots.

These notions were strongly revived in France, in 1718, when Henrion presented to the Academy of Belles Lettres a chronological scale of the human stature, wherein he soberly insisted that Adam was exactly 123 feet 9 inches high, and Eve 118 feet 9¾ inches. According to Henrion's scale, the size of man rapidly diminished from his first fall down to his redemption. The learned author says that Noah was 20 feet shorter than Adam, that Abraham was only 27 or 28 feet high, and Moses no more than 13 feet. Henrion, like a true theorist, is by no means discouraged by the facts of authenticated history: in contempt of all authority, he says Alexander the Great, who was remarked among his contemporaries as being rather a small man, was 6 feet high; but that Julius Cæsar only measured 5 feet.

Under Augustus, our Saviour was born: then the stature of man ceased to dwindle, and then began even to shoot up a little. Here Henrion's scale stops; he having proved, to his entire satisfaction, that in the course of 3000 years man had diminished and lost 118 feet 9 inches of his stature.

The Siamese and other Asiatic people have a religious belief that corresponds with the ingenious Frenchman's scale: they say that since the fall of man he has gradually become less

[*] The Hebrews had several cubits, the most common of which was equal to about half an English yard.

and legs, and that in the end he will not be higher than a magpie!

The Rabbins have written as earnestly on this subject as on the question of our first father's stature. Some of them are convinced that Adam was created a full-grown man, with a good appetite; and that, having no knowledge of cooking, he must have been born in autumn, when the fruits of the earth were all ripe, and edible without any preparation. Other Rabbins, however, maintain, with equal confidence, that he must have been born in spring, the season of youth and hope, and proper to the propagation of birds, beasts, and fishes; and not in autumn, which is the symbol of maturity, decay, and corruption. The hour of the day in which he opened his eyes to this "beautiful visible world" they fix at nine o'clock in the morning exactly. According to the most generally received Rabbinical tradition, Adam transgressed in the very hour of his creation, and only remained six hours in Paradise, being expelled at three o'clock in the afternoon precisely.

The shortness of this time would have interfered with Milton's poem, not allowing of his exquisite description of sunrise and sunset in the terrestrial Paradise. But other Rabbins prolong the term to six, eight, or ten days; while a few are of opinion that Adam remained in Paradise thirty-four years.

"LOT'S WIFE:" PILLAR OF SALT.

Lieut. Lynch, in his official Report of the Exploring Expedition to the Dead Sea, thus refers to this pillar:

April 26. At nine, the water shoaling, hauled more off shore. Soon after, to our astonishment, we saw on the eastern side of Usdun (in the southern part of the sea), one-third the distance from its north extreme, a lofty round pillar, standing apparently detached from the general mass, at the head of a deep, narrow, and abrupt chasm. We immediately pulled in for the shore, and Dr. Anderson and I went up and examined it. The beach was a soft slimy mud, encrusted with salt, and a short distance from the water covered with saline fragments and flakes of bitumen. We found the pillar to be of solid salt, capped with carbonate of lime, cylindrical in front, and pyramidal behind. The upper or rounded part is about 40 feet high, resting on a kind of oval pedestal, from 40 to 60 feet above the level of the sea. It slightly decreases in size upwards, crumbles at the top, and is one entire mass of crystallisation. A prop or buttress connects it with the mountain behind, and the whole is covered with a *débris* of a light stone-colour. Its peculiar shape is doubtless attributable to the action of the winter rains. A similar pillar is mentioned by Josephus, who expresses the belief of its being the identical one into which Lot's wife was transformed. Clement of Rome, a contemporary of Josephus, and Irenæus, a writer of the second century, also mention the pillar.

MANNA OF THE ISRAELITES.

Mr. Giles Mumby has described to the British Association a lichen, found in the kingdom of Algiers, which agrees, at least more nearly than any substance hitherto discovered, with the description of the Manna on which the Israelites fed during their wanderings in the desert. This lichen is found on the sand, and grows during the night, as do many mushrooms. The French soldiers, during an expedition to the south of Constantine, subsisted on it for some days, cooking it in various ways, and even making it into bread.

TIME OF YEAR WHEN OUR SAVIOUR WAS BORN.

The learned have long been divided upon the precise day of the Nativity. In Alford's Greek Testament we read : the Magi were addicted to astronomy, and astronomical calculations prove that a remarkable conjunction of planets took place just before our Saviour's birth. A.U.C. 747, May 20th, there was a conjunction of Jupiter and Saturn in 20° of Pisces, close to the first point of Aries, the part in which the signs, according to the astrologers, denoted glorious and mighty events. On the 27th of October, another conjunction of the same period occurred in 16° of Pisces, and on November 12th a third in 15° of the same sign. On the last two occasions the planets would be so near as to appear as one star of surpassing brightness. Supposing the Magi to have seen the first of these conjunctions, they saw it actually *in the east*, for on the 20th of May it would rise shortly before the sun. If they then took their journey, and arrived at Jerusalem in a little more than five months (the journey of Ezra from Babylon took *four*), and if they performed the journey from Jerusalem to Bethlehem (remaining in Jerusalem to inquire of the Sanhedrim from the October to the November conjunction) in the evening, as is implied, the November conjunction of 15° in Pisces would be before them in the direction of Bethlehem, coming to the meridian about eight o'clock p.m. This calculation would make the Nativity to have occurred about the first of November, reckoning the same interval as between our Christmas Day and Epiphany.

Some have fixed the day of the Nativity at the Passover ; others, among whom was Archbishop Ussher, at the Feast of Tabernacles. It has been observed, that if the shepherds were watching their flocks when it occurred in the field by night, it could hardly have happened in the depth of winter; but the cold is not severe in Palestine, and the ground is never frozen ; and there is no reason to believe that the temperature has changed.* Be this as it may, the 25th of December has been the day most generally fixed upon, from the earliest ages of the church, for "that most venerable, most astonishing of festivals, the fountain whence the other great festivals flowed." Sir Isaac Newton, in his *Commentary on the Prophecies of Daniel*, accounts for the choice of the 25th of December, the winter solstice, by showing that not only the feast of the Nativity, but most others, were originally fixed at the cardinal points of the year ; and that, the first Christian calendars having been so arranged by mathematicians at pleasure, without any ground in tradition, the Christians afterwards took up what they found in the calendars. So long as a fixed time of commemoration was solemnly appointed, they were content.

"CHRIST'S THORN."

From this plant, *Paliurus aculeatus*, the Jews are supposed to have plaited the Crown of Thorns for our Saviour. It is a small shrub, with flexuose shoots directed almost horizontally from the principal stem, and armed with short, stiff, curved spines, which grow in pairs from the base of the leaves. It has small, shining, ovate leaves, yellowish-green clustered flowers, and a broad brown fruit. It is common in the south-east of Europe and in Asia Minor : in England it is often seen in shrubberies, where it forms a beautiful bush when in flower.

THE CROSS OF CHRIST.

It has been stated, but without sufficient authority, that our Saviour's cross was of the form of " the letter Y, or rather V, with a short upright stem affixed, but one of the arms longer than the other ; in fact, a tree with two leafless branches, both springing nearly from the root." It is true that in the Acts and Epistles the cross is spoken of four or five times as "a tree" and "the tree ;" but the word in the original is ξύλον, which strictly and literally means wood, or any thing made of it. Now, in the Evangelists the word used is always "cross," the original being σταυρός, a word evidently used to signify cross, from its reference to the letter T ; and, from the fact of the superscription having been set up over our Saviour's head a very strong inference may be drawn in favour of a middle piece on which to affix it. But there exists evidence as to the true form of our Saviour's cross the most conclusive. In one of the basement-arches of the Coliseum at Rome, and in the second row from the outside, there is a brick on which is (or was in 1844) distinctly visible the figure of an angel holding in the left hand a perfect cross, of what is termed the Latin form.

* See four communications to *Notes and Queries*, 2d Series, vol. III.

Now, as many of the captives brought from Jerusalem by Titus are known to have been employed in building the Coliseum, there can be very little doubt that this brick was carved by one of these captives, who, if not actually present at our Lord's crucifixion, must have been at Jerusalem at the time, and cognisant of the circumstances connected with it. It was placed back behind an arch (now fallen), probably to escape the observation of the Roman overseers; and such a monument of Christian piety amongst the ruins of that pagan and barbarous building is exceedingly affecting.[*]

BROKEN HEARTS: DEATH OF THE SAVIOUR.

The term Broken Heart, as commonly applied to death from grief, is not a vulgar error, as generally supposed. On the contrary, though not a very common circumstance, there are many cases on record in medical works. This affection, it is believed, was first described by Harvey; but since his day several cases have been observed. Morgagni has recorded a few examples: amongst them, that of George II., who died suddenly, of this disease, in 1760; and, what is very curious, Morgagni himself fell a victim to the same malady. Dr. Elliotson, in his Lumleyan Lecture on Diseases of the Heart, in 1839, stated that he had only seen one instance; but in the *Cyclopædia of Practical Medicine*, Dr. Townsend gives a table of twenty-five cases, collected from various authors. Generally, this accident is consequent upon some organic disease, such as fatty degeneration; but it may arise from violent muscular exertion, or strong mental emotions.

The question becomes overwhelmingly interesting from there being sufficient proof that the physical cause of the death of our blessed Saviour was the rupture of His sacred heart, caused by mental agony. Dr. Macbride, in his *Lectures on the Diatessaron*, quotes from the *Evangelical Register* of 1829 some observations of a physician, who considers the record concerning the blood and water as explaining (at least to a mere scientific age) that the real cause of the death of Jesus was *rupture of the heart, occasioned by mental agony.* Such rupture, it is stated, is usually attended by instant death, without previous exhaustion, and by the effusion into the pericardium of blood, which, in this particular case, though scarcely in any other, separates into its two constituent parts, so as to present the appearance commonly termed blood and water. Thus the prophecy, "Reproach hath broken my heart" (*Psalm* lxix. 20), was fulfilled, as were so many others, in the momentous circumstances of the crucifixion, to the very letter.

Dr. Stroud, by the publication, in 1847, of his *Treatise on the Physical Cause of the Death of Christ,* is considered to have thrown a new light upon this solemn inquiry. In this work, the doctor's application of the science of physiology is brought into juxtaposition with the light of revelation; and the two establish the conclusion, that the bursting of the heart from mental agony was the physical cause of the death of Christ. (Selected and condensed from three communications to *Notes and Queries,* 2d Series, No. 25.)

CRITERION OF DEATH.

Physiologists were long at variance as to any certain test of the event of death, or, in other words, no recognised distinction existed between the human body immediately before and immediately after death; until, in 1839, it was communicated to the French Academy, that the blood taken from the body after death is distinguished from the blood before death by its being non-coagulable.

FACULTY OF FEIGNING DEATH.

There are cases on record of persons who could fall spontaneously into death-trance. Monti, in a letter to Haller, mentions several. A priest of the name of Cœlius Rhodaginus had the same faculty. But the most celebrated instance is that of Colonel Townshend, mentioned in the surgical works of Gooch; by whom and by Doctor Cheyne and Doctor Beynard, and by Mr. Shrine, an apothecary, the performance of Colonel Townshend was seen and attested. They had long attended him, for he was an habitual invalid, and he had often invited them to witness the phenomenon of his dying and coming to life again; but they had hitherto refused from fear of the consequences to himself. Accordingly, in their presence Colonel Townshend laid himself down on his back, and Dr. Cheyne undertook to observe the pulse; Dr. Beynard laid his hand on his heart; and Mr. Shrine had a looking-glass to hold to his mouth. After a few seconds, pulse, breathing, and the action of the heart were no longer to be observed. Each of the witnesses satisfied himself on the entire cessation of these phenomena. When the death-trance had lasted half an hour, the doctors began to fear that their patient had pushed the experiment too far, and was dead in earnest; and they were preparing to leave the house, when a slight movement of the body attracted their attention. They renewed the routine of their observation; when the pulse and sensible motion of the heart gradually returned, and breathing and consciousness. The sequel of the tale is strange: Colonel Townshend, on recovering, sent for his attorney, made his will, and died, for good and all, in six hours afterwards.— *Phantasmata,* by R. R. Madden.

Funeral Customs and Ceremonies.

BRITISH MOURNING.

Mourning habits first appear in monuments and illuminations of the reign of Edward III.; and the earliest mention of them seems to be by Chaucer and Froissart. Chaucer, in his *Knighte Tale*, speaks of Palamon's appearing at Arcite's funeral

> In clothes *black* dropped all with tears;

and in his *Troylus and Cresseyde* he describes his heroine,

> In widowes habit large of *samite brown;*

and in another place says,

> Cressoydo was in widowes habit *blacke;*

and in another, when separating from Troylus, he makes her say,

> My clothes everch ono
> Shall *blacke* hen, in tokeynvn (token), herte swete,
> That I am as oute of this worlde agone.

Froissart tells us, that the Earl of Foix, on hearing of the death of his son Gaston, sent for his barber, and was close shaved, and clothed himself and all his household in black. At the funeral of the Earl of Flanders, he says, all the nobles and attendants wore black gowns; and on the death of John king of France, the King of Cyprus clothed himself in black mourning; by which distinction, it would seem that some other colours were occasionally worn, such as the "samite brown" of Chaucer's "Cresseyde." The figures on the tomb of Sir Roger de Kerderton, who died A.D. 1337, represent the relations of the deceased knight wearing their own coloured clothes under the mourning cloak.—*Planché on British Costume.*

PREMATURE INTERMENTS: TRANCE.

The strange circumstance of bodies having been found in coffins with their faces turned to the earth, though referred to by a grave-digger at Bath as part of the ordinary course of decomposition, has drawn attention to the very painful subject of Premature Interment. A Correspondent of the *Notes and Queries* states, that in 1853, during some excavations at the east end of Bristol, many dead human bodies were found with their faces downwards; and, doubting the Bath grave-digger's explanation, another Correspondent infers, that during some raging pestilence, the anxiety of the uncontaminated to avoid infection had induced them to remove their less fortunate fellow-creatures out of the way with so much haste, as actually to bury them alive; and in some convulsive struggle between life and death they had turned themselves over.

The tender Juliet soliloquises :

> How if, when I am laid into the tomb,
> I wake? . . . .
> . . . . there's a fearful point ;

and how prevalent is such a fear, may be gathered from the number of instances in which men have requested, that before the last offices are done for them, such wounds or mutilations should be inflicted upon their bodies as should effectually prevent the possibility of an awakening in the tomb. Dr. Dibdin relates, that Francis Douce, the antiquary, requested in his will that Sir Anthony Carlisle, the surgeon, should sever his head from his body, or take out his heart, to prevent the return of vitality ; and his co-residuary legatee, Mr. Kerrick, had also requested the same operation to be performed in the presence of his son.

In France premature interments have been frightfully numerous; and Bruhier has collected 180 cases, many of which were attributable to hospital negligence. With the view of preventing these sad results, a premium was awarded in 1846, by the Academy of Sciences, for the best treatise on the signs of death, and the means to prevent premature interment.

In 1703 a sermon was preached (and subsequently printed) in the Presbyterian chapel of Lancaster, on *The Duty of the Relations of those who are in dangerous Illness, and the Hazard of hasty Interments;* wherein is the following extract from an address by Dr. Hawes, one of the founders of the Royal Humane Society:

The custom of laying out the bodies of persons supposed to be dead as soon as respiration ceases, and the interment of them before the signs of putrefaction appear, has been frequently opposed by men of learning and humanity in this and other countries. Mons. Bruhier, in particular, a physician of great eminence in Paris, published a piece, about thirty years ago, entitled The Uncertainty of the Signs of Death; in which he clearly proved, from the testimonies of various authors and the attestations of unexceptionable witnesses, that many persons who have been buried alive, and were providentially discovered in that state, had been rescued from the grave, and enjoyed the pleasures of society for several years after. But, notwithstanding the numerous and well-authenticated facts of this kind, the custom above mentioned remains in full force. As soon as the *semblance of death* appears, the bed-clothes are removed, and the body is exposed to the air; which, when cold, *must extinguish the little spark of life* that may remain, and which, by a different *treatment*, might have been kindled into flame.

Mr. Girle quotes, among his " proofs," the case of Mrs. Godfrey, mistress of the Jewel Office, and sister of the great Duke of Marlborough, who lay *in a trance*, apparently dead, for seven days, and was even declared by her medical attendants to be dead. Colonel Godfrey, her husband, would not allow her to be interred, or the body to be treated in the manner of a corpse ; and on the eighth day she awoke, without any consciousness of her long insensibility. The authority assigned for this story is Mr. Peckard, Master of Magdalen College, in a work entitled *Further Observations on the Doctrine of an Intermediate State.*

Stories are also told of a Mr. Holland, improperly treated as dead, who revived,—only to die, however, from the effects of exposure to cold in the grave-dress ; and of a Mrs. Chaloner, a lady of Yorkshire, who was buried alive, and who was found, on the re-opening of the vault in which she was interred, to have burst open the lid of her coffin, and to be sitting nearly upright in it.

Mr. Girle also relates that Dr. Doddridge, on his birth, showed so little signs of life that he was laid aside as dead ; but one of the attendants perceiving some motion in the body, took the infant under her charge, and by her treatment the flame of life was gradually kindled.

We quote the substance of the above from two communications to *Notes and Queries*, Second Series, Nos. 32 and 38. In the former is a list of works upon this painful subject. Several cases are narrated in the Reports of the Royal Humane Society for 1787-9.

We add two narratives. In 1814, Anne Taylor, the daughter of a yeoman of Tiverton, being ill, lay six days insensible, and to all appearance dead: during the interval she had a dream, which her family called *a trance*, an account of which was subsequently printed. On awaking from her stupor, by her request a person wrote down all she had to relate, which she desired her father would cause to be printed. This request he evaded until, as she told him, it would be too late. She died the same evening. Next morning her voice was heard by the person who wrote the narrative, inquiring if it was printed. Between ten and twelve o'clock the undertaker's men placed her in the coffin; and while the family were at dinner her voice was again heard, saying, " Father, it is not printed." This was attested by six witnesses ; but, after her death, Mr. Vowles, a dissenting minister of Tiverton, in a sermon, was considered to have proved the fraud of the whole story.

More veracious is the case of the Rev. Owen Manning, the historian of Surrey, who, during his residence at Cambridge University, caught small-pox, and was reduced by the disorder to a state of insensibility and apparent death. The body was laid out, and preparations were made for the funeral, when Mr. Manning's father, going into the chamber to take a last look at his son, raised the imagined corpse from its recumbent position, saying, "I will give my poor boy another chance;" upon which signs of vitality were apparent. He was therefore removed by his friend and fellow-student Dr. Heberden, and ultimately restored to health. He had another narrow escape from death; for becoming subject to epilepsy, and being seized with a fit as he was walking beside the river Cam, he fell into the water, and was taken out apparently lifeless; Heberden, however, being called in, again became the means of Manning's restoration.

A monument in St. Giles's church, Cripplegate, has strangely been associated with a trance story. In the chancel is a tablet in memory of Constance Whitney, representing her rising from a coffin: and the story relates that she had been buried while in a trance, but was restored to life through the cupidity of the sexton, which induced him to disinter the body to obtain possession of a valuable ring left upon her finger.

Among many strange narratives, is that of Cardinal Somaglia, who recovered from trance for one moment to put away the surgeon's knife, which had begun the preparatory incision before embalming, and then died in agony.

OBJECT OF DOLES.

The distribution of gifts, or *Doles*, whilst the donor was lying at the point of death, or within a short time after his decease, amongst his poorer neighbours, was of frequent occurrence in Roman-Catholic times. The intention appears to have been to excite the recipients to pray for the soul of the dying or recently-deceased person. The practice did not immediately cease at the Reformation; for in 1561, Sir Rowland Hill (said to be the first Protestant Lord Mayor), in his last illness, caused twelve pence to be distributed to every householder in each ward of the City (Machyn's *Diary*, p. 270); and in 1566, Sir Martin Bowes, alderman, gave directions for "thirty pounds, which he kept ready told in a little bag in his iron chest, to be distributed amongst the poor of the ward at the time he was dying." — *Will of Sir Martin Bowes, in the Prerogative Court.*

One of the most celebrated Doles in England was that of the family of Tichborne, who date their possession of the manor of Tichborne, near Alresford, in Hampshire, so far back as 200 years before the Conquest. When the Lady Mabella Tichborne, worn out with age and infirmity, was lying on her death-bed, she besought her living husband that he would grant her the means of leaving behind her a charitable bequest, in a dole of bread to be distributed to all who should apply for it annually on the Feast of the Annunciation of the blessed Virgin Mary. Sir Roger, her husband, promised her the produce of as much land as she could go over in the vicinity of the park while a certain brand or billet was burning, supposing that, from her long infirmity (for she had been bed-ridden some years), she would be able to go round a small portion only of his property. The venerable dame, however, ordered her attendants to convey her to the corner of the park, where, being deposited on the ground, she seemed to receive a renovation of strength, and, to the surprise of her anxious and admiring lord, who began to wonder where this pilgrimage might end, she crawled round several rich and goodly acres. The field which was the scene of Lady Mabella's extraordinary feat retains the name of Crawls to this day: it is situate near the entrance of the park, and contains an area of twenty-three acres. Her task being completed, she was re-conveyed to her chamber, and summoning her family to her bedside, predicted its prosperity while the annual dole existed, and left her malediction on any of her descendants who should be so mean or covetous as to discontinue or divert it; prophesying that when such should happen, the old house would fall, and the family name would become extinct from the failure of heirs male: and that this would be denoted by a generation of seven sons being followed immediately after by a generation of seven daughters and no son. The custom thus founded in the reign of Henry II. continued to be observed for centuries on the 25th of March.
In 1670 Sir H. Tichborne employed Giles Tilberg, an eminent Flemish painter, to represent the ceremony of the distribution. It was usual to bake 1400 loaves for the dole, of 1lb. 10oz. avoirdupois weight each; and if, after the distribution, there remained any persons to whom bread had not been distributed, they received 2d. each in lieu thereof. It was not until the middle of the last century that the custom was abused; when, under the pretence of attending Tichborne Dole, vagabonds, gipsies, and idlers of every description assembled from all quarters, pilfering throughout the neighbourhood; and at last, the gentry and magistrates complaining, it was discontinued in 1796. This gave great offence to many who had been accustomed to receive the dole, and a partial falling of the old house in 1803 was looked upon as an ominous sign of Lady Mabella's displeasure. Singularly enough, the baronet of the day had seven sons; and, when he was succeeded by the eldest, there appeared a generation of seven daughters; and the apparent fulfilment of the prophecy was completed by the change of the name of the baronet to Doughty, under the will of his kinswoman.—Abridged from the *Winchester Observer.*

HELPING THE DYING.

The Rev. John Eagles, in one of his excellent essays contributed to Blackwood's *Edinburgh Magazine,* has the following :

I have often noted a difference in the sympathy with the dying in the rich and in the poor. With the former, there is generally great cau-

tion used that the sick should not think themselves going; if it is to be
discovered, it is rather in a more delicate attention, a more affectionate
look, which the sick cannot at all times distinguish from the ordinary
manner. The poor, on the contrary, tell the sick at once, and without
any circumlocution, that they never will get over it. Is it that the shock
is less to the poor—that they have fewer objects in this world for which
life might be desirable? But this is sometimes dangerous. I was once
going to visit a poor woman; and met the parish surgeon, and inquired
for his patient. He told me the room was full of friends and neighbours,
all telling her she couldn't last long; and he said, "I make no doubt
she will not, for she is sinking because she thinks she is dying; yet I
see no other reason why she should; and I could not get one to leave
the room." I entered; my authority had a better effect. I turned all
but one out of the room, and then addressed the woman, who was apparently exhausted and speechless. I told her exactly what the surgeon
had said, and that she would not die, but be restored to her children
and husband. The woman positively started, raised herself in bed, and
said, with an energy of which I did not think her capable, "What, am
I not dying? Sha'n't I die? No! Then, thank the Lord, I sha'n't die."
I gave strict orders that none should be admitted; and the woman did
recover, and has often thanked me for saving her life. Clergymen
should be aware of this propensity in the poor, that, when mischievous,
they may counteract it.

THE CENOTAPH.

The Cenotaph of antiquity was an empty tomb, erected in
honour of some person deceased, and distinguished from a sar-
cophagus, in which a coffin was deposited. Of cenotaphs there
were two sorts; one for those who had, and another for those
who had not, been honoured with funeral rites in another place.
The sign by which honorary sepulchres were distinguished from
others was commonly the wreck of a ship, to denote the decease of the person in some foreign country.

ANIMALS BURNT AND BURIED WITH THE DEAD.

The late Mr. J. M. Kemble, in a series of interesting instances of the "Animals that were burnt and buried with the
Dead, both in Christian and Heathen Rites," observes, that even
in our time the custom has not entirely disappeared; and refers
to the charger being led at the Duke of Wellington's funeral as
a remnant of the ceremonies practised by our forefathers. As
late as the year 1781, a horse was slaughtered at his master's
grave. Frederick Kasimir, Commander of Lorraine, in the
Order of Teutonic Knights, and General of the Cavalry in the
service of the Palatinate, was buried at Tréves, 13th of February
1781, according to the ritual of his order. An officer led the
charger immediately after his master's bier, and, on the brink
of the grave, a skilful blow with the hunting-knife laid low
the animal, which was then thrown upon the coffin. In Nor-

way a ship was found buried with burnt horses in it. The skull of the horse is frequently found together with the human skeleton. The horse among Northern nations was a sacred animal. Dogs also were found in the ship in Norway; they are mentioned in Homer as being slain on the tomb of Patroclus. Bones of the ox and cow are found buried with human remains. The cow was a sacred animal. The Merovingian kings were drawn in a chariot by oxen. Bones of the hare, of various birds, and the wild-boar, are met with in these interments. The latter animal was sacred to Freya, and forms a conspicuous ornament, probably as a protecting genius, on a bronze helmet discovered at Vulci.

LICH-OWL : LICHFIELD.

The Lich-Owl is the Screech-Owl, so called from the supposed ominousness of its cry and appearance; from the Saxon *lic* or *lice*, a carcass. From the same origin comes *liche-wake*, used by Chaucer for the vigils or watches held over deceased persons; corrupted into *late-wake*, or *lake-wake*, and in Scotland into *like-wake*. Drayton has

> The shrieking litch-owl, that doth never cry
> But boding death, and quick herself inters
> In darksome graves and hollow sepulchres.

The same poet thus gives the etymology of *Lichfield*:

> A thousand other saints, whom Amphibal had taught,
> Flying the Pagan foe, their lives that strictly sought,
> Were slain where Litchfield is, whose name doth rightly sound,
> There of those Christians slain, *dead field*, or burying ground.
>   *Polyolbion.*

BURIAL WITHOUT COFFINS.

Although Coffins have been used for several ages, burial in them as a universal custom in England may be said to have commenced with the last century.

The Romans had coffins of several stones; of bricks covered with tiles; of stone, with urns and lachrymatories in them; they had also leaden and glass* coffins. Of wooden coffins Arthur's is the oldest instance. They frequently occur in British barrows; the skeleton sometimes lying in a shallow wooden case, of a boat-like form. Stone coffins occur among the Anglo-Saxons as early as the year 698, and were not quite obsolete before the reign of Henry VIII. Double leaden coffins, not of plain lead, but folded in a curious manner, occur in the Anglo-Saxon era; and at Farleigh Castle are some adapted to the form of the body, like the cases of mummies, and bearing

* Winkelmann states that glass was used by the Egyptians for coffins; and in 1847 a process was patented in England for making coffins of glass.

on the upper part the figure of a human face in flat relief. Elsewhere there are others of wood and elegant carved work.

In *Reliquiæ Hearnianæ* we find these curious particulars:

Formerly it was usual to be buried in winding-sheets, without coffins, and the bodies were laid on biers. And the custom was practised about threescore years ago (1724); though even then persons of rank were buried in coffins, *unless they ordered otherwise.* Thomas Nailo, of Hart Hall, in Queen Elizabeth's time, is represented in a winding-sheet in Cassington Church. It seems, therefore, he was not buried in a coffin, especially since his effigy in a winding-sheet there was put up in his lifetime. In the monkish times, stone coffins were much in vogue, especially for persons of quality, and for those other distinguished titles, such as archbishops, bishops, abbots, abbesses, &c. Even many of the inferior monks were sometimes so buried;* though otherwise the most common way was a winding-sheet. Yet many persons of distinction, instead of being put in coffins, were wrapt up in leather, as were Sir William Trussell and his lady, founders of Shottesbrook church and chantry, in Berks, as may be seen in my edition of *Leland's Itinerary;* and 'twas in such leathern sheets or bags that others wore put that were laid in the walls of churches.

In the crypt of St. Paul's Cathedral is the life-size marble effigy of Dr. Donne, in his winding-sheet, which Nicholas Stone sculptured from a picture of the Doctor painted on board by his bedside. This effigy was placed in the old cathedral after his death; but, says Mr. Markland, it has never been assumed that the Dean was buried in the vaults without a coffin. Donne uses the word 'coffined' in his poems:

> Let me lie in prison,
> And here be coffined when I die.

Burial in coffins seems to have been early a condition of interment in churches. Among the vestry minutes of St. Helen's, Bishopsgate, is the following (March 5, 1564):

"Item, that none shall be bury'd within the church, *unless the dead corpse be coffined in wood;*" which Mr. Lott, F.S.A., states to be the first sanitary minute with which he is acquainted.

Oak was formerly commonly used for coffins; but this wood contains more acid than any other, and caused the more rapid oxidation and decay of the lead; on which account was substituted as a coffin-wood elm, which contains little, if any, of the destructive acid.

The word *coffin* appears to have been otherwise applied than to the box or chest for dead bodies. It was the name for a mould of paste for a pie. Selden speaks of " the coffin of our Christmas pies (mince-pies), in shape long, in imitation of the cratch," or manger, in which the infant Saviour was laid. A paper case, in the form of a cone, used by grocers, is also called a coffin; as is the wooden frame which encloses the printers' imposing stone. And the coffin of a horse is the whole hoof of the foot above the coronet, including the coffin-bone.

* The lid of a stone coffin, sculptured with the effigy of a monk, was found a few years since upon the site of Swinstead Abbey, in Lincolnshire.

THE ROSARY

is a chaplet or string of beads, the number of which is thus defined by the Abbé Prevost :

It consists (he says) of fifteen tens, said to be in honour of the fifteen mysteries in which the Blessed Virgin bore a part. Five Joyous: viz. the annunciation, the visit to Elizabeth, the birth of our Saviour, the purification, and the disputation of Christ in the Temple. Five Sorrowful: Our Saviour's agony in the garden, His flagellation, crowning with thorns, bearing His cross, and crucifixion. Five Glorious: His resurrection, ascension, descent of the Holy Ghost, His glorification in Heaven, and the assumption of the Virgin herself.

This is good authority. Why each of the fives is multiplied by ten the Abbé does not explain : it is probably to make the chaplet of sufficient length. Others make it consist of 150 Ave Marias and 15 Paters. A modern French Dictionary explains it : "fifteen tens of Aves, each preceded by a Pater."

LIMBO.

This name for the borders of hell—sometimes used for hell itself—is corrupted from *limbus*, the hem or border of a garment. The old schoolmen supposed there to be, besides hell (*infernus damnatorum*), (1) a *limbus puerorum*, where the souls of infants unbaptised remained; (2) a *limbus patrum*, where the fathers of the Church, saints, and martyrs, awaited the general resurrection ; and (3) Purgatory ; to which, in popular opinion, was added, (4) a *limbus fatuorum*, or fool's paradise, the receptacle of all vanity and nonsense. Shakspeare and Spenser use it generally for hell :

> And far from help as limbo is from bliss.
> *Titus Andronicus*, act iii. sc. 1.

> That voice of damned ghost from limbo's lake.
> *Faerie Queene*, b. ii.

Here it is used for a prison :

> Legions of sprites from limbo's prison got.
> *Fairfax's Tasso*, b. iv.

Milton describes

> A limbo large and broad, since call'd
> The paradise of fools.   *Paradise Lost*, b. iii.

THE PASSING BELL.

This Bell was formerly tolled for a person who was dying, that is, *passing* from life. It has been called "the melancholy warning of the death-crier." The practice is of great antiquity, for Bede has the proverb :

> When the bell begins to toll,
> Lord, have mercy on the soul;

and the following couplet occurs in Ray:

> When thou dost hear a toll or knell,
> Then think upon thy *passing* bell.

It seems to have been tolled for all classes; for, in a statute passed late in the reign of Henry VIII., it is ordered "that clarke are to ring no more than the passing bell for poare people, unless for an honest housholder, and he be a citizen; nor for children, maydes, journeymen, apprentices, or any other poare person." In the "Advertisement for due order," &c., 7th Elizabeth, we find:

Item, that when a Christian bodie is *is passing*, that the bell be tolled, and that the curate be speciallie called for to comforte the sicke person; and after the time of his passinge, to ring no more but one shorte peale; and one before the buriall, and another shorte peale after the buriall.

Shakspeare thus alludes to this custom:

> And his tongue
> Sounds ever as a sullen bell,
> Remember'd knolling a departed friend.
>
> *Henry IV.* part ii.

D'Ewes mentions, in 1624, the bell tolling for an individual whom he visited, and who lived some hours afterwards. The canon, however, is express on the subject: "And when any is passing out of this life, a bell shall be tolled, and the minister shall not then be slack to do his last duty."

In most of the Visitation Articles the custom was enjoined, usually in this form:

And when any person is passing out of life, doth he (the clerk), upon notice given him thereof, toll a bell, as hath been accustomed, that the neighbours may thereby be warned to recommend the dying person to the grace and favour of God?

In 1662, the Bishop of Worcester asked, in his Visitation Charge:

Doth the parish-clerk or sexton take care to admonish the living, by tolling of a *passing bell*, of any that are dying, thereby to meditate of their own deaths, and to commend the other's weak condition to the mercy of God?

Mr. Douce thinks the Passing Bell was originally intended to drive away any demon that might seek to take possession of the *soul* of the deceased; on which account it was sometimes called the *Soul Bell*.

Wheatly, in his work on the *Book of Common Prayer*, apologises for our retaining this ceremony, and says:

Our Church, in imitation of the saints in former ages, calls in the minister, and others who are at hand, to assist their brother in his last extremity. In order to this, she directs that when any one is passing out of this life, a bell should be tolled, &c.

Pennant mentions that in his time the peal *after the funeral* was " a merry peal rung at the request of the relations ; as if, Scythian-like, they rejoiced at the escape of the departed out of this troublesome world."

When Sir Walter Scott was writing his *Border Minstrelsy*, in 1803, the Passing Bell was still retained in many villages in Scotland.

TOLLING FOR THE DEAD.

For the Passing Bell we have substituted Tolling the Bell *after Death;* but in former ages both practices were observed. Thus Durand, who lived in the twelfth century, tells us that " bells must be tolled twice for a woman and thrice for a man ; if for a clergyman, as many times as he had orders ; and at the conclusion, a peal on all the bells, to distinguish the quality of the person for whom the people are to put up their prayers. A bell, too, must be rung while the corpse is conducted to church, and during the bringing it out of the church." Mr. Brand considered this to account for a custom preserved in his time in the north of England, "of making numeral distinctions at the conclusion of the ceremony, *i. e.* nine knells for a man, six for a woman, and three for a child; which are undoubtedly the vestiges of this ancient injunction of Popery."

For tolling the largest bell of the church the highest price was charged; because, exclusive of the additional labour, superstition ascribed to its louder sound the property of scaring evil spirits further off, to be clear of its knell, by which the poor soul got so much more the start of them. Besides, being heard further off, it would (in the case of the passing bell) procure the dying man a greater number of prayers.

The dislike of spirits to bells is mentioned in the *Golden Legend*, by Wynkyn de Worde. At Dewsbury in Somersetshire, to this day, a bell is tolled on Christmas Eve, which is called "the devil's knell;" for, it is said, the devil died when Christ was born. This custom was discontinued for many years, but was revived by the vicar in 1828.

WAX-WORK.

That the Romans were acquainted with the art of working in Wax, every scholar knows. It was their custom, at the funerals of great men, to carry with them the effigies of the dead ; and we learn from Pliny, that " their faces, pressed in wax, are disposed in separate closets, so that they may be images which may accompany the funerals of those of gentle blood." These were taken home after the body was burnt, and placed in cases (wooden cases, says Polybius), and exhibited on solemn days in the "atria" of the houses. On them were inscribed the rank and quality of the deceased. In cases of treason, or any great crime, however, these figures were delivered up to the executioner, to be destroyed publicly. The way in which these predecessors of Mrs. Salmon and Madame Tussaud worked in wax is minutely described by Pliny. He says it was the invention of Lysistratus of Sicyon, the brother of Lysippus; that they first took the form of the face in gypsum (plaster-of-Paris), in the way invented by Debutades, and then squeezed wax into this form or mould, and so obtained the likeness. Thus were made the "imagines" which were placed in the Roman halls, like the family pictures in our houses.

Before we speak of wax effigies being carried in funeral processions in England, it should be noticed that a waxen image was a part of the paraphernalia of a witch, by means of which she was supposed to torment her unfortunate victims. In Ben Jonson's *Sad Shepherd*, we find the witch sitting in her dell, "with her spindle, threads, and images:" the practice was, to provide the waxen image of the person intended to be tormented, and this was stuck through with pins, and melted at a distance from the fire.

Of the wax effigies which had been borne in state funerals, a large collection was preserved in Westminster Abbey to our time. Its exhibition was formerly one of the sights of London, and was called "the Play of the Dead Volks," and "the Ragged Regiment." They represented "princes and others of high quality" who were buried in the Abbey. In a description of them a century since, we are told: "These effigies resembled the deceased as near as possible, and were wont to be exposed at the funerals of our princes and other great personages in open chariots, with their proper ensigns of royalty or honour appended. The most ancient that are here laid up are the least injured, by which it would seem as if the costliness of their clothes had tempted persons to partly strip them; for the robes of Edward VI., which were once of crimson velvet, now appear like leather; but those of Queen Elizabeth and King James the First are entirely stript, as are all the rest, of every thing of value. In two handsome wainscot presses are the effigies of King William, and Queen Mary, and Queen Anne, in good condition. The figure of Cromwell is not mentioned in the list; but in the account of his lying-in-state, the effigy is described as made to the life in wax, and appareled in velvet, gold-lace, and ermine. This effigy was laid upon the bed of state, and carried upon the hearse in the funeral procession: both were then deposited in Westminster Abbey; but at the Restoration, the hearse was broken to pieces, and the effigy was destroyed, after it had been hung from a window at Whitehall." In the prints of the grand state funeral-procession of General Monk, Duke of Albemarle, in 1670, his effigy, clad in part-armour and ducal robes and coronet, is borne upon an open chariot beneath a canopy, and surrounded by a forest of banners; on reaching the Abbey, the effigy was taken from the car, and placed upon the body, beneath a lofty canopy bristling with baunerets, and richly dight with armorial escutcheons.

To what may be styled the legitimate wax figures at Westminster were added, from time to time, those of other celebrities, as, for example, Mother Shipton; and the strange collection was shown until 1839, when it was very properly removed.

In France a similar collection of effigies has been made. Mr. Cole, upon his visit to the Abbey of St. Denis, near Paris, November 22d, 1765, says in his *Diary:* "Mr. Walpole had been informed by M. Marietta that in this treasury were several wax figures of some of the later kings of France, and asked one of the monks for leave to see them, as they were not commonly shown or much known. Accordingly, in four cupboards, above those in which the jewels, crosses, busts, and curiosities were kept, were eight ragged figures of so many monarchs of this country to Louis the Thirteenth, which must be very like, as their faces were taken off in wax immediately after their decease. The monk told us, that the great Louis the Fourteenth's face was so excessively wrinkled, that it was impossible to take one off from him."

BURIAL IN A COWL.

A superstitious idea seems to have been formerly attached to the fact of burying the corpse in a monk's Cowl, for which we may, among many other authorities, refer to Holinshed. Speaking of the death of King John, he says: "For the manner was at that time in such sort to bury their nobles and great men, who were induced, by the imagination of monks and fond fansies of friers, to believe that the said cowl was an amulet, or defensitive to their soules from hell and hellish bags, how or in whatsoever sort they died."—Holinshed's *Chronicle*, vol. ii. p. 337; W. M. Wylie, F.S.A., *Archæologia*, vol. xxxv. p. 303. (Has this "defensitive" property of the *cowl* any thing to do with the protection believed to be afforded by the *caul*, described in *Things not generally Known*, First Series, p. 130?)

ROSE-TREES PLANTED ON GRAVES.

In the village churchyard of Ockley, in Surrey, it was formerly the custom of betrothed lovers to plant Rose-trees at the head of the grave of a deceased lover, should either party die before the wedding. Camden, Evelyn, and Aubrey, record this custom, which Mr. Manning considers to have been handed down from the Romans, by whom the rose was so used. The Romans were much at Ockley; and the Roman road (Stane-street Causeway) passes through the village.

𝔥𝔬𝔪𝔢 𝔓𝔯𝔬𝔟𝔢𝔯𝔟𝔰, 𝔖𝔞𝔶𝔦𝔫𝔤𝔰, 𝔞𝔫𝔡 𝔓𝔥𝔯𝔞𝔰𝔢𝔰.

Pumping a Man, i. e. seeking to get information from him indirectly, may be traced to Otway's *Venice Preserved,* act ii. sc. 1, where Pierro says:

> Pump not me for politics.

Virtues of Sage.—In our enumeration at pp. 133 and 134 of the present volume, we omitted the proverbial line: " He that would live for age, must eat sage in May."

Fast and Loose will be found in Shakspeare's *Love's Labour's Lost,* act iii. sc. 1:

> As cunning as fast and loose.

On Tick.—Tick, for credit, is a word at least as old as the seventeenth century, and is corrupted from ticket, as a tradesman's bill was formerly called; and the phrase was originally *on ticket, i. e.* things taken to be put into the bill. Sedley, in the *Mulberry Garden,* 1668, says:

> I confess my tick is not good;

and Oldham (*Poems,* 1683) has:

> Reduced to want, he in due time fell sick,
> Was fain to die, and be interred on tick.

The statute 10 Car. II. against gaming, enacts that " if any person shall lose any sum of money so played for, exceeding the sum of 100*l.* at any one time or meeting, upon *ticket* or credit," &c.

Admiral of the Blue is an old popular term for a tapster, from the colour of his apron:

> As soon as customers begin to stir,
> The Admiral of the *Blue* cries, "Coming, sir !"
> > *Poor Robin,* 1731.

Wild Oats, applied to a very extravagant fellow, is of old date. Lord Bacon speaks of " light brains and wild oats;" and " wild oats" occurs in *How a Man may chuse a Good Wife,* 1602. *Oat-meal* seems to have been a current name for profligate bucks, being mentioned with the Roaring Boys, in a ballad by Ford or Dekker.

Between Hawk and Buzzard is a proverb, meaning perhaps originally, between two equally dangerous enemies, a hawk and a kite. It is now chiefly used to express mere doubt. The *hawk* is tractable, the *buzzard* is not; whence the French put them together in a proverb thus : " You cannot make a hawk of a buzzard."

A Mare's Nest is a cant phrase for a ridiculous discovery. In Ireland, it is said, when a person is seen laughing immoderately without any apparent cause, " O, he has found a mare's nest, and he's laughing at the eggs."

> Why dost thou laugh ?
> What mare's nest hast thou found ?   *Bonduca*, act v. sc. 2.
> Nares's *Glossary*, new edit. 1858.

Giving Quarter originated from an agreement between the Dutch and Spaniards, that the ransom of an officer or soldier should be a quarter of his pay. Hence to beg quarter was to offer a quarter of their pay for their safety, and to refuse quarter was not to accept that composition as a ransom.

To give Pap with a Hatchet was a proverbial phrase for doing a kind thing in an unkind manner, as it would be to feed an infant with so formidable an instrument. An old fellow and a young wife are thus pointed at in a "Discourse of Marriage" (*Harl. Misc.*): " He that so old seeks for a nurse so young, shall have pap with a hatchet for his comfort."

Deaf as an Adder.—There is a Kentish proverb about the Adder which accords with the Scripture allusion to its deafness, " They are like the deaf adder that stoppeth her ear" (*Psalm* lviii. 4):—

> If I could hear as well as soo,
> No man nor beast should pass by me.

The Welkin.—This term, familiar in the phrase " to make the welkin ring," signifies the sky, from *wealcan*, to roll, or *welc*, a cloud, Saxon. Yet it is used also for the cloudless sky. Shakspeare has :

> The sky, the welkin, the heaven.
> *Love's Labour's lost*, act ix. sc. 2.

And Spenser, in his Shepherd's Kalendar,

> The swallow peeps out of her nest,
> And cloudie welkin cleareth.

It has been preserved as a poetical word by Milton, and many other poets.

Eating Humble Pie.—When our forests were stocked with deer, and venison pasty was commonly seen on the tables of the wealthy, the inferior and refuse portions of the deer (termed the "umbles") were generally appropriated by the poor, who made them into a pie : hence "umble-pie" became suggestive of poverty, and was afterwards applied to degradations of other kinds

Piping Hot is taken from the custom of a baker's blowing his pipe, or horn, in villages, to let the people know his bread is just drawn, and consequently "hot" and light.—Lemon's *Etymological Dictionary*, 1783.

Three Blue Beans in a Blue Bladder.—This whimsical word-play is of long standing, and occurs in an old drama, and in the *Alma* of Prior.

The Baker's Dozen : Thirteen.—This was originally called a devil's dozen, and was the number of witches supposed to sit down at table together in their great meetings, or sabbaths. The baker, who was a very unpopular character in former times, seems to have been substituted on this account for the devil. In Cleaveland's *Poems*, 1561, we find the line :

> Hercules' labours were a baker's dozen.

We quote this from the additions to Nares's *Glossary*, new edit. : "Hence the superstition relating to the number thirteen at table ;" the ill luck of which will be found noticed in *Things not generally Known*, First Series, p. 147.

The Owl was a Baker's Daughter was a legendary tale of a baker's daughter transformed into an owl: it is referred to in *Hamlet*. The substance of the tale is, that a baker's daughter, who refused bread to our Saviour, was by Him transformed into an owl, as a punishment for her impiety.

An Owl in an Ivy-bush perhaps denoted originally the union of wisdom or prudence with conviviality ; as, " be merry and wise." It is, however, true, that a bush, or *tod, of ivy* was usually supposed to be the favourite resort of an owl ; the ivy was also sacred to Bacchus.

Odd Numbers lucky.—" They say there is divinity in odd numbers, either in nativity, chance, or death."—*Merry Wives of Windsor*, act v. sc. 1.

The Black Ox has trod on his Foot, denoted that he had fallen into decay and misfortune.

Palermo Razors were celebrated for their excellence before Britain had learnt to excel all the world in cutlery.

A Feather in his Cap.—This saying has been traced to a passage in Lansdowne Ms. 775 (British Museum), in a "Description of Hungary," written 1599, stating, "It hath been an ancient custom among them (the inhabitants) that none should wear a fether but he who had killed a Turk, to whom onlie yt was lawful to shew the number of his slaine enemys by the number of fethers in his cappe."

Hobson's Choice is as old as the younger days of Milton,[*] but its meaning has become perverted in course of use. Its origin is thus given in one of Steele's contributions to the *Spectator*, No. 509 :

> I shall conclude this discourse with an explanation of a proverb, which by vulgar error is taken and used when a man is reduced to an extremity ; whereas the propriety of the maxim is to use it when you would say there is plenty, but you must make such a choice as not to hurt another who is to come after you.
>
> Mr. Tobias Hobson, a carrier, was "the first in this island who let out hackney-horses." He lived in Cambridge, where he kept a stable of forty good cattle, always ready and fit for travelling. But when a man came for a horse, he was led into the stable, where there was great choice ; but he obliged him to take the horse which stood next to the stable-door ; so that every customer was alike well served according to his chance, and every horse ridden with the same justice ; from whence it became a proverb, when what ought to be your election was forced upon you, to say, "Hobson's Choice."
>
> This memorable man stands drawn in fresco at an inn (which he used) in Bishopsgate-street with an hundred-pound bag under his arm, with this inscription upon the said bag:
>
> "The fruitful mother of a hundred more."

The inn is the Four Swans, Bishopsgate-street-without, which remains to this day the most perfect galleried old inn in London ; but the portrait of Hobson—*non est inventus.*

Cooking his Goose.—A speculative Correspondent of *Notes and Queries*, Second Series, vii. p. 252, has found the following among some witty stories in a Ms. of the middle of the seventeenth century, in Sion-College library, which he considers to explain the vulgar phrase of "Cooking his Goose."

The King of Sweden's Goose.

The King of Swedland coming to a towne of his enemyes with very little company, his enemyes, to slight his forces, did hang out a goose for him to shoote ; but perceiving before night that thes few soldiers had invaded and set their chiefe houlds on fire, they demanded of him what his intent was. To whom he replied, "To roast your goose."

Good Wine needs no Bush.—That this proverb alludes to the bush which was usually hung out at vintners' doors; is well known ; but it is not so well known that the bush should be ivy, according to classic propriety, that plant being sacred to Bacchus ; and our old writers specially name the ivy-bush : whereas at public-houses and beer-shops they hang out a branch of elm, hazel, or any other inappropriate tree.

Planet-struck.—The planets were formerly supposed to have the power of doing sudden mischief by their malignant aspect, which was conceived to strike objects ; as when trees are sud-

* Hobson died January 1, 1630. Milton wrote on him an epitaph of eighteen lines.

denly blighted, or the like. Hence the common expression of "planet-struck." The editors of Nares's *Glossary* add this quaint illustration of the superstitious belief in the planet-book, of which our dream-book is a sort of reflex :

> "Go fetch me down my planet-book
> Straight from my private room ;
> For in the same I mean to look
> What is decreed my doom."

> The planet-book to her they brought,
> And laid it on her knee ;
> She found that all would come to naught,
> For poison'd she should be.

With a Theonine Tooth, or the bitterest malice, was derived from Theon, a poor freedman of Rome, in Horace's time ; a man of malignant wit, who, provoking his master, was turned out of his house with the present of a small coin, and told to go and buy a rope to hang himself.—*Horace*, Epist. i. 18-82.

Mad as a March Hare.—Hares are said to be unusually wild in the month of March, which is their rutting time. Hence "as mad as a March hare," which occurs in Heywood's *Epigrams*, 1567.

Placing the Pen behind the Ear.—The practice of thus resting the pen when not in actual use is ancient. According to Wilkinson, the scribe of ancient Egypt would clap his reed-pencil behind his ear when listening to any person on business, as the painter was also in the habit of doing when pausing to examine the effects of his painting. In the Middle Ages also public clerks and registrars carried a pen in the ear.

Wild-Goose Chase was a term used to express a sort of racing on horseback formerly practised, resembling the flying of wild geese ; those birds generally going in a train one after another, not in confused flocks as other birds do. In this sort of race, the two horses, after running twelve-score yards, had liberty, which horse soever could get the lead, to take what ground the jockey pleased, the hindmost horse being bound to follow him within a certain distance agreed on by the articles, or else to be whipped in by the triers and judges who rode by ; and whichever horse could distance the other won the race. This sort of racing was not long in common use ; for it was found inhuman, and destructive of good horses, when two such were matched together. For in this case neither was able to distance the other till they were both ready to sink under their riders ; and often two very good horses were both spoiled, and the wagers forced to be drawn at last. The mischief of this sort of racing soon brought in the method now in use, of only running over a certain quantity of ground, and determining the plate or wager by coming in first at the winning-post. The phrase "Wild-goose chase" is now employed to denote a fruitless attempt, or an enterprise undertaken with little probability of success; such as our early dramatist May has thus pleasantly described:

> Ah me, throughout the world
> Doth wickedness abound:
> And well I wot, on neither hand
> Can honesty be found.
> The wisest man in Athens
> About the city ran
> With a lantern, in the midst of day,
> To find an honest man.
> And when at night he sat him down
> To reckon on his gains,
> He only found—alack, poor man—
> His labour for his pains.

Jack Ketch.—In Lloyd's *Ms. Collection of English Pedigrees* (Brit. Museum) occurs the origin of this notorious cognomen: "The manor of Tyburn* was formerly held by Richard *Jaquett*, where felons were for a long time executed; from whence we have *Jack Ketch.*" There is skill in his art. Dryden observes, with rare humour: "A man may be capable, as Jack Ketch's wife said of her servant, of a plain piece of work, a bare hanging; but to make a malefactor die sweetly, was only belonging to her husband." Another noted hangman, in the seventeenth century, was one *Derrick*, after whom was named the temporary crane formed on board ship for unloading and general hoisting purposes, by lashing one spar to another, gibbet-fashion.

Daines Barrington says that, in his day, when an executioner was wanted in the maritime counties of North Wales, the hangman was always procured from Cheshire, and paid an extraordinary price.

Pigs seeing the Wind.—Pigs have remarkably small eyes, yet are said to be very sagacious in foretelling wind and weather. Thus, in *Hudibras at Court*, we read:

> And now, as hogs can see the wind,
> And storms at distance coming find.

Plutarch remarks, that pigs' eyes are so situated and constructed, that the animal cannot look upwards, and never has a view of the heavens till he is thrown upon his back; and then, clamorous as he is, astonishment and terror silence him in an instant.—Dr. Nash's *Notes to Hudibras.*

---

* Formerly, when a person prosecuted for any offence, and the prisoner was assented at Tyburn, the prosecutor was presented with "a Tyburn Ticket," which exempted him, and its future holders, from serving on juries; and this privilege was not repealed until 6th Geo. IV.

Paid down upon the Nail.—The origin of this phrase is thus stated in the *Recollections of O'Keefe*, the dramatist: "An ample piazza under the Exchange (Limerick) was a thoroughfare. In the centre stood a pillar about four feet high, and upon it a circular plate of copper about three feet in diameter. This was called the Nail, and on it was paid the earnest for any commercial bargains made; which was the origin of the saying, 'Paid down upon the nail.'" Perhaps the custom was common to other ancient towns.—*Notes and Queries.*

Coals to Newcastle is English, of course, in the outer garment which it wears; but in its innermost being it belongs to the whole world and to all countries. Thus the Greeks said, "Owls to Athens," Attica abounding with these birds; the Rabbis, "Enchantments to Egypt," Egypt being esteemed of old the head-quarters of all magic; the Orientals, "Pepper to Hindostan;" and in the middle ages they had this proverb, "Indulgences to Rome."—*Rev. Thomas Wilson on Proverbs.*

Quick Sticks and Inkle-Weavers.—In Lincolnshire, if a person is progressing at a rapid pace on his journey, the trite observation upon the occasion is, "he goes like *quick sticks.*" This expression derived its origin, there can be no doubt, from the rapid growth of the shoots of the *quick* (roots of the whitethorn bush), which in some parts of England are planted to form hedge-row boundaries. The "sticks" extend so "quickly," after the roots have taken hold of the ground, that they are styled *quick roots.* Again, "as thick as Inkle-Weavers" is a very familiar expression, used by persons who mean to imply that "close fellowship" exists between particular parties to whom they might refer. Now *inkle* is an old provincial name for *tape,* which was, nearly a century ago, manufactured to a great extent at Newbury, in Berks. The tape-looms, on which the threads were prepared, were so narrow, and so closely connected in position, that the weavers sat in close proximity to each other. Hence the expression, "as thick as *inkle-weavers.*"

Up with the Sun.—To rise with the sun implies, in common parlance, very early habits, of difficult attainment. But, "we rise with the sun at Christmas: it were but continuing to do so till the middle of April, and, without any perceptible change, we should find ourselves then rising at five o'clock; at which hour we might continue till September, and then accommodate ourselves again to the change of season, regulating always the time of retiring in the same proportion. They who require eight hours' sleep would, upon such a system, go to bed at nine during four months."—*Southey's Colloquies.*

The word *Lover* is nearly equivalent to friend, and was

formerly in common use in that sense. Thus, in *Psalm* xxxviii.
11, we have, in the old version, "My lovers and my neighbours
did stand looking upon my trouble;" and also, in the common
version, "My lovers and my friends stand aloof from my sore."
So afterwards, *P's.* lxxxviii. 18. Brutus begins his address to the
people, "Romans, countrymen, and lovers." Another change
which has been undergone by this and some other words is, that
they are now usually applied only to men, whereas formerly they
were common to both sexes. This has happened, for instance,
to "paramour" and "villain," as well as to "lover." But villain is still a term of reproach for a woman as well as for a man
in some of the provincial dialects; and although we no longer
call a woman a lover, we still say of a man and woman that
they are lovers, or a pair of lovers. The term "lover" is also distinctly applied to a woman in so late a work as Smollett's *Count
Fathom*, published in 1754: "These were alarming symptoms
to a lover of her delicacy and pride" (vol. i. c. 10).—Professor
Craik's *English of Shakspeare.*

He is not worth Powder and Shot, i.e. he is not worth suing,
—it would be a waste of money to go to law with him. This
is the only sense in which the phrase is used among us. The
corresponding Dutch phrase — "The bird is not worth the
shot." *De vogel is het schot niet waardig*—is of more general
application; like the French saying, "The play is not worth
the cost of the caudle," *Le jeu ne vaut pas la chandelle.* Long
before the late controversy on the plurality of worlds, this last
proverb was happily applied by a French writer in the following sentence: "If the stars that people the firmament were
destined only to gladden our sight, *le jeu ne vaudrait pas la
chandelle.*"—*Kelly.*

THE WHETSTONE.

To give the Whetstone as a prize for lying was a standing jest with our ancestors. Ray, among proverbial phrases
denoting a liar, has, "He deserves the whetstone." Nares
considers the jest may have arisen from some such idea as
Randolph's, in his interlude of *The Pedlar*, thus descanting on
a whetstone for sharpening wits:

> Leaving my brains, I come to a more profitable commodity; for,
> considering how dull half the wits of this university [Cambridge] be, I
> thought it not the worst traffique to sell whetstones. This whetstone
> [he continues] will set such an edge upon your inventions, that it will
> make your rusty iron brains purer metal than your brazen faces. Whet
> but the knife of your capacities on this whetstone, and you may pre-
> sume to dine at the Muses' Ordinarie, or sup at the Oracle of Apollo.

Then there were jocular games, in which the prize given for
the greatest lie was a whetstone, which, Lupton says, was "a

silver whetstone." In an old morality, Mendax, the liar, brings
a whetstone in his hand, and blazons his own arms as three
whetstones in gules, with no difference. The Cretans being
always noted for lying, Lyly says: "If I met with one of Crete,
I was ready to lie with him for the whetstone."

Travellers, being always suspected of lying, were compli-
mented with the attribute of the whetstone. Ben Jonson's
traveller, Amorphus, hires a page named Cos (or Whetstone);
and Bishop Hall speaks of

> The brain-sicke youth that feeds his tickled eare
> With sweet-sauc'd lies of some false travellor;
> Which hath the Spanish decades red awhile,
> Or Whetstone-leasings of old Maudevile.

A strange use of the whetstone is recorded by Harington to
have been made by a lying knight; who, while he publicly
acknowledged how he had slandered an archbishop, all the
while carried a long whetstone hanging out at the pocket of
his sleeve, so conspicuous, as men understood his meaning was
to give himself the lie.

This, says Narea, explains the force of Lord Bacon's sar-
casm; who, when Sir Kenelm Digby boasted of having seen the
philosopher's stone in his travels, but was puzzled to describe it,
interrupted him, saying, "Perhaps it was a whetstone."

Butler satirises the newspapers of his time as

> Diurnals writ for regulation
> Of lying to inform the nation,
> And by their public use to bring down
> The rate of whetstones in the kingdom.
>
> *Hudibras*, part ii. can. 1.

So late as 1792 this lying custom can be traced in England.
Budworth, in his *Fortnight's Ramble to the Lakes*, says: "It is
a custom in the north, when a man tells the greatest lye in the
company, to reward him with a whetstone; which is called
lying for the whetstone."

THE WEIRD SISTERS.

The term Weird is from the Saxon *wyrd*, a witch, or fate,
and is used by Scottish writers in that sense. It was particularly applied by Shakspeare to his witches in *Macbeth*, because he found them called *weird sisters* in Holinshed, from
whom he took the history:

> The weird sisters, hand in hand,
> Posters of the sea and land.   *Macbeth*, act i. sc. 3.

The weird sisters meant also the fates with Scottish writers;
and Gavin Douglas so translates *Parcæ* from Virgil. In an old
English ballad, "weird lady" means a witch, or enchantress:

To the weird-lady of the woods,
Full many and long a day,
Through lonely shades and thickets rough
He winds his weary way.   *Percy's Reliques.*

THE THREE SOULS.

The peripatetic philosophy, which governed the schools in the time of our old dramatists, assigns to every man *three souls:* the vegetative, the animal, and the rational. In Huarte's *Trial of Wits,* translated by Carew, there is a curious chapter concerning these Three Souls. Howell says:

After the forty-fifth day of conception, the embryon is animated with three souls: with that of plants, called the vegetable; then with a sensitive, which all brute animals have; and lastly, the rational soul is infused: and these three in man are like Trigonus in Tetragono.—*Letters,* I. ill. 36.

THE NINE WORTHIES.

These are famous personages, often alluded to, and classed together rather in an arbitrary manner, like the Seven Wonders of the World, &c.

The Nine have been thus counted up as the *Nine Worthies of the World* by Richard Burton, in a book published in 1687:

Three Gentiles	1. Hector, son of Priam. 2. Alexander the Great. 3. Julius Cæsar.
Three Jews	4. Joshua, conqueror of Canaan. 5. David, king of Israel. 6. Judas Maccabæus.
Three Christians	7. Arthur, king of Britain. 8. Charles the Great, or Charlemagne. 9. Godfrey of Bullen [Bouillon].

London had also Nine Worthies of her own, according to a pamphlet by Richard Johnson, author of the famous *History of the Seven Champions.* These worthies are: 1. Sir William Walworth, fishmonger; 2. Sir Henry Pritchard, vintuer; 3. Sir William Sevenoake, grocer; 4. Sir Thomas White, merchant-tailor; 5. Sir John Bonham, mercer; 6. Sir Christopher Croker, vintner; 7. Sir John Hawkwood, merchant-tailor; 8. Sir Hugh Calvert, silk-weaver; 9. Sir Henry Maleverer, grocer. Sir Thomas White seems to have been the only quite peaceable worthy among them, whose fame lives in St. John's College, Oxford, and Merchant Tailors' School, London, which school he founded.

From the fame of these personages, Butler formed his curious title of *Nine-worthiness,* meaning, it is presumed, that his hero (Hudibras) was equal in valour to any or all of the nine.

THE FORLORN HOPE.

For centuries (says "An Old Soldier," in *Notes and Queries*, No. 220), the Forlorn Hope was called, and is still called by the Germans, *Verlorne Posten;* by the French, *Enfans perdus;* by the Poles and other Slavonians, *Stracona poéta,*—meaning in each of those three languages a detachment of troops, to which the commander of an army assigns such a perilous post, that he entertains no hope of ever rescuing it, or rather gives up all hope of its salvation. In detaching these men, he is conscious of the fate that awaits them; but he sacrifices them to save the rest of his army, *i.e.* he sacrifices a part for the safety of the whole. In short, he has no other intention, no other thought in so doing, than that which the adjective *forlorn* conveys. Thus, for instance, in Spain, a detachment of 600 students volunteered to become a *forlorn hope,* in order to defend the passage of a bridge at Burgos, to give time to an Anglo-Spanish corps (which was thrown into disorder, and closely pursued by a French corps of 18,000 men) to rally. The students all, to the last man, perished; but the object was attained. Thus far the phrase as a strategy of war. It is, however, employed in a more poetic sense.

"There is great kindliness" (says an able and genial writer in the *Edinburgh Essays*, 1856) "in such phrases as *Enfans perdus, Infante perduto, Gens perdus, Fille perdue,* and the *Forlorn Hope of Humanity.* Our notion of a forlorn hope is destruction to the individuals composing it, but a clear gain to the force from which they are selected. Doubtless an entire army partakes of this character, and we may speak of the whole human race as *Gens perdus,* life being, as some one has acutely observed, the disease of which we all perish: but the phrases are usually applied to persons remarkably and eminently unfortunate, whose work, whether it be called good or evil, attracts general notice; and indicate, when so applied, an unexpressed, perhaps unconscious, judgment, which is well worthy of a little consideration.

"Certain moral critics, however, view the subject in a different light. They have very little patience with the excuses of frailty, and highly approve Randle Cotgrave's definition, in his old dictionary, of the *Enfans perdus,* as 'lost, perished, forlorne, past hope of recovery, cast away, forgorne, omitted, overslipped, run or fallen away; also lewed, naughty, wicked, ungracious, or past grace.' They even regard them with horror, and apply to them that singular passage in the Epistle of Jude, where those who despise dominion, speak evil of dignities, and dream of things to come, are spoken of as 'clouds without water, carried about of winds; trees whose fruit withereth, without fruit, twice dead, plucked up by the roots; raging waves of the sea, foaming out their own shame; wandering stars, to whom is reserved the blackness of darkness for ever.' In this view there is much important truth: it is impossible to deny that many of the most unfortunate men of genius have been great sinners, in the ordinary sense of the word,—have been devotees of him whom Buddha called the Lord of Pleasure and the God of Death, and so have destroyed their own balance and calm."

THE WORD "WORTH."

The able Anglo-Saxon scholar and antiquary, Mr. John Just, of Bury, in a paper read to the Rosicrucians at Manchester, in 1853, gives the following definition of this word:

Wortha, *Weortha*, Anglo-Saxon, a field, &c. *Worth* means land, close, or farm. It does not necessarily imply any residence, although thereon might be a hall or mansion. It likewise sometimes means nothing more than a road or public way. Hence it is connected with the names of many places on our old roads, as Ainsworth, Edgeworth, on the Roman military road to the north; Failsworth, Saddleworth, on the Roman military road from Manchester to York; Unsworth, Pilsworth, on the old road between Bury and Manchester; and Ashworth, Whitworth, Butterworth, on old roads, and connected with old places near Rochdale. Whether originally land, closes, or farms, *worths* were acquired properties. The old expression of "What is he worth?" in those days meant, "Has he land?" "Possesses he real property?" If he had secured a good worth to himself, he was called a *worthy* person, and in consequence had *worship*, i. e. due respect shown him. A *worth* was the reward of the free; and perchance the fundamentals of English freedom were primarily connected with such apparently trivial matters, and produced such a race of *worthies* as the proud Greeks and haughty Romans might not be ashamed of., *Worth* is pure Anglo-Saxon. The Scandinavians applied it not in their intercourse with our island.

THE WORD "CHOUSE"

is derived by Mr. Craufurd from the Persian *kiaus*, intelligent, ingenious, astute. In Persia and Turkey this word is applied to certain public agents, as an honorary title. Mr. Gifford, in a note to his edition of Ben Jonson's Works, says:

In 1609, Sir Robert Shirley sent a messenger, or *chiaus*, (as our old writers call him,) to this country, as his agent from the Grand Signior and the Sophy, to transact some preparatory business. Sir Robert followed him at his leisure, as ambassador from both these princes; but before he reached England, his agent *chiaused* the Persian and Turkish merchants here of 4000*l.*, and had taken his flight,—unconscious that he had enriched the language with a word, the etymology of which would mislead Upton and puzzle Dr. Johnson.

The *Alchemist* of Ben Jonson, in which the word first occurs, was first acted in 1610, the year following the commission of the fraud; and the following is the dialogue:

Dapper. What, do you think that I am a *chiaus?*
Face. What is that?
Dapper. The Turk was here: as you would, do you think I am a Turk?
Face. I will tell the doctor so.
Dapper. Do, good sweet captain.
Face. Come, noble doctor, pray thee, let us prevail. This is the gentleman, and he is no *chiaus.*

The cheat, who in all probability was a Persian, it will be observed, is called a Turk; for our forefathers were not particular in distinguishing Oriental people. Both people wore great turbans, and both professed Mohammedanism; and they used the name that was most familiar to them. At first the word appears to have meant a cosener or cheat; and this seems its natural sense. Dryden uses it as a verb, " to cheat, to cosen;" and Butler for the party cheated, a bubble, a tool;

> A sottish *chouse,*
> Who, when a thief has robbed his house,
> Applies himself to cunning men.   *Hudibras.*

WORTH OF HISTORIC TRADITIONS.

Mr. Buckle, in his *History of Civilization in England,* remarks:

The great historians of the middle ages often trace back events in an unbroken series from the moment when Noah left the ark, or even when Adam passed the gates of Paradise. They say also that the capital of France is called after Paris, the son of Priam, because he fled there when Troy was overthrown.

In the *Notes to a Chronicle of London* from 1089 to 1483, pp. 163-187, 4to, 1827, there is a pedigree in which the history of the bishops of London is traced back, not only to the migration of Brutus from Troy, but also to Noah and Adam. Matthew Paris and Matthew of Westminster trace Alfred to Adam, as does also William of Malmesbury. And Ticknor mentions that the Spanish Chronicles present "an uninterrupted succession of Spanish kings from Tubal, a grandson of Noah."

Even in the seventeenth century, this very remote antiquity of Paris was not extinct; and Coryat, who travelled in France in 1608, describes the name of the city from " Paris, the eighteenth king of Gallia Celtica, whom some write to have been lineally descended from Japhet, one of the three sons of Noah, and to have founded this city."—*Crudities,* 1611.

The middle-age historians also mention that Tours owed its name to being the burial-place of Turonus, one of the Trojans; while the city of Troyes was actually built by the Trojans, as its etymology clearly proves. It was well ascertained that Nuremberg was called after the Emperor Nero, and Jerusalem after King Jebus, a man of vast celebrity in the Middle Ages, but whose existence later historians have not been able to verify. The river Humber received its name because, in ancient times, a king of the Huns had been drowned in it. The Gauls derived their origin, according to some, from Galathia, a female descendant of Japhet; according to others, from Gomer, the son of Japhet. Prussia was called after Prussus, a brother of Augustus. This was remarkably modern; but Silesia had its name from the prophet Elisha, from whom, indeed, the Silesians descended; while, as to the city of Zurich, its exact date was a matter of dispute, but it was unquestionably built in the time of Abraham. It was likewise from Abraham and Sarah that the gipsies immediately sprung.

LEVITY UPON RELIGIOUS SUBJECTS.

There cannot be a more indiscreet error than to talk loosely upon religious and moral obligations before those from whom we expect any sort of obedience or service. This is well exemplified in the following anecdote from the *Memoirs of Garrick:*

Mallet, who was a great freethinker, used on all occasions to advance his sentiments, until, we are told, the inferior domestics in his house became as able disputants as the heads of the family. The servant who waited at table, being thoroughly convinced that for any of his misdeeds he should have no account to render hereafter, was resolved to profit by the doctrine, and made off with the plate and many things of value. He was overtaken, and brought before his master and some select friends. At first the man was sullen, and would answer no questions put to him; but being urged to give a reason for his infamous behaviour, he resolutely said: "Sir, I have heard you so often talk of the impossibility of a future state, and that after death there was no reward for virtue or punishment for vice, that I was tempted to commit the robbery." "Well but, you rascal," replied Mallet, "had you no fear of the gallows?" "Sir," said the fellow, looking sternly at his master, "what is that to you, if I had a mind to venture that? you had removed my greatest terror, why should I fear the lesser?"

PRECIOUS FRAGMENTS OF TIME.

The Hon. Robert Boyle has, in his *Discourse touching Occasional Meditations,* this striking passage:

This way of thinking may in part keep men from the loss of such smaller parcels of time as, though a meer moralist would not perhaps censure the neglect of them in others, yet a devout person would condemn it in himself. For betwixt the more stated employments and important occurrences of humane life, there usually happen to be interpos'd certain intervals of time, which, though they are wont to be neglected, as being singly, or within the compass of one day, inconsiderable, yet in a man's whole life they may amount to no contemptible portion of it. Now these uncertain parentheses (if I may so call them), or interludes, that happen to come between the more solemn passages (whether business or recreations) of humane life, are wont to be lost by most men for want of a value for them, and ev'n by good men for want of skill to preserve them. For though they do not properly despise them, yet they neglect, or lose them, for want of knowing how to rescue them, or what to do with them. But as, though grains of sand and ashes be, apart, but of a despicable smallness, and very oasis and liable to be scatter'd and blown away, yet the skilful artificer, by a vehement fire, brings numbers of these to afford him that noble substance glass, by whose help we may both see ourselves and our blemishes lively represented (as in looking-glasses), and discern celestial objects (as with telescopes), and with the sun-beams kindle dispos'd materials (as with burning glasses); so when these little fragments, or parcels of time, which, if not carefully look'd to, would be dissipated and lost, come to be manag'd by a skilful contemplator, and to be improv'd by the celestial fire of devotion, they may be so order'd as to afford us both looking-glasses, to dress our souls by, and perspectives, to discover heavenly wonders, and incentives to inflame our hearts with charity and zeal. And since goldsmiths and refiners are wont, all the year long, carefully to save the very sweepings of their shops, because they may contain in them some filings or dust of these richer metals, gold and silver, I see not why a Christian may not be as careful not to lose the fragments and lesser intervals of a thing incomparably more precious than any metal, time ; especially when the improvement of them by our meleteticks (or way and kind of meditation) may not only redeem so many portions of our life, but turn them to pious uses, and particularly to the great advantage of devotion.

QUESTIONS FOR THE OLD NATURALISTS.

Thomas Fuller, in his *Holy and Profane State*, unquestionably his greatest work, thus eloquently asks :

Tell me, ye naturalists, who sounded the first march and retreat of the tide, "Hither shalt thou come, and no further." Why doth not the water recover his right over the earth, being higher in nature ? Whence came the salt ; and who first boiled it, and made so much brine ? When the winds are not only wild in a storm, but even stark-mad in a hurricane, who is it that restores them again to their wits, and brings them asleep in a calm ? Who made the mighty whales, which swim in a sea of water, and have a sea of oil swimming in them ? "Who first taught the water to imitate the creatures on land ?—so that the sea is the stable of horse-fishes, the stall of kine-fishes, the sty of hog-fishes, the kennel of dog-fishes, and in all things the sea the ape of the land ? Whence grows the ambergris in the sea ? which is not so hard to find where it is as what it is. Was not God the first shipwright ; and all vessels on the water descended from the loins (or ribs rather) of Noah's ark ? or else who durst be so bold, with a few crooked boards nailed together, a stick standing upright, and a rag tied to it, to adventure into the ocean ? What loadstone first touched the loadstone ? Or how first fell it in love with the north, rather affecting that cold climate than the pleasant east, or fruitful south, or west ? How comes that stone to know more than men, and find the way to land in a mist ? In most of these men take sanctuary at *occulta qualitas;* and complain that the room is dark when their eyes are blind. Indeed, they are God's wonders ; and that seaman the greatest wonder of all, who, seeing them daily, neither takes notice of them, admires at them, nor is thankful for them.

METAPHORICAL SCULPTURES OF EGYPT.

Mr. Bonomi has read to the Syro-Egyptian Society a paper, illustrated by drawings made from the monuments, to show that many metaphorical expressions in the Bible are exactly embodied in some of the sculptures. For instance, the well-known *rilievo* on the towers of the gateways to almost all the temples of Egypt, whether built by a Pharaoh or a Ptolemy, representing the king striking off the heads of a group of supplicants, is not a sacrifice, but a metaphorical sculpture exactly embodying the 40th and 41st verses of the 18th Psalm. So likewise the metaphor contained in the sentence, "Until I make *thine enemies thy footstool*," is constantly embodied in the statues of the Pharaohs, which are usually sculptured in a sitting position, with their feet on a stool or block, on which is engraved a string of captives. But the most speaking evidence of this metaphor, common to both descendants of Heber and Mizraim, is to be found on a mummy in the British Museum, on the soles of whose shoes is painted the figure of a prisoner belonging to a nation the most constant and determined enemy of Egypt. Dr. Bell also illustrates the same subject, to the effect that there is at Constantinople the statue of an emperor on horseback trampling on a prisoner, like the equestrian statue of Marcus Aurelius in the Capitol, which the doctor thinks had at one time a similar statue of a 'man under the horse's feet. The equestrian statue at Constantinople has been removed by some conqueror of that city, who imagined that he would thereby secure the city to himself and his successors for ever. From this prejudice of olden time (illustrated also by the horse-foot found among the terra-cottas of Tarsus) Dr. Bell traces the vulgar belief in the efficacy of a horseshoe, nailed to the door of a house or the mast of a ship, to preserve them and their inmates from peril or misfortune. (See also " Luck of Horseshoes," in *Things not generally Known*, First Series, p. 145.)

ORIGIN OF "PA" AND "MA."

Sir Gardner Wilkinson, in his clever work on Colour and Taste, observes: "The learned are pleased to derive the names *Pa* (or *Ba*) and *Ma* from verbs meaning ' to nourish' and ' to fashion' (neither of which indeed is very applicable), rather than from the two natural and untaught sounds made by infants, to which the signification of father and mother were *afterwards* applied. Again, the mode of reckoning by tens (at once the most obvious and natural, from the ten fingers) is thought to be ' one of the most marvellous achievements of the human mind, based on an abstract conception of quantity, and regulated by a spirit of philosophical classification;' and the child Harpocrates, with its finger to its mouth, has been thought to represent ' Silence,' instead of the idea of 'infancy,' from a common habit of young children.''

𝔚eather-𝔚isdom.

___

THE ANEROID BAROMETER.

THE following information respecting this new instrument is from an official paper published by the Board of Trade :

Aneroid barometers, if often compared with good mercurial columns, are similar in their indications, and valuable: but it must be remembered that they are not independent instruments; that they are set originally by a barometer,* require adjustment occasionally, and may deteriorate in time, though slowly.

The aneroid is quick in showing the variation of atmospheric pressure ; and to the navigator, who knows the difficulty, at times, of using barometers, this instrument is a great boon ; for it can be placed any where, quite out of harm's way, and is not affected by the ship's motion, although faithfully giving indication of increased or diminished pressure of air.† In ascending or descending elevations the hand of the aneroid may be seen to move (like the hand of a watch), showing the height above the level of the sea, or the difference of level between places of comparison.‡

The principle on which it is constructed may be explained in a few words, without going into a scientific or minute detail of its various parts. The weight of a column of air, which in a common barometer acts on the mercury, in the aneroid presses on a small circular metal box, from which nearly all air is extracted; and to this box is connected, by nice mechanical arrangement, the hand visible over the face of the instrument. When the atmospheric pressure is lessened on the vacuum-box, a spring, acting on levers, turns the hand to the left ; and when the pressure increases, the spring is affected differently, the hand being turned to the right. It acts in any position ; but, as it often varies several hundredths with such a change, it should therefore be held uniformly.

The known expansion and contraction of metals under varying temperatures caused doubts as to the accuracy of the aneroid under such changes ; but they were partly removed by introducing into the vacuum-box a small portion of gas, as a compensation for the effects of heat or cold,—the gas in the box, changing its bulk on a change of temperature, being intended to compensate for the effect on the metals of which the aneroid is made. Besides which, a further and more re-

___

* A small turnscrew being applied gently to the screw-head at the back. This is often necessary on receiving or first using an aneroid that has long been lying by, or that has been shaken by travelling.

† It is a good weather-glass—to be suspended on or near the upper deck, for easy reference.—and is unlikely to be injured by mere concussion of air or vibration of wood when guns are fired.

‡ Allowing 0·0011 of an inch for each foot.

liable compensation has lately been effected by a combination of brass and steel bars.*

WORTH OF WEATHER PROGNOSTICATIONS.

Mr. E. J. Lowe, from a multitude of observations, undertaken with a view of ascertaining whether the popular and generally received opinions respecting atmospheric phenomena have in reality any foundation, has arrived at these conclusions: that little or no dependence can be placed upon any of the popular weather-signs or predictions; and that, in most cases, fair weather predominates even when the prognostications indicate rain. The following table of numerous registered observations on phenomena which are said to indicate either rain or fair weather, shows how the result stood:

	Number of Observations.	Followed in 24 hours by Fair	and	Rain.
Solar haloes . . .	204	133	,,	71
Lunar haloes . . .	102	51	,,	51
White stratus in valley .	229	201	,,	28
Distance clear . . .	102	61	,,	41
Distant sounds heard as if near	45	25	,,	20
Aurora borealis . .	76	49	,,	27
Coloured clouds at sunset .	35	26	,,	9
Dew profuse . . .	241	198	,,	43
White frost . . .	73	59	,,	14
Stars bright. . . .	83	64	,,	19
Stars dim . . .	54	32	,,	22
Smoke rising perpendicularly	6	5	,,	1
Sun red and shorn of rays .	31	31	,,	8
Moon shining dimly . .	18	12	,,	6
Flies troublesome . .	22	12	,,	10
Spiders' webs thick on the grass .	13	9	,,	4
Leaves of vegetables drooping	25	5	,,	20

Mr. Leonard Jenyns has the following practical suggestions upon weather-prophecies:

To judge by the weather-almanacs which yearly make their appearance, one might suppose that the science had already made sufficient advances to warrant the predictions of those who set themselves up to be prophets in this matter. But it is hardly necessary to warn the public against placing the slightest confidence in these publications, which have been so often exposed. In some instances these almanacs have acquired notoriety for a time by a few happy guesses about the weather, which have come right by a mere coincidence; but in the long-run, if any one will take the trouble to compare them throughout with what really occurs, their predictions will be found just as often wrong as right, showing that they are grounded upon no trustworthy principles.

* The manufacture of these useful auxiliary instruments (all French originally) has been much improved latterly. The name *Aneroid* is a scientific Greek compound to express the principle of the instrument, namely, a vacuum: from ά, no, ἀήρ, air, and εἶδος, form, with the usual ν (n) interposed in such compounds for the sake of euphony. The French is *anéroïde*.

Some, indeed, pretend to base their foreknowledge of the weather upon the foreknown changes of the heavenly bodies above alluded to. They claim to be listened to on the ground that, the weather being under the influence of the moon and planets, and altering from time to time as these bodies alter their positions in respect of the earth and each other, we may safely draw our inferences about the former from knowing the exact places of the latter on any particular day or month we may have in view. But greater names than any which this class of meteorologists can boast of have utterly discouraged all such theories. Arago, for one, in reference to the common notion of the weather being affected by the moon or comets, has expressed his belief that, if the latter have any influence at all, that influence is so small as to be almost inappreciable, and that consequently "the predictions of the weather can never be a branch of astronomy properly so called."

Mr. Jenyns is equally sceptical with respect to the cycle theory, supposing a succession of changes in a given order dividing regular intervals of time. The truth is, that the more the science of meteorology advances, the less hope there seems to be of our ever being able to foretell the weather with any certainty.

It is even impossible to predict what the weather will be after the lapse of a few hours; for, in order to predict with certainty if it will rain or clear up, a knowledge of the temperature of the upper region is requisite; and as this is wanting, there must always be a great degree of uncertainty in our prognostications.

WHAT IS THE MEAN TEMPERATURE OF THE DAY?

There are two hours in the day at which the temperature is a mean of the day in England: the first occurs at about 9 o'clock a.m., and the last at about 8 hours 15 minutes p.m.; the critical interval, as it is called, being thus about 11 hours 15 minutes.—*Sir D. Brewster.*

THE LONGEST DAY.

June 21 is the longest day, the climax of the greatest range of the sun; after which the beautiful twilight is sensibly shortened. The sun rises at 35m. after 3, and sets at 18m. after 8, giving solar light for 17 hours 33m. in England; in Scotland the twilight remains till the dawn. The beauty of the sunrise at Midsummer is known by but too few, and ought to be more generally witnessed: it is a spectacle, without the aid of either mountains or ocean, quite worth the effort of leaving the bed.

EXTREME HEAT.

June 16, 1858. Early in the morning the temperature of the air in the shade was 61·5 deg.; this increased to 82·7 deg. by 9h. a.m., to 87·5 deg. by 10h. a.m., to 89·0 deg. by 11h. a.m., to 90·0 by noon, to 91·6 deg. by 0h. 45m. p.m., and to 94·5 deg. by 1h. p.m.; decreased to 93·3 deg. by 1h. 20m. p.m., to 91·8 deg. by 2h. p.m., to 90·4 deg. by 3h. p.m., to 7²2 deg. by 9h. p.m., and to 62·0 deg. during the night. The mean temperature of the day was 76·0 deg., exceeding the average for the day by 17·6 deg., being a greater departure from the average than Mr. Glaisher (of the Royal Observatory) has ever experienced.—*The Astronomer Royal.*

TREES STRUCK BY LIGHTNING.

Meteorologists have found in trees struck by lightning no traces of electricity on the upper branches, but it appears to strike at the main trunk. When the colour of the electric discharge is red, it indicates that the electricity is very high.

TREES DEFENSATIVE AGAINST LIGHTNING.

Mr. M'Nab, Fellow of the Botanical Society of Edinburgh, has long noted information regarding lightning-struck trees in Great Britain, in consequence of the generally received opinion that neither the Beech nor the Birch have ever been noticed to be injured by Lightning. Since 1843, he has communicated to the Botanical Society the names of various lightning-struck trees, but neither beech nor birch were among the number. He formerly stated to the Society that the inhabitants of America generally resorted to beech-trees during a thunder-storm, from the fact of their not being liable to be struck with lightning. This he found to be the case through large tracts of country; and it induced him to institute an inquiry in Britain, which up to this period (1859) agrees with the information he received in America.

CAUSES OF FORKED LIGHTNING.

Mr. Grove has proved by experiment, that the effects of rarefaction upon gases, either produced by the air-pump or by heat, tend to render the discharges of electricity more facile, and to enable them to pass across much larger spaces than would otherwise be the case. Thus, when the flame of a spirit-lamp was held near one of the terminal points of a coil-apparatus, the terminals being separated to a distance far beyond that at which the spark would pass in cold air, the spark darted to and along the margin of the flame, and could be curved or twisted about in any direction, giving a perfect illustration of the forked form of lightning, and of the probable reason why it does not pass in straight lines—the temperature of the air being different at different points in its passage, and much of this variation of temperature being, in all probability, occasioned by the mechanical effects of the discharge itself upon the air.

Mr Nasmyth considers that the form usually attributed to lightning by painters, and in works of art, is very different from that exhibited in nature; and he believes the error of the artists to have originated in the form given to the thunderbolt in the hand of Jupiter, as sculptured by the early Greeks.

With regard to the colour of lightning in general, when the discharging clouds are near the earth, the light is white; and when they are at a great height, the light is reddish, or violet.

IS LIGHTNING CAUSED BY RAIN?

In a Report of the Committee of Physics of the Royal Society it is asked, whether the sudden gust of rain, which is almost sure to succeed a violent detonation immediately overhead, is a *cause* or *consequence* of the electric discharge. In support of the former view, it is observed: "in the sudden agglomeration of many minute and feebly electrified globules into one rain-drop, the quantity of electricity is increased in a greater proportion than the surface over which (according to the laws of electric distribution) it is spread. Its tension, therefore, is increased, and may attain the point when it is capable of separating from the *drop* to seek the surface of the *cloud*, or of the newly-formed descending body of rain, which, under such circumstances, and with respect to the electricity of such a tension, may be regarded as a conducting medium. Arrived at this surface, the tension, for the same reason, becomes enormous, and a flash escapes." This view is supported by several observations made by Mr. W. R. Birt, the meteorologist.

BELLS AND LIGHTNING.

The old notion that the ringing of Bells during a storm was defensative has been thus commented on by Fuller:

Bells (says the Church historian) are no effectual charm against lightning. The frequent firing of abbey-churches by lightning confuteth the proud motto commonly written on the bells in their steeples, wherein each bell entitled itself to a sixfold efficacy, viz.

> Men's death I tell by doleful knell,
> Lightning and thunder I break asunder,
> On Sabbath all to church I call,
> The sleepy head I raise from bed,
> The winds so fierce I do disperse,
> Men's cruel rage I do assuage.

Whereas it appears that abbey-steeples, though quilted with bells almost *cap-à-pie*, were not proof against the sword of God's lightning. Yea, generally, when the heavens in tempests did strike fire, the steeples of abbeys proved often their timber, whose frequent burnings portended their final destruction.

Lord Bacon, in his *Natural History*, 1635, thus refers to this notion of superstition and olden philosophy:

It has anciently been reported, and is still received, that extreme applauses and shouting of people, assembled in multitudes, have so rarefied and broken the air, that birds flying over have fallen down, the air not being able to support them; and *it is believed by some, that great ringing of bells in populous cities hath charmed away thunder*, and also dissipated pestilent airs. All which may be also from the concussion of the air, and not from the sound.

WHAT TO DO IN A THUNDER-STORM.

The following remarks on the best means of avoiding the dangers of a Thunder-storm (from De la Rive's valuable *Treatise on Electricity*) cannot be too widely known; they serve to correct many popular errors upon this point.

Man, from the remotest ages, has devised means for protecting himself personally from lightning. We will not examine these various methods, which have only an interest purely historical: we shall confine ourselves to remarking that, among these means, some possess no value; and others—such as not to run, to prevent currents of air, &c.—have all at least a doubtful value. Although an insulating envelope certainly mitigates the danger with which one is threatened, as is proved by the example of a priest, who was preserved from the attack of lightning by the silk vestments with which he was clad, nevertheless we cannot admit that it causes it altogether to disappear; indeed, glass itself is not always respected by lightning, as is proved by several examples of glass broken and reduced to powder by it, and even simply pierced by very defined holes, without adjacent fissures.

It would be better to avoid having about one metallic objects, when fearing to be struck in the time of a storm. Franklin also recommends not to keep oneself too near to chimneys, the soot of which is able to conduct the electric discharge; to keep oneself distant, for the same reason, from metals, from looking-glasses (on account of their tin-foil), and from gildings. The best thing appears, that we should endeavour to keep ourselves in the middle of a room; the less we trust the walls and the ground, the less we are exposed. The surest plan, perhaps, would be to have a hammock suspended by silk cords in the centre of a large room. However, even with these precautions it may happen that, if the lightning does not find a continuous conductor around the chamber, it may dart from one point upon the point diametrically opposed, and may meet in its course the person placed in the middle of the room.

Numerous assemblies of men or animals may increase the danger of being struck by lightning, either by assembling in a given point a greater quantity of conducting matter, or by producing from their breathing an ascending column of vapour, the effect of which is to conduct in preference the discharge towards the place itself whence it emanates. Finally, it is probably also to an ascending current of moist air that may be attributed the fact, observed very generally, that granaries filled with grain and forage are more frequently struck by lightning than other buildings. It also happens sometimes that a single person is struck in the midst of a numerous group, and inversely, that a single person is spared, without our being able to detect any exterior cause of this difference; which is evidently due to the circumstance that, as is proved by direct experiments, there are individuals who are naturally better conductors of electricity than others. Although it would be more prudent not to be situated in the midst of clouds out of which lightning and thunder are escaping in an incessant manner, yet a number of examples of persons who have been placed in this situation, and who have come out safe and sound, show that there is not always danger of death in traversing similar clouds: it is, in like manner, more prudent, in the time of a storm, to keep oneself at a certain distance from telegraphic wires, in order to escape the shock of the sparks that may result, as Professor Henry has demonstrated, from phenomena of induction.

HOW BIRDS BUILD THEIR NESTS WEATHERPROOF.

Mr. M. W. B. Thomas, of Cincinnati, Ohio, has ascertained, by careful observation, the following facts: When a pair of migratory birds have arrived in the spring, they immediately prepare to build their nest, making a careful reconnaissance of the place, and observing the character of the season that is coming. *If it be a windy one*, they thatch the straw and leaves on the inside of the nest, between the twigs and the lining; *if it be very windy*, they get pliant twigs, and bind the nest firmly to the limb, securing all the small twigs with their saliva; *if they fear the approach of a rainy season*, they build their nests so as to be sheltered from the weather; but *if a pleasant one*, they build in a fair open place, without taking any of these extra precautions. In recording these facts, Mr. Thomas has kept duly registered the name of the bird, the time of arrival in spring, the commencement of nesting, the materials of the nest, and its position; the commencement of laying, number of eggs in each nest, commencement of incubation, appearances of young, and departure in autumn.

Pictures, and the Care of them.[*]

THE "FOUR COLOURS" EMPLOYED BY ANCIENT PAINTERS.

It is frequently stated that Apelles and other celebrated Greek painters used only four colours, viz. white, yellow, red, and black. This statement is founded on a passage in Pliny, who has given us, in the 34th, 35th, and 36th books of his *Natural History*, the only connected and critical history of the fine arts we possess by an ancient writer. In practical matters Pliny is, however, confessed on all hands to be an unsafe authority; for, judging from his confused, contradictory, and partial descriptions, he must have been unacquainted with some of the simplest operations in painting.

In regard to the question of the "Four Colours," it is certainly a mistake to suppose the ancient painters were acquainted with no others. Our knowledge, it is true, respecting the colours used in classical times is not very considerable, and is derived chiefly from a few passages in ancient authors. Some information has, however, been drawn from experiments on the colours in ancient paintings; and these data are together sufficient to prove that the ancient painter could command a set of pigments almost as extensive as the modern artist. Unless, indeed, we suppose Pliny to have intended to point out a distinction between the practice of the earlier and later painters, the gossiping amateur contradicts himself; for he enumerates in all no less than five different whites, three yellows, nine reds or purples, two blues, two greens, and one black (*atramentum*), which, moreover, appears to be a generic expression that includes bitumen, charcoal, ivory or lamp black, and probably a blue-black, which, thinned, would supply a blue tint; and a longer list might be made out from other authors. That Pliny intended to point out a sort of metaphorical distinction in the practice of the later Greek painters, who, we know, excelled in colouring, is probable from the fact that all the greatest modern authorities agree that the surest road to fine colouring is through a simple palette. And Sir Humphry Davy very justly says, in the account of his experiments on the ancient colours: "If red and yellow ochre, blacks and whites, were the colours most employed

[*] Communicated by Mr. T. J. Gullick.

by Protogenes and Apelles, so they were likewise the colours most employed by Raphael and Titian in their best styles." From such primary colours innumerable hues and tints may of course be composed.

It must, however, be remembered that classical painting of the best period was more closely allied to sculpture than the modern; and from the superior importance attached to design, great soberness in the use of colours prevailed for a long time in antiquity. And although it is possible to infer the contrary from ancient critics,—and it has been inferred even from the inferior remains of ancient painting preserved at Pompeii and elsewhere,—still we have no direct evidence that painting ever attained the same perfection in Greece as sculpture, or that it ever arrived at the distinctive excellence we admire so much in the works of Titian.

On this subject Müller, in his valuable work on *Ancient Art and its Remains*, observes: " Even the Ionic school, which loved florid colouring, adhered to the so-called *four* colours, even down to the time of Apelles; that is, four principal colouring materials. which, however, had not only natural varieties themselves, but also produced such by mixing; for the pure application of a few colours only belonged to the imperfect painting of the architectural works of Egypt, the Etruscan *hypogea*, and the Grecian earthenware. Along with these leading colours, which appeared stern and harsh to a later age, brighter and dearer colouring materials were gradually introduced."

FRAMING PICTURES.

The object in Framing a Picture is, by surrounding it with one colour, to confine the eye to the work alone, and prevent its being distracted by other adjacent objects. Frames with mouldings inclined inwards are useful in giving greater apparent depth to the distance of a landscape or the background of a figure-subject. The principal lines of a picture are also harmoniously extended and enriched by the frame: thus the round head of a child, or a group consisting of an assemblage of curved lines, reaches the eye more agreeably through a circular frame; so likewise with the repetition of forms in the square or oblong aperture. On the Continent, the practice is frequently adopted of commissioning the artist to paint expressly for a given situation; and the frames are made to harmonise in style with the other ornaments of the apartments, particularly the mouldings and cornices. In this way a unity of effect is secured not otherwise attainable. Frames are usually in bad taste from being overloaded with ornament. In general, the simpler the frame the better. When the horizontal line in a

picture is very evident, there should be no ornaments at the
side of the frame which, from difference of position, may dis-
turb the effect of that line on the eye.   Frames which project
much appear to contract a room.   Massive frames convey a
painful impression of suspended weight; but this is partly ob-
viated by "open-work" patterns.

For water-colour paintings it is especially important that
the frames should not be heavy or too profusely ornamented.
A massive frame will almost destroy the effect of delicate work
in water-colours.   Burnishing small points of the frame is,
however, from their greater vivacity, less objectionable for
water-colours than when the frame is intended to enclose an
oil-picture.   The glass of the frame should not touch the face
of the painting.   The mount or margin intervening between
the water-colour painting and its frame is almost invariably
white; though it might not unfrequently with advantage be
tinted, especially if the painting is merely a vignette, that is to
say, if it has no background.   For all delicate work, light in
tone, a paper mount is preferable; and for such, a simple gold-
bead frame, with a gold edge to the mount next the picture, is
very suitable.   But more powerfully and intensely coloured
water-paintings, especially if warm in tone, might often be
rendered more effective and harmonious by substituting a gold
mount.   In all cases, however, we recommend to allow the
artist to select or advise the choice of frame for his own work;
or to let him know if it is desired that the frame for his picture
should match others, in order that he may paint with a view to
the influence of the frame.

DISTRIBUTION OF PICTURES.

It is very common to see pictures of the most dissimilar
character, even in the houses of collectors, stuck all over the
walls, as if they formed a part of the pattern of the paper.   In
all cases oil-pictures, water-colour drawings, and engravings,
should be separated; for in juxtaposition they greatly injure
each other's effect.   In private houses, and for domestic decoration, pictures should always have relation to the dimensions of
the chamber in which they are placed.   As large pictures apparently diminish the size of a small apartment, the smaller easel
and cabinet pictures have been with good taste preferred for
our contracted English interiors.

In the spacious entrance-halls and corridors of country mansions, large hunting subjects, groups of dead game, and fruit-
pieces, are, however, appropriately placed.   In dining-rooms
also, from the more massive and simple character of the furniture, a few life-size portraits of those who, with a little stretch

of imagination, we may imagine to be partakers of our hospitality, together with, of course, subjects of a cheerful and festive, if not bacchanalian character, are admissible. Pictures of still-life, consisting of eatables, &c., or "breakfast pieces," as they are called, and of which Dutch art has produced such an extraordinary number, are also frequently introduced into dining-rooms. Affection will determine where the portraits of dear relatives should be placed: the study or library suggests itself as the most appropriate locality for their reception. For the drawing-room, subjects of a refined and elegant character would naturally be chosen ; and water-colour drawings form a fitting decoration for a *boudoir*, or an inner drawing-room ; while framed prints may be reserved for sleeping apartments. There is surely no reason, however, why the possessor of pictures, who has a separate apartment for his books, and a conservatory for his flowers, should not also have a gallery, with a suitable light, for the proper display of his pictures.

LIGHTING PICTURE-GALLERIES.

An arched or angular skylight in a roof, springing at such an angle that the light coming through illumes the top equally with the bottom of the wall, is the most suitable for a picture-gallery. The centre skylight on a flat roof of some of our exhibition rooms is very objectionable, on account of the little light which pictures receive placed any where near the ceiling.

PAPER-HANGINGS AND PICTURES.

The Paper of the wall against which pictures are suspended should have no pattern, and be of one uniform colour ; and if borders are introduced, they should not contain flowers, but be of some geometrical or conventional style of ornament. The best colours for the wall-paper are red, inclining to crimson (especially for landscapes), or tea-green. Bright carpets, and all gaudy colours in the hangings, furniture, or elsewhere, are likewise injurious to the effect of pictures.

HANGING PICTURES.

As a general rule in Hanging Pictures, the horizontal line of the picture, which is easily distinguishable in a landscape or a portrait with a background, should be placed level with the eye. In an exhibition, the pictures in this most favourably situation are said to be *on the line.* The artist, be it remembered, when painting, treats his canvas as an artificial opening into space, and fixes the horizontal line (at least, theoretically) on a level with the eye—in fact, the two things are identical ; and he paints accordingly. If the spectator, therefore, does not regard the picture from the same relative position, much of the work will be foreshortened, and the general effect falsified. Hanging pictures low has the additional recommendation of increasing the apparent height of an apartment.

Another rule is to hang a picture as nearly as possible in the same light as that in which it was painted. This may be easily discovered in the picture itself, for the light is gradated from the same side as it actually fell upon the work during its execution. If this is neglected, the general truth of the picture is concealed; we get such unnatural effects as shadows thrown out of window, and much of the spirit and feeling which the artist communicated to his touches are lost. This is still more important in respect to water-colour drawings, on account of the grain of the paper, which converts a highly-finished drawing into a coarse daub if not regarded in the proper light.* Painters in water-colours are so sensible of this, that they frequently inscribe the professional direction, *jour à droite*, or *jour à gauche*, according as the light should be on the right or left. In apartments lighted from the side, the pictures should never slant, as if toppling over; the effect of this on the eye is very disagreeable. Nothing but "an eye for colour" can direct in deciding whether pictures would be mutually improved in effect by contrasting a warm, red, or yellow picture with a cool, green, or purple one, or by placing the warm and cold side by side. The lines which pictures form should also be agreeable to the eye, as well as their colour arrangement, and there should at least be a regular base-line. One would, however, naturally in the first place choose central situations, or the "places of honour," for the works of highest quality. Then, again, a dark-toned picture, dimmed by age and discoloured varnish, will require more light than a modern one.

Pictures should not be suspended from one nail; the diagonal lines formed by the cord have a very discordant effect. Two nails and two vertical cords, or, what is far more safe, pieces of *wire cordage*, should be used. A similar objection exists to the use of strings from brass rods running round the ceiling, particularly when there are two or three tiers. These strings cross the vacant surface above the tiers of pictures with great irregularity. To avoid this, some suspend the lower pictures by hooks fastened into the under side of the frames of the upper row of pictures. But there is an admirable contrivance for concealing the attachment of pictures altogether, and allowing them to be slung forward into the room, so as to receive the full light.

* For a full explanation of the cause of this, together with other directions for Hanging Pictures, we refer the reader to *Painting popularly Explained*, by T. J. Gullick and J. Timbs, F.S.A., pp. 289-292.

CARE OF PICTURES.

It is necessary to keep a dry moderately warm temperature, by means of flues or fires, in rooms containing pictures. Damp is the most insidious enemy to many colours; and pictures have been irrecoverably injured by leaving a window open for some hours on a cold, foggy, wintry day. · Pictures also require light and pure air; the habit, therefore, of covering them up in town-houses, during the many months that families are away, is very pernicious. Where pictures or mirrors are suspended for some time against a painted wall and then removed, a dark mark will be found on the wall; a proof of the ill effects of the practice to which we allude. Light also retards the yellowing of oils and varnishes. Frames should be regularly dusted with a hand-brush made of hackle feathers.

Washing pictures should be undertaken on a warm dry day, and nothing but clean cold water should be used by any but very experienced picture-cleaners. The surface should be wetted with a sponge. or soft leather; but the water should never be allowed to float, and all moisture should be carefully removed by gentle friction with an *old* silk handkerchief. The *backs* of pictures should be frequently cleaned; and it is desirable to protect them and render them air-tight with sheets of tin-foil, or oil-skin. When glass is placed over the face of pictures, it should be glazed like the glass in our window-sashes. When this is not properly done, and the air penetrates, we see the consequence very plainly on framed prints in a gradually advancing stain from the edges. The relining of pictures is often an excellent precaution for their preservation. The ingenious operation of transferring pictures from panel to canvas is too delicate and tedious to be undertaken except for valuable works.

VARNISHING PICTURES.

Picture-purchasers should always be on their guard against the picture-dealers' common practice of giving a meretricious appearance to inferior works by loading them with varnish. Many private persons are, however, fond of what they term "doctoring" pictures, which consists principally of inundating them with varnish. Pictures should only be varnished by thoroughly competent persons. The reason for this is, that to avoid the accumulation of several coats of varnish, it is necessary, before revarnishing, to remove the coat previously laid; and to do this, without disturbing the *glazings* of the picture itself, requires considerable experience. The "glazings" are thin films of transparent colour, frequently difficult to distinguish by the eye from the final varnish which the artist applies

last to obtain his most delicate effects; and if these are removed, the picture of course loses its choicest finishing touches.

The hard varnishes—such, for instance, as copal—are the
more durable; but the soft mastic varnish (dissolved in spirits
of turpentine), now commonly used, may be removed and renewed with less risk. A picture should be thoroughly dry
before varnishing, in order to prevent subsequent cracking.
Varnishing should be performed in fair weather, and in a dry
warm room; for a current of cold or damp air will "chill" or
"bloom," that is to say, give a dull mildewed appearance to
any description of varnish.

PICTURE CLEANING AND RESTORING.

Mr. Leslie, in his excellent *Handbook for Young Painters*,
says: "Pictures, like ourselves, are not only subject to the
inevitable decay of age, but to a variety of diseases, caused by
heat, cold, damp and foul air. Many (and they too are among
the most delicate and beautiful) have, like Leonardo da Vinci's
"Last Supper," and a large proportion of the works of Watteau,
of Reynolds, and of Turner, unsound constitutions given to
them by the authors of their existence, and are thus subject
to premature and rapid destruction. These liabilities, and the
many accidents to which they are exposed, have made picture-
restorers as important a class in art as physicians and surgeons
in life; and, as might naturally be expected, there are many
unskilful among them, and many ignorant quacks."

Picture-doctors are, however, a necessary evil; and to choose
men of well-known respectability is the only advice we can
offer the public, when it is necessary to intrust paintings to
their tender mercies. But "restorations" and "repaintings"
should be avoided as much as possible. The oil in old pictures
has undergone all its changes; not so the oil in the new tints,
which are made to match the old; but as the changes must
take place, after a time the restorations and repaintings necessarily cease to match, and become apparent from their dis-
cordance.

HOW TO LOOK AT A PICTURE.

In viewing Pictures, the proper *focal distance*, which is determined by their size and the character of the execution, should
be strictly observed. The spectator should retire from a large
picture or from apparently coarse painting till it assumes an
appearance of perfect finish. By doing so, he will derive a special pleasure in seeing a perfectly satisfying effect produced by
apparently inadequate means. Velasquez and Gainsborough,
whose bold handling is calculated for being seen at a consider-

able distance, are said to have painted with brushes six feet long. When on one occasion a person was looking closely into a newly-finished work by Rembrandt, the master is reported to have petulantly observed, that his picture was not painted to be smelt, and that the smell of oil-paint was very injurious.

What is called the "fresh eye,"—a phrase meaning the proper perception of colour and form,—is lost much sooner than the general visitor to picture-exhibitions suspects. Inaccuracies of drawing may sometimes be detected, when the eye is too much fatigued to discover them otherwise, by examining a picture reversed in the looking-glass. We all know that, owing to the active influence colours have over each other, it is difficult, in arranging a collection of pictures, to prevent their "killing," as it is termed, or at least injuring one another. It is not, however, so generally known, that when the eye has dwelt for some time on one particular colour, it is temporarily unfitted for correctly distinguishing or properly enjoying other colours. This has been demonstrated by the celebrated French chemist M. Chevreul, in a number of interesting experiments. The prejudicial effects of this to artists in a general exhibition will be instantly understood.

Mr. Sydney Smirke, A.R.A., has recently addressed a letter to Sir Charles L. Eastlake, P.R.A., directing attention to this circumstance, and suggesting a remedy. "Let any one," says Mr. Smirke, "who wishes to receive a full measure of enjoyment in a picture-gallery, hold in his hand a tablet, painted of a neutral tint, on which to rest his eye as he passes from one picture to another. Has his eye become inebriated by some florid colourist? A draught of the neutral tint on his tablet will sober it down, and bring it to the full use of its senses. Has he been contemplating a glowing Italian sunset, or 'A Masquerade at Naples?' a glance at his tablet will prepare him for the next picture, perhaps 'A Mist in the Highlands.' By means of his tablet his eye becomes on each occasion a *tabula rasa*, a cleansed palette, prepared to receive a fresh assortment of colours. Its discriminating powers are restored, its bias corrected; and thus each picture will stand on its own merits." In the case of landscapes, where it is desired that the eye should appreciate tints of green, the writer suggests that "the reverse of the tablet—a blank page in the catalogue, for example, where there is one—should be coloured with a deep, pure, but not bright red. Let the eye absorb a dose from this side before it contemplates a landscape, and it will be at once found to have been brought into a right condition for duly appreciating the artist's labour." We may add, that a set of tints for this purpose is provided for visitors to the National Gallery, and suspended in the main corridor.

WAS OIL-PAINTING DISCOVERED BY JOHN VAN EYCK?

There has been considerable controversy respecting the reputed discovery of the art of painting in oil by the early
Flemish master John Van Eyck. The total absence of all, even
incidental, reference among classic authors to oil-painting, may
be considered conclusive evidence that the ancients were unacquainted with the art. It is now known, however, from the
frequent allusions to them, that during three centuries ante-
cedent to the technical perfection displayed in the works of
the brothers Van Eyck, there were what we may consider ten-
tative efforts in oil-painting. And so distinct is the evidence
of the practice of oil-painting long before the beginning of the
fifteenth century—when the Van Eycks flourished—that the
account of their invention or discovery by Vasari (the Italian
biographer of artists), even understood restrictedly, has been
denied altogether. It appears, however, that oil-painting was
at first only employed for colouring standards, banners, and
pennons with heraldic devices, and for the subordinate, complementary, and decorative parts of pictures—such, for instance,
as draperies and accessories. And no examples of figures or
pictures in the modern sense of the term, entirely executed in
oil, before the time of the Van Eycks, can be proved to exist;
nor is there a distinct record of such works having been executed. As might, therefore, have been expected, recent research has shown that the Van Eycks are entitled to our grati-
tude; not, indeed, for having created the art, but for removing
disqualifications which unfitted it to compete with, much less
supersede, the ordinary tempera—the egg vehicle of the mediæval painters.

IMPROVEMENT OF PUBLIC TASTE.

Sir Gardner Wilkinson, in his work *On Colour*, says, that
he considers the poor "image-men" who wander through our
streets have done more to improve the general taste, to place
copies of known sculpture within the reach of all, and to fa-
miliarise the eye of the English public with what is good, than
any school (which a few only can attend), than any gallery
(which the working classes seldom visit), or any institution in
the country; and when we recollect that English art paraded
(without shame) through the streets was confined to cats with
moving heads, green parrots, wooden lambs covered with cot-
ton-wool, or (if the figure of a man was attempted) a coarse
boor holding an equally vulgar pot of beer, we may feel grateful for the change so unostentatiously brought about by these
humble foreigners.

HOW TO CHOOSE A CARPET.

Regularity of pattern is too much sought after in choosing our carpets. Sir Gardner Wilkinson and others have shown how much more important is the effect of colour in a carpet than that of pattern, and how much more agreeable is the irregularity in the patterns of Eastern carpets than the formal and symmetrical exactness thought so necessary in our own. "Colour, and not the pattern," says Mr. Giles, "is the primary source of interest in such cases, as in the ordinary Turkey carpet, in which no one looks for a pattern; and while our Axminsters, Wiltons, and Kidderminsters, the designs of which have been considered rather than the harmony of their colours, are so distressing in their obtrusive roses and cornucopias, the incomprehensible and often-repeated interlaced design of the old Turkish carpet seems never to weary." Hence this pattern, or one nearest resembling it, is preferable.

THE TERM "CERAMIC."

This is a word of recent introduction into our language, as a generic term including all manufactures of potters' clay. It is derived from κέραμος, the Greek for potters' clay. One of the quarters of the city of Athens, on the south-west side of the Acropolis, was called Ceramicus; and although Pausanias assigns a different derivation, Pliny relates that it was so called from the manufactory of Cholcostrius, a celebrated modeller of statues in clay.

TO CLEAN PRINTS.

Mr. Stannard, in the *Art-Union* for 1847, gives the following method as infallible:

Immerse the print for an hour or so in a lye made by adding to the strongest muriatic acid its own weight in water, and to three parts of this mixture adding one of red oxide of lead, or black oxide of manganese. A print, if not quickly cleaned, may remain in this liquid twenty-four hours without harm. Indian-ink stains should, in the first instance, be assisted out with hot water. Pencil-marks should be taken out with India rubber or day-old bread, carefully, so as not to injure the engraving. If the print has been mounted, the paste on the back should be thoroughly removed with warm water. The saline crystals left by the solution may be removed by repeated rinsings with warm water.

Inventions and Discoveries.

A FEW OF THE WONDERS OF INDIA-RUBBER.

THAT the produce of a tree found in vast luxuriance in the dense forests of Southern America should, within comparatively few years, by the applications of skill, be brought into manifold uses,—alike characterised by their ingenuity and importance,— is certainly one of the marvels of our scientific age. Such, in brief, is the history of India-Rubber, or *Caoutchouc*, as it is now called, and its manufactures. India-Rubber was first brought to England in 1767, and is thus mentioned in a letter from Sir Joseph Banks to Mr. Canton, in the archives of the Royal Society: "With this you will receive two balls of the new Elastick Substance" (Weld's *Hist. Royal Soc.* vol. ii. p. 106). In 1772, Dr. Priestley thus speaks of the new substance, in his *Introduction to Perspective:*

I have seen a substance excellently adapted to the purpose of wiping from paper the marks of a black-lead pencil. It must therefore be of singular use to those who practise drawing. It is sold by Mr. Nairne, mathematical-instrument maker, opposite the Royal Exchange. He sells a cubical piece of about half an inch for three shillings; and he says it will last several years.

Many persons (says Mr. Thomas Hodgskin, the experienced writer on subjects of political and commercial economy) yet alive remember when India-Rubber was only known as a part of a stationer's stock, in the shape of little black flexible bottles, more or less ugly, and when it was only used to rub out pencil-marks. Now it fills a large place in the arts. Instruments to relieve pain and carry on war; toys to amuse children, and buffers quietly and smoothly to stop the impetuous railway-train; the softest and most yielding of all beds, the most impermeable of clothing; the most flexible of tubes; the valves which approach the nearest to the most delicate and exquisite contrivances of nature to carry on the functions of life, but rudely imitated in the most ingenious of our contrivances, pumps and steam-engines, &c.,—are all now made of India-Rubber. Hardly any business of life is carried on without its aid. It is used in our printing-offices, it forms a link in telegraphic communication, and is indispensable on railways; it guards the traveller from atmospherical evils; it enables the diver to traverse the bottom of the ocean; it is essential to balloons; it stretches and contracts like our own skin, and is a necessary part of the most useful, convenient, and graceful dresses. Without it civilisation would have been as effectually stopped as we by its means stop the train; and the discovery of it and its many uses, like the discovery of gold and its great use as money, the best known and most precise measure of all the services which men render one another, is a necessary part of human progress.

Nevertheless, one of the most extensive of these useful applications was known in South America upwards of a century since, where cloaks were then waterproofed with India-Rubber; and disinclined as we are to rob Mr. Macintosh of the merit of his adaptation, the invention must be awarded to another age; indeed, it is almost one of the antiquities of the New World. In a work entitled *La Monarchia Indiana*, printed at Madrid in 1723, we find a chapter devoted to '' Very profitable trees in New Spain, from which there distil various liquors and resins.'' Among them is described a tree called *ulguahuall*, which the natives cut with a hatchet, to obtain the white, thick, and adhesive milk. This, when coagulated, they made into balls, called *ulli*, which rebounded very high when struck to the ground, and were used in various games. It was also made into shoes and sandals. The author continues: ''Our people (the Spaniards) make use of their *ulli* to varnish their *cloaks*, made of hempen cloth, *for wet weather*, which are good to resist water, but not against the sun, by whose heat and rays the *ulli* is dissolved.'' India-Rubber is not known in Mexico at the present day by any other name than that of *ulli;* and the oiled-silk covering of hats very generally worn throughout the country by travellers is always called *ulli*.

Shoes (worn in some countries as *over-shoes*) have also long been made of Caoutchouc in its native country. Edwards, in his *Voyage up the Amazon*, witnessed the process of making these India-Rubber shoes, which he thus describes: First, the lasts are made of wood from the United States; they are smeared with clay to prevent adhesion, and the leg of each is a long stick, to serve as a handle. The lasts are dipped into the Caoutchouc-milk, and are then held over the smoke of a fire made with a species of palm-nut, which dries the surface at once. The lasts are then redipped; and the process is repeated until the shoes are of sufficient thickness, a greater number of coatings being given to the bottom or sole. A shoe is thus made in a very short time. It is then placed in the sun for a few hours, and changes from a yellowish hue to a reddish brown; it is next figured by girls with small sticks of hard wood, or the needle-like spines of palms, and is fit for sale.

M. Claussen, the botanist, when travelling in South America, found the *Hancornia speciosa*, a tree which produces India-Rubber, growing on the high plateaux, at from 3000 to 5000 feet above the sea-level. It bears a fruit in form not unlike a bergamot pear, and full of milky juice, which is liquid Caoutchouc. To be eatable, this fruit must be kept for two or three weeks after being gathered, in which time all the India-Rubber disappears, or is converted into sugar; and it is then in taste one of the most delicious fruits known, and regarded by the Brazilians as superior to all the other fruits of the country.

DIVISIBILITY AND CONSUMPTION OF GOLD.

Gold-leaf is beat out so thin, that 50·7 square inches of it weigh only one grain. Now the 1000th part of a line or inch is easily visible through a common pocket-glass. A square inch of gold, therefore, is divisible into a million of parts, each visible through a common microscope. Hence it follows, that when gold is reduced to the thinness of gold leaf, $\frac{1}{50700000}$th of a grain of gold may be distinguished by the eye. But Reaumur has shown that one grain of gold, of the thinness which it is upon silver wire, will cover an area of 1400 square inches. It is plain that in this case $\frac{1}{71000000000}$th of a grain of gold may be rendered visible. But small as this particle is, we have no reason for believing that it does not constitute a considerable number of atoms.

An ounce of gold upon silver wire is capable of being extended more than 1300 miles in length; and nineteen ounces of gold, which in the form of a cube would not measure more than an inch and a quarter on each side, will completely gild a silver wire in length sufficient to compass the *whole earth* like a hoop.

Gilt wire is drawn from bars of silver covered with gold; of which it requires but the 8,640,000th part of an ounce to cover an inch of wire. If this gilt wire be dipped in nitric acid, the silver within the coating will be dissolved, but the hollow tube of gold which surrounded it will still remain suspended. This beautiful illustration of the divisibility of matter requires to be shown by aid of a powerful microscope.

Faraday thus illustrates the minute diffusion of this wonderful metal. The quantity of gold in the film or solution by which the ruby tint is obtained is very small. Suppose that a leaf of gold which weighs about 0·2 of a grain, and will cover a base of nearly ten square inches, were diffused through a column having that base, and 2·7 inches in height, it would give a ruby fluid equal in depth of tint to a good red rose, the volume of the gold being about the $\frac{1}{10000}$th part of the volume of the fluid. Another result gives 0·01 of a grain of gold in a cubic inch of fluid. These finely-diffused particles have not as yet been distinguished by any microscopic power applied to them.

Some idea of the consumption of gold and silver in articles of luxury may be formed from a calculation given by Jacob, who estimates it for Europe at an annual value of five millions and three-quarters sterling. How much of these precious metals must disappear by wear, leaving no trace! Would it be surprising to find traces of gold and silver in the soil of all human dwellings in the course of time? How circulating coin must be continually worn away by friction, the elements of the gold and silver being scattered throughout the whole world in invisible particles! What chemical or galvanic magic may one day collect them together again, to decorate the crevice of some rock with their brilliancy, or to raise some bed of sand to honour, we know not; but we are certain they are not destroyed, although they may be lost to us.—*Kobell's Mineral Kingdom.*

Mr. R. Hunt, keeper of the Mining Records, states, that for the uses of the arts not less than 1000 ounces of fine gold are used in Birmingham alone every week, and that in the United Kingdom the weekly consumption of leaf-gold is as follows: London, 400 oz.; Edinburgh, 35 oz.; Birmingham, 70 oz.; Manchester, 40 oz.; Dublin, 12 oz.; Liverpool, 15 oz.; Leeds, 6 oz.; Glasgow, 6 oz.: total, 584 oz. Of this, he states, on the authority of an eminent gold-refiner, that not one-tenth part can be recovered; and he adds, that for gilding metals by the electrotype, and the water or wash-gilding processes, not less than 10,000 ounces of gold are required annually. One establishment in the Potteries employs 3500*l.* worth of gold per annum, and nearly 2000*l.* worth is used by another. The consumption of gold in the Staffordshire Potteries, for gilding porcelain and making crimson and rose colour, varies from 7000 oz. to 10,000 oz. per annum.—*Chemistry, Theoretical and Practical*, by Dr. Muspratt.

Large quantities of gold are used in gilding portions of the exteriors of modern public buildings.* Thus the gold-leaf used in decorating the clock-tower of the New Houses of Parliament, and the labour, cost upwards of 1500*l.* Sir Charles Barry states, that for the sake of durability he used fine or pure gold of treble the thickness of ordinary gold-leaf, when difficulties arose from

* The regilding of the outer golden gallery of St. Paul's Cathedral cost the late Dean 6*l.*, and the triple regilding of the vase of flames on the Monument cost the Corporation of London 120*l.*

the galvanic action between the gold and the metals in contact with it; to remedy which a composition has been applied, which, besides advantages as to durability and colour, constitutes a perfect insulation between the gold and the metals which it covers.

The above, however, is but a trifling quantity compared with the gold used in gilding the five crosses, as well as the cupola, of the new church of St. Isaac at St. Petersburg, which required a mass of 247 pounds of gold, and are seen glittering at a distance of forty wersts (about twenty-seven miles) from St. Petersburg.

A curious fact is mentioned by Mr. John Phillips, in his geological lecture in Victoria, namely, that great use may be made of the honeysuckle in gold-finding; a tree, or line of trees, on the side of a hill indicating au arenaceous bed on the bottom, as witnessed in a steep hill on the Loddon or Kangaroo diggings, where gold was found, as Mr. Phillips had predicted three years before.

The great gold discoveries of recent years will be found noticed in *Things not generally Known*, First Series.

THE VALUE OF IRON.

To show how cheaply iron is obtained, and how the mechanical skill and labour expended upon it exceed the price, a writer in the *British Quarterly Review* gives the following calculations:

Bar-iron worth 1*l*. is worth when worked into—

	£ s.		£
Horse-shoes	2 10	Polished buttons and buckles	897
Table-knives	36 0		
Needles	71 0	Balance - springs of watches	50,000
Penknife-blades	657 0		

Cast-iron worth 1*l*. is worth when converted into—

	£		£
Machinery	4	Neck-chains	1,386
Larger ornamental work	45	Shirt-buttons	5,896
Buckles and Berlin work	600		

Thirty-one pounds of iron have been made into wire upwards of 111 miles in length; and so fine was the fabric, that a part was converted, in lieu of horse-hair, into a barrister's wig. The process followed to effect this extraordinary tenuity consists of heating the iron, and passing it through rollers eight inches in diameter, going at the rate of 400 revolutions per minute, down to No. 4 on the gauge. It is afterwards drawn cold down to No. 33 on the same gauge, and so on till it obtains the above length in miles.

WHAT IS TUTENAGUE?

The exact nature of Tutenague is still a problem. Some state that Tutenague is a name given by the Chinese to zinc; others consider it to be an artificial mixture of different metals; the Tutenague which was formerly exported from the East Indies is, however, pure zinc, without any alloy of lead. M. De Guignes affirms, that it is a native mixture of lead and iron, peculiar to China. It has frequently been confounded with the white copper of China, which is of a different composition, and not allowed to be carried out of the empire. Upon the authority of a merchant trading between India and China, Tutenague was an article of very extensive commerce between those countries until the year 1820, when it was superseded by the introduction of German spelter into India.

ANCIENT PLOUGHS.

The kind of Plough in use among the early Greeks, so far as we can collect from the description given by Hesiod, and from certain drawings which have come down to us, was not materially different from that of the ancient Egyptians. It is at least probable that the Plough described by Hesiod had no wheels; and perhaps it may be concluded that this was the commoner form even in Italy at the time when Virgil wrote, since Pliny describes the addition of wheels to have been but recently introduced. But of whichever description the Roman or Grecian Plough is considered to be, little improvement in its construction seems to have been effected since that remote period till a very recent epoch; for when we examine the implements employed for ploughing in most nations of modern Europe, we still find them of a construction as rude and clumsy as those represented in the sculptures and models that have come down to us or are described by the writers of antiquity.—Dr. Daubeny's *Lectures on Husbandry.*

The ancient Lombard Plough is still in use in Piedmont. It has probably not changed its form since the days of the Georgics; it has no wheels, and the ploughshare is inserted in the shaft.

PLOUGHING WITH HORSES' TAILS.

Barrington notes: "Notwithstanding an Irish statute of Charles I., that opprobrium of the Irish, with regard to ploughing by the horses' tails, still continues in the north-western parts, as it does in the north-western Highlands of Scotland. It arises, I should imagine, from not being able to purchase collars, or more convenient harness. As, however, for the barbarity, the custom which prevails in Somersetshire and the north of England, to pluck the feathers from live geese, seems equal to it.

ZINC MILK-PANS.

Zinc pans have been much recommended for use in dairies, as the milk speedily coagulates in them, and the quantity of cream is great. But if the milk becomes sour while in them, the acid acts upon the zinc and forms unpleasant, though perhaps not poisonous compounds. Upon the whole, porcelain or glass is the best material for milk vessels.

Zinc, it is well known, prevents other metals with which it is in contact from *rusting*. Many instances suggest themselves in which much manual labour might be saved by the simple contrivance of appending either a ring or slip of zinc to the metal to be preserved bright. It would be specially applicable in the case of bayonets and rifle-barrels; and a zinc edging to a scabbard would prevent the rusting of a sword.

HOW TO EXAMINE A WATCH.

To one who has never studied the mechanism of a watch, its main-spring, or the balance-wheel, is a mere piece of metal. He may have looked at the face of the watch, and while he admires the motions of its hands, and the time it keeps, he may have wondered in idle amazement as to the character of the machinery which is concealed within. Take it to pieces, and show him each part separately; he will recognise neither design, nor adaptation, nor relation between them; but put them together, set them to work, point out the offices of each spring, wheel, and cog, explain their movements, and then show him the result: now he perceives that it is all *one* design,—that notwithstanding the number of parts, their diverse forms and various offices, and the agents concerned, the whole piece is of *one* thought, the expression of *one* idea. He now rightly concludes that when the mainspring was fashioned and tempered, its relation to all the other parts must have been considered; that the cogs on this wheel are cut and regulated—*adapted*—to the ratchets on that, &c.; and his final conclusion will be, that such a piece of mechanism could not have been produced by chance; for the adaptation of the parts is such as to show it to be according to design, and obedient to the will of *one* intelligence.—*Maury.*

EGYPTIAN AND CHINESE LOCKS.

The earliest lock of which the construction is known is the Egyptian, which was used 4000 years ago. In this lock three pins drop into three holes in the bolt when it is pushed in, and so hold it fast; and they are raised again by putting in the key through the large hole in the bolt, and raising it a little, so that the pins of the key push the locking-pins up out of the way of the bolt. The security of this lock is very small, as it is easy to find the places of the pins by pushing in a bit of wood covered with clay or tallow, on which the holes will mark themselves; and the depth can easily be got by trial.

Mr. Chubb, the well-known lock-maker, possesses a wooden Chinese lock, which is very superior to the Egyptian, and, in fact, is founded on exactly the same principle as the Bramah lock, which long enjoyed the reputation of being the most secure one ever invented; for it has sliders or tumblers of different lengths, and cannot be opened unless they are all raised to the proper heights, and no higher. Until about eighty years ago, we had no lock so good as this in England.—*E. B. Denison*, *Q. C.*

THE PEDOMETER.

The Emperor Napoleon I. had a watch which wound itself up by means of a weighted lever, which rose and fell at every step he took; and having a gathering click to it, it wound up a ratchet attached to the barrel, if it was not then fully wound up. The instrument called the *Pedometer* is on the same principle, though its object is different, being merely to count the number of steps you take while the instrument is in your pocket. It is capable of adjustment according to the number of steps which the wearer usually takes in a mile, which he must first count, and set the instrument accordingly, when it will indicate the distance walked; but without such adjustment it affords no measure of distance at all.—*E. B. Denison, Q. C.*

CURIOUS USE OF THE MICROSCOPE.

Lately, on one of the Prussian railways, a barrel, which should have contained silver coin, was found, on arrival at its destination, to have been emptied of its precious contents, and filled with sand. On Professor Ehrenberg being consulted on the subject, he sent for samples of sand from all the stations along the different lines of railway through which the specie had passed, and by means of his microscope identified the station from which the interpolated sand must have been taken. The station once fixed upon, it was not difficult to hit upon the culprit among the small number of *employés* on duty there.

PRINCE RUPERT'S DROP.

To this celebrated personage is to be attributed the invention of the toy that bears his name as "Rupert's Drop,"—that curious bubble of glass which has long amused children and puzzled philosophers" (Lord Macaulay's *England*, vol. i. p. 409).

This philosophical toy was introduced by Rupert into England in 1660, and communicated by Charles II. to the Royal Society at Gresham College. It was so well known when *Hudibras* was written as to be used in popular illustration. In part ii. canto 2, we have,

Honour is like that glassy bubble
That finds philosophers such trouble,
Whose least part crack'd, the whole doth fly,
And wits are crack'd to find out why.

This bubble is in form somewhat pear-shaped, or like a leech distended; it is formed by dropping refined green glass, when melted, into cold water, and its thick end is so hard that it can scarcely be broken on an anvil; but if the smallest particle of its taper end be broken off, the whole flies at once into powder. The theory of this phenomenon is, that its particles when in fusion are in a state of repulsion, but on being dropped into the water its superficies is annealed, and the particles return into the power of each other's attraction; the inner particles, still in a state of repulsion, being confined within their outward covering (*Philosophical Transactions*, vol. xlvi. p. 175). These drops are difficult to make; but they may be bought for a trifle at toy-shops, or of philosophical instrument makers.

CANDLE-BOMBS.

Candle-Bombs are old; and are described by Beckmann as small glasses, hermetically sealed and containing a drop of water, which, when placed on hot coals, burst with a loud report, and therefore are called fulminating glasses. Hooke speaks of them in his *Micrographia*, 1665.

CORKED BOTTLES FILLED BY PRESSURE OF THE SEA.

That empty bottles, securely corked and let down into the sea, at various depths, have been drawn up filled with water, without any appearance of the corks having been displaced, has long been well known, but has been attributed to various causes.

The Rev. John Campbell, in his *Travels in South Africa*, in 1815, relates:

We drove a cork very tight into an empty bottle. The cork was so large that more than half of it could not be driven into the neck of the bottle. We then tied a cord round the cork, which we also fastened round the neck of the bottle, to prevent the cork sinking down, and put a coat of pitch over the whole. By means of lead we sunk it in the water. When it was let down to about the depth of 50 fathoms, the captain said he was sure the bottle had instantaneously filled; on which he drew it up, when we found the cork driven down into the inside, and of course the bottle was full of water.

We prepared a second bottle in the same way, only with the addition of a sail-needle being passed transversely through the upper part of the cork, which rested on the mouth of the bottle, and all completely pitched over. When about 50 fathoms down, the captain called out as before, that he felt by the sudden increase of weight that the bottle was filled; on which it was drawn up. We were not a little surprised to find the cork in the same position, and no part of the pitch broken; yet the bottle was full of water. . . . The porousness of the glass seems to be the only consideration by which we can account for the fact.

In 1854, Captain Spowart, of the *Wilberforce,* corked, wired, and sealed a bottle up tight, and tied tarpaulin over all, the bottle being empty: this he sank 90 fathoms, and on being hauled up, it was full to within two inches of the cork of water, the cork being still tight.

Dr. Buckland, in his *Bridgewater Treatise,* says :

Captain Smyth, R.N., found that a claret bottle filled with air, and well corked, was burst before it descended 400 fathoms. He also found that a bottle filled with fresh water, and corked, had had the cork forced in at about 180 fathoms.

Sir Francis Beaufort made the experiment with bottles empty and filled, but with various results.

The empty bottles were sometimes crushed; at others the cork was forced in, and the fluid exchanged for sea-water. The cork was always returned to the neck of the bottle; sometimes, but not always, in an inverted position.

The results, of course, vary with the depths to which the bottles are sunk. Sir Henry Delabeche computed the pressure at a depth of 100 feet to be sixty pounds to the square inch, including that of the atmosphere; while at 4000 feet, the pressure would be about 1830 pounds to the square inch. By some the phenomenon is referred to the *porousness of the glass;* but this has been disproved by experiments with glass balls being submitted, in Bramah's hydraulic press, to a weight of 3,360 pounds on the square inch, when the balls were uninjured. We rather incline to the opinion that in the bottle experiments, although the pressure might not be sufficient to break the glass, it might reduce by compression the size of the cork and the covering of pitch or wax, and thus afford space for the water to enter, which it would do through the minutest inlet under such pressure : "the wire would keep the cork in its original position, and on being drawn up, the expansion to its former bulk would be instantaneous." Such is the opinion of a Correspondent of *Notes and Queries,* Second Series, No. 32. At all events, the elasticity of the cork is better proved than the porosity of the glass.

"CANST THOU TELL HOW AN OYSTER MAKES HIS SHELL?"

says the Fool in *King Lear;* to which Lear replies, "No;" and the Fool rejoins, "Nor I neither."

Now the shell of the oyster consists of concentric layers of membrane and carbonate of lime, the marks of which we see in its rough outer surface. That which now forms the centre and utmost convexity of the shell, was, at an early age, sufficient to cover the whole animal; but as the oyster grows, it throws out from its surface a new secretion, composed of animal matter and carbonate of lime, which is attached to the shell already formed, and projects further at its edges. Thus the animal is not only protected by this covering, but as it increases in size, the shell is made thicker and stronger by successive layers. It is also shaped with as curious a destination to the vital functions of respiration and of obtaining food as any thing we can survey in the higher animals. We cannot walk in the streets without noticing that, in the fish-shops, the oysters are laid with their flat sides uppermost. They would die were it otherwise. The animal breathes and feeds by opening its shell, and thereby receiving a new portion of water into the concavity of its under shell; and if it did not thus open its lid, the water could neither be propelled through its branchiæ, or respiratory apparatus, nor sifted for its food. It is in this manner that oysters lie in their native beds: were they on their flat surface, no food could be gathered, as it were, in their cup; and if exposed by the retreating tide, the opening of the shell would allow the water to escape and leave them dry, thus depriving them of respiration as well as food.—Abridged from *Lord Brougham and Sir Charles Bell's Notes on Paley's Natural Theology.*

The Hon. Robert Boyle has left us a curious reflection "upon the Eating of Oysters." "We impute it," he says, "for a barbarous custom, to many nations of the Indians, that like beasts they eat raw flesh. And pray how much is that worse than our eating raw fish, as we do in eating those oysters? Nor is this a practice of the rude vulgar only, but of the politest and nicest person amongst us, such as physicians, divines, and even ladies. And our way of eating them seems more barbarous than theirs, since they are wont to kill before they eat, but we scruple not to devour oysters alive, and kill them, not with our hands or tooth, but with our stomachs, where (for aught we know) they begin to be digested before they make an end of dying. Nay, sometimes, when we dip them in vinegar, we may, for aught to one bit, devour alive a shoal of little animals, which whether they be fishes or worms I am not so sure as I am that I have, by the help of convenient glasses, seen great numbers of them swimming up and down in less than a saucerfull of vinegar."

POMPEIAN AND LONDON PAVEMENT.

The roads of Pompeii were usually raised some height above

the ground, and consisted of three distinct layers of materials : the lowest, stones mixed with cement ; the middle, gravel, or small stones, to prepare a level and unyielding surface to receive the upper layer, which consisted of large masses accurately fitted together. It is curious to observe, that after many ages of imperfect paving in London, we have returned to the same plan. The roadway is based in the same manner, upon broken granite instead of loose earth, and a further security against its working into holes is given by dressing each stone separately to the same breadth, and into the form of a wedge, like the voussoirs of an arch, so that each tier of stones spans the street like a bridge. This is an improvement upon the Roman system, which depended for the solidity of construction on the size of the blocks, which were irregularly shaped, although carefully and firmly fitted.

THE TURNPIKE

originally meant what is now called a Turnstile ; that is, a post with a movable cross fixed at the top, to *turn* as the passenger went through. Ben Jonson, in his *Staple of News*, has,

> I move upon my axle, like a turnpike.

This seems originally to have belonged to fortifications, the points being made sharp, to prevent the approach of horses : they were therefore *pikes* to *turn* back the assailants.—Nares's *Glossary*, new edit.

VARIETIES OF IVORY.

Ivory is principally obtained from the western coast of Africa and Hindostan, Camaroo Ivory being considered the best, on account of its colour and transparency : in some of the best tusks, the transparency can't be discovered on the outside. A third kind of Ivory, called the Egyptian, is lower in price than the Indian, but is uneconomical in working. Great quantities of Ivory are consumed in Sheffield in making handles for cutlery : to make up 180 tons' weight, a year's consumption, there must be about 45,000 tusks, whose average weight is nine pounds each, though some weigh from sixty to one hundred pounds. According to this, the number of elephants killed every year is 22,500 ; but, allowing that some tusks are cast and some animals die, it may be fairly estimated that 18,000 elephants are killed every year for their Ivory, which is contrary to the usual belief, that the Ivory used comes from the tusks cast by living elephants.—Jameson's *Journal*, No. 07.

The finest specimens of elephants' tusks sent to the Great Exhibition were a pair weighing 325 pounds, from the *Elephas*

Africanus, obtained from an animal killed near the newly-dis-
covered Lake Ngami, in South Africa; each tusk measured
eight feet six inches in length, and twenty-two inches in basal
circumference. A single tusk, weighing 110 pounds, from the
same locality, was associated with them.

TO RESTORE DECAYED IVORY.

A few years since, Mr. Layard sent to England from the
ruins of Nineveh some splendid Ivory carvings, which, on being
unpacked, were found crumbling to pieces very rapidly. This
decay, Professor Owen suggested, was owing to the loss of albumen in the Ivory; and upon his recommendation, the articles
were boiled in a solution of albumen, when the Ivory became
as firm and solid as when first entombed.

HOW THE CHINESE CONCENTRIC IVORY-BALLS ARE CARVED.

The Rev. W. Milne, in his popular work on China, thus
explains the mystery of these Concentric Ivory-Balls,—ten,
twelve, or more, cut out one within the other.

It has been conjectured that the balls are originally cut into halves,
and are so strongly or nicely gummed or cemented together, that it is
impossible to detect the junction; and attempts have been made to dissolve the union by soaking and boiling a concentric ball in oil, of course
to no purpose. The explanation, obtained by Mr. Milne from more
than one native artist, is as follows:

A piece of ivory, made perfectly round, has several conical holes
worked into it, so that their several apices meet at the centre of the
globular mass. The workman then commences to detach the innermost
sphere, by inserting into each hole a very sharp tool with a bent point.
This instrument is so placed as to cut away or scrape the ivory through
each hole at equi-distances from the surface, thus working until the
incisions meet. In this way is separated the innermost ball; and to
smooth, carve, and ornament it, the faces are one by one brought opposite one of the largest holes. The other balls, larger as they near the
surface, are each cut, wrought, and polished precisely in the same
manner; the outermost ball being of course the last. The implements
employed, the size of the shaft of the tool, as well as the bend of its point,
depend on the depth of each successive ball from the surface.

RUSSIA-LEATHER

derives its well-known odour, and its power of withstanding the
attacks of insects and the progress of decay, from its being
manufactured with oil obtained from the destructive distillation
of the bark of the birch.

THE FIRST POSTAGE-ENVELOPE.

M. Piron tells us that the idea of a Post-paid Envelope

originated, early in the reign of Louis XIV., with M. de Velayer, who, in 1653, established (with royal approbation) a private penny-post, placing boxes at the corners of streets for the reception of letters wrapped up in Envelopes, which were to be bought at offices established for that purpose. M. de Velayer also caused to be printed certain forms of *billets*, or notes, applicable to the ordinary business among the inhabitants of great towns, with blanks, which were to be filled up by the pen with such special matter as might complete the writer's object. One of these *billets* has been preserved to our time. Pelisson, Madame de Sévigné's friend, and the object of the *bon-mot* that "he abused the privilege which men have of being ugly," was amused at this kind of skeleton correspondence, and under the affected name of Pisandre, he filled up and addressed one of these forms to the celebrated Mdlle. de Scuderi, in her *pseudonyme* of Sappho. This strange *billet-doux* is still extant; one of the oldest, we presume, of penny-post letters, and a curious example of a prepaying envelope.—*Quarterly Review*, No. 128.

The invention of stamped postage-envelopes is, however, claimed for Sweden; for in 1823 a Swedish artillery-officer, Lieutenant Trekenbor, petitioned the Chamber of Nobles to propose to the Government to issue stamped paper specially for envelopes for prepaid letters: but the proposition was rejected by a large majority.

CIPHER-WRITING.

The art of Secret Writing, or Writing in Cipher, was, according to Polybius, invented by Æneas, the author of a Treatise on Tactics, and other works. He produced twenty methods of writing in cipher, which no person could unfold; but we doubt much whether they would preserve this quality at the present day. The article "Cipher," in *Rees's Cyclopædia*, by Mr. Blair, a surgeon, is an admirable treatise on the subject. It is no less strange than true, that this art, so important in diplomacy, as long as couriers are liable to be intercepted, was held in abhorrence by the Elector Frederic the Second, who considered it as a diabolical invention. Trithemius, abbot of Spanheim, had composed several works to revive this branch of knowledge; and Boville, an ignorant mathematician, being unable to comprehend the extraordinary terms he made use of to explain his method, published that the work was full of diabolical mysteries. Poissevin repeated the assertion; and Frederic, in a holy zeal, ordered the original work of Trithemius, which he had in his library, to be burned, as the invention of the devil.

THE BEST WRITING-INK.

Dr. J. Stark, of Edinburgh, has manufactured upwards of 230 different inks, and tested the durability of writings made with these on all kinds of paper. His numerous experiments show that no salt of iron, and no preparation of iron, equal the common sulphate of iron, or green copperas, for ink-making; and that even the addition of any persalt, such as the nitrate or chloride of iron, although it improves the colour, deteriorates the durability of ink. The ink Dr. Stark prefers for his own use is composed of 12 oz. of the best blue galls; 8 oz. sulphate of indigo; 8 oz. copperas; a few cloves, to prevent mouldiness; and 4 or 6 oz. of gum-arabic, for a gallon of ink. Dr. Stark recommends that all legal deeds or documents should be written with quill-pens, as the contact of steel invariably destroys more or less the durability of every ink. The author shows that a good copying-ink has yet to be sought for; and that indelible inks, which will resist the pencillings and washings of the chemist, need never be looked for.

We appear to have lost the art of making writing-ink permanent. Manuscripts of the eleventh and twelfth centuries, now in our State-Paper Office, are apparently as bright as when first written; while those of the last two hundred years are more or less illegible, and some of them entirely obliterated. We have seen a document of the time of Richard II. (1377-99) in which the ink is as fresh as if written last week.

ARQUEBUSADE WATER.

This preparation of olden pharmacy was formerly the remedy for a wound from an *arquebusade*, or shot from an arquebuse or hand-gun, first mentioned by Philip de Comines, in his account of the battle of Morat, in 1470. In England, on the first formation of the Yeomen of the Guard, in 1485, half were armed with bows and arrows, the other with arquebuses; and a large party of arquebusiers are seen in the picture in Windsor Castle which represents King Henry the Eighth's procession to meet Francis the First between Guisnes and Ardres. Though invented for the purpose from which it is named, the *Eau d'Arquebusade* is still occasionally applied to sprains, bruises, &c.

The French still prepare it very carefully from a great number of aromatic herbs. In England, where it is the *Aqua Vulneraria* of the pharmacopœias, the formula is: Dried mint, angelica tops, and wormwood; angelica seeds; oil of juniper and spirit of rosemary: distilled with rectified spirit and water.

RAZOR-PAPER

supersedes the use of the ordinary strop. By merely wiping

the razor on the paper, to remove the lather after shaving, a keen edge is always maintained without further trouble; only one caution being necessary,—that is, to begin with a sharp razor, and then the paper will keep it in that state for years. It may be prepared thus : First, procure oxide of iron (by the addition of carbonate of soda to a solution of persulphate of iron), well wash the precipitate, and finally leave it of the consistency of cream : secondly, procure some good paper, soft, and a little thinner than ordinary printing-paper; then, with a soft brush, spread over the paper (on one side only), very thinly, the moist oxide of iron; dry it, and cut the paper into pieces two inches square; it will then be fit for use.

ANTIQUITY OF " MARKING-INK."

In 1852, Mr. Herapath, in unrolling an Egyptian mummy, discovered on one of the linen bandages hieroglyphical characters, in colour similar to those of the present " marking-ink." Mr. Thornton Herapath next examined with a microscope the stained fibres of the bandage; and on making comparative experiments with a piece of the linen wrapper recently "marked" in the usual way with a solution of nitrate of silver, the fibres presented a very similar appearance to that of the ancient stained cloth. Hence it is concluded that the Egyptians were really acquainted with nitric acid, and employed the nitrate of silver as a "marking-ink," just as we do at the present day. "If," said Dr. Camps to the Syro-Egyptian Society, "this were admitted, we must then allow the Egyptians to have had a more intimate acquaintance with chemistry and chemical preparations than is generally assigned even to that very clever, intelligent, and ancient people."

The ink of the Egyptians has been imitated. Mr. Joseph Ellis, of Brighton, states, that by making a solution of shellac with borax in water, and adding a suitable proportion of pure lamp-black, an ink is producible which is indestructible by time or by chemical agents, and which on drying will present a polished surface, as with the ink found on the Egyptian papyri. Mr. Ellis has made ink in the way described; and proved, if not its identity with that of ancient Egypt, yet the correctness of the formula—which had been given him by the late Mr. Charles Hatchett, F.R.S., the eminent chemist.

SECRET IN GLASS-BLOWING.

One of the Glass-workers' secrets is, to simply moisten the mouth with a little water before blowing; when the water will be converted, in the interior of the drop, into steam, which greatly aids the breath in extending the " bell."

HUMAN MECHANISM AND THE BRAIN.

The determination between two lines of action is well exemplified by Mr. Cotton's Weighing-machine. This machine is
destined to separate light sovereigns from those which are heavy ;
the light ones being thrown into one till, the heavy ones into
the opposite. So perfect is this contrivance, that the mechanism will weigh accurately sovereigns to $\frac{1}{100}$th of a grain; and, of
course, more rapidly and correctly than could possibly be effected
by the ordinary process. When Professor De la Rive saw the
mechanism at work, he said it was the perfection of mechanics ;
and truly it is a most wonderful sight to witness the series of
these machines at work in the Bank of England. When the
sovereign is light, the scale-beam rises, and the coin is thrown
by a contrivance into one till, made to receive it; if the sovereign
is heavy, the beam descends, and the coin is thrown into an
opposite box. By this mechanism a selection is made between
the heavy and the lighter coin. The machine decides between
these two states; and in that way its action is analogous to
judgment in the animal kingdom.

Mr. Smee, from whose work on *Instinct and Reason* we quote
this illustration, adds, that when man solves problems by his
brain, he has not simply to decide two things, the rise or fall of
the beam, as in the judgment exhibited by the Weighing-ma-
chines, but his determination is formed upon all the knowledge
he possesses, and upon a vast variety of circumstances; and in
this respect the comparison well illustrates the relative capacity
of the mechanism of man and the structures devised by an Infinite Power.

" THE PATENT RESPIRATOR."

When a person, going out of his house into the cold air of
winter, ties a bulky woollen handkerchief, called a "comforter"
or "fear-nothing," around his neck and face, or holds any such
porous mass over the mouth, his warm breath, going out through
the handkerchief or other mass, or between the internal surface
of the mass and the cheek, leaves warmth there, and then the
cold pure air, drawn towards the mouth through the heated
mass, absorbs a great part of the detained heat, and enters the
chest of the individual much less cold than the air of the atmosphere around. In 1836, a useful modification of this simple
process was pressed on public notice by Mr. Jeffry, a medical
practitioner recently returned from India. The same proposal,
however, had been made, executed, and published, forty years
before, by Dr. Thomas Beddoes, of Bristol, in whose laboratory
Sir Humphry Davy got some of his early lessons in chemistry
and philosophy. The description of Dr. Beddoes' expedient,

"put," says Dr. Arnott, "as a working direction into the hands of any adroit mechanician, would produce a good form of what has been sold as the Patent Respirator." Mr. Jeffry substituted for the handkerchief folds of fine wire-gauze, or pierced plates of metal, which, being heated by the warm breath passing out, give up the heat so acquired to the pure air coming in.

In all the published prints of soldiers in the field exposed at night during a winter campaign, as in that of the Crimea in 1854-5, the men are shown with bulky neck-wrappers rising high over the lower part of the face. These wrappers are commonly thought to serve merely to protect the face from the cold; but they are also potent breath-warmers.

HOW TO SPLIT A SHEET OF PAPER.

If the sheet is sized, soak it in hydrochloric acid, much diluted with water, till the size is rendered perfectly soluble in moderately warm water. When well washed, press it gently between blotting-paper; while still damp, lay it between two sheets of smooth firm paper, previously coated with a solution of isinglass or clear size on one side. Press the sheets well together, and leave them till perfectly dry. Now, by carefully separating the two outer sheets, the middle one will be evenly ruptured, or otherwise, according as one sheet is bent more than the other during the process of separation.

Or, procure two rollers or cylinders of glass, amber, resin, or metallic amalgam; strongly excite them by the well-known means, so as to produce the attraction of cohesion, and then, with pressure, pass the paper between the rollers: one half will adhere to the under roller, the other to the upper roller; when cease the excitation, and remove each part.

HOW TO DETECT FORGED BANK-OF-ENGLAND NOTES.

A very simple way of Proving a Note is by slightly damping it with the tongue: then holding it up to the light, if genuine, the water-mark appears more distinctly on the part damped; if forged, the pretended water-mark disappears. This easy test would prevent many spurious notes from getting into circulation.

INVENTION OF THE RAILWAY.

Nearly two centuries since Railways were employed in the Newcastle collieries. Lord-Keeper North, in 1676, writes: "The manner of the carriage is by laying *rails of timber* from the colliery to the river exactly straight and parallel: and bulky carts are made with four rollers fitting these rails, whereby the carriage is so easy, that one horse will draw four or five chaldron of coals—and is an immense benefit to the coal-merchants." Cast-iron rails date a century later; for George Stephenson tells us, from the books of the Coalbrook-Dale Iron Company, that in 1767, between five and six tons of cast-iron rails were made at these works, but only "as an experiment, on the suggestion of one of the partners." The use of *cast-iron rails* is stated by Mr. Carr to have been first introduced at the colliery of the Duke of Norfolk, near Sheffield, in 1776.

A striking suggestion of uniting railway communication into a "system," as connecting lines are now called, will be found in Sir Richard Phillips's *Morning's Walk from London to Kew*, published in 1813. On reaching the Surrey Iron Railway, at Wandsworth, where a train of carriages was drawn by one horse, Sir Richard says, "I thought of the millions which have been spent at Malta, four or five of which might have been the means of extending *double lines of iron railway* from London to Edinburgh, Glasgow, Holyhead, Milford, Falmouth, Yarmouth, Dover, and Portsmouth. A reward of a single thousand would have supplied coaches, and other vehicles, of various degrees of speed, with the best tackle for readily turning out; and we might ere this have witnessed our mail-coaches running at the rate of ten miles an hour, drawn by a single horse, or *impelled fifteen miles an hour by Blenkinsop's steam-engine*." The writer of these sagacious remarks lived until 1840; so that he had the gratification of witnessing a triumph greater than his long-cherished hope.

In the interval was published the first *Treatise on Railways*, by Nicholas Wood, of Killingworth, wherein the writer deprecates any attempt at a greater speed than fourteen miles an hour upon railways. Yet this shortsightedness was exceeded by a writer in the *Quarterly Review* :

What (said the reviewer) can be more palpably ridiculous than the prospect held out of locomotives travelling twice as fast as stage-coaches! We should as soon expect the people of Woolwich to suffer themselves to be fired-off upon one of Congreve's ricochet rockets, as trust themselves to the mercy of such a machine going at such a rate. We will back old Father Thames against the Woolwich Railway for any sum. We trust that Parliament will, in all railways it may sanction, limit the speed to eight or nine miles an hour, which we entirely agree with Mr. Sylvester is as great as can be ventured on with safety.

The Locomotive Steam-engine dates long after the Railway; and the directors of the Liverpool and Manchester Railway were for some time undetermined as to the kind of motive power which they should adopt, ere they decided upon the Steam-locomotive.

In Great Britain, there were in 1859, 9500 miles of Railway; and taking, at a rough calculation, one locomotive engine, with a force of 200 horse-power, to every three miles of railway, and assuming each to run 120 miles per day, we might thence calculate the distance travelled over by trains to be equal to 380,000 miles per day, or 138,000,000 miles per annum.

GENERAL INDEX.

THE END.

A LIST

OF

POPULAR WORKS

PUBLISHED BY

LOCKWOOD & CO.

7 STATIONERS'-HALL COURT, LONDON, E.C.

The Boy's Own Book: A Complete Encyclopædia of all the Diversions, Athletic, Scientific, and Recreative, of Boyhood and Youth. With many hundred Woodcuts, and Ten Vignette Titles, beautifully printed in Gold. New Edition, greatly enlarged and improved, price 8s. 6d. handsomely bound in cloth.

N.B.—This is the original and genuine 'Boy's Own Book,' formerly published by Mr. Bogue, and more recently by Messrs. Kent and Co. Care should be taken, in ordering the above, to give the name of either the former or present publishers, otherwise some inferior book, with a nearly similar title may be supplied.

The Little Boy's Own Book of Sports and Pastimes. With numerous engravings. Abridged from the above. 16mo. price 3s. 6d. cloth.

Merry Tales for Little Folk. Illustrated with more than 200 Pictures. Edited by MADAME DE CHATELAIN. 16mo. 3s. 6d. cloth elegant. Contents:—The House that Jack Built—Little Bo-Peep—The Old Woman and Her Eggs—Old Mother Goose—The Death and Burial of Cock Robin—Old Mother Hubbard—Henny Penny—The Three Bears—The Ugly Little Duck—The White Cat—The Charmed Fawn—The Eleven Wild Swans—The Blue Bird—Little Maia—Jack the Giant Killer—Jack and the Bean Stalk—Sir Guy of Warwick—Tom Hickathrift, the Conqueror—Bold Robin Hood—Tom Thumb—Puss in Boots—Little Red Riding-Hood—Little Dame Crump—Little Goody Twoshoes—The Sleeping Beauty in the Wood—The Fair One with Golden Locks—Beauty and the Beast—Cinderella; or, the Little Glass Slipper—Princess Rosetta—The Elves of the Fairy Forest—The Elfin Plough—The Nine Mountains—Johnny and Lisbeth—The Little Fisher-Boy—Hans in Luck—The Giant and the Brave Little Tailor—Peter the Goatherd—Red Jacket; or, the Nose Tree—The Three Golden Hairs—The Jew in the Bramble Bush.

Victorian Enigmas; being a Series of Enigmatical Acrostics on Historical, Biographical, Geographical, and Miscellaneous Subjects; combining Amusement with Exercise in the Attainment of Knowledge. Promoted and encouraged by Royal Example. By CHARLOTTE ELIZA CAPEL. Royal 16mo. cloth, elegantly printed, price 2s. 6d.

☞ The idea for this entirely original style of Enigmas is taken from one said to have been written by Her Majesty for the Royal children, which, with its Solution, is given.

'A capital game, and one of the very best of these commendable mental exercises which test knowledge and stimulate study. To the Queen's loyal subjects it comes, moreover, additionally recommended by the hint in the title-page and the statement in the preface, that it is a game practised by Her Majesty and the Royal children, if indeed it were not invented by the Queen herself.'—CRITIC.

'A good book for family circles in the long and dreary winter evenings, inasmuch as it will enable the young to pass them away both pleasantly and profitably.'
CITY PRESS.

JOHN TIMBS'S POPULAR WORKS.

'Any one who reads and remembers Mr. Timbs's encyclopædic varieties should ever after be a good table talker, an excellent companion for children, a "well-read person," and a precious lecturer.'—ATHENÆUM.

Things Not Generally Known. By JOHN TIMBS,
F.S.A., Editor of 'The Year Book of Facts,' &c. In Six Volumes, fcp. cloth, 15s.; or, the Six Volumes bound in Three, cloth gilt, or half-bound, 18s.; cloth, gilt edges, 18s. 6d. Contents:—General Information, 2 Vols.—Curiosities of Science, 2 Vols.—Curiosities of History, 1 Vol.—Popular Errors Explained, 1 Vol.

•.• The Volumes sold separately, as follows:—

Things Not Generally Known Familiarly Explained.
(General Information). 2 Vols. 2s. 6d. each, or in 1 Vol. 5s. cloth.

'A remarkably pleasant and instructive little book; a book as full of information as a pomegranate is full of seed.'—PUNCH.
'A very amusing miscellany.'—GENTLEMAN'S MAGAZINE.
'And as instructive as it is amusing.'—NOTES AND QUERIES.

Curiosities of Science, Past and Present. 2 Vols.
2s. 6d. each, or in 1 Vol. 5s. cloth.

'"Curiosities of Science" contains as much information as could otherwise be gleaned from reading elaborate treatises on physical phenomena, acoustics, optics, astronomy, geology, and palæontology, meteorology, nautical geography, magnetism, the electric telegraph, &c.'—MINING JOURNAL.

Curiosities of History. Fcp. 2s. 6d. cloth; or, with
'Popular Errors,' in 1 Vol. 5s. cloth.

'We can conceive no more amusing book for the drawing-room, or one more useful for the school-room.'—ART JOURNAL.

Popular Errors Explained and Illustrated. Fcp.
2s. 6d. cloth; or, with 'Curiosities of History,' in 1 Vol. 5s. cloth.

'We know of few better books for young persons; it is instructive, entertaining, and reliable.'—BUILDER.
'A work which ninety-nine persons out of every hundred would take up whenever it came in their way, and would always learn something from.'
ENGLISH CHURCHMAN.

Knowledge for the Time: a Manual of Reading,
Reference, and Conversation on Subjects of Living Interest. Contents:—Historico-Political Information—Progress of Civilization—Dignities and Distinctions—Changes in Laws—Measure and Value—Progress of Science—Life and Health—Religious Thought. Illustrated from the best and latest Authorities. By JOHN TIMBS, F.S.A. Small 8vo. with Frontispiece, 5s. cloth.

'It is impossible to open the volume without coming upon some matter of interest upon which light is thrown.'—MORNING POST.
'We welcome this attempt to preserve the bright bits and the hidden treasures of contemporary history. It is with keen pleasure we bear in mind that this learned collector's eye watches our journalism and the daily utterance of scholars, determined that no truth shall be lost.'—LLOYD'S NEWS.

Stories of Inventors and Discoverers in Science and
Useful Arts. By JOHN TIMBS, F.S.A. Second Edition. With numerous Illustrations. Fcap. 5s. cloth.

'Another interesting and well-collected book, ranging from Archimedes and Roger Bacon to the Stephensons.'—ATHENÆUM.
'These stories by Mr. Timbs are as marvellous as the *Arabian Nights' Entertainments*, and are wrought into a volume of great interest and worth.'—ATLAS.

JOHN TIMBS'S POPULAR WORKS—*continued.*

Walks and Talks About London. By JOHN TIMBS,

F.S.A., Author of 'Curiosities of London,' 'Things not Generally Known,' &c. Contents:—About Old Lyons Inn—Last Days of Downing Street—Walks and Talks in Vauxhall Gardens—Last of the Old Bridewell—The Fair of May Fair—From Hicks's Hall to Campden House—Talk about the Temple—Recollections of Sir Richard Phillips—Curiosities of Fishmongers' Hall—A Morning in Sir John Soane's Museum—A Site of Speculation—Changes in Covent Garden—Last of the Fleet Prison—Forty Years in Fleet Street—Changes at Charing Cross Railway London—Blackfriars Bridge—Raising of Holborn Valley—An Old Tavern in St. James's. With Frontispiece, post 8vo. cloth gilt, 8s 6d.

'The London of the last generation is, day by day, being rent away from the sight of the present, and it is well that Mr. Timbs is inclined to walk and talk about it ere it vanishes altogether, and leaves the next generation at a loss to understand the past history of the metropolis so far as it has a local colouring, as so very much of it has. Much of this has now gone for ever, but our author has watched the destructive course of the "improver," and thanks to his industry, many a memory that we would not willingly let die, is consigned to the keeping of the printed page, which in this instance, as in so many others, will doubtless prove a more lasting record than brass or marble.'—GENTLEMAN'S MAGAZINE.

Things to be Remembered in Daily Life. With

Personal Experiences and Recollections. By JOHN TIMBS, F.S.A., Author of 'Things not Generally Known,' &c. &c. With Frontispiece. Fcp. 3s. 6d. cloth.

' While Mr. Timbs claims for this volume the merit of being more reflective than its predecessors, those who read it will add to that merit—that it is equally instructive.'—NOTES AND QUERIES.

' No portion of this book is without value, and several biographical sketches which it contains are of great interest . . . . " Things to be Remembered in Daily Life " is a valuable and memorable book, and represents great research, and considerable and arduous labour.'—MORNING POST.

' Mr. Timbs's personal experiences and recollections are peculiarly valuable, as embodying the observations of an acute, intelligent, and cultivated mind. " Things to be Remembered " carries with it an air of vitality which augurs well for perpetuation.'—OBSERVER.

School-days of Eminent Men. Containing Sketches

of the Progress of Education in England, from the Reign of King Alfred to that of Queen Victoria; and School and College Lives of the most celebrated British Authors, Poets, and Philosophers; Inventors and Discoverers; Divines, Heroes, Statesmen, and Legislators. By JOHN TIMBS, F.S.A. Second Edition, entirely revised and partly re-written. With a Frontispiece by John Gilbert, 13 Views of Public Schools, and 20 Portraits by Harvey. Fcap. 6s. handsomely bound in cloth.

☞ Extensively used, and specially adapted for a Prize-Book at Schools. 'The idea is a happy one, and its execution equally so. It is a book to interest all boys, but more especially those of Westminster, Eton, Harrow, Rugby, and Winchester; for of these, as of many other schools of high repute, the accounts are full and interesting.'—NOTES AND QUERIES.

Something for Everybody; and a Garland for the

Year. By JOHN TIMBS, F.S.A. Author of ' Things Not Generally Known,' &c. With a Coloured Title, post 8vo. 5s. cloth.

' This volume abounds with diverting and suggestive extracts. It seems to be particularly well adapted for parochial lending libraries.'—SATURDAY REVIEW.

' Full of odd, quaint, out-of-the-way bits of information upon all imaginable subjects is this amusing volume, wherein Mr. Timbs discourses upon domestic, rural, metropolitan, and social life; interesting nooks of English localities; time-honoured customs and old-world observances; and, we need hardly add, Mr. Timbs discourses well and pleasantly upon all.'—NOTES AND QUERIES, July 30, 1881.

BOOKS FOR NURSERY OR MATERNAL TUITION.

The First or Mother's Dictionary. By Mrs. JAMESON (formerly Mrs. MURPHY). Tenth Edition. 18mo. 2s. 6d. cloth.

, Common expletives, the names of familiar objects, technical terms and words, the knowledge of which would be useless to children, or which could not well be explained in a manner adapted to the infant capacity, have been entirely omitted. Most of the definitions are short enough to be committed to memory; or they may be read over, a page or two at a time, till the whole are sufficiently impressed on the mind. It will be found of advantage if the little pupils be taught to look out for themselves any word they may meet with, the meaning of which they do not distinctly comprehend.

School-Room Lyrics. Compiled and Edited by ANNE KNIGHT. New Edition. 18mo. 1s. cloth.

La Bagatelle; intended to introduce Children of five or six years old to some knowledge of the French Language. Revised by Madame N. L. New Edition, with entirely New Cuts. 18mo. 2s. 6d. bound.

This little work has undergone a most careful revision. The orthography has been modernised, and entirely new woodcuts substituted for the old ones. It is now offered to parents and others engaged in the education of young children, as well adapted for familiarising their pupils with the construction and sounds of the French language, conveying at the same time excellent moral lessons.

' A very nice book to be placed in the hands of children; likely to command their attention by its beautiful embellishments.'—PAPERS FOR THE SCHOOLMASTER.

' A well-known little book, revised, improved, and adorned with some very pretty new pictures. It is, indeed, French made very easy for very little children.' THE SCHOOL AND THE TEACHER.

Chickseed without Chickweed: being very Easy and Entertaining Lessons for Little Children. In Three Parts. Part I. In words of three letters. Part II. In words of four letters. Part III. In words of five or more letters. New Edition, with beautiful Frontispiece by Anelay, 12mo. 1s. cloth.

A book for every mother.

Peter Parley's Book of Poetry. With numerous Engravings New Edition, revised, with Additions, 18mo. 1s. 6d. cloth.

This little volume consists, in part, of extracts from various publications, and in part of original articles written for it. It is designed to embrace a variety of pieces, some grave, and some gay; some calculated to amuse, and some to instruct; some designed to store the youthful imagination with gentle and pleasing images; some to enrich the mind with useful knowledge; some to impress the heart with sentiments of love, meekness, truth, gentleness, and kindness.

Cobwebs to Catch Flies; or Dialogues in short sentences. Adapted for Children from the age of three to eight years. In Two Parts. Part I. Easy Lessons in words of three, four, five, and six letters, suited to children from three to five years of age. Part II. Short Stories for Children from five to eight years of age. 12mo. 2s. cloth gilt.

, The Parts are sold separately, price 1s. each.

DELAMOTTE'S WORKS

ON ILLUMINATION, ALPHABETS, &c.

A Primer of the Art of Illumination, for the use of Beginners, with a Rudimentary Treatise on the Art, Practical Directions for its Exercise, and numerous Examples taken from Illuminated MSS., and beautifully printed in gold and colours. By F. DELAMOTTE. Small 4to. price 9s. cloth antique.

'A handy book, beautifully illustrated; the text of which is well written, and calculated to be useful...... The examples of ancient MSS. recommended to the student, which, with much good sense, the author chooses from collections accessible to all, are selected with judgment and knowledge, as well as taste.'—ATHENÆUM.

'Modestly called a Primer, this little book has a good title to be esteemed a manual and guide-book in the study and practice of the different styles of lettering used by the artistic transcribers of past centuries....An amateur may with this silent preceptor learn the whole art and mystery of illumination.'—SPECTATOR.

'The volume is very beautifully got up, and we can heartily recommend it to the notice of those who wish to become proficient in the art.'—ENGLISH CHURCHMAN.

'We are able to recommend Mr. Delamotte's treatise. The letterpress is modestly but judiciously written; and the illustrations, which are numerous and well chosen, are beautifully printed in gold and colours.'—ECCLESIOLOGIST.

The Book of Ornamental Alphabets, Ancient and Mediæval, from the Eighth Century, with Numerals. Including Gothic, Church-Text, large and small; German, Italian, Arabesque. Initials for Illumination, Monograms, Crosses, &c., &c., for the use of Architectural and Engineering Draughtsmen, Missal Painters, Masons, Decorative Painters, Lithographers, Engravers, Carvers, &c. &c. Collected and Engraved by F. DELAMOTTE, and printed in Colours. Sixth Edition, royal 8vo. oblong, price 4s. cloth.

'A well-known engraver and draughtsman has enrolled in this useful book the result of many years' study and research. For those who insert enamelled sentences round gilded chalices, who blazon shop legends over shop-doors, who letter church walls with pithy sentences from the Decalogue, this book will be useful. Mr. Delamotte's book was wanted.'—ATHENÆUM.

Examples of Modern Alphabets, Plain and Ornamental. Including German, Old English, Saxon, Italic, Perspective, Greek, Hebrew, Court Hand, Engrossing, Tuscan, Riband, Gothic, Rustic, and Arabesque, with several original Designs, and Numerals. Collected and Engraved by F. DELAMOTTE, and printed in Colours. Royal 8vo. oblong, price 4s. cloth.

'To artists of all classes, but more especially to architects and engravers, this very handsome book will be invaluable. There is comprised in it every possible shape into which the letters of the alphabet and numerals can be formed, and the talent which has been expended in the conception of the various plain and ornamental letters is wonderful.'—STANDARD.

Mediæval Alphabet and Initials for Illuminators. By F. G. DELAMOTTE. Containing 21 Plates, and Illuminated Title, printed in Gold and Colours. With an Introduction by J. WILLIS BROOKS. Small 4to. 6s. cloth gilt.

'A volume in which the letters of the alphabet come forth glorified in gilding and all the colours of the prism interwoven and intertwined and intermingled, sometimes with a sort of rainbow arabesque. A poem emblazoned in these characters would be only comparable to one of those delicious love letters symbolised in a bunch of flowers well selected and cleverly arranged.'—SUN.

The Embroiderer's Book of Design, containing Initials, Emblems, Cyphers, Monograms, Ornamental Borders, Ecclesiastical Devices, Mediæval and Modern Alphabets and National Emblems. By F. DELAMOTTE. Printed in Colours. Oblong royal 8vo. 2s. 6d. in ornamental boards.

The Fables of Babrius. Translated into English Verse from the Text of Sir G. Cornewall Lewis. By the Rev. JAMES DAVIES, of Lincoln Coll. Oxford. Fcp. 6s. cloth antique.

' " Who was Babrius?" The reply may not improbably startle the reader. Babrius was the real, original Æsop. Nothing is so fabulous about the fables of our childhood as their reputed authorship.'—DAILY NEWS.

' A fable-book which is admirably adapted to take the place of the imperfect collections of Æsopian wisdom which have hitherto held the first place in our juvenile libraries.'—HEREFORD TIMES.

NEW ANECDOTE LIBRARY.

Good Things for Railway Readers. 1000 Anecdotes, Original and Selected. By the Editor of ' The Railway Anecdote-book.' Large type, crown 8vo. with Frontispiece, 2s. 6d.

' A capital collection, and will certainly become a favourite with all railway readers.'—READER.

' Just the thing for railway readers.'—LONDON REVIEW.

' Fresh, racy, and original.'—JOHN BULL.

' An almost interminable source of amusement, and a ready means of rendering tedious journeys short.'—MINING JOURNAL.

' Invaluable to the diner-out.'—ILLUSTRATED TIMES.

Sidney Grey : a Tale of School Life. By the Author of ' Mia and Charlie.' Second Edition, with six beautiful Illustrations. Fcp. 4s. 6d. cloth.

The Innkeeper's Legal Guide : What he Must do, What he May Do, and What he May Not Do. A Handy-Book to the Liabilities, limited and unlimited, of Inn-Keepers, Alehouse-Keepers, Refreshment-House Keepers, &c. With verbatim copies of the Innkeeper's Limited Liability Act, the General Licensing Act, and Forms. By RICHARD T. TIDSWELL, Esq. of the Inner Temple, Barrister-at-Law. Fcp. 1s. 6d. cloth.

' Every licensed victualler in the land should have this exceedingly clear and well arranged manual.'—SUNDAY TIMES.

The Instant Reckoner. Showing the Value of any Quantity of Goods, including Fractional Parts of a Pound Weight, at any price from One Farthing to Twenty Shillings; with an Introduction, embracing Copious Notes of Coins, Weights, Measures, and other Commercial and Useful Information: and an Appendix, containing Tables of Interest, Salaries, Commissions, &c. 24mo. 1s. 6d. cloth, or 2s. strongly bound in leather.

☞ Indispensable to every housekeeper.

Science Elucidative of Scripture, and not antago-nistic to it. Being a Series of Essays on—1. Alleged Discrepancies; 2. The Theories of the Geologists and Figure of the Earth; 3. The Mosaic Cosmogony; 4. Miracles in general—Views of Hume and Powell; 5. The Miracle of Joshua—Views of Dr. Colenso: The Supernaturally Impossible; 6. The Age of the Fixed Stars—their Distances and Masses. By Professor J. R. YOUNG, Author of ' A Course of Elementary Mathematics,' &c. &c. Fcp. 8vo. price 5s. cloth lettered.

' Professor Young's examination of the early verses of Genesis, in connection with modern scientific hypotheses, is excellent.'—ENGLISH CHURCHMAN.

' Distinguished by the true spirit of scientific inquiry, by great knowledge, by keen logical ability, and by a style peculiarly clear, easy, and energetic.'

NONCONFORMIST.

' No one can rise from its perusal without being impressed with a sense of the singular weakness of modern scepticism.'—BAPTIST MAGAZINE.

Mysteries of Life, Death, and Futurity. Illustrated

from the best and latest Authorities. Contents:— Life and Time;
Nature of the Soul; Spiritual Life; Mental Operations; Belief
and Scepticism; Premature Interment; Phenomena of Death;
Sin and Punishment; The Crucifixion of Our Lord; The End of
the World; Man after Death; The Intermediate State; The Great
Resurrection; Recognition of the Blessed; The Day of Judgment;
The Future States, &c. By HORACE WELBY. With an Emblematic
Frontispiece, fcp. 3s. cloth.

'This book is the result of extensive reading, and careful noting; it is such a
common-place book as some thoughtful divine or physician might have compiled,
gathering together a vast variety of opinions and speculations, bearing on physiology, the phenomena of life, and the nature and future existence of the soul. We
know of no work that so strongly compels reflection, and so well assists it.'
                                                        LONDON REVIEW.

'A pleasant, dreamy, charming, startling little volume, every page of which
sparkles like a gem in an antique setting.'—WEEKLY DISPATCH.

'The scoffer might read these pages to his profit, and the pious believer will be
charmed with them. Burton's "Anatomy of Melancholy" is a fine suggestive
book, and full of learning; and of the volume before us we are inclined to speak in
the same terms.'—ERA.

Predictions Realized in Modern Times, Now first

Collected. Contents:— Days and Numbers; Prophesying Almanacs; Omens; Historical Predictions; Predictions of the French
Revolution; The Bonaparte Family; Discoveries and Inventions
anticipated; Scriptural Prophecies, &c. By HORACE WELBY.
With a Frontispiece, fcp. 5s. cloth.

'This is an odd but attractive volume, compiled from various and often little-
known sources, and is full of amusing reading.'—CRITIC.

'A volume containing a variety of curious and startling narratives on many
points of supernaturalism, well calculated to gratify that love of the marvellous
which is more or less inherent in us all.'—NOTES AND QUERIES.

Tales from Shakespeare. By CHARLES and MISS

LAMB. Fourteenth Edition. With 20 Engravings, printed on toned
paper, from designs by Harvey, and Portrait, fcp. 3s. 6d. cloth elegant.

The Tongue of Time; or, The Language of a Church

Clock. By WILLIAM HARRISON, A.M., Domestic Chaplain to H.R.H.
the Duke of Cambridge; Rector of Birch, Essex. Sixth Edition,
with beautiful Frontispiece fcp. 3s. cloth, gilt edges.

Hours of Sadness; or, Instruction and Comfort for

the Mourner; Consisting of a Selection of Devotional Meditations,
Instructive and Consolatory Reflections, Letters, Prayers, Poetry,
&c. from various Authors, suitable for the bereaved Christian.
Second Edition, fcp. 4s. 6d. cloth.

The Pocket English Classics. 32mo. neatly printed,

bound in cloth, lettered, price Sixpence each:—

THE VICAR OF WAKEFIELD.	SCOTT'S LADY OF THE LAKE.
GOLDSMITH'S POETICAL WORKS.	SCOTT'S LAY.
FALCONER'S SHIPWRECK.	WALTON'S ANGLER, 2 Parts, 1s.
RASSELAS.	ELIZABETH; OR, THE EXILES.
STERNE'S SENTIMENTAL JOURNEY.	COWPER'S TASK.
LOCKE ON THE UNDERSTANDING.	POPE'S ESSAY AND BLAIR'S GRAVE.
THOMSON'S SEASONS.	GRAY AND COLLINS.
INCHBALD'S NATURE AND ART.	GAY'S FABLES.
BLOOMFIELD'S FARMER'S BOY.	PAUL AND VIRGINIA.

WORKS BY THE AUTHOR OF 'A TRAP TO CATCH A SUNBEAM.'

'In telling a simple story, and in the management of dialogue, the Author is excelled by few writers of the present day.'—LITERARY GAZETTE.

A Trap to Catch a Sunbeam. Thirty-fifth Edition, price 9d. cloth; 6d. sewed.

'*Aide toi, et le ciel t'aidera*, is the moral of this pleasant and interesting story, to which we assign in this Gazette a place immediately after Charles Dickens, as its due, for many passages not unworthy of him, and for a general scheme quite in unison with his best feelings towards the lowly and depressed.'—LITERARY GAZETTE.

☞ *A Cheap Edition of the above popular story has been prepared for distribution. Sold only in packets price 1s. 6d. containing 12 copies.*

Also, by the same Author, each price 9d. cloth; 6d. sewed.

'COMING HOME;' a New Tale for all Readers.
OLD JOLLIFFE; not a Goblin Story.
The SEQUEL to OLD JOLLIFFE.
The HOUSE on the ROCK.
'ONLY;' a Tale for Young and Old.
The CLOUD with the SILVER LINING.
The STAR in the DESERT.
AMY'S KITCHEN, a VILLAGE ROMANCE: a New Story.
'A MERRY CHRISTMAS.'
SIBERT'S WOLD. Third Edition, 2s. cloth, limp.
The DREAM CHINTZ. With Illustrations by James Godwin. 2s. 6d. with a beautiful fancy cover.

Sunbeam Stories. A Selection of the Tales by the Author of 'A Trap to Catch a Sunbeam,' &c. Illustrated by Absolon and Anelay. FIRST SERIES. Contents:—A Trap to Catch a Sunbeam—Old Jolliffe—The Sequel to Old Jolliffe—The Star in the Desert—'Only'—'A Merry Christmas.' Fcap. 3s. 6d. cloth, elegant, or 4s. gilt edges.

Sunbeam Stories. SECOND SERIES. Illustrated by Absolon and Anelay. Contents:—The Cloud with the Silver Lining—Coming Home—Amy's Kitchen—The House on the Rock. Fcap. 3s. 6d. cloth elegant; 4s. gilt edges.

Minnie's Love: a Novel. By the Author of 'A Trap to Catch a Sunbeam.' In 1 vol. post 8vo. 6s. cloth.

'An extremely pleasant, sunshiny volume.'—CRITIC.
'We were first surprised, then pleased, next delighted, and finally enthralled by the story.'—MORNING HERALD.

Little Sunshine: a Tale to be Read to very Young Children. By the Author of 'A Trap to Catch a Sunbeam.' In square 16mo. coloured borders, engraved Frontispiece and Vignette, fancy boards, price 2s.

'Just the thing to rivet the attention of children.'—STAMFORD MERCURY.
'Printed in the sumptuous manner that children like best.'—BRADFORD OBSERVER.
'As pleasing a child's book as we recollect seeing.'—PLYMOUTH HERALD.

THE FRENCH LANGUAGE.

M. de Fivas' Works for the Use of Colleges, Schools, and Private Students.

The attention of Schoolmasters and Heads of Colleges is respectfully requested to the following eminently useful series of French class-books, which have enjoyed an unprecedented popularity. A detailed prospectus will be sent on application.

De Fivas' New Grammar of French Grammars;

comprising the substance of all the most approved French Grammars extant, but more especially of the standard work 'La Grammaire des Grammaires,' sanctioned by the French Academy and the University of Paris. With numerous Exercises and Examples illustrative of every Rule. By Dr. V. DE FIVAS, M.A., F.E.I.S., Member of the Grammatical Society of Paris, &c. &c. Twenty-eighth Edition, price 3s. 6d. handsomely bound.

' At once the simplest and most complete Grammar of the French language. To the pupil the effect is almost as if he looked into a map, so well-defined is the course of study as explained by M. de Fivas.'—LITERARY GAZETTE.

. A KEY to the above, price 3s. 6d.

De Fivas' New Guide to Modern French Conver-

sation; or, the Student and Tourist's French Vade-Mecum; containing a Comprehensive Vocabulary, and Phrases and Dialogues on every useful or interesting topic; together with Models of Letters, Notes, and Cards; and Comparative Tables of the British and French Coins, Weights, and Measures: the whole exhibiting, in a distinct manner, the true Pronunciation of the French Language. Sixteenth Edition, 18mo. price 2s. 6d. strongly half-bound.

' Voulez vous un guide aussi sûr qu'infaillible pour apprendre la langue française, prenez le Guide de M. de Fivas: c'est l'indispensable manuel de tout étranger.'
L'IMPARTIAL.

De Fivas, Beautés des Écrivains Français, Anciens

et Modernes. Ouvrage Classique à l'usage des Collèges et des Institutions. Dixième Édition, augmentée de Notes Historiques, Géographiques, Philosophiques, Littéraires, Grammaticales, et Biographiques. Twelfth Edition, 12mo. 3s. 6d. bound.

' An elegant volume, containing a selection of pieces in both prose and verse, which, while it furnishes a convenient reading book for the student of the French language, at the same time affords a pleasing and interesting view of French literature.'—OBSERVER.

De Fivas, Introduction à la Langue Française;

ou, Fables et Contes Choisis; Anecdotes Instructives, Faits Mémorables, &c. Avec un Dictionnaire de tous les Mots traduits en Anglais. À l'usage de la jeunesse, et de ceux qui commencent à apprendre la langue française. Seventeenth Edition, 12mo. 2s. 6d. bound.

' By far the best first French reading book, whether for schools or adult pupils.'
TAIT'S MAGAZINE.

De Fivas, Le Trésor National; or, Guide to the

Translation of English into French at Sight. Third Edition, 12mo. 2s. 6d. bound.

☞ Le 'Trésor National' consists of idiomatical and conversational phrases, anecdotes told and untold, and scraps from various English writers, and is especially intended to produce by practice, in those who learn French, a facility in expressing themselves in that language.

. A KEY to the above. 12mo. 2s. cloth.

NO MORE LAWYERS' BILLS!

Just published, 8th Edition, much enlarged. 12mo. cloth, price 6s. 8d.
(saved at every consultation).

Every Man's Own Lawyer: a Handy Book of the

Principles of Law and Equity. By a BARRISTER. Comprising the
Rights and Wrongs of Individuals, Mercantile and Commercial
Law, Criminal Law, Parish Law, County Court Law, Game and
Fishery Laws, Poor Men's Law; the Laws of

Bankruptcy	Merchant Shipping
Bets and Wagers	Mortgages
Bills of Exchange	Settlements
Contracts	Stock Exchange Practice
Copyright, Patents, and Trade Marks	Trespass, Nuisances, &c.
Elections and Registration	Transfer of Land, &c.
Insurance (Marine, Fire, and Life)	Warranties and Guarantees
Libel and Slander	Forms of Wills, Agreements, Bonds,
Marriage and Divorce	Notices, &c.

Also Law for

Landlord and Tenant—Master and Servant—Husband and Wife—Executors and
Trustees—Heirs, Devisees, and Legatees—Guardian and Ward—Married Women
and Infants—Partners and Agents—Lender and Borrower—Debtor and Creditor—
Purchaser and Vendor—Companies and Associations—Friendly Societies—Clergymen, Churchwardens, &c.—Medical Practitioners, &c.—Bankers—Farmers—Con-
tractors—Stock and Share Brokers—Sportsmen, Gamekeepers—Farriers and Horse-
dealers—Auctioneers, House Agents—Innkeepers, &c.—Bakers, Millers, &c.—
Pawnbrokers—Surveyors—Railways, Carriers, &c.—Constables—Labourers—
Seamen—Soldiers, &c. &c.

'What it professes to be, a complete epitome of the laws of this country,
thoroughly intelligible to non-professional readers. The book is a handy one to
have in readiness when some knotty point requires ready solution, and will be
found of service to men of business, magistrates, and all who have a horror of
spending money on a legal adviser.'—BELL'S LIFE.

'A clearly worded and explicit manual, containing information that must be
useful at some time or other to everybody.'—MECHANIC'S MAGAZINE.

'A work which has long been wanted, which is thoroughly well done, and which
we most cordially recommend.'—SUNDAY TIMES.

---

*New Book by one of the Contributors to ' The Reason Why' Series,
and Assistant Editor of ' The Dictionary of Daily Wants.'*

Now ready, Second and Cheaper Edition, 1 vol. crown 8vo, pp. 384,
2s. 6d. cloth.

The Historical Finger-Post: A Handy Book of

Terms, Phrases, Epithets, Cognomens, Allusions, &c., in connexion
with Universal History. By EDWARD SHELTON, Assistant Editor
of ' The Dictionary of Daily Wants,' &c. &c.

'A handy little volume, which will supply the place of " Haydn's Dictionary of
Dates" to many persons who cannot afford that work. Moreover, it contains some
things that Haydn's book does not.'—BOOKSELLER.

'It is to the historical student and antiquarian what " Enquire Within" is to the
practical housewife—not dispensing with stores of hard-acquired and well-digested
knowledge, but giving that little aid which, in moments of hurry and business, is
the true economiser of time.'—VOLUNTEER SERVICE GAZETTE.

'The idlest reader would find it convenient to have it within reach.'
PUBLISHERS' CIRCULAR.

'Really a very useful work; and, at the present day, when everybody is expected
to be up in everything, as good a handy-book for cramming on the current subjects
of conversation as any that we know. About 8000 subjects have all their place in
this extraordinary collection, and although termly given, the account of each is
sufficient for ordinary purposes.'—ERA.

'A very desirable companion, as containing a variety of information, much of
which could only be got by diligent inquiry and research. . . . Deserves a place as
a book of reference on the shelves of the study or library.'
NAVAL AND MILITARY GAZETTE.

'This most useful and admirably arranged handy-book will in most cases greatly
lighten the labour of investigation, and obviate a long and tedious search through
voluminous publications.'—WEEKLY TIMES.

THE GERMAN LANGUAGE.

Dr. Falck Lebahn's Popular Series of German School-books.

'As an educational writer in the German tongue, Dr. Lebahn stands alone; none other has made even a distant approach to him.'—BRITISH STANDARD.

Lebahn's First German Course. Third Edition.

Crown 8vo. 2s. 6d. cloth.
'It is hardly possible to have a simpler or better book for beginners in German.'
ATHENÆUM.
'It is really what it professes to be—a simple, clear, and concise introduction to the German Language.'—CRITIC.

Lebahn's German Language in One Volume. Seventh

Edition, containing—I. A Practical Grammar, with Exercises to every Rule. II. Undine; a Tale: by DE LA MOTTE FOUQUÉ, with Explanatory Notes of all difficult words and phrases. III. A Vocabulary of 4,500 Words, synonymous in English and German. Crown 8vo. 8s. cloth. With Key, 10s. 6d. Key separate, 2s. 6d.
'The best German Grammar that has yet been published.'—MORNING POST.
'Had we to recommend the study of German, of all the German grammars which we have examined—and they are not a few—we should unhesitatingly say, Falck Lebahn's is the book for us.'—EDUCATIONAL TIMES.

Lebahn's Edition of Schmid's Henry von Eichen-

fels. With Vocabulary and Familiar Dialogues. Seventh Edition. Crown 8vo. 3s. 6d. cloth.
'Equally with Mr. Lebahn's previous publications, excellently adapted to assist self-exercise in the German language.'—SPECTATOR.

Lebahn's First German Reader. Fifth Edition. Cr.

8vo. 3s. 6d. cloth.
'Like all Lebahn's works, most thoroughly practical.'—BRITANNIA.
'An admirable book for beginners, which indeed may be used without a master.'
LEADER.

Lebahn's German Classics; with Notes and Complete

Vocabularies. Crown 8vo. price 3s. 6d. each, cloth.
PETER SCHLEMIHL, the Shadowless Man. By CHAMISSO.
EGMONT. A Tragedy, in Five Acts, by GOETHE.
WILHELM TELL. A Drama, in Five Acts, by SCHILLER.
GOETZ VON BERLICHINGEN. A Drama. By GOETHE.
PAGENSTREICHE, a Page's Frolics. A Comedy, by KOTZEBUE.
EMILIA GALOTTI. A Tragedy, in Five Acts, by LESSING.
UNDINE. A Tale, by FOUQUÉ.
SELECTIONS from the GERMAN POETS.
'With such aids, a student will find no difficulty in these masterpieces.'
ATHENÆUM.

Lebahn's German Copy-Book: being a Series of Exer-

cises in German Penmanship, beautifully engraved on Steel. 4to. 2s. 6d. sewed.

Lebahn's Exercises in German. Cr. 8vo. 3s. 6d. cloth.

'A volume of "Exercises in German," including in itself all the vocabularies they require. The book is well planned ; the selections for translation from German into English, or from English into German, being sometimes curiously well suited to the purpose for which they are taken.'—EXAMINER.

Lebahn's Self-Instructor in German. Crown 8vo.

3s. 6d. cloth.
'One of the most amusing elementary reading-books that ever passed under our hands.'—JOHN BULL.
'The student could have no guide superior to Mr. Lebahn.'
LITERARY GAZETTE.

Just published, in a closely-printed Volume, in a clear and legible type, post 8vo. 6s. cloth.

The Domestic Service Guide to Housekeeping;

Practical Cookery; Pickling and Preserving; Household Work; Dairy Management; the Table and Dessert; Cellarage of Wines; Home-Brewing and Wine-Making; the Boudoir and Dressing-room; Invalid Diet; Travelling; Stable Economy; Gardening, &c. A Manual of all that pertains to Household Management: from the best and latest authorities, and the communications of Heads of Families; with several hundred new recipes.

'A really useful Guide on the important subjects of which it treats.'—SPECTATOR.
'The best cookery-book published for many years.'—BULL'S MESSENGER.
'This "Domestic Service Guide" will become, what it deserves to be, very popular.'—READER.
'This book is characterised by a kindly feeling towards the classes it designs to benefit, and by a respectful regard to religion.'—RECORD.
'We find here directions to be discovered in no other book, tending to save expense to the pocket, as well as labour to the head. It is truly an astonishing book.'—JOHN BULL.
'This book is quite an encyclopædia of domestic matters. We have been greatly pleased with the good sense and good feeling of what may be called the moral directions, and the neatness and lucidity of the explanatory details.'—COURT CIRCULAR.

Just published, with Photographic Portrait and Autograph, and Vignette of Birthplace. fcp. cloth, price 3s. 6d.; Cheap Edition, without Portrait, 2s. boards.

Richard Cobden, the Apostle of Free Trade: a

Biography. By JOHN McGILCHRIST, Author of 'The Life of Lord Dundonald,' &c.

'The narrative is so condensed, and the style at once so clear and vigorous, that the volume is eminently entitled to a popular circulation. . . . We trust it will find its way to the book-shelves of thousands of working men.'—MORNING STAR.
'The mind of Cobden, as it gradually developed itself, is unfolded before us, and the volume brings to a focus many most interesting expressions of the deceased statesman's views.'—LONDON REVIEW.
'Those who wish to know something of Richard Cobden will find instruction and interest in the book.'—READER.

The Robinson Crusoe of the Nineteenth Century.

Just published, handsomely printed, post 8vo. with Portrait and Sketch Map, 3s. 6d.

Cast Away on the Auckland Isles: a Narrative of

the Wreck of the 'Grafton,' and of the Escape of the Crew, after Twenty Months' Suffering. From the Private Journals of Captain THOMAS MUSGRAVE. Together with some Account of the Aucklands. Also, an Account of the Sea Lion (originally written in seal's blood, as were most of Captain Musgrave's Journals). Edited by JOHN J. SHILLINGLAW, F.R.G.S.

The TIMES Correspondent (December 19, 1865) says that Captain Musgrave's Diary 'is almost as interesting as Daniel Defoe, besides being, as the children say, "all true."'
'It is seldom, indeed, that we come upon a sea narrative now-a-days as interesting as this.'—LLOYD'S NEWSPAPER.
'Does anyone want to measure the real gulf which divides truth from fiction, let him compare Captain Musgrave's narrative with "Enoch Arden."'—READER.
'Truth is here stranger than any fiction.'—NEWS OF THE WORLD.
'A more interesting book of travels and privation has not appeared since "Robinson Crusoe;" and it has this advantage over the work of fiction, that it is a fact.'—OBSERVER.
'Since the days of Alexander Selkirk, few more interesting narratives have seen the light.'—MELBOURNE SPECTATOR.
'A stern realisation of Defoe's imaginative history, with greater difficulties and severer hardships.'—COURT CIRCULAR.

WORKS IN ENGINEERING, ARCHITECTURE, MECHANICS, SCIENCE, &c.

THE YEAR-BOOK of FACTS in SCIENCE and ART.
Exhibiting the most important Improvements and Discoveries of the past year in Mechanics and the Useful Arts, Natural Philosophy, Electricity, Chemistry, Zoology and Botany, Geology and Mineralogy, Meteorology and Astronomy. By John Timbs, F.S.A. (Published Annually.)

☞ This work records the proceedings of the principal scientific societies, and is indispensable for such as wish to possess a faithful picture of the latest novelties of science and the arts.

AIDE-MEMOIRE to the MILITARY SCIENCES; framed from Contributions of Officers of the different Services, and edited by a Committee of the Corps of Royal Engineers, 3 vols. royal 8vo. upwards of 300 Engravings and Woodcuts, in extra cloth boards, and lettered, £4. 10s. ; or may be had in six separate parts, paper boards.

THE HIGH-PRESSURE STEAM-ENGINE. By Dr. Ernst Alban, Practical Machine Maker, Plan, Mecklenburg. Translated from the German, by William Pole, C.E., F.R.A.S., Assoc. Inst. C.E. 8vo. with 30 fine Plates, 16s. 6d. cloth.

A PRACTICAL and THEORETICAL ESSAY on OBLIQUE BRIDGES. With 13 large Folding Plates. By George W. Buck, M. Inst. C.E. Second Edition, corrected by W. H. Barlow, M. Inst. C.E. Imperial 8vo. 12s. cloth.

THE PRACTICAL RAILWAY ENGINEER. By G. Drysdale Dempsey, Civil Engineer. Fourth Edition, revised and greatly extended. With 71 double quarto Plates, 77 Woodcuts, and Portrait of G. Stephenson. One large vol. 4to. £2. 12s. 6d. cloth.

ON IRON SHIP-BUILDING ; with Practical Examples and Details, in Twenty-four Plates, together with Text containing Descriptions, Explanations, and General Remarks. By John Grantham, C.E., Consulting Engineer, and Naval Architect. (*New Edition in preparation.*)

A TREATISE on the PRINCIPLES and PRACTICE of LEVELLING. By Frederick W. Simms, M. Inst. C.E. Fourth Edition, with the Addition of Mr. Law's Practical Examples for setting out Railway Curves, and Mr. Trautwine's Field Practice of Laying out Circular Curves. With 7 Plates and numerous Woodcuts, 8vo. 8s. 6d. cloth.

☞ Trautwine on Laying out Circular Curves is also sold separately, price 5s. sewed.

PRACTICAL TUNNELLING. By Frederick W. Simms, M. Inst. C.E. Second Edition, with Additions by W. Davis Haskoll, C.E. Imperial 8vo. numerous Woodcuts and 16 Folding Plates, £1. 1s. cloth.

TABLES for the PURCHASING of ESTATES, Annuities, Advowsons, &c., and for the Renewing of Leases ; also for Valuing Reversionary Estates, Deferred Annuities, next Presentations, &c. By William Inwood, Architect. Seventeenth Edition, with considerable additions. 12mo. cloth, 7s.

THE STUDENT'S GUIDE to the PRACTICE of DESIGNING, MEASURING, and VALUING ARTIFICERS' WORK ; with 43 Plates and Woodcuts. Edited by Edward Dobson, Architect and Surveyor. Second Edition, with Additions on Design, by E. Lacy Garbett, Architect. One Vol. 8vo. extra cloth, 9s.

A GENERAL TEXT-BOOK, for the Constant Use and Reference of Architects, Engineers, Surveyors, Solicitors, Auctioneers, Land Agents, and Stewards. By Edward Ryde, Civil Engineer and Land Surveyor ; to which are added several Chapters on Agriculture and Landed Property. By Professor Donaldson. One large thick vol. 8vo. with numerous Engravings, £1. 5s. cloth.

THE ELEMENTARY PRINCIPLES of CARPENTRY. By Thomas Tredgold, Civil Engineer. Illustrated by Fifty-three Engravings, a Portrait of the Author, and several Woodcuts. Fourth Edition. Edited by Peter Barlow, F.R.S. One large Volume, 4to. £1. 1s. in extra cloth.

HINTS to YOUNG ARCHITECTS. By George Wightwick, Architect, Author of " The Palace of Architecture," &c. Second Edition, with numerous Woodcuts, 8vo. extra cloth, 7s.

WORKS IN ENGINEERING, &c.—*continued.*

A MANUAL on EARTHWORK. By ALEX. J. S. GRAHAM,
  C.E., Resident Engineer, Forest of Dean Central Railway. With Diagrams.
  12mo. 7s. 6d. cloth.

THE OPERATIVE MECHANIC'S WORKSHOP COM
  PANION; comprising a great variety of the most useful Rules in Mechanical
  Science, with numerous Tables of Practical Data and Calculated Results. By W.
  TEMPLETON, Author of 'The Engineer's Common-Place Book,' &c. Seventh Edition,
  with 11 Plates. 12mo. price 5s. bound and lettered.

THEORY of COMPOUND INTEREST and ANNUITIES,
  with TABLES of LOGARITHMS for the more difficult computations of Interest, Discount, Annuities, &c., in all their Applications and Uses for Mercantile and
  State Purposes. By F. THOMAN, of the Societé Crédit Mobilier. 12mo. 5s. cloth,

THE ENGINEER'S, ARCHITECT'S, and CONTRAC-
  TOR'S POCKET BOOK (Lockwood and Co.'s, formerly Weale's), published
  Annually. With Diary of Events and Data connected with Engineering, Architecture, and the kindred Sciences. The present year's Volume is much improved by
  the addition of various useful articles. With 10 plates, and numerous Woodcuts, in roan tuck, gilt edges, 6s.

THE BUILDER'S and CONTRACTOR'S PRICE BOOK
  (Lockwood and Co.'s formerly Weale's), published Annually. Containing the
  latest prices for work in all branches of the Building Trade, with items numbered for
  easy reference. 12mo. cloth boards, lettered, 4s.

THE TIMBER MERCHANT'S and BUILDER'S COM-
  PANION. Containing new and copious TABLES, &c. By WILLIAM DOWSING,
  Timber Merchant, Hull. Second Edition, revised. Crown 8vo. 5s. cloth.

A SYNOPSIS of PRACTICAL PHILOSOPHY. Alpha-
  betically Arranged. Designed as a Manual for Travellers, Architects,
  Surveyors, Engineers, Students, Naval Officers, and other Scientific Men. By the
  Rev. JOHN CARR, M.A., of Trin. Coll. Camb. Second Edition, 12mo. cloth, 5s.

THE CARPENTER'S NEW GUIDE ; or, Book of Lines
  for Carpenters, founded on the late PETER NICHOLSON'S standard work. A New
  Edition, revised by ARTHUR ASHPITEL, Arch. F.S.A.; together with Practical Rules
  on Drawing, by GEORGE PYNE, Artist. With 74 Plates, 4to. price 41 1s. cloth.

TREATISE on the STRENGTH of TIMBER, CAST
  IRON, MALLEABLE IRON, and other Materials. By PETER BARLOW, F.R.S.
  V.S., Hon. Mem. Inst. C.E., &c. A New Edition, by J. F. HEATHER, M.A., of the Royal
  Military Academy, Woolwich, with Additions by Prof. WILLIS, of Cambridge. With
  19 Illustrations, 8vo. 18s. cloth.

MATHEMATICS for PRACTICAL MEN ; being a Com-
  monplace Book of Pure and Mixed Mathematics, for the Use of Civil Engineers,
  Architects, and Surveyors. By OLINTHUS GREGORY, LL.D. Enlarged by HENRY
  LAW, Fourth edition, revised, by J. R. YOUNG, Author of 'A Course of Mathematics,' &c. With 13 Plates, 8vo. £1 1s. cloth. .

THE LAND VALUER'S BEST ASSISTANT, being
  Tables on a very much improved Plan, for Calculating the Value of Estates. By
  R. HUDSON, Civil Engineer. New Edition, with Additions and Corrections, 4s. bound,

A MANUAL of ELECTRICITY. Including Galvanism,
  Magnetism, Dia-Magnetism, Electro-Dynamics, Magno-Electricity, and the
  Electric Telegraph. By HENRY M. NOAD, Ph.D., F.C.S., Lecturer on Chemistry at
  St. George's Hospital. Fourth Edition, entirely re-written. Illustrated by 500 Wood-
  cuts, 8vo. £1 4s. cloth. Sold also in Two Parts : Part I. Electricity and Galvanism, 8vo.
  12s. cloth. Part II. Magnetism and the Electric Telegraph, 8vo. 10s. 6d. cloth.

DESIGNS and EXAMPLES of COTTAGES, VILLAS,
  and COUNTRY HOUSES. Being the Studies of Eminent Architects and
  Builders, consisting of Plans, Elevations, and Perspective Views ; with approximate
  Estimates of the cost of each. 4to. 67 Plates, £1 1s. cloth.

THE APPRAISER, AUCTIONEER, and HOUSE-
  AGENT'S POCKET ASSISTANT. By JOHN WHEELER, Valuer. Second
  Edition, 12mo. cloth boards, 5s. 6d.

PRACTICAL RULES on DRAWING, for the Operative
  Builder, and Young Student in Architecture. By GEORGE PYNE, Author of
  'A Rudimentary Treatise on Perspective.' With 14 Plates, 4to. 7s. 6d. boards.

THE BOOK FOR EVERY FARMER.

New Edition of Youatt's Grazier, enlarged by R. Scott Burn.

The Complete Grazier, and Farmer's and Cattle Breeder's Assistant. A Compendium of Husbandry, especially in the departments connected with the Breeding, Rearing, Feeding and General Management of Stock, the Management of the Dairy, &c.; with Directions for the Culture and Management of Grass Land, of Grain and Root Crops, the Arrangement of Farm Offices, the Use of Implements and Machines; and on Draining, Irrigation, Warping, &c., and the Application and Relative Value of Manures. By WILLIAM YOUATT, Esq., V.S., Member of the Royal Agricultural Society of England, Author of 'The Horse,' 'Cattle,' &c., Eleventh Edition, enlarged, and brought down to the present requirements of Agricultural Practice by ROBERT SCOTT BURN, one of the Authors of ' The Book of Farm Implements and Machines,' and of ' The Book of Farm Buildings,' Author of ' The Lessons of My Farm,' and Editor of ' The Year-Book of Agricultural Facts.' In one large 8vo. volume, pp. 784, with 213 Illustrations, price £1 1s. strongly half-bound.

' The standard, and text-book, with the farmer and grazier.'
FARMER'S MAGAZINE.

' A valuable repertory of intelligence for all who make agriculture a pursuit, and especially for those who aim at keeping pace with the improvements of the age. . . . The new matter is of so valuable a nature that the volume is now almost entitled to be considered as a distinct work.'—BELL'S MESSENGER.

' The public are indebted to Mr. Scott Burn for undertaking the task, which he has accomplished with his usual ability, making such alterations, additions, and improvements as the changes effected in husbandry have rendered necessary.'
SPORTING MAGAZINE.

' A treatise which will remain a standard work on the subject as long as British agriculture endures.'—MARK LANE EXPRESS.

' The additions are so numerous and extensive as almost to give it the character of a new work on general husbandry, embracing all that modern science and experiment have effected in the management of land and the homestead.'
SPORTING REVIEW.

' It is, in fact, a compendium of modern husbandry, embracing a concise account of all the leading improvements of the day.'—NEW SPORTING MAGAZINE.

The Lessons of My Farm: A Book for Amateur Agriculturists; being an Introduction to Farm Practice in the Culture of Crops, the Feeding of Cattle, Management of the Dairy, Poultry, Pigs, and in the Keeping of Farm-work Records. By ROBERT SCOTT BURN, Editor of ' The Year-Book of Agricultural Facts,' and one of the Authors of ' Book of Farm Implements and Machines,' and ' Book of Farm Buildings.' With numerous Illustrations, fcp. 6s. cloth.

' A very useful little book, written in the lively style which will attract the amateur class to whom it is dedicated, and contains much sound advice and accurate description.'
ATHENÆUM.

' We are sure the book will meet with a ready sale, and the more that there are many hints in it which even old farmers need not be ashamed to accept.'
MORNING HERALD.

' A most complete introduction to the whole round of farming practice. We believe there are many among us whose love of farming will make them welcome such a companion as this little book in which the author gives us his own experience, which are worth a great deal.'—JOHN BULL.

' Never did book exercise a more salutary effect than " My Farm of Four Acres." Mr. Burn has followed suit in a very practical and pleasant little work.'
ILLUSTRATED LONDON NEWS.

SPOTTISWOODE AND CO., PRINTERS, NEW-STREET SQUARE, LONDON.